Endorsements for *Eastbound From Flagstaff*

"an amazing level of authenticity in this coming of age story."

Michael Bishop
Author of *A MURDER IN MUSIC CITY*

"From rural Kentucky to Detroit's industrial supremacy—to the vastness of the American West in the early 1900's, Annette Valentine weaves a powerful story of resilience and recovery. A quest filled with brutal tragedies explores the depths one endures and the path that ultimately leads to redemption."

Peter Rosenberger
Radio Host, Author of *HOPE FOR THE CAREGIVER*

"Once in a while an opportunity comes along to impact someone else's life in a profound way. I believe in the power of this story to do exactly that. It's a refreshing mix of thought-provoking and gratifying episodes with an enormous backdrop of colorful relationships — a wonderful read."

Darrell Waltrip
Three-time NASCAR Cup Series champion, author, national television broadcaster, American motorsports analyst, and former racing driver.

"Debut novelist Annette Valentine has written a well-developed saga dealing with the relationships of her characters. She makes the reader root for the triumph of the personalities."

Cherie Feinberg
Attorney

"Annette Valentine has a genuine gift for allowing her fiction to ask the toughest of theological and existential questions, while telling an enthralling story. *Eastbound from Flagstaff*, based on the author's father, is a beautiful and often heartbreakingly poignant tale of courage, tragedy, grace and coming home."

Joy Jordan-Lake
Author of the bestselling novel *A TANGLED MERCY* and other books

"Refreshing. Powerful. A fervently told story with plenty of dramatic twists to stir your emotions. I felt I'd truly gotten to know a man of grace and courage."

Dr. Hal Hadden
Founder of Christian Leadership Concepts (CLC)
and Becoming Like Jesus (BLC), Author of *LOVE JESUS*

"In this her first novel, Annette Valentine has crafted a wonderful story that weaves together universal themes of fathers, sons, waywardness, and reconciliation within the context of a rich Southern heritage. Together they combine to tell of a journey, not unlike the one we are all on – one with ups and downs, turns and detours, and questions with sometimes fleeting answers. In the end, however, the journey reveals an overarching purpose and plan, making redemption not just something possible but probable.

David A. Hofmann
Senior Associate Dean for Academic Affairs and Hugh McColl, Distinguished
Professor of Organizational Behavior, UNC's Kenan-Flagler Business School

"*Eastbound From Flagstaff* spans an era where innocence, aspirations, and a longing for adventure beat in the chests of a generation of young men. Annette Valentine writes with nostalgic tenderness in this coming of age story."

Karen Pashley
Inspirational speaker and author of *PRECIOUS IN HIS SIGHT*

"She's given us a standout creation with a worthy appeal. Fascinating, genuinely eloquent."

Marie C. Thursby
Visiting Scholar, Laboratory for Innovation Science at Harvard
Regents' Professor Emeritus, GA Institute of Technology

Eastbound from Flagstaff, A Novel

Eastbound
FROM
Flagstaff

a novel

Annette
Valentine

NEW YORK

LONDON • NASHVILLE • MELBOURNE • VANCOUVER

Eastbound from Flagstaff
A Novel

Published in New York, New York, by Morgan James Publishing. Morgan James is a trademark of Morgan James, LLC. www.MorganJamesPublishing.com

ISBN 9781642793345 paperback
ISBN 9781642793352 case laminate hardcover
ISBN 9781642793369 eBook
Library of Congress Control Number: 2018913143

Cover Design by:
Rachel Lopez
www.r2cdesign.com

Interior Design by:
Christopher Kirk
www.GFSstudio.com

Disclaimer: This is a work of fiction. All incidents and dialogue, and all characters with the exception of some public figures, are the product of the author's imagination or are used fictitiously and are not to be construed as real. Any resemblance to actual persons, whether living or dead, or actual events is purely coincidental. Accounts of incidents and their locale are not intended to portray anything beyond an entirely fictional setting.

Morgan James is a proud partner of Habitat for Humanity Peninsula and Greater Williamsburg. Partners in building since 2006.

Get involved today! Visit
MorganJamesPublishing.com/giving-back

For my husband, Walt,
whose encouragement sustains me.

For my father whose integrity paved the way
and gave me a reason to write.

For my family and friends without whose support
I would not have dared to dream.

PART ONE
Chapter 1

—➤◆◆◄—

The erratic clomp of footsteps struck what sounded like the first, second, and third treads on the staircase leading to my apartment. No mystery surrounded the identity of the individual who was wasting little time getting to the second floor. A thud hit the fourth bare wood step and echoed in the stairwell. It had to be the foul-mouthed tenant who lived below me, coming to give me a piece of his mind, again. I could hear him cussing up a blue streak as he ascended. One by one: stomp, swear, stomp, swear until I could almost feel his hot breath in my face. A few feet away at the entrance to apartment number 202—mine—a floorboard yielded its familiar creak under the man's weight.

I unplugged the carpet sweeper cord and wrapped it in tidy circles along the side of the deflated Hoover bag and glanced through the open window over the kitchen sink. Albuquerque's slight October midday breeze moved the desert air, rippling the loosely gathered curtain that hung from the sash. Clouds floated idly above craggy slopes of the Sandia Mountains in the distance. Out there, from all appearances, 1929 was lazing past.

After a sufficient delay to show my lack of respect, I answered the hostile knock on my door.

A young man with beer breath and disheveled clothes stood looking at me. His height was a few inches shy of mine. He'd chosen an indignant look to greet me. The toe of his shoe crossed the threshold. "That your Model T parked out front?"

"It is."

"Well, its tire is on my bed of . . ." He faltered, caught his balance against the doorframe, and offered a cheeky smile. "Did I say a good morning to you, Mr. Simpson?"

"The name's Hagan. Not Simpson. Simon Hagan. Guess I didn't catch yours."

"Hagan?" He eyed me with an enlightened stare. "You've run your vehicle over a stretch of my grass, Mr. Hagan. My property since it's under my window—" A bad-mannered and energetic belch escaped the pooching cavern of his belly.

I reacted, backhanding my tweed vest to avoid the spew.

The man took little notice. "And the noise from whatever machine you're using to ratchet the floors has disrupted my sleep."

"That would be a carpet sweeper, a present for my wife who'll be coming—"

"Had no idea you were married."

"Never mind. Allow me a look-see, and if that's the case concerning my automobile, I'll make amends. Otherwise, you've made an unnecessary trip up here. Now if you'll excuse me, I'm in a hurry." I checked my wristwatch. "Wife's bus is due from Flagstaff in just over an hour. But as long as we're having this little discussion, I'd be much obliged if you'd put your trash out back where it belongs. Couldn't help noticing you've left a bit of it outside your door. Might make a better impression on her if it were gone."

He blinked with no response. My comments seemed to be totting up for consideration somewhere behind bleary eyes.

"The trash," I said, raising my volume, "gone, perhaps? No later than noon."

"Your vehicle . . . off my grass, perhaps? The sooner the better."

"Fair enough, mister."

"The name's Reagan. Ronald Reagan. Don't let me keep you."

I nodded and closed the door, having permitted my tipsy neighbor to get the last word. His interruption was not about to foil my efforts to put a shine on the apartment. Today was much too favorable to be pettifogging minor details anyhow, with my bride's bus arriving soon. I hustled off to the kitchen in a tailspin, cleared the dishes from the drainboard, wiped down the counter, and proceeded to do a once-over through the rest of the place, rehearsing my lines for the part I'd gotten at the local theatre as I went.

In the bedroom, a small vase crammed full of flowers sat on the nightstand. Next to it, her photograph beamed back at me with a reassuring smile. The comforts she'd become accustomed to during the last several months, however, living at her sister's, had me wondering about my adequacy.

There was no mistaking it: the love we'd gotten back was real, and it filled me with everything worth living for. Wasted days I'd imprinted with guilt were gone. Gone, too, was my powerlessness and the futile hours of worry over my brother's whereabouts. And gone was my reproach for an earless God because of what he had not done while I trod inexhaustible deep waters. Like a giant ship in a slow turn on the ocean, I'd felt my indifference to my father changing course. Over time it had become clear that he'd been the anchor during my struggle to stay alive, and I no longer felt like a disappointed child unfairly denied a safe port in the storm. The lamp was on. I turned it off, then back on again to prove to myself that I wasn't dreaming.

I strutted to the living room, waving my arms in the air, dramatizing my scrip, not about to cave in to the outright temptation to smoke a cigarette. Acting came naturally, and so much about the idea of a masquerade did as well. Today in particular, rehearsing suited me, or the walls in the tiny burrow that was my apartment would have closed in around me.

I sat down on the couch and continued to recite with nervous energy the words that let me ignore the question of how I would find time to work my job at the Franciscan Hotel—moreover, how I could afford *not* to. But I was in love, and my physical reserves to press on with classes at the university, acting, and my dishwashing duties at the hotel were bolstered by it. Eager to be on my way, I stood up. Unimaginable as it was, solid truth that the woman I loved had married me gave me courage.

Her bus trip would be taxing, so better my being early than late to the station. I plumped the seat cushion that I'd made a mess of and straightened out the wrinkles, then walked to the window. Past it, New Mexico's peaks touched a magnificent sky.

I jingled the keys in my pocket and was out the door with plenty of answers to the question of where I was going. From my quiet source of dev-ilment, I anticipated the likelihood of running into Mr. Reagan. At the bottom of the stairs I could see that I had, in fact, encroached on his property. Also, that his trash was unmoved. Not wanting to start a rift, I situated myself in my secondhand Model T, pulled the choke lever, then hopped back out and went to the front end to crank her up.

My father-in-law would be pleased to know I owned one again, old as it was. We'd had our history, Charlie and I, and sitting in the driver's seat of my Model T—similar to the one he'd taught me to drive—felt mighty good. I crept backwards off of Mr. Reagan's grass, switched gears, and gave the T some gas.

After crossing Railroad Avenue, I went east where farmers grazed their sheep on the Grand Mesa. Lying ahead, the sand dunes marked the eastern edge of the floodplain, and the mesa rose gently up to the foothills of the Sandia Mountains. I followed the ruts in the road, moving at twenty-five miles an hour toward the station, avoiding the rocks that might cause me to veer off to the side. The mild wind played havoc with the waves in my hair, and my linen cap bounced on the seat beside me.

Within half an hour and right on time, I was waiting at the station. I paced from one end to the other, on the lookout for the rounded, cream-col-ored top of the motor coach. My eyes were peeled for the first glimpse of the eastbound bus from Flagstaff.

Minutes passed. I took a look at my wristwatch again, holding its face so the intermittent sun's glare didn't distort its hands: 11:39. The bus was overdue. I went to the desk for the third time.

"No, sir," the clerk said, "please be patient. They're just a few minutes behind schedule. It's usually on—"

The ring of the telephone behind him got his attention.

He pressed his ear to the receiver and, without turning his head, shifted his gaze toward me as he listened. Then froze. His faraway look made my blood run cold. The ring of another telephone cut through the close space like a shrill omen, taking from me the air that I breathed.

And once again I felt powerless.

Chapter 2

When America entered the twentieth century, almost half of its population lived on a farm, and I was birthed on a rugged one without my consent in rural Kentucky. That's where I was in 1902, a babe in my mother's arms in a one-room clapboard house. Our home sat on the vast abundance of hilly pastureland where my father's father had staked his claim to the land he handed down to his only son. It was there that Geoffrey Newton Hagan at twenty-four years old and Nellie Virginia Keenan Hagan at eighteen became the second generation of the Hagan clan, and I, Simon Newton, was their firstborn.

My folks worked an eighty-acre farm from the minute the sun came up to the minute it went down. By the time I was eight, I did the same. Sometime during my youth, it became evident that farming rendered a hard life, but I had absolutely nothing to compare it to. It wasn't until much later that I came to recognize the breadth of trials and the depth of toil required to run a self-contained farm on the outskirts of nowhere.

My being entrusted as a scrawny kid with the supervision and care of the prized buckskin stallion named Soot was testimony enough of the responsibility I carried. Fortunately, for me, ol' Soot had a gentle disposition, which enabled me to handle him, and that alone justified his having been gelded. I knew early on what it meant that the horse had been deprived of his vigor, and not wishing the same fate to befall me as a result of my own spirited behavior, I aimed to please.

So as a youngster, both Soot and I had temperaments that qualified us as docile males. He was destined for a lifetime of submission, but my compliance lasted only till I was eighteen. Until then, there was no reasonable excuse for a strapping youngster like me to refuse to do a man's share of the work.

Every able-bodied person in our house and the sharecroppers on our land went about doing what we were supposed to, and the older I got, the more chores there were to be done. Little else till now had done as much to toughen the sinews of my armor.

—⋙◆⋘—

Sheer habit, not the restless night, rousted me out of bed long before five a.m. I hit the floor with both feet, flung the covers over my younger brother Alan so he could continue sleeping another hour or so, and stumbled to the washstand. I poured water into the basin and splashed a freezing-cold handful on my face, then got dressed in an unheated and pitch-black corner of the room.

I'd have been hard-pressed to find an area in our home that was heated or lighted, for while having grown over the years from one room to several, it was far enough in the country to be lacking in electrical advantages enjoyed by city folk. Adding to the austerity was the warped floorboard that chose today to catch the end of my bare toe. Cussing was not part of my vocabulary, for otherwise this would have been an ideal chance to use it. Not one of my younger brothers gave any indication that my annoyance disturbed them. Alan merely rolled over, but neither Mason, Raymond, nor Seth stirred in the bed that the three of them shared across the room. They slept, and I left without a word, closed the door behind me, and descended the stairs.

Already Mother was up, kindling a fire in the kitchen stove. Dried apples were piled high in the pot, ready for stewing.

I brushed past her with my displeasure full-blown and airing. "I'll be sleeping in the hayloft from now on," I said. "Don't see a single reason not to."

"Good morning to you, too." Her lighthearted chuckle had its peculiar way of disarming me. She bent over to stoke the fire. "If you've a mind to, Simon, then do it. Nothing's stopping you. But for this day, tackle it with a good attitude, as unto the Lord," she said, dropping a hint at salvation. "I'll rustle up hotcakes and sausage, and all you can eat of those apples. It'll be ready before your chores are done." She straightened up, and I caught the glint in her eye. "Now, Simon, go."

She was beautiful to me, with a smile that could lift my burdens, and the love I felt for her was as deep as the well at the back of the house. One by one, when she'd scarcely reached the age of thirty-six, my siblings and I—eight sons and daughters—drained strength and energy from her on a regular basis. Alan, Mason, Mary, and then Raymond. My siblings had kept on coming: Seth, Charlotte, Lewis.

The girls' room was across the hall upstairs. Lewis was still sleeping in a crib in my parents' room next to the parlor. On this particular Sunday in late March, it was at least an hour before daybreak. With a second chance at starting it off on a pleasant note, I planted an affectionate kiss on Mother's cheek. Her delight was worth the awkwardness. We both laughed.

My boots awaited me at the back door. I pulled them on at the stoop, grabbed an oil lantern, and lit the wick. The morning felt brisk as I set out for the cattle barn, holding the canister high to see my feet in front of me. Beyond its beam, without electricity, I couldn't see a darned thing.

Dad had begun the milking. He didn't look up as I rounded the corner and hung my lantern on a penny nail protruding over the gate to the hogpen. The assortment of livestock was pleading loudly to be let out to pasture. I put oats and corn into the troughs and then brought a pail full of swill to add to the feed.

The farm's routine went on without much variation, no matter which day of the week. A smoothly run farm depended upon everyone pitching in, and all but the very youngest of us tended to early morning duties, the same as we did before going to school on other days. The fact that we would be going to church today merely positioned it as top priority.

The minute I opened the gate to let the pigs loose to go inside their loafing area, they clamored for feed, their flat snouts rooting for a place in front of or beside a bristly-haired competitor at the troughs. They were a sight to behold, but I had little time to waste on unproductive amusement. Dad would by now be shooing the cows out to graze, anticipating my help to carry bucketfuls of milk to the house.

We hoisted them from the mire and came up past the well, circling the back side of the pump near the house. I toted the lantern in one hand, trying not to slosh the contents of the bucket in the other. Mother met us at the door, holding it wide to let me follow Dad inside.

He had his hat hung on a hook almost before the screen slammed shut behind me. He stepped close enough to give my mother a peck on the forehead, and in a few words assured her that he'd be polished and in his Sunday best before breakfast. She was preparing to strain the milk even before he was out of sight.

It was still plenty dark outside. Daylight was only just beginning to break in the east. Even so, I left the lantern behind and with ease walked down to the barn three hundred feet away, trailing the scent of manure and wet straw into the stalls. Ol' Soot was eyeing me from the far end of the barn, near where the buggy was kept. I approached with an outstretched hand, took a minute to stroke his muzzle, and then kept on going out of the barn, swinging an empty pail.

The pond had thawed, and the stream was freely running into it. I crossed the muddied embankment to get at the water and lowered my pail. Pieces of morning light quietly reflected blues in the rippling current.

The winter crops had made it through. Turnips, kale, carrots. They'd held, but the aftermath of a tough winter hovered in the mist over the trees to the north. The tobacco barn and sharecroppers' houses stood in jagged shapes against the horizon on the eastern boundary. There was plenty of room for the tobacco to grow and pasture enough for the half-dozen steers left there at night.

My mind was engaged as I trudged toward the barn, hashing out my list of responsibilities following breakfast. I'd need to call the sheep and pen them once the mares were out and the stalls were clean, and I'd need to lay down fresh straw—all before church. And there was the need to mend the fence later today.

As I looked back at the house, I could see Mother walking in the direction of the chicken coop. I went inside the barn as usual, but Soot whinnied and pawed the ground as if I'd startled him by coming near his stall. My touch and the tone of my voice eased his jitters.

I set the pail down so he could drink and stood close to him, admiring my prize of a horse, combing his mane with my fingers, patting his sooty buckskin coat. He adored the attention and responded better to me than to anyone else.

———⋙◆⋘———

It was getting late. Most likely nearing six o'clock by now. Sunup. Time to get on back to the house for breakfast.

Whistling a tune, I stepped with Soot out into the open. I'd led him out of the barn hundreds of times. It's what I did, but something was amiss, and not the wet soil, and not the plow or the mule or the haystacks. Spooked, he gave a spirited headshake, and as the breeze came at us, his nostrils flared. He was moody and aloof, so I held his bridle firmly, and we neared the trees at the fencerow.

I spotted Mother just as I opened the gate—past the dirt-capped hillside that awaited March's covering of new grass, back by the chicken coop, gathering eggs. It was part of her morning routine, and part of mine was leading the stallion to pasture, so I held even tighter to Soot's bridle. Already he'd sensed danger, and when my mother's cry reached us, it was impossible to hold him. Terror, the likes of which no words can describe, sent him galloping off as wild as the wind. He bolted from my grasp, and panic seized every nerve in my body, for there in the distance an odd blur of coloration—my mother's wispy form—appeared. Close to her, reared up on its hind legs, was an enormous black bear.

Nothing in my seventeen years on earth had prepared me for the sight. The only thought racing through my head was to save my mother. I made a dash for the barn, tearing around the corner to where the shotgun hung from a strap on the doorframe. I gripped the gun firmly behind the trigger, jerked it from the nail, and darted back outside. From three hundred feet away I halted, trying to keep my arms from shaking, and pulled the shotgun to my shoulder.

The rising sun blinded me, and the bear continued to move erratically, taking from me the sliver of hope I had of shooting him. There was no mistaking the gap that had narrowed between him and Mother. She was barely visible. I squinted, trying to spot him and keep from hitting her, knowing the profound risk with a shotgun at that distance.

Instinct told me to run instead as if there were a chance I could physically stop him in his tracks, pull him limb from limb. But with my cheek planted firmly against the stock, I stared down the sight and fired, feeling the recoil as the shot rang out and echoed through eternity. The bear went down.

Nothing could tell me whether I'd struck a fatal blow or if he'd merely dropped on all fours. I took off running after him, stumbling, regaining my balance, running again, calling out to God, desperate to shorten the distance and lessen the incline that stretched to the chicken coop. Every step carried dead weight, and the pounding in my chest sucked the air from me, but I ran wildly, narrowing the distance between us, unable to make out if the bear was alive, unable to see my mother.

At less than a hundred feet from me, the great beast rose again to its feet. Before I could draw my gun, the back door burst open, and Dad flew out of the kitchen. From the stoop he racked his rifle, aimed, and fired, and the bear dropped onto its side.

Within seconds I reached the level area that surrounded the house, gasping for breath, and stopped as if something had paralyzed me on the spot. Near the boughs of evergreen trees lay my mother, motionless. Blood gushed from the side of her face, and her arm was severed.

Out of the corner of my eye, I watched Dad coming down the steps toward us, barefooted, absorbed, both eyes fixed straight ahead. His trousers hung from his shoulder by a single suspender. The rifle tumbled from his hand and fell behind him in the dirt. I opened my mouth to speak, but the words didn't follow. He walked past me as if I were invisible and slumped beside her. The unrestrained howl of agony that poured from him tore through all outdoors.

Sweat ran down my face and covered the palms of my hands. I couldn't feel myself rushing to their side. Neither could I feel myself sliding my arms under Mother's limp frame as my father reached out with both hands to touch her. Nor could I feel myself lifting her in my arms from the pool of blood beneath her. Every sensation I possessed turned to ice. The earth stopped moving. Dazed, I carried her toward the house.

My brother was as rigid as a fence post, stricken and speechless at the top step, holding the door. He gawked at the awful sight.

"Quick, tear some rags. Anything!" I shouted. The sound of my own voice was foreign.

Openmouthed, Alan stared at me as if the urgency of my command had bypassed his understanding.

"Move, Alan. Rags," I said, and our eyes met with fire passing between them. "Go!"

I caught the door with the heel of my boot and eased Mother inside, through the kitchen's stifling heat, through the dining room, cutting gingerly past the huge cherrywood table and into the parlor. Dad came up behind us as I laid her on the sofa. I stood still, anticipating his courage to bolster me, but he dropped to the rug and knelt down beside her, unable to stand, unable to speak. Not a speck of color showed in his face. Lines, chiseled in his brow, had erased his unshakable hope that typically registered even in the worst of circumstances.

We both knew there was none. She panted in shallow gasps and, never having opened her eyes, breathed her last.

Alan flew into the room and abruptly came to a standstill a few feet from the sofa where Mother lay. A wad of rags to stop her bleeding fell from his hand. Given our obvious emotion, he gazed incredulously at me and then at Dad. Frozen, he didn't move a muscle.

I was the first to stand after being crouched beside her body, and Dad was behind me, distraught. He pushed himself up from the floor and slowly rose to his feet. Alan fell into my arms and sobbed.

Dad began staving off the younger children who were wandering into the room, sleepy-eyed and confused, as if they weren't sure whether they were late or early for breakfast. But Mason and Mary were old enough to know there was more to the commotion. They had both come too close not to catch a glimpse of torn flesh and the horror that could not be masked. With Alan distraught, they burst into tears.

"Mason," Dad said, hiding his bloodied hands behind his back, "I want you and your sister to go with the children to my room. And Mary, get the baby from the crib and hold him. Rock him. I'll be there shortly." His voice was soft, his smile forced and weak. "Understood?"

"Yes, sir," Mason said, taking instructions with the maturity his thirteen years afforded him. He wasted no time redirecting the youngsters to the bed-room, and all but Alan and Mary left the room. Mason remained composed, nonetheless, flexing his two-year seniority over her. "Come on, Mary. Let's go," he said in earnest and the same distinctive nod of his head as Dad's.

She was having none of it. "Can I talk to Mummy?" She watched, wait-ing for Dad to formulate an answer.

But answers weren't going to flow easily, and a room full of dispersing children offered no reprieve for Dad. He kept his arms behind his back and swallowed so hard his Adam's apple bobbed under his collar.

"Mary," I said, squatting next to her with Alan still clutching me, "first, go to Mother's room and find her favorite dress. Stay there with it till I come and get you. Then you can talk to her about it."

The suggestion came out of nowhere. Mary turned and was out of sight. Dad crumpled in a heap at Mother's side. Alan peeled himself from me and did the same.

I was not equipped for such pain—not as the eldest sibling, not as the strongest. There was no justice to point to and no provision to lean on. I broke down and cried. At seventeen years old, I sat on the floor and cried like a girl.

Chapter 3

Whether we were ready or not, Alan and I grew up in that spring-time while I was still seventeen and Alan was fifteen. When we got out of bed that Sunday morning in March of 1920, we were boys. That night when we turned down the oil burners and went to sleep, we were old men. We and our siblings had lost the only person we could ever call Mother. The day—the year—left its indelible mark.

"Help me out, Simon." Dad had his hand on my shoulder. He'd come and stood next to me without my knowing, and the two of us huddled close to my mother's lifeless body. "I've sent Alan to saddle up one of the horses. We have a job to do while he's gone off to fetch Doc Orr. Go in and talk to the rest," he said, referring to the younger children. "I'll cover her best I can. They can come say their goodbyes. Give me a few minutes alone with her." After looking at my bloodstained overalls, he handed me a rag. "Take this and clean up first. Change your clothes."

I went through the motions of climbing the stairs to the boys' room. The place had been left with unmade beds and unattended chamber pots. There was no time to linger or spend unnecessary amounts of time in an effort to make myself presentable. I did what I could and went back down.

Dad had propped Mother at an angle on her side with a cushion. Only one side of her face showed. He'd covered her with the quilt she typically kept across the back of the sofa. It was folded under her chin. The pattern of bright green squares somehow gave life to her skin color. Every telltale sign of her encounter with the bear was concealed. I wasn't sure how. I didn't dwell on it.

13

He gently moved his fingers over her eyelids to close them and then tucked her hair under her head as if it had never been ripped out of the neat bun she had worn twisted at the back of her neck. Her bare feet poked out from the quilt's end, her muddy shoes lay beside her on the floor. As untroubled as she appeared, she could have been sleeping.

But she wasn't sleeping, and outrage smoldered in my gut. Emotions threatened to swallow me. *God in heaven*, I muttered. *You let this happen.*

"Dad?" I made sure he was hearing me. I made sure I wasn't shouting at him the way I wanted to shout at God. "Should I go get Mary and the others?"

"Sure, son. And keep them close to you." He touched Mother's cheek with the back of his hand, and I could hear him whispering to her, calling her Lacy. And then he looked at me, his eyes dripping. "Let them talk to her. I'll go out to the coop. Do what I have to do out there."

He shuffled out, and I wound my way through the hallway to my parents' bedroom, where the children had been instructed to wait, and then led them through the narrow hall and into the parlor. The sun shone brightly through the window on the far side, and I was sure only I was noticing the beams radiating through the dust particles that haloed on the wood floor within a few feet of the sofa where we stopped.

We stayed there, looking at her. I couldn't trust myself to speak.

"Will she open her eyes?" Mary's little voice was hardly audible. She had seen more than her eleven-year-old mind could understand, and Charlotte, only just five, had surely missed seeing anything of Mother's encounter with the bear.

I hoped so. "She'll open them when it's time to see Jesus," I said. "For now, she's waiting. Maybe take Charlotte's hand, Mary." It was clear enough they were both terrified.

Mason handed off the baby to me and took Mary's hand, and she in turn took Charlotte's, and the three of them crept forward.

"Mummy?" Mary began to speak. Tears poured from her eyes and ran down her cheeks like a dam flooding its banks. "Mummy, we don't want you to . . . please don't die."

The three younger children, it seemed, were crying because the older ones were. Raymond and Seth snugged up beside me like ducks under a

—————◆—————

mother's wing, and the finality of death was heard in the cries of Nellie Virginia Keenan Hagan's sons and daughters. Alan, when he returned with the doctor, would complete the circle of offspring that she held dear, only to mourn her loss.

"I laid your church dress on the bed," Mary said, releasing Charlotte's hand. She took a step closer to our mother.

In a split second I had to decide whether to let Mary express her heart or keep her from going closer—let her have the last time she would ever see Mother unfold as a sweet memory or take a chance that she or her sister might suddenly rush over to give Mother a hug.

I weighed the trauma associated with such an action.

"Charlotte," I said, "you and Mary and Mason keep real still, right where you are. Let's take turns telling Mother how pretty she'll look in her favorite dress." I swallowed hard and took a deep breath. "Me first." I aligned myself with the others, still holding Lewis, who had quieted as if he recognized we were standing on holy ground. "Mother," I said, "I think you'll look like an angel in your favorite dress." I nearly choked on the lump in my throat. The parlor was so quiet that I could hear the saliva going down.

I waited for the others to speak of their own accord.

Mason spoke first. "You are so pretty, Mum." But he stopped short—to cough.

Charlotte claimed the pause for herself. "I yike it, Mummy. Pretty."

I wasn't sure Mary could say anything more. Tears continued down her cheeks. She wiped them with her free hand and held tightly to Charlotte's with the other.

My siblings looked to me, every one of them. Didn't matter the circumstance, they just did. Even Lewis, wriggling in his sopping wet pajamas, still in my arms, had pulled away from my chest and was looking at me, rheumy-eyed.

I was coming up short. At six foot three, I was short. Short of the mark. Short on answers. "Mason, how about you and Mary take the little ones on upstairs." It seemed a reasonable way to lead them from the parlor and make way for Doc Orr when he arrived. "Everybody, go get dressed. Stay there till you're called. I'll rustle up some breakfast. By then Alan should be back."

It was another twenty minutes or more before Dad returned to the house from out back. I could hear him coming up the steps. He came on inside, roughed up, his thick head of sandy-colored hair tussled. It was obvious he needed to change clothes, but at least now if one of the children wandered outside or near the chicken coop, it wouldn't be a scene for them to contend with. He turned without looking in the parlor and went straight down the hallway leading to the bedroom.

I doubted if I was man enough to have gone and done the necessary task that he had, out by the chicken coop. But I was not the man my dad was, nor did I sense that I had the stamp of his nature. There was no other excuse for why I had missed being able to shoot the bear, why I hadn't held my arm steady, why I hadn't aimed better and killed it.

I watched from the parlor as Dad disappeared into his room, knowing I would never be able to look myself in the mirror or answer why I hadn't been capable of killing the bear with my bare hands—or why Mother had to be the one to die.

Chapter 4

Lewis had bawled for so long he'd worn himself out. His head rested on my shoulder in complete surrender. He gasped for air between blubbers, drooling on the thumb in his mouth. I shifted him from one side of my body to the other. Lewis, not yet three—and a thirty-five-pound millstone—was content for now to sleep.

I had made my way to the kitchen with the thought of preparing food when I noticed Alan through the window, on horseback, galloping down the lane on his return trip from Doc Orr's. Quickly, I pried Lewis off me and laid him on some flour sacks in the corner, praying he would stay asleep. Word that a crisis had occurred at the Hagan farm would generate some help with meals later and whatever else God-fearing people did to alleviate the strain at such a time, but right now we were on our own. I took a skillet from the sideboard.

Alan came through the back door, huffing and puffing. I was thankful the others were off getting cleaned up and dressed. He was a mess, and his hair, I could have sworn, was redder than usual and hung down like alfalfa in his face. But something besides hair had scratched him, to the point of drawing blood in parallel lines down the side of his nose, almost as if he had done it to himself. He rushed to the parlor and stood next to our mother.

He spoke but made no sense. "She's got to get up! We're going to church."

I felt ashamed for wondering if he'd snapped. Lewis was somehow still asleep. I put the skillet down and followed after Alan. "Alan," I said, and he looked through me as if I were invisible. "Alan, where's Doc Orr?"

He glared at me for a minute or more and then took hold of the front of his shirt and pulled until he'd ripped it off. His shoulders were stiff as a board. "Hurry, Simon! Save her!"

"Alan," I said as calmly as I could, "the others have gone upstairs. You're needed. So, go on now. Be strong."

He hung back, unready to give up.

I prompted again.

That was when he started upstairs, his shoulders drooping, and I returned to the kitchen. I heard him on the stairway. "Doc's coming," he said. "Doc's coming."

The milk had been sitting all morning. Mother had strained it and would have taken it to the root cellar by now, but in an instant everything that would have been—and *should* have been—was not.

Hotcake batter awaited eggs that never came, and I didn't know what else belonged in the mixture. It was destined for the slop bucket. The apples had cooked to a pulp. I turned off the flame underneath them, savoring for a brief moment their sweet smell, as if it were the last fragment of grace to be found, then moved them aside. One look at the mound of ground pork and I turned away, repulsed. The sight of it made my legs want to fold.

They might have, had Dad not entered the kitchen. "Sausage. Good," he said, emotionless.

He had dressed himself in church garb and fresh layers of peacefulness, but deep in his eyes was the truth of his suffering. They were swollen and bloodshot, and their rich brown was watered down. "We'll need something solid to keep us going," he said.

No remnant of his personality remained. Nothing of his easy smile that so often seemed to stifle itself just short of an outright laugh. I wondered if there was a chance in a million I'd ever see it again.

He reached toward me with his rough hands, working hands, shaking as they were, and we embraced. It was not something we did as a routine—just part of the flow of pain as it passed between two broken hearts.

He pulled back, his hands still on my upper arms. I could feel his breath and see where his beard had been shaved clean.

He looked me straight in the eye. "We'll make it, Simon. We'll make it through."

With that said, he went to the parlor to wait for Doc Orr, and I set the skillet over the open flame and began frying the sausage.

⬅◆➡

Dad stood stoically on the day she was buried, perhaps to convince himself of the strength he possessed to face it. I wasn't sure if his posture was a sign of his faith or a measure of his stubbornness, but my honor was due him. It wasn't for me to question my father, and truth be known, I'd been around him long enough to be certain he wasn't questioning God.

I, on the other hand, was questioning God and not terribly inclined to carry the weight that was trying to bend me to the ground.

Dad's lips didn't move. Nothing did. But I heard his voice in my mind, saying to her the way he often did: *You're my bright and morning star, Lacy.*

Part of me wanted to know how he'd come to call her Lacy, why the kiss on her forehead caused her to shrug off the attention as if she didn't require it.

I braced myself next to her coffin, wondering if she'd become Lacy—in place of her given name Nellie—because of the delicate collars she'd crocheted for herself, and table doilies, and little coats for the new babies soon after they were born. Often it seemed that Dad had plucked her right out of the nest that held her childhood, as if he'd whisked Mother from under her own father's nose.

Story had it the whole-souled, good ol' Presbyterian missionary had nary a say about Geoffrey Newton Hagan taking a liking to his only daughter, and Dad owned up to it. On occasion, he filled in bits and pieces regarding Grandfather Josiah Henry Keenan.

Grandfather had traveled on horseback through the Southern Alleghenies, eventually making his way southwest to Kentucky, and later he'd gotten the itch to pack up his family and migrate them to Todd County. "That put them within arm's reach," Dad had said with a laugh, recounting how he, at twenty-one, had simply laid eyes on Mr. Keenan's fifteen-year-old girl. Hadn't wasted any time claiming the young Scottish Highlander for his bride.

And now Dad's face was turned toward the treetops. The sun shone full, a glorious morning. Unfair as it was, we left my mother in Glen Haven Cemetery under an endless canopy of blue heaven. Better if a darkened sky had opened up and dropped buckets full of rain to acknowledge the searing loss that my family was enduring.

The preacher, so placid, contrasted sharply with Alan, so irrational. And the youngsters lacked understanding that they would never again see their mother. Not feel her warmth, not touch her skin, not smell her fragrance. It probably hadn't crossed their minds—the reality of walking the rest of the days of their lives without ever again experiencing her love, her gentleness, and her sweet smile.

We stayed a long while. I had no idea how long, but every eye was red with the unmasked evidence of our world being shattered. There was no answer for what could possibly make life go on. The best part of it had changed.

I pulled a curtain of denial around me, shutting out reminders of opportunities I'd squandered, things I should have done but hadn't, words I could have said but hadn't.

But her death didn't end the cycle of life on the farm. The cows needed milking. The horses needed to be brought in from the pasture. Everything that breathed needed something. Dad needed his Lacy. And I, the eldest at seventeen, couldn't say it, but the rest of us needed our mama.

Chapter 5

In the days to follow, from all appearances, the butterscotch stone bungalow situated high on an embankment six miles outside Elkton, Kentucky, housed a typical family—*my* family—who lived in it in the spring of 1920. Its steeply pitched roof swept down over the deep porch, and the chimney jutted above it at the east end like the protective arm of God. Gatherings had commenced under its broad stretch in the years I'd lived there, and family members, neighbors, and churchgoers had come to spend time, standing under its shelter, sitting in its rockers.

Three sharecroppers lived on the land with their wives and their children in tiny dwellings on the north side of the acreage. They managed the wheat fields and whatever else needed to be done, whether in or out of the planting season or during the time of harvesting. They'd done more than their duty in the days following the funeral, and the hired hands had hacked down the buffer of trees by the chicken coop.

I'd watched as they axed every last evergreen and tore apart the chicken coop, dismantling the wood frame, plank by plank. Fragments of the wire cage lay twisted on the ground. I didn't care to know what, but the men had done something with the bear carcass. Dad had seen to it.

For the time being, anyway, the chickens were distributed among the sharecroppers, save the one striped hen. That one was Mary's. She'd coddled it since the day it was hatched.

As the sun set over the cleared-off parcel, I looked out to the vacant patch where a part of me would always remain. A storm had begun brewing.

I came around the side of the house and noticed how swiftly a haze had settled out to the west beyond the pond. Behind it, the sun was steadily fading, like embers aglow in a dying fire. I studied it once more, deep in thought. Something caught my eye farther off to the north. The longer I stared, the more certain I was of a woman walking across the wheat fields in my direction. A minute or two passed, and there was no doubt. A woman, one of the sharecroppers' wives, was moving intentionally, lifting her long dress to dodge last year's twigs and branchlets. On her arm was what looked like a basket.

She came into full view, attentively choosing her steps. Head down, she appeared to pay no heed to the gray clouds forming in a violet sky.

Other ladies had come out to the house from neighboring farms, bringing food, being sympathetic. Some had stayed to help with the wash and other household chores, the ones eleven-year-old Mary couldn't do, the ones the rest of us were trying to add to our routines. But none had come on foot—until this woman.

I shouted to Dad that one of the womenfolk was on her way up to the house.

"I'll see to her!" he shouted back from somewhere in the house. "Secure the barn, Simon. Get everyone inside." He was matter-of-fact. "Storm's a'coming."

I struck out toward the barn, yelling for Alan and Mason to give me a hand at corralling the animals, although it was plain enough the horses were not in the pasture. An eerie emptiness covered the fields. Except for the cows mooing as they returned to the barn and a lone bird chirping on a fence post, little more than a sweet-scented stillness filled the air.

Mason flung open the barn door before I'd gotten fifty feet, waving his straw hat, motioning me off. Alan was prodding the last of the cows into the barn.

I entrusted my brothers with the animals and started back the way I'd come. A sandy tornado sky hung over the house.

I reached the stoop at the back door, took off my boots, and came through the kitchen, barefooted. Dad's voice became louder the closer I got to the parlor window, and it was easy to see the form of a woman standing at the edge of the front porch. I hastened past in an effort to go unnoticed.

Dad caught a glimpse of me and motioned. Respectfully, I obeyed. The screen door snapped shut behind me as I went out. The sharecropper's wife leaned against one of the large, pyramid-shaped columns, its square base serving as a place for her to prop her basket while she caught her breath.

"Good day, Mrs. Brody." I nodded politely, self-consciously covering one bare foot with the other, trying to remain steady in the process. "You've walked quite a piece."

She paid no attention to my teetering and began to speak as she handed me the basket of baked bread and churned butter. That and fresh eggs were nestled in the folds of the red-checkered towel.

Dad listened intently, his gaze fixed on her face. His eyes glistened, and his hands hung at his sides while she expressed her sadness for our loss. She didn't look at me as she spoke of Mother, and I was hesitant to comment.

From one of the back rooms inside, the baby's crying broke an awkward tranquility. The three of us forced a smile. There didn't seem anything more to be said.

"You're most kind, Mrs. Brody," Dad said. "I would invite you in, but the sky has me a bit uneasy. Looks like we might have us a squall on our hands."

Mrs. Brody turned to see where Dad pointed. Menacing black clouds were sandwiching a funnel of light between their layers and the earth, pushing darkness toward us from the west. Debris swirled in a rush of warm air from the south.

And then the first drops fell. At first, it was a musical rain—gentle, with a special fragrance all its own. Clean, fresh. But already the wind was blowing wisps of brown hair from the twisted knot at the nape of Mrs. Brody's neck. Her flour sack dress flapped against her thin frame. She peered helplessly at Dad through rimless glasses. Alarm registered in her eyes.

"You can't walk back across the field now, you hear?" Dad said. "I'll saddle up Beauty and run you home. Otherwise, that husband of yours is gonna worry till you're back safe and sound."

Thunder rolled, long and low, far off to the west.

"I'll get Beauty and bring her up, Dad," I said, referring to his mare. I rushed inside and made a beeline for the stoop to get my boots. I left the basket in the kitchen sink and took my boots with me back through the house.

The door slammed behind me. "Dad, why don't you let me go?" I sat on a rocker, pulled on the right boot, picked up the left. "I'll get Soot."

A steady drizzle was underway.

"Dad?"

He shook his head with a confident smile and took hold of the woman's arm. "No, get Beauty. She's up to it, and we'll depend on the Lord to guide us through."

I pulled on the boot and started across the porch, wondering what Lord he was gonna depend on. *The one*, I thought, *that disregarded me*?

"Best hurry, son." His voice was grave.

I took off for the barn, running past Dad and Mrs. Brody and down the stone steps to where a mighty oak tree towered nearby. Fierce winds were assaulting it. The smaller limbs had begun to sway. The rest of it remained unyielding.

I made a run for it. The barn door was shut. I pushed it open with brute force and slowed to a fast walk as I came near the stables. The horses were edgy. Soot saw me coming and whinnied as I passed his stall and crossed over to the tack room for a saddle and bridle, then returned to the stall next to his. Beauty nodded her red head above the door.

"Come on, girl. Don't be grumpy tonight." I flopped the saddle on Dad's chestnut mare and let the straps down. "Easy there. That's it." With the straps tied, I grabbed the reins, put my foot in the stirrup, and threw my leg over the saddle. "Good girl. Let's go."

Beauty had seen worse weather. This, however, was awful. Thunder continued to rumble in the distance. Lightening cracked. She put her head to the wind, and we galloped up to the house. I jumped off, drenched, still holding the reins while Dad helped Mrs. Brody mount.

She hiked up her dress and climbed on Beauty's hindquarters. Dad mounted with a confidence I could never match and situated himself in the saddle in front of Mrs. Brody. Off they rode in the pouring rain, across the sloping mounds of mud and through the back fields, with the woman clinging to his middle.

He was probably right about her husband, Willie, being worried about his wife. I had no right to question Dad's judgment, but I did.

I rushed back inside and flew through the parlor, past the dining room, and on into the kitchen. The dishes clanged in the sideboard as I raced to the window, my eyes hunting through the downpour for a glimpse of Dad. I remained there, dripping on the linoleum floor, and listened to the rain pelting the tin roof as it fell on the deep dormers and ran onto the roof below.

A sudden, violent gust of wind and a clap of thunder brought Alan running down the stairs from the second floor. Five-year-old Charlotte followed a moment later, dragging her blanket, thumb in her mouth.

"Where's Dad going in this weather?" Alan was utterly shaken, as if some sort of horrific catastrophe was about to repeat itself.

I wanted to reassure him it wasn't, but I could not.

Another gust of wind, savage in its fervor, swept across the landscape from the southwest to northeast, shrill and whistling from one end of the house to the other. It rattled the window panes as it went, and outside, fledgling trees bent to the ground in submission.

"He and the Lord are taking Mrs. Brody home," I said. "Let's get the others into the root cellar."

Alan's mouth dropped open. "On horseback?" He stumbled backward in disbelief. I had good sense enough to get to the house ahead of the storm. But you're all wet, Si. Why didn't ya stay up at the house?"

"Alan! Listen to me!" I gave him a no-nonsense look just as another zap of lightning hit. "Get going! Round everybody up. I'll fetch a lantern."

I charged back outside, hurried over to the cellar door, and after a struggle, finally pulled it open against the driving rain. Wooden steps led down to absolute blackness. I ran back to the house for the lantern, yelling like a madman for Mason, who hadn't come back from the barn with Alan.

Within minutes, the eight of us were huddled at the back door, waiting for a word from me to take us out into the storm and a few feet away, down the cellar steps. Every face was upturned, every eye on me. Mary's hen strutted about, its gobble wagging in the wind, its head jabbing this way and that.

"Mary, give me the baby and hold on to Seth. Alan, hold on to Charlotte." I was panting. Water dripped from the end of my nose. "Raymond, hold on to my pants leg. Mason, take the lantern."

"Lucy!" Mary screeched for her hen. "We can't leave Lucy!"

"Go ahead, Mason. Lead the way," I said, directing the pack. "Let me pick up Lucy. Light it when you're down. I'll bring up the rear. Let's go."

We tromped down the back stairs and stayed close to the house, moving as fast as we could without slipping on the muddy path. Then, one by one, we descended the stairs. I clutched the baby in one arm and held the chain on the door with my other hand while the protesting hen I'd stuffed into my overalls clawed at my chest. Mason lit the lantern and set it on the floor, freeing himself to take the baby, and I pulled Lucy out by her feet with her wings flapping in terror. Using both hands now and gradually lowering the plank door above me, I backed down the stairs.

Inches before it shut, I heard the muffled strikes of hooves on the ground. I waited, holding the door far enough open to peer outside. Within seconds, Dad and the chestnut mare were visible, the well-ridden beast rounding the house, striding at full speed for the barn.

It was everything I could have prayed to see. But I had not prayed. I supposed I never would again. I required something more, something Dad did not: a reason, an explanation for Mother. A *justifiable* one. But there was none. And the storm raged on.

Fate alone brought Dad through it, I thought, and my mind wouldn't accept a different truth.

I let go of the cellar door, and it slammed shut with a watery bang. The illogical notion that a caring God had guided Dad home followed me down the wooden stairs.

The lantern flickered, and shadows danced on the stone walls of the foundation. I didn't hear a peep out of anyone.

There was very little headroom, and with so little space, it felt like a damp tomb. The eight of us, wet to the bone, sat on the cool dirt floor. Huge oak logs, bigger than my arms could have wrapped around, lay in rows above us, hewn on one side to form the flooring inside the house. A few canned tomatoes and other jars of last season's vegetables sat stacked on the freestanding shelves against the back wall. As far as I knew, no one had asked who would preserve the fruits and vegetables when the time came for canning.

Mary cradled her black-and-white-striped hen, smoothing its feathers, touching its red wattle, talking to it in a lower-toned voice as if that would soothe the wildness in its beady, black eyes.

Reasoning wasn't going to make the fear go away. Not fear of the storm, not fear of the future. And nothing was going to comfort us in our sorrow— neither churned butter nor baked bread. How naive I'd been to trust a God whose room at the top had very little to do with the rest of us down below in this pit. He'd hurled his power or withheld it—I couldn't be sure which. Either way, his actions had left us motherless, and Dad still called him Lord. What exactly was I missing in my understanding?

The pain divided me into two people. One I knew, and one I didn't.

Maybe ten minutes passed before curiosity got me up off the floor and made me climb the stairs and lift the door to take a peek at the weather. The wind outside was blowing like I'd never seen before.

"Sit tight," I said. "It's not over."

During my trek up the stairs and back down, the puddle my wet clothes had left on the floor had chilled. I parked my butt in it anyway, and we waited out the storm. The roar of the wind was deafening. But God—as far as I could tell—was silent.

Chapter 6

Outside it was quiet. The high winds had let up. The storm, for the moment, was over.

I lumbered through the kitchen door. Dad, freshly dressed in dry clothes, was moving down the hall at a fast but unassuming gait—his sinew undisguised: burly, over six foot.

Alan and the rest of my siblings came inside behind me and scattered off to their rooms to change out of wet clothes. I hung back, no longer dripping but soggy and whipped, needing to hear what evidently was on Dad's mind.

"That was some twister," he said, his brow furrowed. "Beats all." He shook his head dolefully, but his eyes held their ever-present optimism. "Just thankful to get Mrs. Brody home safely. And glad to get off that horse alive." His brow relaxed. "You know, son, God got us there and back again."

I felt my spine stiffen, perturbed by his reference to a fickle God. "You're the one, Dad. You rode out the storm." With a stranglehold on the basket, I snatched it from the sink and pulled the bread loaf from inside it.

"That one, son, was a tornado for sure," he said, taking a deep breath, ignoring my impudence. "Bigger than any storm we've seen around these parts." He blinked hard, took the basket from me, and gently set it down on the sideboard.

I took an egg from the folds of checkered cloth. "I'll fix us some supper. Scramble—"

"That thing," he emphasized with a headshake, "moved outta the southwest, Simon. Coming at me full force." He gazed into my eyes until I was certain he could see my soul and continued, recounting the details. "Then suddenly it doubled back." He traced an exaggerated circle in the air with his right arm. "Had to have touched down just south of here. But Beauty and I were in the barn by then." His arm dropped limply. His voice cracked. "God's power spared us."

I wanted to accept that, but I couldn't. My lips tightened in defiance.

He pressed on, blind to the conflict flaring inside me. "Lord knows the children don't need that kinda loss. Their mother . . ." Dad's voice trailed off.

I reminded myself of the egg I held in my hand and resisted the urge to crush it. The rest of me stiffened, intent on holding back the sarcasm that was bound to erupt. "So, God picks and chooses?" I heard my voice rise.

Dad flinched at the mockery. "If that's a serious question, son, then ask it of God. You've got a lot of healing to do. We *all* do. But remember this: God is sovereign." His chest swelled under the arch of his broad shoulders. "We're at liberty to ask our questions, but God's sovereign."

I could feel the grind of my teeth and the muscles in my face tightening. Contempt layered in the recesses of my stomach. Sovereign? Really? I wasn't even sure I knew what that meant. At least not where my mother was concerned. I, too, would have preferred a good God as much as the next guy, but I'd just walked past the lingering fragrance of Mother's calico apron still hanging next to the stove. *Where was God's power when—*

Dad rested his hand on my shoulder.

It occurred to me that I needed to keep my mouth shut. I had no right to demand to know what force had molded him into the hardened rock that kept him believing. I couldn't fall in step with his faith in a callous God, and I felt myself slipping away, as if I were molasses spilled between the crevices of the back-porch floorboards. I tried to run from the awareness that we had drifted apart. I was his son, but his God was not one I could trust.

"I'll be riding down south a ways before it gets any darker," he said. "See what I can see. Maybe if anybody's needing help."

He left without eating, and I went about doing what I could to cook food for the rest of us, glad I hadn't smashed the eggs. We needed them, as well as the butter and the bread. I hated to think Mrs. Brody had risked her life to bring the basket across the field on foot. Dad had risked his, though, to put a meal on the table.

With supper finished, I saw to the children's toilet needs. Alan and Mason helped tend the regular chores with the livestock, which left only the milking yet to be done.

I was spreading hay when Dad rode into the barn on Molly. It was after dark. The mare was breathing hard. He slid off her and hitched her to the post. Beauty gave a jealous snort in her stall down the way.

Mason walked over from the hogpen.

"Wipe her down for me, Mason." Dad was as breathless as the animal he'd just ridden in. He gave Mason a dismissive nod. "We don't want to put her away wet. Thanks, son," he said as my brother led Molly away. He turned to me. "They've been hit at the Petersons' place."

Alan was coming our way and saying something—too far away for us to hear him.

"That twister's killed Zack Peterson," Dad said in a hushed voice before Alan reached us.

Alan meandered over and opened his mouth to speak, but Dad interrupted. "I do need to get at those cows now, don't I, before they burst. Alan, son," he said in a kind and persuasive tone, "how's about you go on up to the house and rustle up a bite for me? I'll be more than ready to eat a plateful of anything once I'm done here."

I couldn't even look at Dad. The worm had turned in the Hagans' neck of the woods, or so it seemed. How, I wondered, in less than two weeks, could life in one small segment of rural Kentucky change so drastically?

⟫•◇•⟪

Cold scrambled eggs awaited on a plate, covered with Mrs. Brody's red-checkered cloth. I was the only one who hadn't gone to bed, and Dad was long overdue for supper—such as it was. It was approaching eleven. I was relieved to hear him clamber up the back steps.

He stopped long enough to take off his boots, then came through the kitchen doorway. "My heart's heavy, Simon," he said as he crumpled on a dining chair and picked up his fork. "*Too* heavy. Zack Peterson was caught." He spoke between mouthfuls of eggs and lukewarm sausage gravy. "That young wife of his is beside herself, naturally. Small son he has, maybe Raymond's age, can't begin to understand." He swiped some bread through the gravy and stopped short of eating it, looking up from his plate. His eyes brimmed with tears. "Tragic. We know how they feel, don't we?"

I doubted he expected an answer—a reverent groan at the most.

"Did they lose their house?"

"No, the tobacco barn. My guess is he ran there for cover. Could've had business in there, though. Whole thing just lifted up." Dad got up, plate in hand, and took it to the sink. "I'm turning in, Simon. Tomorrow's another day."

"I'll scald the milk and take it to the cellar. Night, Dad."

"Turn in soon. You look beat. Get some good rest."

With the last of the chores done and the final trip to the cellar, I made the climb to my room. Quite possibly, I was asleep before my head hit the feather pillow.

———◈———

With or without the rooster's crow the next morning, the necessity to pee got me out of bed. I was dressed and out to the barn, back to the grind.

The storm had moved on through, and a significant part of all outdoors was enveloped in the sweet bouquet that followed a simple spring rain. My walk down the hill gave me a whiff of the damp earth, further confirming the intense deluge that had struck the land.

Dad was seated at a cow's side, milking, undeterred by my entrance. I headed over to Soot's stall and then moved out toward the pasture with my stallion plodding along beside me.

It was an hour before I finished wrapping up the predawn chores. More than once it crossed my mind to do them "as unto the Lord" as Mother had prompted, but I mingled suffering with anger, trying to hold up under the guilt as I clomped back through the barn.

Dad had positioned himself at the other end, outside at the gate, with his foot wedged between the lowest two slats in the fence. His elbow rested on his bent knee and his ragged straw hat perched itself on the back of his head. A milk pail sat on the ground next to the fence post. "Morning, son. Just taking in the splendor of the sun coming up." He raised his arm and brushed his hand across the sky as if it were a canvas on an easel. "Yonder, just look at it!"

I could see it plainly, as well as the fields to the north where sharecroppers had tilled and plowed the soil into rows to form firm seedbeds for planting.

On the ridge beyond, trees were aligned in flawless symmetry, and the sun in all its glory was rising. But I was not satisfied to watch the sun coming up. I wanted to take Dad's pulse. *Maybe*, I chided, *it's just me, dousing myself with self-pity.*

The fields had taken a beating. Seeds that had been planted earlier in the month were now blown to smithereens. Boards had been blown from the barn. Limbs were down. The retaining wall up near the house that held back our cascading yard was strained, threatening to break and forever scar us with moist and mildewed memories.

Nothing, however, compared to the devastation that had gone on at the Petersons' place a mile or so south. I understood the humbleness I'd heard in my father's comment—*"If ever I needed church, it's tomorrow"*—but I couldn't reckon with the thought of sitting in church.

"Yessir," was all I said.

"I'll swing around, get Mrs. Brody's basket to her on the way back home."

"No need, Dad. I'll take it across later this morning."

"Fine, but plan on church. And plan on walking there with Alan and Mason."

"I'm pretty much a man. Guess it's 'bout time I start making some of my own decisions."

A glance—his—darted at me from beneath his hat's brim. He scraped the bottom of his boot on the fence board and straightened his broad shoulders. "Your mother's place was next to me on the buckboard. And now Mary and Charlotte will be sitting next to me in Lacy's place, boys in the back. We'll go as a family, Simon. And we'll worship as a family."

Chapter 7

⟫◆⟪

The sky was wide open and blue and around noontime when I rode north across the plowed wheat fields to the Brody house, guiding Soot out to the perimeter of the seedbeds as I went.

There'd been no reason for me to go over to the Brodys' in the past, making this the first time I'd seen the tiny, graying timber houses occupied by the share-croppers. These were people who stayed to themselves, and I guessed my folks were, as well. It had taken a tragedy to alter the order of things. Mrs. Brody's kind gesture at the mercy of a tornado had shortened the distance between us.

I sat tall in the saddle. Mrs. Brody's basket, which I'd tied to the saddle horn, flopped against Soot's black mane as he plodded along. The red-check-ered cloth was neatly folded inside.

We picked up the pace as we cleared the fields and trotted on the wagon path, a barking dog on our heels, past two little dwellings situated about fifty yards apart. Their sloping red tin roofs swooped down over the houses and bent outward along the front edges, covering the modest porches where the Mullins and the McKinneys lived. These and other tenants had been around as long as I could remember.

Mrs. Brody was tenaciously hoeing the red clay in the side yard at the third house. Seeing her assured me I had the correct indistinguishable prop-erty. She stopped long enough to fold back the brim of her bonnet and then held to the long arm of the hoe and watched as I rode in on Soot.

"Good day to you, Mrs. Brody!" I shouted back at her and, like the caw of a crow, it broke the tranquility of the setting.

The tethered goat lurched on the rope that held him to the post at the far end of the porch. Mrs. Brody straightened her glasses and dropped the hoe to look me over.

"Simon. It's Simon Hagan here, returning your basket. Don't mean to startle you."

She came running from the near side of the house to greet me. "Not a'tall, Mr. Hagan," she said as I got off Soot and unfastened the basket. "Not a'tall! Please come sit a spell."

A primitive-looking bench sat next to the only window. Mrs. Brody rushed to the entry. A crude frame had been nailed around its opening.

I swung the reins over the narrow handrail to secure Soot and then started up the four stairs, unsure if the rickety boards would hold my weight, ducking underneath the overhang as I went.

The door stood slightly ajar. A bed and a chest of drawers were visible in one room, a table, three chairs, and washstand in the other. From my angle it looked like the Brody family had devised a way for these two rooms to be enough.

With no need to go inside and not wanting to, I set the basket on the bench. "I sure want to thank you, Mrs. Brody. Thank you for your generosity."

Her rimless glasses caught a beam of sun and reflected the light as she looked up at me. "Don't mention it, not a'tall. Your mama came across those fields many a time, bringing me this, bringing me that."

She raised a hand over her forehead to shield her eyes from the sun but paid no attention to the black, scraggly-haired goat, which was screaming like a human, tongue hanging from its mouth. "She was a good woman, your mama. Now Willie . . . he's out to the field with the mule. Will you be needin' to see him?"

I looked out past the house to where the mule pulled the plow. Mr. Brody walked behind, steering it, tromping the ground, repairing the windblown field.

"No, ma'am. I'll be on my way now," I said, feeling like I had more than my share of abundance—or less than my share of a mother. In the short week since I'd lost her, I'd discovered it took more strength than I had. My world had changed in a single morning, and now this unearthing of economic disparity had me buffaloed. I covered the guilt with a throaty laugh. "We're much obliged for your help, Mrs. Brody."

Her bonnet was low over her eyes before I was down the steps, and the hoe was in her hand before I rode out of sight.

I needed to be alone, making tonight a fine one to act on my decision to sleep in the hayloft. I thought I might also find it a relief to miss out on Alan's moaning and his fits of sleeplessness. And by church time tomorrow, my head would be clear.

———◆———

We'd gotten to church in the usual way, along with the unusualness of not having Mother on the front seat of the buckboard. Molly pulled the four-wheeled wagon up to the churchyard. Her prancing gait seemed to have put the girls in a feisty frame of mind. The younger boys on the back seat punched and poked at each other. The baby sat between them.

Dad jumped down and jiggled Molly's bridle and hitched her to the post. Mason, Alan, and I brought up the rear, walking at a clip that put us not that far behind. With everyone in tow, Dad led the way past the blossoming apple trees alongside the white picket fence to the one-room, steepled building.

A small crowd had gathered. More parishioners were arriving. Women clustered to one side, talking to each other in dainty voices, correcting their children in more forceful ones.

I stayed in step with Dad as he joined the handful of men, some in their Sunday best, others in their mud-free overalls. I'd managed a pair of pleated trousers, a waistcoat, and a tie for the day, which had begun fairly mild. Following the brisk walk beside, sometimes behind, the loaded-up buckboard, I fanned my white shirt—pushing and pulling its top button like I was priming the pump—to keep it from sticking to the sweat on my chest.

The talk amongst those in the know was all about the outcome of the week here in Todd County. The rest of the men listened intently to the subdued chatter about the twister and the horror of Zack Peterson's misfortune, which had occurred in its path. Then came the subject of the bear that had come out of hibernation, and the topic of the two untimely deaths was laid out for everyone within earshot, children included.

"You makin' it through, Geoffrey?" The gray-haired older gentleman couldn't seem to make eye contact with Dad. He gave a weakly kick to a dirt clod under his foot.

Some things should have been left unsaid. We were, however, on the lawn of the Lord. Where else was a person to talk about their dead if not here?

Dad's inscrutable countenance gave little away. With his head erect, he looked straight at Mr. Granville. "We're doing the best we can." His left shoulder twitched a mite as he formulated the remainder of his answer. "It's a tough row to hoe, yes sirree. Mighty tough."

I felt the weight of his powerful hand on my back, like a vise at the base of my neck.

"Mighty tough," he said again and moved a step closer to me, as if in our standing closer together we might draw on each other's strength.

I was silent, expecting the heat of his flesh to melt clear through to my spine. From somewhere down the tree-shrouded lane, the sound of a motorized vehicle grew louder, unmistakably the ta-ta-ta of a Model T approaching.

"How 'bout you, Simon?" Mr. Granville asked. "Gotta be hard."

"Yes, sir." I raised my voice over the noise of the engine as the Model T rolled closer. "Thank you for asking, Mr. Granville. It's been one day at a time." I wanted to pull away. Better to stay put. I nodded, fiddling with my tie. "Todd County's seen a lot of suffering this past week."

The engine shut down. The automobile's door opened, and Mr. Robert Maxwell, whose fine style and uppity good looks were a sight to behold, emerged. His left foot touched the ground slowly, with the dignity of a superior breed.

"Good, lad. Good," Mr. Granville said.

But already heads were turning in the other direction. Chatter broke off at the sight of the novel automobile.

A few seconds passed. Mr. Maxwell stood and unfurled.

I could feel the warm syrup of his political agenda sliding down the backs of the men in their less-than-stylish Sunday attire. I'd not had a cynical bone in my body until now, further confirming I did not belong in this yard, not on these premises, not anywhere close to God's house. But I liked the automobile, and more than once I caught myself admiring the notable curve of the shiny black fenders above the front tires, the sleek, sassy top, and the angled steering wheel that showed through the driver's window like a magic wand in a make-believe glass carriage. It made our simple buckboard—and everyone else's, too—look pathetic.

Mr. Granville hadn't finished his prattle. "Me and the missus are praying for you folks."

I didn't share Mr. Granville's nor his wife's devotion to prayers. But letting that fact be known seemed wrong, for I liked to think I'd been brought up better than that. Expressing my growing doubt in a God that even cared was equally unnecessary. "Very kind of you, sir."

The men's talk of the bear who'd come out of hibernation, hungry and aggressive, was successfully squelched by the sight of Mr. Maxwell's enviable possession. Behind me, little Mary tugged on my waistcoat.

"Perhaps, gentlemen," Mr. Granville continued, "we ought to take a look at that automobile."

Dad looked relieved. He hung back while the others went to inspect the Model T and then gently tried to pry Mary's fingers from my waistcoat. "Mary, angel, let me have your hand," he said. "We're obliged to offer some comfort to Mrs. Peterson. She and her boy had a great loss, same as us."

Mary, still gripping my clothing, didn't take her eyes off me. "You'll tell me about that bear, Simon. Won't you?"

I didn't answer. I couldn't have given her an answer even if I'd had one. Not now. Not ever.

Dad spoke tenderly to her. "Go with me, won't you, Mary, before church starts?"

I could feel her grasp loosen.

"Right off the assembly line." Mr. Maxwell was puffed up enough to pop the buttons off his suit coat. "Why, up there in Detroit—well, *near* there— they're pushing these babies out right and left." He brought a cigarette to his mouth and inhaled deeply. "By the thousands every day." He exhaled a puff of smoke into the air above his dazzled onlookers. "Henry Ford's paying five dollars a day to mass produce them on the assembly lines. Good work, good pay." His smile broadened. He mashed his cigarette in the dirt with the toe of his shoe. "Good automobile!"

Every head bobbed in unison, mine included, and the bell rang from the modest steeple tower. Parishioners began moving toward the open door of the church.

"Mr. Hagan," Mr. Maxwell said, taunting me as I turned to go, "she'd look good on you, lad! Bet you'll own one yourself someday."

"Do tell?" I gave a brief smile, conscious of the array of horses that stood tied to the apple trees.

Beautiful as she was, Miss Molly was still an old nag by comparison, and the horse-drawn buckboard could never be so stylish as the only glossy-finished Model T in front of the clapboard church.

It wasn't my place to begrudge him his automobile or blame him for the undeserved humiliation it had imposed on ol' Molly and me, but I could taste a world of possibilities. That world, most likely, wasn't going to come to the idyllic pastureland in Todd County, Kentucky.

"I thank you for that prediction, Mr. Maxwell." I nodded a good day to him and followed the parade of ladies into the building.

They were the same ones who'd come out to the house, the good folk that Mother described as the salt of the earth. And after the service they'd be the ones to give prolonged hugs to the Hagan clan and to Mrs. Hannah Peterson and her son. It was that kind of parish. Then we'd make our way back to our respective farms and resume our chores without missing a beat.

⟫◈⟪

Alan had been scarce as hen's teeth during the entire gathering. As we walked home, he picked up a good-sized stick and, with every step he took, beat the ground with it.

"Were you even in church?" My tone was guarded. Even so, not the right words. "Dad wants us inside the building at least, Alan, if not in the same pew."

Alan, riled, broke the stick over the wheel of the buckboard as it rolled close to us.

"Listen, Alan, we need—"

"I'm listening!" His eyes were intense, searching, with no sign of his dimples on a troubled face. "You have all the answers, don't you?" He jutted his peach-fuzzed chin in defiance.

Mason left us and walked on ahead, up toward the front of the carriage. With the clomp-clomp of Molly's hooves, I was certain Dad couldn't hear me or Alan. The boys in the back seat faced forward.

"Calm down, hear? We're gonna have to pull together, Alan. For the sake of the little ones." I was searching my mind for a way to defuse his frustration. "How about you spending tonight in the barn with me in the hayloft. We can talk."

Alan whipped his head in my direction, and his curly red hair blazed in the sunshine. Dimples buried themselves deeply into both cheeks. "Yeah!"

He pitched the stick, and we walked in silence the remainder of the way home.

My head had not cleared as I'd hoped, not in the abandonment I'd chosen for myself in the barn, not on the haystacks where I'd laid my body last night. I wondered if it ever would. And tonight, in inviting Alan into my torment, I was as inadequate as a non-swimmer trying to rescue a drowning man. Between the volatile conversation and the vicious circle of determining why things happened the way they did, I could see his pain. And I felt his pain. We wept. He was on edge. I couldn't brush him off. Nothing short of a fairy godmother was going to help, and I didn't see one coming.

The last blinking star seemed to fade off in the corner of the loft's opening. There in the country air, with the smell of manure in my nostrils, my thoughts held to the question of how to shield Mary. For the rest of her life.

Alan moaned, and the sound of him wrestling his demons on the bed of hay finally slacked off in the night, and I must've catnapped, knowing I was needed here, needed back at the house, needed when only God could have helped.

I awoke with a start, but not a thing had changed. It had to be way after midnight. Alan was snoring. I thought of the splendid automobile and the rows of shiny Model Ts on a city street—nothing more than a dream. The quarter moon had set like another world in space. Clouds floated above the hilly landscape. I had a sinking feeling it was one I'd never get past.

Chapter 8

⟨⬥⟩

I'd rarely gone inside the church all spring. Dad couldn't have missed them—those times I'd obediently walked with my brothers to church but hadn't gone inside. For me, the fascination was none other than Mr. Robert Maxwell and his automobile and the fact that he was running for state senator. He, too, showed up every Sunday.

Dad's reason for church was God, but there'd not been any doubt about the eye he had out for Miss Hannah—as opposed to my whereabouts. I'd seen the interest blossoming as far back as May, when the peonies had been there for the picking. And he had. For her. I doubted I was the only one to notice.

Just prior to the service, he joined me next to the elm tree, where I was city-talking with Mr. Maxwell about the four-cylinder engine on his automobile. I generally looked forward each week to such conversations but sensed this one was quickly coming to an end. Dad had a smile for us but didn't show any interest in our ongoing discussion of automobiles. There was a lull, and the two men shook hands and exchanged niceties before Mr. Maxwell turned to go. I'd have followed like a lost hound at his heels if it hadn't been apparent that Dad had a purpose in singling me out.

He held his straw hat by the brim with both hands and, turning it slowly, looked up at me. "I'm not gonna insist you go inside, son. You're eighteen." His smile had vanished. His fingers worked their way around his hat, nimbly turning it in circles. "Almost eighteen anyway." The hat rotated in his hands. "A man. But you need to know this—and know it well." He didn't take his eyes off me. "Your fight with God is one-sided." His eyes pleaded.

If God isn't to blame for what happened at the chicken coop, I thought, *then I am! I could have protected her, saved her*. I could feel myself grimace.

Dad took a step toward me and laid a hand on my shoulder.

Instinctively, I backed off, unable to face him, scared he might see straight through to my shame.

Resigned, he covered the beads of perspiration on his head with his hat, turned, and slowly walked toward the building. Mrs. Peterson stood at the entrance, waiting alone.

I couldn't bring myself to go inside the door and sit there, respectfully regarding the traditions of faithful churchgoers. Instead, I parked myself on a rock under the tree and waged my one-sided fight with God.

Mother had been gone only a few short months. No one would have judged Dad's need for a woman at his side, and widow Hannah Peterson was there. Once again, the season of burley tobacco was at hand while he cultivated a new love elsewhere.

The longer days of June, dry as they were, allowed us to work in the fields with the black men he'd hired, dropping the seeds that would—if the laws of nature cooperated—emerge in a matter of ten days.

By July there was no doubting the strength of the crops or the growing relationship between Dad and Mrs. Peterson. It wasn't for me to question. I could see it in his eyes. I knew him well, although he shared nothing of what was on his mind when it came to Hannah Peterson. I knew what was happening.

July was hot, unusually hot. The tobacco plants were maybe a foot tall, and the flower heads were ready to be bagged for seed production. Days in the fields were dreadfully long. We covered the young plants before the flowers opened in order to maintain the purity of the variety and then topped and suckered the leaves. But there was always the possibility of bad weather, plant disease, or insects that could take out an entire crop in a matter of days, if not minutes. Plenty of farmers had lost their farms or their status as cash or share tenants because of crop failures. We'd been lucky. The land was ours, but weather didn't pick favorites. Farming necessitated plowing the rows, treading our existence, awaiting seed that might never produce.

I lit a cigarette and considered the futility as the smoke streamed from my mouth and nostrils. It was something over which I had no control. The unpredictability made me want something more.

It must've been the gander I'd taken at the sharecroppers' situation that had stuck in my craw. I pondered the effort it took for the Brodys to provide sustenance and an income through the sale of a smidgen of surplus on the small parcel they worked. I'd witnessed the poverty.

As for Miss Hannah, though, the twister had left her to bury her dead husband, step over the tombstone, and hike on. She and the Brodys were caught and, in the aftermath of the storm, I had come face-to-face with the devastation. It had forced them to start over.

But now, two months after replanting, leaves sheltered the head of the wheat berries on forthcoming stalks, and the field swished and swayed in a blaze of color beneath the warm sun. As part of the cycle of life, the expected crop would burst forth. Mature wheat. Golden, pristine, and unscathed.

I felt out of place. It wasn't the burden of failure. Rather the putrid smell of guilt. I had to count the cost of rotting on the farm. My roots were stagnating in shallow ground.

Chapter 9

⟫⟩◈⟨⟪

The chirpy-voiced widow of Zack Peterson moved into our house with her nine-year-old son, Marly, on the second of September. It was a Thursday afternoon. The wedding had been one of good logic and suitability, mildly acceptable if not overwhelmingly agreeable to those who had a say-so.

Hannah Peterson seemed like a decent person.

The pink flower in her hair held her thick brown locks to one side. Other than that, she would have passed for an average-looking woman walking down the aisle of the small church. Sun poured through the round window above the arched door as if it were an anointing. Pink ribbons lay in the sills of the eight-paned sashes, three on a side. Her plain pink dress ruffled at the top of her neck, covered her wrists, and came down to the floor.

Mary was one of those who'd been mildly accepting of the marriage proposal. She had clung to her striped hen when Dad had chosen to tell her the news, and in the heat of the July day when he broke it to her, a backdrop of hollyhocks stood in support like colorful soldiers behind her. She stroked the clucking fowl with one hand and wiped away tears with another. Dad pulled a sunshine-yellow blossom from the stalk and held it out for her. She rewarded him with a brave little smile at the peace offering.

For Alan, there had been no opportune time to learn the news, and he was still ranting on the morning of the wedding. "Why? Tell me why she's so important. We don't need her here."

One after another, he fired off his questions, but Dad's explanations weren't enough to satisfy Alan. It didn't matter that Dad needed a mother for his children, that he felt lonely, or that running a farm without a wife and helpmate was a hardship.

"I want her for my wife, Alan. It comes down to that."

All reasoning went unheard. Alan stomped the ground while I waited for a chance to intervene.

Dad walked away from him and left him swinging his arms in the air. And the wedding went forward.

Dad was a head taller than Miss Hannah and probably twelve or fourteen years her senior. She had a dark complexion and wide, expectant eyes, which made me want to know what she saw that I didn't. Her peppy smile had managed to catch Dad's attention at every church service since April. But it was, after all, their wedding day, a blustery afternoon. The ceremony was over in a matter of a few minutes, and all in attendance were happy as larks. For Miss Hannah, the full import of becoming the mother of nine children, including her son Marly, in one afternoon had apparently not sunk in.

She leaned on Dad's arm as they stood for their vows. I turned away when he kissed her on the lips at the pronouncement that they were man and wife. They rode off in the buckboard with the both of them snuggled in the seat, which on normal occasions Dad occupied all by himself. I figured they'd gone straight to the house, since there was no other place they could go. It was pointless to ask such a question.

Under the watchful eye of Mrs. Brody, my siblings and I were kept distracted for two hours at the church with yard games, pink punch, and endless plates of cookies. By the time we caught up with the newlyweds back at the house, it was later in the day. Dad couldn't have seemed more triumphant if he'd brought home a new horse. Miss Hannah, bustling around in an unfamiliar kitchen, looked like an adolescent girl in a mature lady's housedress. It had been six months since I'd heard so many pots and pans rattling this close to suppertime.

The youngest children were wild. The rest of us had chores left to do before sitting down to a meal. I changed into overalls and went to the barn. Miss Hannah was nowhere to be seen as I came through the kitchen on my way out. A couple of hired hands were taking up the slack created by our attendance at the wedding. I finished up what needed to be done and went on back to the house.

Mary had set the table, someone had gathered flowers, and the orang-ish-brown dog who had taken up residence just in time to be a best friend for Raymond and Marly was barking at the back door. All three bounded into the house as I made my way inside carrying a pail of milk. Dad followed behind me with another, a liveliness in his step.

It wasn't yet four o'clock. The cows had never been milked this early. Neither had supper ever come so early, but it was ready. A mound of boiled potatoes, a mess of greens, and a slab of pork sat on the Lazy Susan that was being circled in the middle of the cherrywood dining table. Miss Hannah made the spread seem like it was as easy as falling off a log. Her boy and Raymond had paired up at one section of the octagonal table. Huddled together, they were having their own conversation about whatever nine-year-old stepbrothers talk about.

I didn't know Miss Hannah's history. I doubted Dad did, either. She looked far different from my mother, who had been a fairly tall woman with light skin and reddish hair—whose descent and nationality I'd duly concluded was Scotch. And Highlanders, from a native mountaineer's viewpoint, were thought to have come down from Pennsylvania, but my dad wasn't a Kentucky mountaineer. He was just a simple farmer with a third-grade education.

Whatever my mother's ancestry, it had more or less dissolved in her marriage to my dad. She'd shed the label of a circuit rider's daughter to become Dad's Lacy, soft-spoken and tender but subtly strong. Much of the time her blue eyes did the talking. And after they eloped, Geoffrey Newton Hagan took his bride to his parcel of Kentucky land, where some mighty fine roots took hold.

I wasn't about to graft on to Miss Hannah's. Hannah had two strikes against her. She wasn't Lacy, and she wasn't my mother.

At least that was what I'd thought until the day they were married. It was then that our household lit up with her presence, and hope moved in where there'd been scarcely any for quite some time.

Dad was stretching his arms and yawning before the sun went down. Miss Hannah blushed so deeply it turned her cheeks rosy.

Chapter 10

I tiptoed out to the front porch and, hoping to go unnoticed by any of the family, made sure the screen door closed quietly behind me. I needed to sit a spell in solitude. Maybe smoke a cigarette. Weeks had passed since the wedding. The end of September was drawing near, and the daylight hours were waning. Evenings were bordering on balmy, this one in particular. I sat in the rocker and pulled out my Camels. It looked like ten or eleven of the twenty still remained.

The mutt that Raymond had fostered—and was now sharing with his new stepbrother—came up the steps, meandered over to where I sat, and laid his pointed face on my knee. Raymond and Marly, each nine years old, had cleverly named him Ninety-nine, but the dog was just Niney now.

I took a puff and exhaled into the night. The lovable little mongrel looked up at me for attention.

"What is it about your neck that needs so much scratching, Niney?"

In my opinion, I'd earned a moment alone to breathe in the night air and savor the tobacco that I hadn't personally had to plant, plow, or harvest—unless I had without knowing it. We owned fifteen or more acres of it. I'd smelled the light, air-cured leaves of tobacco since I was knee-high to a duck, and this season I'd taken on the planting season "as unto the Lord," but Mother's admonition hadn't lightened the load. I stretched my arms over my head, trying to get the kinks out and relax, and then took another couple of puffs and rubbed the dog's mottled coat of fur.

Satisfied, Niney sat down at my feet.

Burley tobacco sustained our family and, as the landowners, the planting and harvesting required the Hagans to produce, even with the help of the hired hands. With them and five tenants, Dad, Mason, Alan, and I farmed the eighty acres. It hadn't made a farmer of me yet. Dad still seemed to think it would.

I stretched again, taking a moment to rub my *own* stiff neck.

Despite the drought we were having, the tobacco plants had grown to three feet in the low-lying areas, and they had ripened from deep green to yellow before turning brown as harvest time approached. We had followed a pair of mules through the tobacco patches back in June, pushing the worn plow handles and stumbling over the newly turned-up earth. And after it was laid by and we plowed again with a two-point plow, there was still no dirt in my veins. But it flowed through Dad's. He was a natural-born hustler. I respected that.

His honest living came from digging it out of the soil, and now that we'd come to the harvest—the tobacco sticks had been driven into the ground between the rows of mature tobacco, and the leaves had been cut and wilted—we'd be spearing them and moving each pole into the open-sided barn to dry. Every bit of it would eventually go into the production of cigarettes, and the biggest amount was produced right here in Kentucky. It was our main crop, our cash, our livelihood. That and barley.

After a couple more puffs, I put out the cigarette with my foot and kicked it to one side. Niney sighed. We were both enjoying the peacefulness when Alan rushed out to the porch.

"I've been looking everywhere for you!" His disdain was matched only by his uncouth interruption. "I'm sleeping in the hayloft with you tonight." His chest heaved with anxiety.

The dog stood up, smelling trouble.

I kept my seat, eyeball to eyeball with Alan. "No, Alan, you're not." I paused to gather my wits. "Mary should have someone a little older than Mason to oversee things—with Marly and all. That would be you." I figured a role with more authority would sit well with him.

Mary had cleared a corner of the boys' bedroom for Raymond and Marly to call their own to ensure Marly would fit in with his new stepbrothers, especially Raymond, since they were the same age.

"I'm counting on you to leave Dad alone and keep everyone else from bothering him and Miss Hannah. You up to it, Alan?"

"I most certainly am," he said smugly. "Gimme a cigarette, Si." He pulled a rocker up close and sat next to me, grinning.

I handed over a cigarette. It made some sense, not a lot, but if it boosted his confidence, then well and good. Considering the price of cigarettes—ten cents a pack—I savored every last one of them, doling out only this one.

His eyes searched my face. The soft, adolescent hair growing in profusion on his upper lip shone in the moonlight.

"Oh, you need a light, too?" I struck a match and held it out for him. "Here, this is the way you do it—"

"You're babying me! Stop. I mean it." He promptly choked as he inhaled, gagging and coughing.

It was funny, but I never looked his way. I'd probably been just like him, appearing just as green to Mr. Maxwell when he'd given me my first. Except I wasn't in the same league as Mr. Maxwell—or capable of dreaming of a Model T with big-city headlights.

"You should shave, Alan, or you'll set that mustache on fire." I wasn't sure if he saw me wink through the swirling smoke. "Better be careful."

"Needling me. I don't like it." He stifled a cough, and the evening got quiet, except for the howl of a distant coyote and the muted goings-on inside the house. "You like Miss Hannah?" Alan's voice was meek, dead serious, as if the mention of her name had sapped vital juices from him.

My heart needed to wrap around him. It begged. He looked like a lost fawn, left to scavenge for himself. Things weren't the same as they'd once been, but we were managing. There was hope. The girls, in particular, required a mother, and like Dad had told me, we had no choice but to go on. We'd traded one life for another—same as Miss Hannah had. It wasn't supposed to be this way, but it was the best we could do. That was what I was thinking, anyway, before Mary showed up at the door.

She opened it and stuck her head out. "Dad's gonna have you out to the woodpile, Alan. I'm telling." She was standing in front of us now, hands on her hips.

"You will not, Miss Mary," I said, rising, trying to quiet the barking dog.

"And I'll sic this mad dog on you!" Alan snapped at her as he stood up.

"Enough of this. You'll wake everyone." They were both looking to me, and I wasn't about to squander the privilege that went with my age. "Alan, you're not out of the woods yet. Why don't you help Mary wrap up in the house. That's what next oldest does. It's time for you to take charge." I expected him to salute at any moment, eager as he was to face the challenge. "You can see, I'm really too old to share a room with three young boys—four including Marly—and you're turning sixteen. So now, Alan, when we finish here, I'll just head on down to the barn—alone."

Alan couldn't take the drafts in the elevated loft anyhow. I liked it that way and wouldn't have thought of leaving, except that with winter coming on, I'd have to give some consideration to moving back into the house.

Mary went inside. Alan looked as if there was a loose end still dangling.

"To answer your question, I like Miss Hannah." It was good to hear myself say it. "I think after, lo, these three, four weeks, we should let Dad keep her. Don't you?"

I had coaxed a smile out of Alan, albeit a fleeting one. Perhaps with the levity, we both felt some relief from the weight we'd been carrying on our shoulders.

It was nice to have a woman in the house—someone to have a meal waiting, someone to make the children laugh, someone to move Dad's heart in a new direction. She was good for Dad, good for us all. Alan, even.

A large number of chickens were being housed in a new coop beyond where the old one had stood. I rounded the house and passed the mighty oak where I would have seen the coop's old location if I'd gone any farther, but I didn't. I couldn't. I walked the long way 'round just to burn off nervous energy and went down to the barn with minutes of dim daylight left to show me the pine needles that had turned from tawny to amber. Early signs of autumn were apparent in a fallen leaf here and there, and Niney sniffed each one. The long-blooming flowers that had survived the hot summer were seeing their last days, fading in color, awaiting another wind to whisk away their petals.

I was plenty tired but pent up, trapped in a world that would have me leading the horse to pasture from now on, going my way to sleep in the hay-loft, trying to remember a God that gave a hoot. And I was stuck here, for there was no place else to go.

Chapter 11

⟨⟩⟨⟩⟨⟩

In the smattering of days that remained of September, the temperature dropped to the fifties at night. It was all that was saving the crops from burning up.

I was already sweating like a hog before the sun was overhead. Not a cloud in the sky, not a breeze blowing in any direction. By noon it was back up in the low eighties, and later on it must've been close to ninety degrees.

The eighty-acre Hagan farm was taking a beating from the heat and lack of rain, just like every other homestead in the area. The tenants, farmhands, and even the women were working the fields. Pastureland was parched. Livestock grazed in the shade of a few trees along the fence in the afternoon and sat in the pond during the better part of the day.

In the fields, men in straw hats and women in bonnets fought the heat— their heads bobbing in unison as they harvested the matured wheat for the animals and grain for replanting. Straw from wheat stems had been dried, baled, and stacked in the upper level of the tobacco barn to be used for bedding for the barnyard animals. Below the straw bales were the wagons, the tractor, and plows. Alfalfa hay had been cut, dried, and baled for feed and stored in the hay barn, and the sweet, powdery smell of dried grains was everywhere. Diesel exhaust billowed from the farm equipment and hung in the air. Tobacco was nearly ready to be speared and strung up from the rafters to dry.

Some of the hogs had come up to the back gate through the field. I went to see what was wrong and found that the cows had torn the fence down again. They, too, were in the wheat field, so I drove them a few hundred feet and turned them in with the other cattle and then bucked up and repaired the fence before moving the stock to fresh pasture. Niney nipped at my trouser leg the entire way.

A blustery wind had picked up by late afternoon, blowing dust and dirt. I went in through the kitchen carrying an armload of acorn squash. Supper was already on the stove, and Dad had come inside to eat before going back down to the hay barn. His straw hat lay on the sideboard.

We ate, too exhausted to say very much. Charlotte did most of the chattering, and Lewis wasn't far behind. Miss Hannah came in, having fastened up the chickens for the night. I couldn't ignore the obvious: Alan was not present. His usual fretful state must have taken him off somewhere to sulk. The rest of us were accounted for. Peanut-sized Marly was sniffling and coughing.

Dad handed him a handkerchief and patted him on the back.

I respected Dad for the kindnesses I'd seen him show Miss Hannah's round-faced, big-eared boy. Marly was withdrawn and shy. Perhaps he'd been that way before the twister took his father's life. If any of us had seen a talkative side of him, it was Raymond.

Dad finished blessing the food and asked where Alan was.

"I yelled for him," Hannah said, smiling as she passed the fried corn.

I couldn't imagine her bird-weight voice reaching much farther than the back of the house, let alone wherever Alan had hidden himself.

"Not like him to miss supper, is it?" she said. "Didn't hear anything."

"Yeah," Dad said to Hannah. "Sometimes it is. He's in a state. Needs a little time, I guess. Leave him be for now."

Miss Hannah had been living this close to Alan for less than a month. She was still trying to unravel the threads of his quirkiness, some of which had come undone to show themselves, harmless as most of them were.

Dad finished and pushed back his chair. "Fine vittles, Hannah." Weary as he must have been from day after day of long hours in the field, he managed a hardy laugh that made the rest of us smile. Dad laughed at most anything slightly worthy. It seemed to renew his vigor, but the deep furrow in his brow made him look tired. "Tomorrow's another day, Lord willing. I'll see you 'fore sundown with a pail of milk."

He was talking to Hannah, but the rest of us were listening.

A pail of milk before sundown was unremarkable, but the obvious affection between Dad and Hannah wasn't. I couldn't help thinking how youthful and energetic in comparison to our own mother she was, but she'd had seven fewer children to birth and raise. An unruly tinge of resentment struck a sour note with me.

But she had been good, and the girls were drawn to her. Charlotte clung to her long skirt as Miss Hannah tried to clear the table.

"Mary, if you'll help with the dishes, I'll sit here for a minute with her." Miss Hannah's deep-set eyes were gentle—like those of a fragile doll—and she looked down lovingly at five-year-old Charlotte, waiting to be held. "Then we can dry them together."

"That's good, very good." Dad gave the girls a peck on the cheek and turned to go. "Men," he said with a motion for us to follow, "best be winding up down at the barn."

Tomorrow promised to be another earlier-than-usual day and would begin at four in the morning. Dad, leading the way, had his straw hat in hand. He'd milk the cows before turning in for the night.

I walked briskly down to the hay barn, picking corn bits from my front teeth with a piece of straw. The horses were out to pasture, and their stalls needed cleaning. The hogs, meanwhile, needed slopping. The routine was as clear as the veins on the back of my hand. Mason ran past me as if he had a pressing assignment up ahead, pausing just long enough to slug my shoulder for the heck of it. I saw Alan in the distance loafing near the tobacco. I waved for him to come help and continued my duties without him. Experience told me he'd come in his own time.

With the stalls cleaned and the hogs tended, I went out the far end of the barn toward the pasture. The gate was ajar, but the horses were oblivious to the freedom that was theirs. Alan's carelessness didn't have a name. No matter, I thought. All was well.

I whistled for the horses. Beauty pranced up to the gate, eager to be led out. Something had put her in a good mood. Soot and Molly weren't far behind.

"You'll have to wait," I told them.

It was after six o'clock, and the sun was easing down in the west. In another hour or so, it would start to get dark. Dad would finish milking before that and would come along with a filled pail for me to carry.

I hustled Beauty along. She went peaceably into her stall, and I brushed her down and closed the door. I started back to the pasture for the other two horses, walking out in the open.

Alan had not shown up. I could see him sitting with his back against the slider on the tobacco barn. He didn't appear to be doing anything, although it wasn't easy to be sure at seventy or eighty yards away. Odd as it was, I went to check on him. If he saw me coming, he didn't acknowledge it. The closer I got, the more certain I was of the kerosene lantern next to him—a low-burning flame, dancing.

I broke into a run, jumping over tobacco sticks, yelling his name.

He was on his feet by the time I reached him and holding what looked like a homemade cigarette, which he'd rolled in a chewing gum wrapper.

"Are you crazy—"

He tossed it on the ground, and it fell apart. "They won't light!" he screamed like a wounded animal. "They won't!" Thoroughly agitated, unable to stand in one place, flailing and thrashing about, he pointed to several attempts he'd made. Strewn wrappers lay in the straw at the entrance to the barn.

Dry as it had been, we might as well have been sitting on a powder keg. I stomped on every wrapper and kept on stomping. "So foolish! This could have been a fire!"

I picked up the lantern, about to snuff it out, when Alan rushed at me. He hit my chest with his fists, and the lantern dropped. The flames erupted on the dry straw. They leapt up, spreading like thick orange marmalade, darting across patch after patch of waiting combustibles.

"Dad!" I yelled with such great volume I could feel the pressure resounding in my head, bursting on my ears. "Dad! Fire!"

Over and over, I yelled as I raced from the front of the barn to the side—berserk—praying I'd find water inside the cistern, praying it wasn't bone-dry, praying it was filled with water from the spring. I grabbed the single bucket, dunked it below the water's surface in the tank, and tore back to the flames, dousing and stomping with all my might.

Alan stood motionless, like a stick in a frozen pond.

"Alan! Buckets! Run!" My voice boomed. Blood pulsated through my temples. Sweat poured down my face. "Buckets!"

I could hear Dad yelling as he ran. I could hear the neighing horses still left in the pasture.

"Alan! To the pond!" Two buckets swung violently from Dad's hands.

Horrified, I raced for the cistern, back and forth, desperate to contain the crackling flames—spiraling with the speed of the wind toward the barn's entrance. But in seconds they were shooting underneath the slider and raging through the spaces in the boards. They licked up under the roof, engulfing it in flames as if a torch had lit every corner of the barn.

Dad, Mason, and Alan were flying, their buckets of water sloshing. Frantic, they ran toward the blazing building like midgets in the presence of a leaping, gyrating giant performing a wicked dance. Brilliant yellow melded with deep orange as the flames pointed higher and higher, pumping white, gray, and black smoke into the darkening blue sky.

"Open the slider! Save the tractor—anything!" Dad yelled as we pushed open the door.

Wham! came the blast from the barn, and we were thrown thirty feet by the back draft from inside. Mason and Alan ran to us, got us to our feet. We tried desperately to move the equipment, but flames poured from both ends of the overhangs. Seconds later, the rafters came tumbling down. Smoke telescoped funnels at the top of the gables. The noise ripped and rumbled with a deadening pitch, every bit as fierce as the torturous twister.

"Get back! Back!" Dad hollered over the roar of the inferno. He waved his arms at Alan and Mason, who were carrying harnesses, to move out. Then he pushed me away from the wagon, which I'd gotten only partway out of the barn. "Get down!" he bellowed and pushed me again.

I could feel fire burning my back. He seized my shoulders like a madman and forcefully threw me to the ground beyond the flames, booting me, rolling me until the fire that had crept up the leg of my overalls was out. For an instant, I was stunned, but his outstretched hand was there for me to grasp, and I was back on my feet, retreating, stumbling, staggering, ducking as the back of the barn blew apart.

Help was arriving—several men at breakneck speed—up the lane. The nearest neighbor was barely a mile away, but already they were coming. They rode on horseback, and the sound of hooves pounded across the fields. One by one, they dismounted with buckets and sprang to action. Tenants, too. And men on foot. The women ran behind them, yelling.

"Douse the hay barn!" Men were belting out instructions to each other. "Save the horses."

The heat was intense, blistering. Its vapors distorted the scene.

"Just let it burn!" Dad shouted. "Save the tobacco! Can't do anything here!" His straw hat was missing, his face soot-covered.

Through the billowing smoke, I couldn't see Soot or Molly in the pasture, but I could hear panic in their shrieking neighs. I kept swinging pond water, flinging it to the left, to the right—feverishly, not stopping—from the loosely formed bucket brigade. It had come out of nowhere, it seemed, crisscrossing the tobacco sticks nearest to the moving flames. Every instant counted.

Miss Hannah and Mary stood at a distance, hugging, holding on to the smaller children, staying close to each other as the smell of burning wood and the sound of crackling grain filled the night.

It had been no more than twenty minutes, but already the barn had been devoured. The flames slowly dwindled on the ground, the surrounding area having been soaked with water. Embers above still smoldered on a cross-beam or two and downward on a couple of vertical anchors, like glowing crosses against a desolate setting. Through the veil of smoke, the sun was dropping in the western sky.

The fire died down, having been contained to the tobacco barn. I over-heard Dad say how thankful he was that there had been no gusts of wind to fan the flames. The others agreed. We had been fortunate.

Alan was nowhere in sight.

Without a word, I went to the pasture. Molly was running wildly. Soot pawed the ground near the gate as I approached. For a time, I stood there, unmoving, confounded and shaken by the destruction. My clothes were seared. My forearms and hands were black. My thighs ached. I leaned against the fence post and cursed the emotion, dropping my head to my chest until I could pull myself together.

"Come on, Soot." I took him by the bridle. He flicked his ears and bobbed his head, nudging me with his muzzle, and together we walked to the hay barn.

The mighty oak tree up near the house silhouetted against the darkening sky as I returned to the pasture for Molly.

Miss Hannah and the little ones had come on down to what was left of the barn. The men from the neighboring farms had ridden off, leaving charred lumber and mooing cows.

A calm descended upon the farm, as if the fire had never happened, and the dismembered skeleton of our tobacco barn that had awaited the Kentucky barley harvest stood in the haze on its stone foundation.

Chapter 12

⇒◆⇐

It was a heavy loss. Only the crops that were air-curing in the barn had been spared, and the voice of the raging fire was one I was sure I'd never forget.

Dad and I, along with a few of the hired hands, walked the area until after midnight, digging trenches, shoveling dirt on any possible remains of dangerous debris. Alan was sent to milk the cows over in the hay barn, and Mason brought fruit and salami to sustain us during the night. Everyone was doing his part. Miss Hannah kept us supplied with cider and fresh water. No one said much. We just kept up the pace for as long as necessary. Not a word had passed between Alan and me. His shoulders slumped, and his gait was measured as he took off to do the milking.

All of us were worn out.

"Be sure to bring a pail from over there, son," Dad said, and he kept on digging. "Reckon they were all taken earlier."

"You be needin' help with the hogs?" I wiped my brow and stretched my back. "I can come over in a bit, just in case."

"Nah," Alan said. "I'll do it."

Within a minute or two, Alan was out of sight. I was sure Dad wanted to ask about the fire. I wished there was a way to make the consequences less, but nothing could undo the truth. He didn't ask a thing.

Then came the morning. Dad was up and at it, dressed and downstairs, same as every other day at four o'clock when there was extra work to be done. Breakfast wouldn't be until sunup. I followed behind him, sharing the light of his lantern in the short, predawn hike to the barn.

We reached the cows, and he squatted on a wooden stool beside Bessie.

"What happened out there yesterday, son?"

Intent as I was on getting over to Soot's stall, I knew Dad deserved to know how the fire had started. I stayed with him, the two of us milking. "Guess I'd have to say it was my fault." I cleared my throat, recalling Alan's ambush, and tried to sound plausible. "Careless and dropped the lantern." I couldn't see past the cow teats between us—couldn't tell if he showed any inkling of suspicion regarding exactly whose actions were careless.

He kept on milking. "It shouldn't even been lit."

There was a hush except for the squirting of milk in the pail.

"Nope, probably not. Not sure what came over me, Dad." I left it at that, knowing there was a groundswell of thoughts that pictured me leaving the farm.

And the rhythmic squirts continued. We finished the milking, and Dad stood up. "I'll take this up to the house. You can get on with your chores. Then we best be at the rebuilding, soon as we can."

"Yessir." I took a step toward him, wanting to make him understand the brawling bitterness inside me that wouldn't go away. "I've been thinking." I cleared my throat. "Pretty much all night."

His gaze leveled with his impenetrable eyes on me . . . He set the pail down, waiting.

"Simon?"

I ran my fingers through my hair, not answering.

"Simon, what's going on?"

"After the harvest . . . after the barn's rebuilt . . ." I backed down like the coward that I was. I'd failed him. That much I could see. I felt his disappointment. It leaked over me, slowly, like pus from a lanced boil. "Didn't sleep a wink last night."

He hesitated, then picked up the pail and looked away, tugging at his earlobe. "Lost my hat, you know. Darn hat."

"I'd best take Soot out to pasture," I said, unable to unravel the knot that was choking me or stop the rabid scenes attacking my mind—those unfair events and disasters that had taken lives and hard-earned crops, futures, and hopes and dreams while the Creator stood by.

We weren't prepared for emergencies, not the way we should have been, considering how common barn fires were. We kept the combustibles well separated from each other, but we hadn't counted on Alan being one of them.

"What'd you tell Dad?" he asked, rounding the corner at Soot's stall.

I glanced up from bridling the horse. "Nothing, Alan. Nothing. What's done is done."

Fidgety, he stepped aside to let me lead my stallion out of the barn and past the buckboard and carriage.

Beauty whinnied across the way.

"At least the horses are good," he offered. "And the crops."

"Yep. They're good. Why don't you go get the other two and lead them on out to pasture."

"Why didn't you tell Dad?"

"Alan, get the horses." I kept on walking past the sixty or so stacked bushels of milo maize, trampling underfoot a busted one, with Alan leaping around me like a leprechaun. "Get going, Alan. We have work to do."

I wandered into the pasture, not wanting to let Soot get far from me.

Last night's disaster had me thinking there weren't enough buckets of water to drown my decision to leave the farm. My instinct to imitate Dad's life as a farmer was smoldering like the sickening sight of the barn nearby. My search for meaning needed to go past the fences that surrounded me. I had to make the break.

Dad stood a ways off, watching as I released my stallion, and then walked over to take a look at the stack of worthless tools and burned-out farm implements. It was one of those times I might have had a cigarette, but it would have been a bad idea, even if I'd had a pack with me.

"We saved four sets of work harnesses. That's about it." Dad shook his head and picked up a log that looked like a black alligator. "Lost the tractor. The wagon. Tom Brody's jitney." He pulled out a handkerchief and blew his nose. "I've got two concerns. One: if we have a frost before we can get the tobacco into the barn." He looked up at me and then smiled. "These warm days, cool nights we're gettin' are perfect to cure the burley, and we have lots to be thankful for, but we're talking days, if not weeks, to rebuild the barn."

Alan rode Molly bareback at a gallop toward us, across the field, holding to the harness, and jumped off. Beauty was trotting up on her own. "Y'all, we've got lots of help on the way, for sure."

Dad pointed to the burned rubble and distorted wagon wheels that the farmhands had collected. "That's good information, Alan. Can you start hauling that pile to the wood's edge? Hitch up Molly first and get Beauty back where she belongs. We're gonna get through this. Disaster's no match for the Hagans. Right, Alan?" He gave him a hefty pat on the back.

Dad turned to me and continued. "The other thing, Simon, is this: pulling enough men out of the fields to clear off and rebuild. But there's always hope. Like Alan said, help's on the way. This time 'round we'll seal it with linseed oil, mix in some milk and lime, ferrous oxide. We'll have us a red barn." He tried to smile. "Lord willing, maybe add a silo."

There was plenty to sort out, standing in the midst of this bad luck. Dad was cut to the heart, I could tell. His vitality, drained. The crops weren't lost, but they were in grave danger. With the end of the harvesting and the share-croppers to pay, the pushing and pulling required to make life go on had to be wearing him down.

But I'd made up my mind about leaving.

⧫

By mid-afternoon, the men who'd assembled near the burned-out barn were ripping down what was left standing. We shouldn't have been surprised to have so much help. That was what good folks did for each other. Hired men stayed long hours, and it took only days to rebuild. Mr. Brody was there every minute. Mrs. Brody helped Hannah. Together they brought food to the work area, but we hardly stopped to eat. Finishing the barn, getting the tobacco in and hung—those were the all-important tasks. Most of the desire to pull my share had been shattered. Headstrong as I was, I did it anyway.

Good farm ground was a prized possession in rural towns, and the smell of a field of rich, dark, fertile soil was a gift, but I'd made my decision. I was leaving. Reasoning through made it clear enough: I had little to offer by staying. I was a waterless pit.

"We've put in a good day's work, son. What say we head on up to the house?"

It was approaching nightfall. Dad and I trudged up the hill toward the house.

I didn't look at him. "We've put in a lot of 'em lately."

"Yep. And I'm grateful for a good harvest. After all's said and done— been a hard year—but God's good."

Memories were not that easily shed. I let the comment slide, trying not to openly balk again at his beliefs, and we walked in silence for a bit.

"God is not mocked. Whatever you sow, that's what you'll reap. The Bible says it."

"I've kinda given up on what the Bible has to say, you know."

"Just beware your wrath doesn't trap you, Simon. Sure hate to see you cherish that anger."

The kitchen door shut behind us.

"You might one day find what you're looking for in your own backyard. Yep, come to your senses and find it right there."

Come to my senses? I had no tricks up my sleeve. Except for the matter of God in my way, I knew the direction, and it was far from this farm.

Chapter 13

With the coming of the end of October, the temperatures cooled. The season ended, and the sharecroppers were due their portion. Dad was a generous man. Where other landowners shared a third, he gave more. Half of the wheat harvest was theirs, and half was his.

In town, James Carver had supplied them credit, and the croppers drew food and supplies from his grocery and hardware store all year long. Seed for the next wheat crop also came from Carver's Grocery and Hardware. Dad sold the sharecroppers' harvest for them and settled their debt to Mr. Carver.

As for me, a hired hand could take my place, and Hannah's young boy, Marly, was filling the gap. I wanted to accept that my place on the farm had changed—how very quickly it had changed—and would forever be different.

"Something's eating at you, son." Dad cranked the Lazy Susan on the dining table until a bowlful of eggs came around and was staring me in the face. "Help yourself there."

"Me next," Mason said. "Some grits, too."

Miss Hannah was smiling her perpetual smile. "Plenty for the lot of you."

The entire family didn't need to be involved in my personal turmoil, and breakfast time was no time to discuss what was eating at me. I took a large scoop of eggs and set the bowl back.

The Lazy Susan spun and stopped at Mason. "Simon took more than his share!"

"Looks like most things are my fault," I blurted, missing my chance to keep quiet.

Dad took a swig of coffee, eyeing me over the top of the cup. "No excuse for that kinda talk, son."

I got up without finishing, flung my napkin on the table, and turned to go. Dad did the same. "Y'all excuse us."

We stepped out the kitchen door and into the brisk morning air. I was down the back steps before the screen slammed shut. He was right behind.

"Don't, Dad. Please. Let's not go into it. I'm sorry. Poor judgment."

"What fault? Why, son? Why are you running?"

"Running? *Running!* Not r*unning*, actually." I could feel my temples throbbing and my heels grinding the hard earth beneath them. "I'm walking off. Leaving, Dad. It's time. Not planning to shirk responsibility here, but there'll always be some season: a planting, a harvest, or something else. The barn's a beauty. Silo turned out well, too."

He rolled down his sleeves. I scarcely noticed the chill.

"Let me talk to the Lord about this, son. Give me some time."

"I need to leave, Dad. I can't stay. Not here. Not on this place. Not in these parts."

"Don't be listening to lies, Simon. No one's blaming you for anything. You're a fine son. A mighty fine son."

"Just not a farmer. And I can't stay here when so many pieces don't fit anymore."

He shook the wooden post next to him. "Well," he said, "a man's gotta do what a man's gotta do. I'm not holding you back. Where'd you plan on going?"

"Don't know just yet. We can talk later. I'll get on down to the barn now."

——◆——

Maxwell and his Model T were at the center of it all.

Pumpkins were lying on the vines at the side of the house. Mary's striped hen stalked the backyard. Leaves from the mighty oak had fallen and covered the front yard. I'd have given anything for a day to spend with the chirping birds. The cool, early morning hours had flown.

Miss Hannah was reading the newspaper when I came up to the house. The *Todd County Standard* was spread out on the dining table. I approached her, not intending to dillydally.

"What do ya make of it?" she asked. "Mr. Maxwell's giving Keating a run for his money, don't you think?" Her hair was disheveled from the bonnet she'd worn since early morning, thick locks of it fell erratically on her cheeks. She didn't seem to care.

Miss Hannah was a source of joy and mirth in the midst of striving. With her peppy voice and ready smile, I had to laugh. I walked over to her and hunched down to look over her shoulder. Robert Rutherford Maxwell's name was splashed across the headlines. Apparently, he was proving to be a formidable opponent for the incumbent state senator.

I straightened up and took a seat on the edge of a chair beside her. "Attaboy, Mr. Maxwell! Guess we won't know till November, will we?" There was no time for idleness, but I could sit for a minute. I felt a certain pride in Mr. Maxwell. "He's looking good. That's just around the corner. You voting, Miss Hannah?"

"If I have a leg I can stand on, yes! Want this?" She handed over the single page that amounted to the middle section of the paper.

Miss Hannah wasn't a practical woman—and a farmer's wife needed to be—but I'd been watching her with reverence. She had put out feed and water for the chickens and milked the cows while I'd seen to the hogs and taken the horses to pasture. She seemed to be managing on her own terms. Lewis was too young for school, but the other children were washed and gone. I doubted that their toilet was attended to, and there was still churning to be done. Pails of milk sat on the sideboard.

I gave the paper a shake to make it rigid while I took a look at the news. "Detroit's got that Ford factory up there. Paying five dollars a day, like Mr. Maxwell said." I reread the article aloud. "Interesting."

Miss Hannah raised her eyebrows and peered at me over the top of the page. "Hmm. Opportunity? You're looking for that, aren't you?"

I laughed. "What I'd really like is a Model T."

She laid the paper aside and, with a predictable smile, folded her dainty hands on the table. "Your father's told me how unhappy you are, Simon." She looked apologetic. "I don't know you well, but I think I can see it in your spirit: a deep search for meaning." She sighed, and her shoulders slumped a bit, but she kept on talking. "When we're family, we're like a body of one flesh and blood, and when one is taken from us—"

Lewis waddled into the room, naked from the waist down, carrying his underpants.

"Oh dear!" Miss Hannah said in her high-pitched voice and laughed out loud. "Let me run and get him situated! I'm falling down on the job." She chased after him. "Come here, baby!"

She caught him and took him by the hand, and I lost sight of them down the hallway, my little brother's bare butt bopping along as he tried to keep up with Miss Hannah.

Her suffering was no different from our family's. I hadn't known Zack Peterson before the tornado had killed him, but I knew by now that he'd married a special woman.

Miss Hannah waltzed back through the hallway and into the room. "Simon," she said as she sat down, "I think what I wanted to say is this: you need to follow your dream. Your mother would have wanted that for you." She smiled down at Lewis, still needing her attention. "Whatever it is, find it and follow it. We both know life is too short not to."

Chapter 14

⊰⊱◆⊰⊱

Mason barreled out the front door of our house, skipped the bottom step, and kept on running until he got to our father. Alan wasn't far behind him. Both my brothers braved the bitter cold to meet me beside the waiting buggy. The horse, startled by the ruckus, whinnied and held his head rigid and high.

"Simmer down, boys. You're spooking ol' Soot. We certainly don't need a runaway carriage today." Dad untied the reins and nodded to me to get a move on.

All but the very youngest of my siblings and Miss Hannah watched from the window in the parlor, their send-off erupting with wonder. Waving hands, visible even from a distance, wobbled through the frost on the glass panes. It was no ordinary day. Otherwise, we would have been going about our chores.

This was no time for nostalgia. Even so, I took one last look at the miles of rugged rock wall that marked the boundary of the Hagan farm.

Stones, stacked knee-high, cut through the tree-lined backdrop, behind which the chicken coop had stood. Nothing could ever make me go back there. Mother's screams still rang in my ears. They—and the instant the bear attacked—were locked in the crevices of my mind. No amount of self-talk was going to erase the damage. No clock was going to turn back time.

I turned away before the rush of sentiment had a chance to overwhelm me, pausing to absorb the view of the house that had fostered me, known me well, and held a part of me still. The new tobacco barn sat alone in the distance, with the silo gleaming nearby against the morning sky, and in its own way offered itself as a memorial to quiet closure. It marked the end of an era for me. The finality felt like closing the lid on a casket.

I couldn't have explained to Alan the significance of the occasion. He slid around on the frozen ground, unable to stand still. His eagerness to be in the middle of the action as I made ready to depart was obvious. Mason rushed ahead of his older brother, determined to be beside the carriage, the last one to bid me adieu.

Dad rooted around in his pocket and pulled two silver dollars from a folded pouch. "There's this, Simon." He pressed the coins into the palm of my hand. "They're from 1884. More of a memento than anything else." While still holding the reins, he hoisted himself up to the carriage seat. "You have the name of the boarding house, don't you?"

"Yes, sir. Got it right here," I said and patted my coat pocket. "Guess I'm 'bout ready."

Alan arched his shoulders and puffed out his chest like a pompous child. "You'll be sorry," he warned, pointing a stiff finger at my face. "I'm not staying around here, either. Not for long. No, sir, not me."

I walked to the other side of the carriage, leaned my bag against the seat, and turned to my brothers. Both were under my nose, and Alan was still huffing. "Pipe down, Alan. There are reasons a mile high for me to go. But you need to stay right here. First of all, you're barely sixteen." I stopped short of reminding him we'd already had this discussion. "A kid, Alan. You're a kid."

I could hear the impatience in my voice, but the time had come to simply say goodbye. It was time to break out of my cocoon.

"You're never coming back, Si," Alan said, lunging at me with outstretched arms, tripping over my feet, and nearly knocking me over. "I know it. You're not coming back."

"Once I get settled in, working in the factory, making automobiles," I said, "I'll get myself established in Detroit. Maybe I can send for you. You and Mason. The two of you can come up together and visit."

Mason remained silent, but when I looked at Alan, I could tell the seed I'd planted was taking root somewhere in his skull. He was stubborn as a mule—and unpredictable—but his arms fell limp at his sides.

He locked eyes with mine. "You'll find me right behind you."

My leaving was hurting Alan but feeling sorry for him wasn't going to alter the fact. I was choosing a path of my own. I wasn't a rebel—I was a Hagan.

As hard as Dad had tried to carry on, home had become a different place after Mother's death. The sweep of changes since that day in March was as real as the new-fallen snow that covered the fields beyond the fence. I let my hand drop heavily on Alan's shoulder and pulled him toward me. Mason waited his turn.

"Mark my words," Alan said, fighting back tears, "there's a world out there, and I'm going to see it."

I could see him kicking loose rocks while I gave Mason a handshake and exchanged parting words with him. I climbed up to the seat next to Dad and didn't look back.

Dad didn't look back, either. He pointed to the leather valise that sat between us on the floorboard. "There's some beef jerky wrapped up, and I put a few thoughts down on paper for you, Simon. They're stuck inside there." He took hold of the reins. "Giddyup, Soot."

The carriage's wheels creaked as we turned and made the loop. Alan yelled something as we rolled away, but I couldn't make out the words.

<hr/>

I was not a farmer. Geoffrey Newton Hagan had accepted that.

Dad and I sat in stoic poses on the buggy seat as it ambled down the dirt road through the Kentucky backcountry toward the train station in Hopkinsville, nineteen miles away. My departure was scheduled for twelve o'clock.

The wind whipped. It was about the norm for an early November morning. The temperature had continued to drop.

Dad threw back his head and laughed. "You're a sight to behold, son. I've got to hand it to you. You look every bit a man, stylish flat cap and all. Grown up before my eyes. If you're a'needin' to fool somebody, I think you can do it. Just don't be a fool while you're at it."

Laughter rarely accompanied his wisdom. He was a straightforward man when seriousness called him to be. He could have fought my leaving.

But he hadn't. He'd given his all: his presence, the two silver dollars, the beef jerky. His support felt good.

"It helps being tall," I said. "And I've got plenty of muscles. The farm-hand kind."

"You're gonna need more than that. I put a Bible in there, too." He nodded toward the bag on the floor. "I expect you to be driving a Model T back home before too long, son. Three hundred dollars, maybe less, will buy you one. You're gonna make that much fairly soon. Probably not by Christmas."

"It's factory work," I said. "All part of being in the big city. I'm ready for it, but I'll miss y'all. Sure hope I get back here to spend Christmas."

We rounded a turn, and my valise tipped over. "So that's what's weighting down my baggage," I said, picking it up. "Your old Bible?"

"No, son, it's your mother's." He glanced over at me, and for a few seconds, the sad history passed between our eyes. "And what I wrote down for you—it's inside there."

Myriad thoughts crept in, and I asked myself if this plunge could have waited until spring. Was it bravery or plain stupidity, going from Kentucky's backwoods to the heart of Detroit? I'd come to this point on my own, through sleepless nights, weighing the consequences, wrestling with what my absence might mean for the ones I'd left behind.

Dad cleared his throat, but neither of us said a word. I was trying to mask the reality that this day had arrived, and in spite of the bitter cold, we continued to move on my decision in our buggy going toward Hopkinsville. What would happen if I got all the way to Detroit and became seriously ill? What if . . . ?

The train rolled into the station just as our carriage pulled up at the opposite end. Dad gave a quick tug on the reins and shouted for ol' Soot to hold up. I was first to step down from the carriage. Dad climbed down and took only seconds to secure the horse's reins to a post.

Steam whooshed from behind the train's brakes as the engine came to a halt. There was no urgency. We were right on time, but both of us hurried. I was saving some last moments for our goodbyes. I guessed he was, too. With my baggage in tow, I moved toward the ticket booth, bypassing clusters of white folk who were standing around talking. Black folk had congregated at the far end of the depot.

I reached the counter and felt for my wallet. "Now then," I said to the station clerk, "I'll be able to make the necessary transactions for my connection from Cincinnati to Detroit once I arrive at the Cincinnati terminal. Am I right?" It sounded to me like I was traveling into eternity, even as I spoke of the distant towns.

"Yup," the clerk said. "Goin' to Detroit, are ya? That's quite a haul, young man." He pushed a ticket across the wooden counter. "Here ya are. You're set to go."

"Thank you, sir." I stooped down to lean my valise against my ankle and smiled at the clerk. "You're right. Quite a haul. All the way to Detroit." I tipped my hat, took the ticket, and then went to find my father.

As I rounded the corner of the building, the two of us came face-to-face, the cold air turning our breath into curling vapors. Neither of us were openly affectionate, but this was different.

He embraced me and held me close. After a time, he stepped back and looked me over, authoritatively, the way only Geoffrey Hagan could. "I'm proud of you, son. Mighty proud. Always will be."

The whistle blared, and he gave a nod. There wasn't much else to be said.

I boarded, hat in hand, and walked halfway down the aisle and seated myself in a forward-facing pair of chairs. I could have sat anywhere—or slept in any one of the beds that could be screened from the aisle by a curtain, for that matter, for I was virtually alone in the passenger section. Except for the porter and a woman with a child near the front, there weren't many people traveling north on this wintry Friday afternoon.

Within minutes, the train was off with a steady, slow surge of power, bound for Cincinnati. My father's last wave was lost in a puffing smoke as the train pushed out of the station. I laid my head on the back of the seat and tried to relax.

Chapter 15

⟫◆⟪

The train arrived at Central Union Station. I stepped off and joined the hustle and bustle of passengers going in every direction. Porters pushed baggage on wheeled carts along the tracks, stopping them to unload in hazardous-looking areas. Crisscrossing tracks ran in dizzying patterns for as far as I could see across the lowland—so low, I supposed, that if the Ohio River flooded, they'd all be underwater.

I had to climb several steps before reaching the platform. I hesitated on every tread, unsure where to go once I got to the top. Compared to how I had been during my fresh, crisp start several hours earlier, I was worn out and unaccustomed to the drastic turnabout of my surroundings. A baggage man zipped in front of me, his arms loaded with suitcases. He missed me by inches.

"Excuse me," I said, flinching, but he paid no attention and was lost in the crowd.

The Cincinnati terminal seemed like a carnival compared to the mild activity I'd left at Hopkinsville's station. I must have looked like a lost giraffe in the middle of it. I started off in one direction, thinking of coffee and a cigarette, and then changed my mind and took a different direction to settle my transportation priorities. I turned without warning and walked headlong into a custodian trying to get out of my way.

"Watch where you're going, fella," he muttered.

"My sincere apology, sir," I said and continued unswervingly on my path through the corridor, past the area marked COLORED WAITING ROOM, and into a hall overflowing with bystanders. Departures were listed on a board behind the ticket counter. The next train to Detroit would put me there before midnight. I was looking at more than a three-hour wait.

When my turn came, I stepped up to the booth and asked the agent behind the wire window about a ticket to Detroit. "Fine, fine," I said, listening to the particulars of the fare. "I understand it's one price plus the Pullman charge and a little extra for a lower berth. So, I'll go with the upper one and save a speck there. But a compartment to myself. Good thing I'm traveling light."

He made no comment in response but simply gave me my change and handed over my ticket.

I took off to the coffee shop, craving a bite to eat. The place was cramped. Every person there had his head behind a newspaper or bowed over a plate of food. It was noisy, but my mouth was watering. I waited for an empty stool at the counter and then ordered corned beef hash and black coffee and swiftly finished so someone else could have my place.

The waiting area was across the hall. I got there with plenty of time to spare before my train was due. Before I knew it, I'd dozed off on a bench.

I wasn't sure how much time had passed when a noise—the thump of a broom under my bench—woke me. I seized my valise from the floor and my hat from my lap as if we were endangered.

"Wouldn't want you to miss your ride, fella," the custodian said. "You kinda stick out in a crowd, being as tall as you are. I ran into you earlier."

"I recognize you," I said, getting to my feet. "But I believe it was the other way 'round. I ran into *you*. Much obliged for waking me." I pulled my watch from my pocket. Its chain dangled below it while I checked the time. "Yes, sir. Much obliged. My train's bound to be out there."

"Watch where you're going, fella," he said with a smile.

I flipped him a nickel and was on my way and out the door, ticket in hand.

The Pullman car was down the line and marked *SLEEPING CAR*. I went as quickly as I could without breaking into a run across the wood platform, down the stairs, and toward the dark green Pullman that awaited.

It took only a short time to settle in and feel the luxuriousness of the deep-buttoned fabric under my butt. Compared to the sparse interior of the Tennessee, Kentucky and Northern Railroad I'd arrived on, this was going to be a comfortable ride.

I felt the thrust of the train as it began to roll—slowly, steadily, power-fully. My cheeks flushed with excitement as the cars began to fly faster and faster. We were moving north, leaving Cincinnati far behind, climbing mile after mile across frozen terrain.

A whistle sounded every time the train approached a crossroads, and the mournful wail rippled through the air like ribbons in a breeze. I shifted in my seat and sat straighter, confidently, getting more and more accustomed to the realization there was no turning back now.

Not a soul had encouraged me to leave. I'd come to this on my own, bank-ing on what the newspapers had said. The big city of Detroit had attracted me, and a job at Ford with three times the wages other manufacturing plants were paying for unskilled labor—sounded good to me.

I breathed deeply and closed my eyes. An hour passed, then another, and somewhere between the train's constant huff-sweep-huff-huff and the whir of its engine, I drifted off again. Not until the porter gave my shoulder a jostle did I consider moving to the upper berth for some undisturbed sleep.

When I woke, the sun had gone down. A distant echo called from some-where in the deep darkness of night, like the voice of home relinquishing its hold on me.

—◇—

It was pitch-black outside when the train clamored into Michigan Cen-tral Station, but the whole place was lit up. I gathered my belongings and stepped down to the pavement near the grand entrance. Across the street in Roosevelt Park, lights flickered in darkness through the trees.

Inside the depot, I took just long enough to get my bearings and absorb the splendor of the massive arched ceiling, the dome-capped pillars, and enormous bronze chandeliers. The rumble of incoming trains could be heard over the click of my shoe heels striking the marble floors. I walked on, almost unable to get past the waiting room without gawking at its opulence, and located the coffee shop.

It was an inviting place, incubator-warm with a low tin ceiling and jet-black counters. A whiff of cooked food and coffee hurried my step.

I situated myself on a stool at the counter, set my valise down on the footrest in front of me, and removed my cap, planting it on my knees below the counter.

Not a minute passed before a perky little gal in a white dress and ruffled apron came over to wait on me. I ordered a cup of black coffee and reached inside my pocket for Dad's piece of paper, upon which was scribbled the name of a boarding house. I sat there, studying the address. It had to be several streets from the main thoroughfare, since very little in the way of structures was nearby. Catching a streetcar made perfect sense. Otherwise, I'd be walking close to a mile on Michigan Avenue to get into town.

With that settled, I gulped down the last of my coffee and bought a newspaper and tucked it under my arm. At a vending area, I picked up a two-cent stamp and a picture postcard with the mighty Beaux-Arts architecture of the train station, dashed off a note to the folks back home, and dropped it into the brass mailbox.

And I was on my way, apprehensive but headstrong—out into the night.

———◆———

I arrived at the boarding house on Clark Avenue, and immediately felt ill-advised to stay. My first impression of the section of town was a disappointment. Even in near darkness, I couldn't mistake the ramshackle house for a decent one, and its broken-down, shabby appearance seemed to typify the others on the street.

From what I judged, the dilapidated neighborhood might have been a good one to avoid, but the day had been long, and it was now far into the night. Despite feeling a warning sensation in the pit of my stomach, I stepped inside.

My entrance roused the sour-faced landlady, who wasn't the least bit interested in small talk. The message was clear: show her the money and find a room on the next floor. She smelled of strong drink, and the unsavory gent who stumbled into the entryway did, also. They made a decrepit pair, clinging to a broken-down desk, and I was more than glad to keep the conversation brief.

I climbed the stairs and fell into bed, suspicious that the picture on the wall was that of a harlot. Moonlight cast a shadow across the meagerly furnished room.

Sometime after I'd fallen into a deep sleep, I awoke. A critter was crawling on my lip, and the rest of the bunch of cockroaches were trooping across the bare, worn mattress. With no option but to stay the night, I got out of bed and sat in a chair by the door, wondering where Dad would have come up with the name of this place. Then I remembered the note he'd written. Too uncomfortable to sleep, anyway, I went to my valise and took it from Mother's Bible.

Scrawled down the center of a piece of paper was his message:

"I sustained you in a desert land, in a howling wilderness, and shielded you, cared for you, guarded you as the apple of my eye."

Those are God's words, son, not mine. Don't ever forget them.
—Dad

I eventually fell back to sleep.

The first glimmer of morning light woke me with a rude beam aimed at my eyelids. My feet came off the chair rungs and hit the floor with a thud. My head was still in a fog, and my neck was stiff as a board. I wiped drool from my chin and set the chair on all fours, then picked up the note and returned it to a spot between two yellowed pages of Mother's Bible.

I needed to pee so bad I couldn't stand it.

All the doors down the hall were closed. I assumed the bathroom was behind one of them. With only a dim bulb hung from the ceiling, I left my door open to allow for some daylight while I knocked on the door across the hall.

Not a sound.

I hesitated and then knocked again.

"Go to the devil!" came the aggravated voice from the other side.

Not wanting to spend any more time here, I hastily found the bathroom, thinking all the while that the person responsible for giving Dad the name of this establishment should be shot. There wasn't much point in belaboring the whole thing. Soon enough I was outside, looking for a streetcar that would take me into town.

Chapter 16

It was Monday morning. The streets of downtown Detroit were buzzing. Every Model T on the road caught my eye, and there were dozens, all with attitude, motoring along with their noses stuck in the air.

I got off the streetcar at the corner of Woodward and Michigan Avenues and stood dumbfounded on the curb, staring first at the traffic light and then at a Model T speeding past. Then another and another, their engines fluttering.

Watching the traffic light change from red to yellow to green left me spellbound. Not only me, but others. Even with the morning chill, bystanders lingered to exchange opinions about the world's first four-way, three-color traffic light of its kind. I stood through a couple of full rounds of it changing colors on all four sides of the intersection and then started on my way, energized by the city's hubbub, sensing the opportunity, which was here for the taking.

I went inside Kingsley Drug Store for a pack of Camels and was out again, cigarettes in hand, and ducked into an alleyway to light one before continuing along Woodward until I spotted an eatery.

The diner was packed with people eating, talking, smoking, and laughing. Filled booths occupied the middle of the room. Others lined the wall below the windows. The front side sported a row of red leather stools. A policeman—a burly black man with huge, rounded shoulders—sat next to the only vacant one. He was perched like a very large bird on a wire and showed no interest in me.

"Good morning," I said, wrapping my leg over the chrome-rimmed cushion. Without waiting for the policeman's response, I pulled a menu from between the salt and pepper shakers. "Any recommendations?" I suspected I might be pushing my luck.

He turned with a scowl, and I got a good look at the shiny brass on his otherwise all-black uniform. "Where ya from, preacher-boy?" He might as well have dared me to move. His grip could have crushed me like a bug. I hadn't offered my hand. I'd merely opened my mouth to speak.

A waitress stepped up before I could. "What are you having this morning, handsome? You'd probably like the steak and hash browns. It's up to you, of course."

"Hash browns and steak, it is," I replied. "And keep the coffee comin', if you would."

"A southerner. I like that." She turned to the cop. "He's a southerner, Roman. Use some manners, would ya?"

He dished up a simple nod. "Like I said earlier, where are you from, Mr. Preacher-boy?"

"Just rolled in on the train from Cincinnati. Looking for work. How can a fella get a job at the Ford place?"

"You ain't from Cincinnati, boy. Who in blazes are you trying to fool? You're from Dixie. Where 'bouts?"

"Kentucky. By way of Cincinnati. Any hints on getting a job at the Ford Motor Company?"

The cop sized me up and took a swig of his coffee. "I'm going to do you a favor, Mr. Preacher-boy, and you'll thank me for it. You see that streetcar out there? You get on it the minute you finish those Yankee hash browns and head out Woodward to Highland Park. They're hiring. Get your white b-hind out there. They're hiring anybody with a lick of sense. Five dollars a day."

"Much obliged, sir," I said. "This is some town you have here. Yes, sir. Some town."

I was itching to see more of Detroit before going out to Highland Park, but I had no time to waste. Neither did I have the money. Breakfast was served up inside of five minutes. I gobbled it down, talking to the waitress and policeman in between bites of steak and potatoes, and finished a third cup of coffee.

"Better be going, but y'all have a nice day now." I slid off the stool and directed my attention to the policeman. "By the way, my name's Hagan.

Simon Hagan. I might run into you again, and if I do, well, I won't forget the favor . . . or the face."

He looked at me over the top of his mug. If he said anything in response, I didn't catch it.

I was out the door with my sights set on boarding the streetcar. If things went my way, I'd get another chance to flex my muscles in this town of a million people, but it wasn't going to be today.

The streetcar rode me along Woodward Avenue, making me soon realize Detroit wasn't confined to city limits. Tall buildings and crowded traffic defined the heart of it. Long-skirted ladies and top-hatted men densely populated its streets. Smokestacks and windowed structures by the dozens lined Woodward on both sides, and the city's perimeter merely changed from one shade of industrial bleakness to another. Detroit just kept on expanding as the streetcar continued humming along.

I was the only one among the ten or eleven passengers in the car who had his eyes glued to the windows, taking in every sight as if I'd come into town from the country for the first time. I was alone in my amazement and glad to have some space.

Highland Park was less than a ten-mile ride away, maybe only six. The closer we got, the more enchanting the bungalows became, and remnants of farmland in patchwork patterns popped up to remind me of home. Leaving Kentucky's homegrown ruralism, exchanging it for a faster pace, was more about scraping off cow manure than rebelliousness. Highland Park, as far as I could tell, was as good a place as any to start.

When Woodward Car House and Woodward Terminal came into view, the thrill made me feel ten feet tall. It was all I could do to sit in my seat and not yell whoopee. The facility looked like it went on for two or three blocks to the west of Woodward Avenue. And then, there it was: Ford Motor Company's Model T plant. The names of the buildings were displayed over the entrances and on signs at the front. I seized the handle on my valise and sat on the edge of my seat, unsure which stop to take, and then got off at Hamilton, hoping it was the place to start. I was more than willing to take any job they'd give me.

It was colder than what for, and the walk from the streetcar to the entrance of the Model T plant hadn't warmed me a darn bit. I went inside and removed my hat, letting every inch of my six-foot-three frame speak for itself.

High windows and plastered walls were unlike anything I'd ever seen. And as sure as I was standing, I had never been around so many people in one place, all of them doing the same thing at the same time. No one looked up. Every person in the brightly lit center section was hunkered over a desk, every head bowed over a typewriter. It was not yet ten o'clock.

I set my valise on the floor and positioned my hat over its handle, hoping to make my baggage look like ordinary attire, but my presence didn't capture anyone's attention. My going unnoticed was getting me nowhere. I pulled a handkerchief from my coat pocket and coughed.

From somewhere in the midst of clacking typewriters, someone told me to take a seat if I was job hunting. The only person who raised her head gave me a dismissive nod. I wasn't the only one hoping to land a job. Probably eight or nine people—men and women—sat in a row of chairs, apparently awaiting an interview. I took my things, walked over, and sat down in the closest available seat.

At the stroke of the hour, a man with a loud voice and eyes like a hawk started giving us instructions. He strutted back and forth in front of us as he shouted what to fill out, where to go, who to speak with, and when to go through the hallowed door for whatever reason.

Two and a half hours later, I walked out the same way I'd entered. I had no experience as a skilled laborer and was not an electrician, pipe fitter, or machinist. Nevertheless, I had a job and a small metal badge to prove it.

It remained to be seen exactly what type of work I'd be doing. Whatever the Ford Motor Company wanted me to do, as long as it was legal, I would show up at the factory at seven o'clock the next morning to start doing it, and I'd be wearing my ID badge to get myself in the door.

But I had no place to stay the night.

Chapter 17

—⟫◆⟪—

Never before had I knocked on doors to ask for a spare room or anything else for that matter, but I needed a room for the night. How I'd chosen Manchester Street to begin looking was now a mystery, one that was beginning to rub me the wrong way. Its close proximity to the factory had made it a reasonable place to start. I'd simply gotten off the streetcar along with a person who had gotten on when I had—at Manchester. That had made sense at the time, but now? Not so much.

More than an hour went by without success. Door after door, knock after knock. I had to find room and board nearby. And soon. It was that or freeze to death on the sidewalk.

"Yes, a room," I said to the umpteenth person at the umpteenth front door, my teeth chattering. "I'm single, mild-mannered. Won't be a bit of trouble."

Finally, a logical person answered my knock. "No, young man. You need to try a different street. My sister's house." The lady gave me an address, told me her sister had recently emptied a room, and offered me coffee. As tempted as I was to take her up on a hot cup of coffee, I couldn't miss the sound of the streetcar as it came clanging down the rail. I thanked her profusely and made a run for it.

"I need to get to Pasadena Street, please," I said, hopping aboard. I panted for air. "Seventy-three Pasadena, to be specific."

"Take a seat," the conductor said. "I'll call out your stop."

I looked around. There was no seat. The crowd aboard pushed one way and then another as more passengers climbed on. Still holding my valise, I grabbed an overhead strap to hold on to with my free hand as the car moved forward.

In the push, I stepped on someone's foot. "Excuse me, ma'am. I think I caught your foot there." Still very much out of breath and half frozen, I must have sounded like a roadster to the woman.

She jerked her head at my apology. "Set your bag here on the floor." She was seated. She indicated with a nod the spot next to her foot. "It'll be out of the way. Pasadena's not far from here."

I veered forward when the car came to a stop and more people jammed on board. "Thanks, ma'am. I'll hang onto it. At this rate, I'm going to be on the floor anyway."

"Welcome to the neighborhood."

I couldn't gauge her politeness but considered it perfectly all right to nod in return. Conversation in any event was next to impossible. Workers from the factory quickly overloaded the car. All appeared tired. I tried looking out a window at the passing scenery, but armpits and bad breath stood between me and an exterior view. I focused on my valise's buckle instead, as if it were a prize. The woman got off at the next stop. Mine followed hers.

The house at 73 Pasadena Street was a respectable one. The tip I'd gotten from the lady on Manchester looked promising. I rapped on the front door and soon saw the curtain move slightly. The latch turned ever so slowly, and the safety chain caught the door.

An eyeball appeared in the space between it and the frame. "How can I help you?"

"My name is Simon Hagan. Your sister sent me. I've gotten a job at the factory." I smiled convincingly. "I'm needing room and board." I let that sink in. "Here's my ID. Gets me in at Ford's."

I wasn't about to hand over my badge to her. I figured she could see it well enough from where she stood.

"How'd you know my sister?"

I waved my hand in the direction of her sister's place. "Over on Manchester. She was good enough to steer me here. I don't know her—just knocked at her door. She said you might have an empty room." I tried not to let my teeth chatter, but the truth be known, they were about to start.

"She did, did she?" She showed fully one side of her face, exposing more than the one beady eye. Her small mouth and pointed nose were visible, pressed against the opening in the door. I couldn't tell if her inspection of me was good or bad until she slammed the door. I assumed that was the end of it, but before I got to the edge of the porch, she opened the door wide. "For Pete's sake, you're not taking off, are you? Come on. Get inside." Her hand never left the doorknob.

The entry was wide and the ceiling high. A patterned rug was within two steps. The wood floor creaked under me. A faint smell of mint wafted past me.

I set down my valise and removed my hat. "Could you take in a boarder? I sure could use a place to stay."

She pushed the door closed. She was a short, well-fed lady and had both hands propped on her hips. She cocked her head to one side and fixed her eyes on my coat lapels. "Short-term or long-term?"

"I expect to be here long-term," I said, offering a smile. "It's hard to say but looks like Detroit is home for a while." The information came out sounding vague. I smiled again. "That's what I'm hoping, anyway."

She gave me the once-over—twice—looking up at me as if I were the tallest tree in the forest. "How about a cup of coffee? We'll talk over some particulars. Mainly, how much I get for a room and my expectations, considering you'll be in my house. Sit there."

She pointed to a chair, and I sat.

It was a cozy room, rather dark, with overstuffed chairs and delicately figured paper on the walls. Some pictures that might have been of her family were randomly arranged over the divan.

After sitting a spell over a cup of coffee, we had a deal. She would wash my clothes and sheets. She served breakfast and dinner except on Sundays. If she invited me on one of those off days, that was, of course, a different matter altogether.

"The bathroom, you'll share with two . . . well, no, one other tenant—a man. It's on the same floor as your room. Month to month, not week to week. No ladies, no rowdy living, no rowdy talk. And I'm Mrs. Butcher. Ready to take a look at the room?"

Her name was befitting her sharp-edged manner. I followed her up the stairs, leaving a few steps between us so her rear end could swing as freely as need-be.

She unlocked the door and marched into the spare bedroom. It was dark and smelled a bit musty. I waited at the threshold while she went directly to the bedside table and lit the kerosene lamp with a match from the box beside it. The space was large, painted blue as the sky, and rather bare. Cheery curtains hung from a narrow rod. On the far wall, a bowl and big white pitcher sat on a washstand. A mirror was fastened above it.

I got the distinct feeling Mrs. Butcher would have aired it out had she been expecting a tenant. For me, though, finding such a place felt lucky. I was ready to settle in.

She drew back the curtains with a quick tug. "I'll just crack it open for a few minutes—and find you a chair somewhere." She looked all around the room. "Used to be one over there. Must have put it elsewhere." She turned, as if she'd simply lost it, and then stopped, distracted by the lacy thing under the table lamp. "You'll be needing more matches . . . later. One day when I can afford it, I'll get electricity up here. Supper's at six. Breakfast at six. You can pay me now," she said with the palm of her hand extended.

I proceeded to pull the money from my wallet while she fished for the key in the pocket of her dress.

"Half a month will do till you get your first pay."

"That's mighty considerate of you, Mrs. Butcher. I think our arrangement is going to work well." I handed her the money and offered another smile, which she tried to ignore.

"Go ahead and put your things in there." She pointed to the armoire. "Sheets are clean. No bedbugs."

"Now that's a relief." I laughed as I said it, but my attempt at humor didn't seem to have struck her as such.

She turned as if she'd been wrenched and was out the door with a comment on the importance of my promptness for dinner at six. Not much else could have sounded better.

⎯⎯⎯⎯⎯◆⎯⎯⎯⎯⎯

Dinnertime was approaching. Rather than miss my place at the table, I showed up a little early in the dining room and walked over to the pie safe to have a look at the collection of framed photographs before the other tenants arrived.

"That one's been dead awhile now," someone said in a husky voice behind me. "Aye. Other one's her brother. Whar ye from, laddie?"

I spun around, startled and less than thrilled at being addressed as an adolescent.

The man wobbled on a stout cane as he made his way over to me and stopped just under my nose. He was heavyset, with bushy eyebrows that, like his short beard and handlebar mustache, were graying. He smelled like mint. I backed away to give us some space. "Kentucky. Todd County. Mrs. Butcher was kind enough to take me in."

"Been here years, laddie," he said, looking up at me in protest. "The woman hasn't been kind yet. And I'm the one that should know. Whar ye say you're from, laddie? Got me a hearin' problem. Got lots of others to go along with it."

I offered my hand to greet him. "Kentucky, sir."

"I'll not be shaking your hand. Mine's been useless since . . . can't remember when. And you can see I need this other one." He shifted his weight on the cane. The entire left side of his upper body remained rigid.

"I'm from Todd County," I said, raising my voice, "in Kentucky." I faced him squarely, letting him read my lips through thick eyeglasses that bridged the end of his nose. "Came in over the weekend," I said, even louder. "Looking for work."

"Why don't ye like work?" He paused to take a deep breath, brandishing his cane in my direction. "Don't ye be staring at me, laddie, or I'm gonna wallop ye with this thing."

Mrs. Butcher came in by way of the swinging door and closed it with a hip shove. A platter of food swayed precariously between her outstretched arms. "You won't do anything of the kind, Mr. Begbie. Prop that thing over here and sit down, the both of you."

"Let me help," I said. "That looks heavy."

"Thought ye didn't like work, laddie."

"No, sir, I—"

A slender, middle-aged man had made his entrance. "He never said such a thing, Begbie. I've been standing here listening to the whole conversation. He never said he didn't like work. Said he came here *looking* for work." The man's baggy trousers flapped as he stepped closer. His greased-down black hair and the bow tie snugged up at his throat gave him an air of sophistication. He thrust his hand in my direction. "The name's Edgar Palmer. You might want to sit at the far end, out of Begbie's way."

Mrs. Butcher set the platter down and waved her arms in exasperation. "Okay, menfolk, this is my home, and you're coming here under this roof to eat my cooking and sleep in my house." She wiped her hands on an already soiled apron. "Beyond that, makes not one iota of difference to me who likes work and who doesn't. This is Mr. Hagan. Now, you men can eat or you can squabble, but you'll do your squabbling outside." She sat down in the chair at the head of the table.

"How do you do?" I said.

Mr. Palmer met my greeting with a smile and a firm handshake. He seemed a mannerly sort.

Mr. Begbie, on the other hand, seemed a bit rough around the edges. After passing around the food, we ate our dinner with his slurps and a burp breaking the silence.

He finished first and after a lull spoke up. "That was fit for a king. Ye make the best corned beef this side of Glasgow, Mrs. Butcher. Ye agree, Mr. Hagan?"

"Yes, in fact I do. It was a delicious meal." I pushed back from the table. "So, if you'll excuse me, I'm going to turn in early. It's been a long day."

Mr. Begbie looked amused. "Got yourself a girlie along the way, did ye? Now that's a fine how-d'ye-do!" He keeled over on the table, laughing, an elbow in his plate. "And here I've been thinking you're a hundred-percent greenhorn. Aye."

Speechless, I checked first Mrs. Butcher's reaction, then Mr. Palmer's.

Mr. Palmer rose from his chair, walked over to Mr. Begbie's, and folded his arms across his chest. "Now see here, Begbie. You know darned well that's not what Hagan said. You're a cantankerous sweaty sock trying to pick a fight."

Mrs. Butcher banged about between the chairs, loading her tray with empty dishes, her eye on me. "Showing off. That's what they're doing."

Begbie reached for his cane. "Am not." He turned to Mr. Palmer. "But you're a daffy whippersnapper, wet behind your ears. Aye. No respect whatsoever. Now move outta me way. Believe I'll have a few puffs." He stood up, bracing himself on the arms of his chair. "Awfully cold in here. May need me shawl."

I watched, thinking the two men were going to have at it.

Mr. Palmer stood his ground, unfolded his arms, and straightened his bow tie. "No. I'm just not going to let Mr. Hagan here be buffaloed by a bitter old Scot."

I'd had enough. "Good night, everyone. Fine meal, Mrs. Butcher."

"Good," Mrs. Butcher said. "Go on about your business. Their bickering . . . skip it."

"Now *she's* a keeper. Aye." A wink escaped Mr. Begbie's drooping eyelids and targeted Mrs. Butcher. "Thirteen years. I should know it."

His words fell on deaf ears, or so I let him believe. I left it at that, withholding an inappropriate comeback, and started up the stairs.

Chapter 18

Next morning, Tuesday, a half hour before the alarm went off, I was awake. My farm routine could have taken the blame on another day, but not this one.

My feet hit the floor. I could see my breath and went to the window, convinced it'd been left open all night. I pulled a blanket from the bed and wrapped it around me and took off for the bathroom, barefooted.

Mr. Palmer and I passed in the hall with a lackluster greeting and continued on in our respective directions. He was robed up, strolling in fancy slippers like he was enjoying a summer walk. I would have given a body part to have had those slippers, and as I stood in front of the john, I recalled the colder-than-kraut Kentucky mornings in the privy. Michigan had any one of them beat by a country mile.

Back in my room, I got myself together while, across from me and hanging in the armoire, my clothes swayed in the drafts whipping through the house. I was dressed before six o'clock and downstairs, where I found Mr. Begbie already sitting at the table.

"Mornin'!"

"How are you, Mr. Begbie?"

"I'm fine, laddie! And ye?"

Mrs. Butcher burst through the door from the kitchen. "Good morning to the both of you," our landlady said. "And to you, too, Mr. Palmer. Right on time. Sit, sit. Breakfast will be out shortly."

Mr. Palmer reached the bottom of the stairs wearing a plaid robe and a frown. His hair was uncombed and his face unshaven. "I beg your pardon.

Overslept this morning," he said, sounding like he'd been deflated some-time during the night. He dropped himself on the chair. Last evening's over-starched demeanor had vanished. "Hope you had a good night's rest."

His comment was directed at no one in particular. My short answer followed, and we ate without speaking. The only sound came from forks on plates.

I finished quickly and folded my napkin. "A terrific day to each of you," I said, laying it aside. After giving a compliment to Mrs. Butcher, I bundled up and walked to the front porch.

Freezing air stung my face as I hurried against the wind and arrived at the streetcar that was barreling down the track. I stood in the aisle for an uneventful ride to the factory and made it inside shortly before seven o'clock.

The noise level was shocking. Giant machines jam-packed the barn-sized building, stamping out parts with a deafening *boom*, vibration, *boom*. Not since lightning had struck a box of rifle shells in the hay wagon several summers ago had I heard such a din. Every row resounded in the systematic operations of greasy automobile parts in the making. Undistracted personnel worked like madmen. The smell of grease and oil gagged me.

My badge was pinned to the lapel of my coat, clearly indicating that this self-respecting Simon Hagan belonged inside this Model T plant. Nothing else about me did. I stood a head taller than any other person, and the choice I'd made to wear pleated trousers was a bad one. I snatched a work apron from one of the long tables, shed my coat, tied the apron around me, and re-pinned my ID to the strap. No one spoke.

Down the line of aproned laborers walked a muscular gent, his mouth going nonstop. He appeared to be inspecting the output and was vigorously commenting. I couldn't hear a word he said over the noise until he got closer to me.

"You'll be casting and forging rods," he said, mechanically turning out well-oiled instructions. "The rod connects the piston to the crank." He gave me a look to see if what he said was sinking in. "It comes out red-hot. You've been warned. That rod'll be hotter than Hades—and twisted. Get it on the surface plate. Here." He pointed. "Flatten it with this." He picked up a hammer and shoved it in my hand. "I'm the foreman. Got 'ny questions?"

"No, sir. I've got it. I'll go ahead and get started."

By a quarter after seven, I was going at it with a ten-pound hammer. My height, coupled with brawn from years of laboring on the farm, worked in my favor. Easily, I was proving I could do the job a smaller man couldn't.

I swung the hammer with a mighty blow, again and again, passing one rod after another from the furnace to the surface plate. And the beat went on. The stack of rods I'd flattened kept mounting, and my eardrums vibrated with each slam of the hammer. I lost track of time as I focused entirely on what I was doing, paying no attention to the workers to my left or right. A single slipup and I'd be out of work, burned to a pulp.

⟫◇⟪

When four o'clock came, I couldn't lift my arm any higher than my chest, not even to put on my coat. It didn't matter. I was burning up, and my shift was done. I left through the rear door, sweating like a pig in a bacon factory. I was breathing hard as I rounded the corner of the building, still so hot that I carried my coat.

The streetcar was filling up quickly. I made a run for it, fully intending to be aboard. Plenty of other people had the same idea. In the push and shove taking place near the track, half a dozen of us missed it entirely, and the packed streetcar rolled away.

I stepped back, fumbled for my lighter and cupped a cigarette away from the stiff wind until I could get a satisfactory draw. It would be a matter of minutes before the next car.

"Did you find Pasadena Street?" The woman's voice was muffled, her hat swung low over one eyebrow. Most of her face was hidden behind a scarf.

"Excuse me?" I eased my coat on over sore shoulders with the Camel wagging between my tightened lips.

She didn't budge. "Your search," she said. "Did you find the house?"

I had to have looked astonished.

"Yesterday!" She laughed. "On this route, standing in the aisle in your city clothes, baggage in hand."

"Oh, of course. Yes, I found the boarding house. Much obliged. Even lasted my first day on the job. Might be the end of me."

We both had a good laugh and then became intent on keeping warm. When the next streetcar came to a stop in front of us, we were the first to get on. The pint-sized lady plopped down on the seat to her left. I sat across the aisle and kept my arms close to my sides, certain I could smell my own body odor through my coat. My innards growled in protest after doing a hard day's work on a reasonable breakfast at the crack of dawn and a puny lunch later on.

"Where are you from?" She loosened her scarf and kept on talking. Her accent was Michigan-distinct, her tone confident. "I hope you don't mind my asking." She angled this way and that, trying to wedge her question between the passengers that moved between us. "You're new around here, aren't you?" Her head poked out from behind the person between us so she could see me.

"All of three days new. Just came in on Sunday from Todd County." I could tell by the tilt of her head it wasn't a place she'd heard of. "In Kentucky."

The last of the crowd boarded and stacked up between us, preventing further chitchat. At the next stop, she waved goodbye and threaded her way through the bodies that blocked the exit and got off. It was impossible to see where she went after that, and the streetcar pulled away.

Chapter 19

With a few full days of work under my belt, I was glad for Friday and unable to imagine other factory workers felt any different. We didn't talk and complaining about a job was kind of useless if a person wanted to keep it. My shift was in full swing, the continuous noise from the assembly line assaulting my ears. Automobile production ran like the well-oiled machine that it was, and from all indications, not a person was giving anything less than his all. None of us made eye contact. I rarely looked up.

The job was a toilsome one with a wracking monotony that left me wanting more—more satisfaction, more of a challenge. There was no end in sight to pulling the rods and pounding the hammer, and the foreman was tough as nails, yelling, swearing, making threats. I hadn't seen him flaunt his musculature, but he didn't disguise it, either. His neck was as wide as his face, and his arms bulged beneath his shirtsleeves. When he was mad, his entire torso turned crimson.

This morning it was crimson. With his quota for the week's output falling short, the morning was souring in a hurry.

But for me, any job was a start. Despite the foreman's tirades, the thought of earning enough money to buy a Model T kept me going. Picturing one of those doozies gave me plenty of push. I was as stoked as if someone had put extra coals in the furnace, and by noon I'd produced a stack of flattened rods well beyond yesterday's. That was my perception, anyway.

The foreman came around about three-thirty and, judging by the angry look in his eyes, saw things differently. "You call this acceptable? Well, let me give you a piece of advice. You either quit putting out garbage like this, or I'll shove your job where the sun don't shine. This is stinking pitiful. Inferior! And not you or anybody under me is going to get paid for stuff like this."

He shouted over the noise, calling me every name in the book. "Now do it right and do it faster. That's the way it's done at Ford. You figure out how to make that come together or get out!" He took a step toward me and finished his rant. "Do I make myself perfectly clear?"

I expected him to slug me, but the showdown ended, and I started in again, pulling the rods, pounding the hammer, praying to God as if he and I had a personal relationship.

I was teachable, and I understood quotas and Fridays, but if there was a better way to do the job, the foreman hadn't bothered to demonstrate it. Doing the job faster—trying harder—was my plan for keeping it and taking home my earnings, so I stepped up the pace, swinging my arm faster and faster through the motions.

The gong sounded for the shift to end. I hadn't heard otherwise, so I assumed my job was intact. I got in line at the payroll window and waited with every other worker for what was due us. One by one, with dollar bills in hand, the crowd filed out of the factory.

The November temperature wasn't much above freezing. Forty, maybe. The wind chill made it feel colder. It felt terrific after being hot for so long. My eyes watered in its bite. No one looked in my direction. Not a ray of sunshine showed itself.

I boarded the streetcar and took a seat alongside people I didn't know— working-class people on our working-class commute. The woman I'd met days before wasn't among the passengers who'd gotten on ahead of me. I craned my neck in search of her maroon hat and scarf-covered face. She was nowhere to be seen—and hadn't been since Tuesday. I would have welcomed her sunny personality and friendly chatter to brighten my mood after the day I'd had at the factory.

Sitting—withdrawn—I felt the brunt of the foreman's criticism. Deserved or not, I didn't like being flicked off like an ant in the preserves. I consoled myself with an aim to redouble my efforts and work harder in the future.

I'll get the strength from the same place I've gotten it before, I told myself. *I'll be man enough to do the job better, and if it's ambition that brought me here, I won't let one day's failure stand in the way.*

I tasted the humiliation while passenger after passenger came aboard. Loaded to the gills, the car left Woodward Terminal, and the Ford Motor Company disappeared from view. I kept quiet, not wanting to talk to anyone, and watched from the window as automobiles and people, trees and sky trespassed on my thoughts. I scanned the memories, toying with the peculiarity of the switch I'd made from the country to the city, rehashing the urgencies I'd confronted to keep human and beast alive. They had been nothing spectacular, just farm life, complex and impossible to minimize—from my fledgling effort as a youth to rescue a calf at the heifer's first birthing to the foolhardy attempt to save the barn from devastating fire and the unforgivable failure to save my mother. Juggling livelihood in rural Kentucky and keeping it in balance had caused living to go deep. Hammering iron bars for hours on end in a factory, by contrast, impressed me as downright unremarkable.

The streetcar came to a stop. I checked again, but the woman was not among the strangers who entered or exited, and the doors closed.

—◆—

I spoke to the people in my path, stepped off the streetcar, and crossed to the other side of Dexter Avenue, dodging a Model T coming my direction.

Dang! What a beauty.

A couple blocks later, I started down the sidewalk that led to Mrs. Butcher's house, taking in Michigan's blustery winter afternoon, revering frozen limbs on barren trees as I went—capable of feeling akin to most anything, from the apple blossom in spring to the cow pie under my foot. I reckoned I wasn't yet rid of the farm.

Nearing the boarding house, I picked up my pace and was inside the door when Mrs. Butcher met me in the front hall, plump package that she was. She held tenaciously to an apple pie, loosely wrapped in a dish towel. Her blend of disapproval and cocked head made her amusing. She had an impish way of enforcing the rules, and I had no reason to buck them.

"Good afternoon, Mrs. B." I removed my hat and coat. "And how is your afternoon going?"

"Apple pie." She came straight at me and lifted the pie toward my nose. "From a lay-dee."

Our eyes locked.

"Not from anyone I know," I said with a smile that put a twinkle in her eye. "Maybe one of my sisters is in town."

"It wasn't your sister, Mr. Hagan," she said, glowering. "The lay-dee was a Mrs. Mallory who stopped by. Said you were new in town, had moved to this house." She plonked her free hand on her hip. "Humph. Did you tell her I don't feed you enough?"

"Mrs. Mallory? Odd. I didn't tell anyone anything of the kind, Mrs. B."

My denial didn't change her expression. She stood her ground.

"I think you're scolding me. I don't even *know* a Mrs. Mallory. What do you make of it?"

"Well, I'm sure I have no idea." Mrs. Butcher curtsied with a snappish knee bend and took off toward the kitchen, brandishing the pie as she went. "But we'll be sharing it at dinner." She tromped out of sight before I could tell her I wouldn't be dining in.

I followed. "Oh, Mrs. B?" I stuck my head through the kitchen doorway and surveyed the place. Strewn pots and pans covered every horizontal surface. Carrot tops and turnips lay in the vicinity of an assortment of knives. "I know this is short notice. My apologies. But don't count on me for dinner. I'm going to get cleaned up, take a bit of a rest. Then I'll be going into town." That was when I spied the pair of chickens that lay lifeless on the drain board. "Your ladies look divine. I truly hate to miss out."

She cut her eyes at me from the center of the room and put the pie down with a disrespectful smack on a large wooden chopping block. "Out of my kitchen, Mr. Hagan," she ordered, waving her arms. "Out. Out. Go! Suit yourself. Leave. But the rest of us will eat your lay-dee friend's pie. And don't come back wanting a crumb."

The door swung shut between us. A whiff of the spicy-sweet pie had me thinking of home.

"My sister!" I hollered back. "Must'a been my sweet sister, all the way from Kentucky!"

Our little send-up had taken only minutes to smooth the edges off a jagged finish to my week.

But, a lay-dee? I mulled over the imagery as I climbed the stairs.

I was floating when I reached my room, wise to the fact that along with a pie had come a woman's attention. But *missus*?

This much I knew: she and I were unrelated. Surely Mrs. B had not believed I was serious.

I settled into my stance at the front of the washstand, considering what might have prompted the gift. I lathered my face and ran my safety razor down the side of it, scraping off fresh stubble.

My thoughts shifted to the possibilities for the weekend. Friday night was straight ahead. Detroit would be waiting. I'd take a streetcar into the city center and find some excitement.

Chapter 20

I was still wrestling with the mysterious visit from the woman named Mrs. Mallory when the streetcar rolled into bustling downtown Detroit. Right on schedule, it deposited me at the corner of Woodward and Michigan Avenues.

The city was coming to life. I walked up Michigan Avenue toward Griswold Street feeling like I owned the night. One after another, Model Ts motored past in swarms, flaunting its engine's ta-ta-tas to taunt me. Honking, spitting, puttering. All of it sounded musical to me. My juices were flowing. Headlights blinded me, and store lights distracted me.

Toward the last block of Griswold, a cross street turned into an alley. Jazz trumpeted through the narrow passageway straight ahead and ricocheted off the backs of tightly packed buildings. I tunneled between mortar and brick walls, walking at a good clip. The closer I got to the music, the faster I walked, keeping step with the beat until I reached the speakeasy and went in.

Smoke clouded the air. My eyes took several minutes to adjust to the dimly lit room. The crowd was alive with action, crammed in, having a fine ol' time. Patrons sat or milled about or danced in the tiny space toward the back of the room. Stubby candles dripped on the tabletops. A small chandelier hung in solitude from the low ceiling.

I elbowed my way through the red-hot cigarette butts that dotted the air like fireflies on a June night.

On the platform near the back of the room, a trombone, sax, and trumpet were blaring. Sweat streamed down the black faces of the trio of men who played them, their bodies rhythmic, their musical instruments gyrating.

Off to the side, at a hopping upright piano, sat a woman whose dark hands danced with gusto across its ivory and ebony keys.

I loosened my tie and lit a cigarette and was letting the razzle-dazzle pump through my veins when I noticed a couple of young women nearby looking in my direction. One in particular caught my eye.

Without my having expected such, a sizable gal—her mighty cleavage squirming, her bracelet-covered wrists waving, her hips swaying—sashayed across the platform to the microphone. She took hold with both hands and began to belt out a song.

I felt the floor vibrate.

The young woman seated at the table stood up. I observed her as she made a move, her dress jiggling in all the right places, and sauntered toward me. She nudged my chest with an alluring shoulder and looked fixedly up at me. Her lips puckered, hinting that my cordial reception would be welcome.

I had no idea in which direction to turn.

"Hey there, good-looking," she said. "Wanna dance?" Her face was painted an appealing shade of rose, and a feather jutted from the band that circled her forehead. Multiple strands of beads wrapped her slender neck. She was ready to dance.

I gave no consideration to refusing. My flight from the backwoods of rurality had me hankering to be the sophisticated gent and put hay wagons and barns behind me. "Hey there yourself, doll." I mashed my cigarette in a nearby ashtray and—in a snazzy, smooth movement—wrapped my arm around her waist. "Let's give it a whirl."

"You do the Charleston, honey?" She batted her long eyelashes, the likes of which I'd not seen, and continued her sweet talk. "Come on!" she whispered so close to my ear that I could hear it over the trumpeter. "I like that sexy twang of yours, honeybunch." Her nose wrinkled as if she were a bunny in the meadow.

"You're teaching," I said. "The Charleston's new to me."

The dance and a whole lot more were equally new. Being on my own, being in charge of my future. And all of it new. My ambition had opened a new door, given me a desire for new territory. It had put me on the Hopkinsville train and taken me about as far away from Kentucky as I could go.

Regardless of unshakable thoughts about the farm, my dream didn't include living on one. Quietly, I was planning on conquering the world.

"Look here, southern man, and do what I do. All right?" Her hips were in fierce motion. Her scanty dress struggled to keep up.

"Yes, ma'am." I kicked up my heels to the rousing razzmatazz and the trumpeter's loud rendition of "Sweet Georgia Brown."

My lady and I were cutting a pretty mean rug when a guy emerged from a curtained doorway not far from us and skillfully maneuvered his tray of drinks to dodge us.

There wasn't a way for me to know what might be happening behind the scene. I was unaffected by the possibilities. Prohibition spawned lots of secrets. Illegal alcohol was just one of them. Besides, the lady with me was plainly making a play for my undivided attention. For now, she was all the novelty my inexperience could handle. Common sense had me believing we'd at least be smart enough to scramble if the police raided.

In the meantime, there was no need to curtail my personal liberty. I was laughing, dancing, and carrying on, and before I knew it, the lady and I were arm in arm and approaching a table near the bandstand. We seated ourselves as close to each other as the chair legs would permit.

"What's your name? Let me guess," I said with a wink and extended my hand with the best-looking smile I could spread on my face. "And I'm Simon."

"Really? Well, hello, Mr. Simon. Tell me more." Her flattering fixation, with eyes like dark, enticing pools, had me acting like a simpleton. I spoke softly so that only she could indulge herself in a Kentuckian's remarks.

A skinny, middle-aged guy with greasy black hair stopped at our table. He balanced on his bony arm a tray full of drinks, and in the next minutes I was sipping dark liquor over a few ice cubes, bewitched by the lady sipping hers.

"So, tell me more," she said again.

I persisted. "Helen or Sarah. Which is it?"

She twisted herself around on her chair and pouted like a child. "Neither. Guess again," she said with puckered lips. It was anybody's game. She turned and cut her eyes at me across her mostly bare shoulder. A single spaghetti strap stood between it and me. "Let's dance," she said.

"Okay, Frances. Is it Frances?"

She gave me a noncommittal but flirtatious shrug and was on her feet, her hand outstretched. "Yeah, if that sounds good to you, sugar."

We danced—and the happy part of me was unleashed—until the musicians took a break. The gaiety continued uninterrupted as trays of glasses with tinkling ice and alcohol were brought from the back room. The nod "Frances" gave our server brought him hustling another round to our table. He set down napkins and distributed our drinks one by one.

My lady made a playful dash for a chair. The server didn't react—just kept on transferring the glasses, his spiderlike reach going from the tray to the table. I beat her to it and, with a rather dramatic flourish, caught her in my arms as she landed on my lap.

The skinny server finished off-loading the drinks and handed me the tab—no smile, just an expectant look as he ran his fingers 'round the edge of the tray and waited.

Frances moved from my lap to the vacant chair next to me and looked on with interest as I pulled out my wallet and peeled off some dollar bills. A day's earnings took a nose dive as I handed the money to the skinny guy.

Toasts were made all around.

Mine went high in the air and stayed there longer than the others. "Anyone of y'all know this lady's name?"

My question brought boisterous laughter. I was the entertainment.

I lit up a cigarette, inhaled deeply, and exhaled slowly, as if there was a powerhouse within me. Smoke rose in the air above us and hovered over our table like a canopy in the dim candlelight.

The band started up again, and the black gal took her place at the piano. The singer took hers atop the platform, and her low-pitched voice began to ooze a soulful melody—like the big brass trombone. Her body writhed to a slow-grinding tempo. The trumpet and sax pushed through like faraway rolling thunder.

It got me humming. "Frances," I said, tapping my oversized shoe against the pedestal at the table's center, keeping time with the music, pitching my final attempt at her name. "It's not Frances, is it?"

Ever so slowly, she slithered off her chair and stood up. "How'd you know?" She tugged at the glass in my hand. Ice jangled in objection till I let it slip from mine into hers. She set it out of my reach. "Come on, sugar. Let's dance this one."

I was in no shape to resist my nameless lady's coaxing. She had me convinced I could stand up. One last puff on my cigarette, and I was up, unsteady but ready to dance.

The other couples nearby were snugged up to each other, moving slowly in circles, but my lady and I were edging across the floor toward the platform. She was leading me, not the other way 'round, and it wasn't long before I was up there singing a lonesome tune with the black gal. The words of the ballad rolled off my tongue like a redneck's song in a wheat field. I seemed to be entertaining the lot of them with my unrestrained performance.

For the condition I was in, I was holding my own, and I alone knew I was overstepping the boundaries of the only personality I had, covering my inadequacies with glib talk and artificial confidence. No one was stopping me.

If Miss Nameless minded, she wasn't letting on. And if her name was really Frances, I didn't find out. The evening went a different direction from there. The music was still going like notes from a faraway horn, and her hands were all over me. That's what I remembered.

Light shone through the gap in the curtain, through which people came and went—night after cheap, careless night, most likely—to the room on the other side.

In the end, I was back there, alone.

Chapter 21

I awoke in the speakeasy to the sound of clanging cans coming from beyond the curtain. The noise grated on my ears. I staggered to my feet, groping in the near darkness, eventually making out a narrow table with liquor bottles, lots of them, and the sofa where I'd been. After buttoning my shirt with one hand, I felt for my wallet with the other and found it between the sofa cushions, unsnapped, and all but empty. The silver dollars Dad had given me fell from the crumpled mess that was my coat.

I was uncertain what all I'd done or how I'd done it, but certain I'd crossed over from the fringes of youthful curiosity to full-blown manhood. I stepped away from the implication, wanting to cover my deeds and make believe it wasn't so, and hide it from my conscience. My tight morals had been reversed in a single night.

It's high time I was growing up, I told myself, but an unfashionable model of right and wrong tottered in my mind. *How very short-lived the rules when character doesn't matter. How shallow the crass assumptions men make.*

I raked my fingers through my matted hair and swallowed hard, trying to rid my mouth of the awful taste of greasy lipstick and stale alcohol, and then stumbled into the poorly lit space where we'd danced. It reeked of disgusting odors. I lifted my eyes. The candles had all burned down. A janitor was sweeping the floor. He never looked up, just minded his own business. I turned and backtracked through the curtain to sleep the night on the floor, too tipsy to know where else to go, and the lingering nightmare returned to remind me that there was no way I could undo what had been done—no more than God could have changed what I'd begged him to change on a single morning last spring. We both had failed on all counts.

⟫◆⟪

The shameful sensation was still lodged in my brain when I awakened. That and the urge to get up and slither out of the mess I'd let Detroit's nightlife make of me.

Willfully, I'd pulled out of Kentucky with the precise purpose of abandoning my roots, leaving them in tainted soil that had no business trying to hold me and mold me or make me a reasonable God-fearing man. I'd come to town to have fun, and the evening proved to have no shortage of enticements. Then all had fizzled. The lady, for a piddling sum, had succeeded in her ploy and was gone. I didn't even know her name. I don't think she knew mine.

With no more than enough money to ride the streetcar home, I closed the door and was out of the speakeasy into the alley on a day not yet light, hoping to resurrect the farm boy that had grown up with country-loving decency. Even so, I had no plans to go back home to face a mediocre existence over which I had no control. With disdain for the speakeasy fixed in my mind, I stuffed my tie into my coat pocket and walked on, repeating, "Seventy-three Pasadena Street," aloud as if I were a drunk old man who needed reminding.

⟫◆⟪

Morning's glow radiated behind the rooftops, cutting between the houses like a beacon in the fog. I crept up the porch steps at Mrs. B's, unable to feel my feet, having spent one of the worst nights of my life after thinking it would be the best. I could only hope to slip inside the house undetected, with no one to question or judge me. But if anyone heard me going up the stairs to my room, they must've known better than to deter me or make innuendos about where I'd been all night.

The only sounds came from the clank and clunk of Mrs. B's pans in the kitchen.

I closed the door, flung my coat onto the bed, and groped around in the dark for matches on the bedside table. My head had cleared, but something about the damp darkness felt deserved, as if I were a child again and had ignored the warnings to stay out of the forbidden cave at the farm.

I was so parched I felt like I'd swallowed a rusty hinge, but the thought of breakfast made my stomach heave. My hand bumped the matches and knocked them to the floor. I knelt to gather them up, keenly aware of my stupor.

It mattered not where my next meal came from. Skipping today would be fine. Sunday, too, unless Mrs. Butcher offered an invitation. Otherwise, it would be Monday morning. House rules.

Even so, I wasn't going to starve. I lit the lamp, singed the hair on my finger, and blew out the match with a disparaging huff. The idea of staying cooped up in my room for the remainder of the weekend was also fine—and not an altogether bad idea. With enough light to see, I went to the armoire, rummaged through my valise, and took out a five-dollar bill. Doing so reduced my stash to five dollars plus one of the two silver dollars Dad had given me. The other, I decided, would remain in the pouch that I kept in the breast pocket of my coat.

I rationed out a piece of jerky to last me the day, set it aside, and put the rest back where I'd found it. But before I could close the valise, I noticed Mother's Bible. The gold inscription, nearly illegible from years of her handling it, left me with an unusual sense of her presence. Touching it in the condition I was in smacked of sacrilege. I questioned why Dad ever believed I'd want to keep it with me—as if its powers could somehow cause me to measure up to his principled ways.

Whipped, I put the Bible back where it belonged. Without removing my shirt, I went to the washstand and doused my face and neck with water, wishing I could reconnect with the convictions he'd given me in the beginning.

The woman who had dripped honey all over me left me no victory to relish. The conquest belonged to her, and I had played the fool, a country boy under her spell. Robbed in more ways than one, I felt like the victim of the greatest heist to date. More than the loss of the contents of my wallet bothered me. The core of my dignity had been struck and, in a matter of a few hours, had all but rotted away.

Chapter 22

When Monday morning rolled around, I was ready to get back on track. Breakfast couldn't come soon enough. I paced in my room, waiting for six o'clock to go downstairs.

"We've got eggs and sausage coming right up." Mrs. Butcher's announcement could be heard from one end of the house to the other.

I moved quickly. The notion that I could subsist on beef jerky had proved unfounded. I was famished and outrageously thirsty.

Mr. Begbie had taken his place at the table. I'd successfully avoided him all weekend, having stayed in my room for two days, but I could no longer skirt the inevitable face-to-face.

"Good morning, sir. Breakfast smells delicious." I took a seat and mentioned Monday's workday ahead, steering clear of Mr. Begbie's girly comment from our last conversation. In whatever way he chose to pronounce it, the topic was going to remain off-limits if I had any say-so. "Hope you're doing well."

"Where'd ye be all weekend, laddie?" He leaned forward, his hand cupped behind one ear, as if some affair, of which he might want to make a bizarre translation, would be forthcoming.

I hesitated, sizing up the seriousness of the glint in his eye. "Here and there. Into the city and about."

He smirked in defeat, sorting out the details I'd not mentioned.

I could have left it at that, but I didn't. "Wrote letters to the folks back home, too," I said, spelling out the less colorful part of my weekend's whereabouts in a voice loud enough to avoid having to repeat.

I stood up as Mrs. Butcher entered with a tray in hand. "Good morning, Mrs. B. May I help there?"

"Mrs. B, is it?" Handicap aside, Mr. Begbie had already ratcheted himself in opposition, bound to make something of it.

"You don't mind that, do you?" I looked to Mrs. Butcher to get her reaction.

She shoved a bowlful of eggs past my nose. "Sit, sit. Have this. I don't. Mind, that is. My late husband called me such." She contemptuously waved off Mr. Begbie. "That man is trying to get your goat. I'll be right back with sausage." She disappeared into the kitchen.

Mr. Begbie and I sat without speaking. I had my thoughts, and he had his. I pulled my cigarette pack from my breast pocket and set it on the table, my line drawn in the sand. He looked off into space, drumming the table with the fingers of his good hand—first on his water glass, then on his plate.

Mrs. Butcher returned with a platter of sausage and a plate with a small piece of apple pie. "Have some, Mr. Hagan. We've been enjoying it in your absence. That last slice is yours."

"Husband. Aye." Mr. Begbie shot a disagreeable glance at her and reached for the pie.

She took offense, or pretended to, and let loose with a smack across the back of his hand—a warning to him for his impudence. Their banter continued while I took the slice for myself.

"Decent of you to save some," I said, downing a mouthful with a tall glass of water as Mr. Palmer came into the room and tightened the sash on his robe. "Good morning." I nodded to him and reached for the pitcher.

He shuffled in, his slippers scraping the floor until he got to the rug's edge. "I smelled the sausage," he said, "and came on down." He pulled up a chair and helped himself to sausage and eggs. "Overslept. Good morning."

"Aye. Again."

I poured more water, minding my own business.

"Any excitement this weekend?" Mr. Palmer talked as he rubbed his whiskers. He looked across at me for an answer—a simple one, I surmised—that would fall somewhere between typical end-of-the-week activities and mildly adventurous ones.

I kept chewing sausage and gulping water, not ready to respond. Excitement, by my definition, didn't include being duped by a zany lady, particularly one I'd never see again. And I was convinced Mr. Begbie's portrayal of the weekend's excitement would provide entertainment at my expense, like calling me a namby-pamby or whatever name the Scots use to refer to moral men. I swallowed hard on the probable implication, feeling sure he'd exploit my Friday night episode in its entirety if he were informed. I was in a tight spot.

"No," I finally answered. "No excitement, Mr. Palmer. Hate to eat and run, but I must. Simply delicious, Mrs. B."

Each of them turned to watch me stand and push my chair up to the table, and their going-over followed me as I left the room.

Getting to the factory and putting the disgrace of the foreman's berating behind me required another fresh start. The past few days alone had me bent on clobbering the loss of self-respect on two counts. I didn't need to sit at the table and make it three. This morning, I'd be on the assembly line, moving on.

I took off up the stairs. When I came back down, the breakfasters interrupted their conversation long enough for us to exchange brief niceties. Then I was on my way, straight out through the front door, ready to take on the morning.

Chapter 23

Ford Motor Company's production level was demanding: the rods, the hammer, the sweat. My back and neck were so sore at the end of the day I couldn't have touched them with a feather without wincing.

High expectations hadn't signaled a new way of doing things, and I didn't ask myself if they could be met. I'd learned it from Dad—a lifestyle—and I owed it to him. Measuring up was about keeping farm life going, maintaining a good work ethic, and knowing the satisfaction of a job well done. He had expected the most from me and carrying my share of the load hadn't earned me a reward. A farmer didn't expect one.

With the last release of my hammer for the day, I called it quits. I'd worked my butt off from the minute I'd gotten to the factory and put on my apron.

I made my way to the nearest exit in hopes of finding in the crowd of workers the person to thank for the apple pie. Halfway to the streetcar stop, I spotted her in the distance. The familiarly bundled figure clad in a maroon hat and scarf bobbed through the bland sea of featureless commuters in dark overcoats.

"Wait up there, ma'am!" I shouted, picking up speed in friendly pursuit.

Either she didn't hear me or chose to ignore me and walked on. I hustled to get to her, racing into the cold wind. We reached the streetcar at the same time.

The close-fitting hat hung low on her forehead, the brim cut away at the back. She spoke rather gruffly through the scarf. "Do I know you?"

I was breathless. White streams of vapor spewed from my mouth. I must have looked like a fire-breathing monster. "Good afternoon, ma'am! You don't remember?"

The corners of her eyes crinkled. "Just kidding." She laughed and raced to the streetcar. "Mr. Todd-County-Kentucky," she yelled over her shoulder as I hurried to catch up, "how was your weekend?"

"Please . . ." I motioned for her to get aboard ahead of me and followed her to a seat. "I believe you might be responsible for a delicious apple pie. Am I right?"

"Consider it a neighborly deed. I hope you enjoyed it."

"What little of it I actually got to eat was delicious. Thank you for being so kind." As uncomfortable as it was, I kept talking. "Actually, you don't know me. I'm Simon Hagan."

"And I'm Virginia Mallory. It's nice to know you, Mr. Hagan."

"Please, call me Simon," I said with a tip of my hat. "Mrs. Mallory, right? You don't ride in the mornings?"

"No. I don't ride in the mornings. My husband gives me a lift before he goes in to take care of early morning duties at the church. He does that, then gets back home in time to fix breakfast for our girls before they head off to school." She smiled.

"Of course. Of course." I nodded to a passenger who brushed by me. "That makes perfect sense."

She unwrapped the scarf that had shielded most of her face on every occasion since I'd first seen her, showing a pert little nose and a pronounced chin, but no less attractive because of it. The telltale lines of a frequently used smile might have resembled my mother's, had she reached the age of forty. I guessed Virginia to be near that.

I stood up as the streetcar neared her stop. "I sincerely appreciate your neighborliness. Thank you. Perhaps I'll see you tomorrow, Mrs. Mallory."

"Virginia. Just plain Virginia. You have a wonderful evening, Simon." She eased past me, rewrapping her scarf around her face and neck.

The aisle had cleared, and the streetcar was starting to move.

Without thinking, I made a dash for the exit and jumped off while I still had the chance. "Mrs. Mallory! Virginia! Hold up!" I yelled, running after her. "There's something you need to . . . I need to tell you."

She wasn't that far ahead. Still, I was huffing against the cold as I caught up to her.

"What is it? Are you ill?"

"No. No, of course not. The pie. It's the apple pie."

"Was it bad? What, Simon?"

"No, as I said, it was delicious. I just wanted you to know it meant a lot. I think it was . . . well, homelike. I don't know, Virginia."

"Come. It's too cold." She had already begun traipsing down the sidewalk. "See me home."

"I really need to catch the next car. I just had to thank you for that. You'll be all right, won't you?"

"Come on," she said from fifteen feet away. "I'm freezing."

I was freezing too, and the splintered memories of last weekend were now not much more than a pinch. Sober, I was a better judge of character, and Virginia's invitation was innocent. I was certain of it. But going to her place was not something I'd planned.

Chapter 24

 ━━━◆━━━

A modest two-story bungalow, painted rust-red boasted a wide dormer that overhung a narrow porch. It sat a short distance back from the tree-lined street. Virginia led the way up the steps and through the front door.

The man I took to be her husband jumped to his feet and dropped a newspaper on the seat where he'd been sitting next to the fireplace. He was a gangly man with a square jaw and a ruddy complexion. "Virgie, hi, darling. And who's this young fella?"

"This is Mr. Todd County," Virginia said, unwinding her scarf. "A real Kentucky gentleman. But you can call him Simon. Simon Hagan."

He came right over to me with a nonstop smile and a ready handshake. Droopy eyelids hung over large blue eyes, and a well-placed cowlick marked his hairline. "Charles Mallory," he said. "It's great to have you in our home."

I immediately took a liking to him. "How do you do, sir?"

"Well, last time I checked, I was doing just fine. Have a seat, Simon. Here. Over here, by the fire. Let me take your coat and hat."

"Honey, Simon works at the factory. I don't think he has family in Detroit." Virginia removed her maroon hat and turned to me. "Do you?" Her curly dark hair fell loose with a quick jerk of her head.

"No, ma'am. It's just me—at the house on Pasadena for the time being." She wasn't quite old enough to be my mother, but all of a sudden, I felt like a child. "No, I only meant—" I collapsed on the chair, not certain what I did mean.

She smiled first at me, then at Mr. Mallory. "I took over a pie, honey.

He's staying where Randy Chalmers used to live."

Mr. Mallory took his chair. "Where do you go to church?"

Whoa, I thought. *Coming here was not smart.* "She surprised me. The pie, I mean. I was surprised to receive it."

Virginia left the room, handing me over to her inquisitive husband.

"And church?" His expression was polite as he waited.

I loosened my collar. The heat from the fire had me burning up. My insides were blistering. *Church, sir? Eight months ago, for your information, God conveniently looked away while a bear ended my mother's life, sir. Me, church?*

The pounding in my chest had to be audible. "No! Uh, church? I don't, sir. Guess you could say I'm rambling around so far. Only been here one Sunday. Maybe once I get my feet firmly planted."

He was quick. "That's how you get them planted. You aren't Catholic, are you?"

"No, sir. My folks are Methodist." I got to my feet, frustrated and ready to be on my way.

"Stay for dinner, Simon," Virginia said from the kitchen. "There's always extra."

"Thank you for your hospitality. I'd better catch the next ride. I'll be expected at the boarding house for dinner. Very nice meeting you, Mr. Mallory."

"You'll not do anything of the kind," he said. "I'll give you a lift. But first things first. I'm Pastor Charlie, not Mr. Mallory, unless you don't go to church. Then I suppose I'm Mr. Mallory." He laughed and stood up, motioning me to follow. "And not sir. Come on out the back way and meet our girls. Automobile's out there."

We passed Virginia peeling carrots at the kitchen sink.

"I'm sorry you're leaving so soon," she said and followed us into the hall.

"Well, I do appreciate the dinner invitation," I said. "Just telling Mr. Mallory—Pastor Charlie—I need to be back at the boarding house."

I hoped my use of the word pastor hadn't earmarked me as a churchgoer.

"If not dinner tonight, what about Thanksgiving? Plans?" Virginia studied my face for an answer.

"Well, I—"

"Mom?" The loud, singsong voice came from behind a closed door. "What's for dinner?"

Pastor Charlie excused himself. "Rachel," he said, knocking on the door, "you and Celeste come on out. We have a guest."

The door opened, and two girls bounded out, giggling and tickling each other unmercifully.

"Rachel, honey, this is Mr. Hagan." Her father took a step back, allowing her center stage. "And Celeste, Mr. Hagan. Simon, our daughters." He moved again, not at all reluctant to show his pride. His smile was broad. The distinctive overlap of his teeth made it broader. "Perhaps you girls could give your mother a hand with dinner while I run Mr. Hagan home."

"Very nice to meet y'all, Rachel." I turned to Celeste. "I have two sisters in Kentucky. One's eleven. The other's five."

"Well, *I'm* sixteen," Rachel informed me, her voice a touch on the haughty side, "and she's thirteen."

Rachel was the spitting image of her mother, although her eyes were deep brown, not green, sparkling, and bored right through me. Dark curls fell to her shoulders. For a sixteen-year-old, she exuded enough confidence to convince me she was older. She was a looker, more woman than girl, notwithstanding her juvenile entry.

But Celeste wasn't ruffled by her sister's uppity response. She swept like a breeze in front of Rachel and firmly planted both hands on her hips. She clearly had a bone to pick. "I'm going on fourteen. And did you really say *y'all?*"

Celeste was tomboyish, with a charming knack for battle and a lean athletic build to support it. I could see Virginia pause behind her, perhaps to take a ringside seat for the showdown.

"Umm, I guess I did. Y'all's just another way of saying—"

"Where in Kentucky?" Celeste was feisty, ready to challenge me. Her eyes had a childlike innocence that made me want to pat her on the head as if she were a hungry puppy awaiting a scrap of food. I managed to keep my composure. Rachel and her father exchanged knowing glances.

"Todd County," Virginia explained before I could answer. "He can tell you exactly where that is when he comes for turkey dinner," she said with a finality meant to ensure my acceptance.

"Your mother told me he's *Mister* Todd County," Celeste's father said. "Sounds interesting, doesn't he?"

"Now y'all are taking this Todd County thing too far, don't you think?" I suddenly felt myself getting in over my head. If I needed to defend my Kentucky roots, this was the time. I turned to Virginia for reinforcement.

Determination sparked in her eyes. "Right, Simon. And you'll join us for turkey at three o'clock on Thursday?"

"You're taking on a perfect stranger?"

"It's Thanksgiving!" Pastor Charlie said. "Go on. Say yes so I can get you to your house. I'll go out and prime the crank." He turned to leave and motioned for me to follow.

"That would be very nice. Thank you. Looks like I'll be seeing you soon, ladies. Until then, have a pleasant evening."

The three of them, having said their goodbyes, were busily scurrying about the kitchen before I could get started down the back stairs.

The passageway was narrow. Pastor Charlie had rushed on ahead. I got to the bottom step and beyond the landing, through to the outside, before putting on my hat. The night had chilled significantly. I was getting a feel for my surroundings when Pastor Charlie yelled from the lean-to shed at the side of the house. I whipped around, looking in the direction of his voice. His Model T was waiting.

He laughed from the driver's seat. His head hung out the window of the center-door sedan. "Get your Kentucky carcass in here!" He blinked the headlights and tooted the horn.

The sky had darkened, but I could see the automobile's beautiful silhouette. I wanted to act normal. I simply could not.

The preacher had opened the door and was standing on the running board. As soon as I got there, he was at the front of the automobile. I watched in earnest as he cranked her up, salivating at the sight of the procedure and the sound of the engine as it started.

He had her running and quickly jumped in and turned the key. I ducked my head as I got in beside him for my first automobile ride, and we sat in near darkness on cold seats for a couple of seconds, feeling the power beneath us.

Our smiles bespoke the love affair we shared.

"Mind if I smoke?" I asked.

His eyes narrowed in concentration as he pushed a pedal to the floor with his left foot. He adjusted the gas lever and gripped the steering wheel. "Go ahead. Have a smoke."

Once he let up on the brake, we were off. And the twenty-two-horse-power, four-cylinder baby with thin black wheels scooted along two frozen dirt tracks, off the preacher's property—down the road to Pasadena Street.

Chapter 25

Thanksgiving morning felt like any other day, except I could smell the bird. Even before noon, the baking turkey had my mouth watering. The aroma filled Mrs. Butcher's house and masked the nauseating stink of mint that on any other day would have taken down a strong man, not to mention a weak one.

Mr. Begbie didn't fit either category, being a specimen all to himself, and his mint pipe tobacco was best not discussed—not today. Following a hearty breakfast that would have to last me till three o'clock, I went to the parlor for some peace and quiet. The view from the window had me thinking about how lucky I was to have found the Mallory family.

"Thankful are ye, laddie? Aye." Mr. Begbie hobbled into the room, planting his cane out front as he went. With all his ceremony, he claimed the chair across from me and lit his pipe.

"I am. And how are you aware of that, Mr. Begbie?"

"It's what the day is. Tree-dition. Your President Lincoln set today aside for it." He tamped his pipe and looked at me with telling eyes. "Immigrating here and all. I'm grateful. Tree-ditions are the fabric of America. Aye."

I sat without moving a muscle and stared at my hands. An unlit Camel hung from my lips. "What brought you over?" The cigarette fell to the floor.

Mr. Begbie laughed out loud. "Ye *are* a greenhorn. Aye." He straightened up, curled his mustache, and faced the window. "The year was 1908, laddie. Came for life itself. Durn near lost it. Aye." He puffed for a moment and looked out over his glasses. "Where ye be for the turkey?"

"The Mallory home. Across the way. Pastor Mallory will come by for me. Very generous folks."

"Indeed!" Mrs. Butcher had been quiet until now. "Must be. First the apple pie. Now this. Go on. Have yourself a fine time. Mr. Begbie and I will do well without you and Mr. Palmer. He's got his old mother to be with."

Mr. Begbie squinted at her and winked. "A fine ol' time."

"I'm going to let the two of you work this out," I said and retrieved my cigarette. "Think I'll take a brisk walk." I pulled out my watch and had a look—the perfect time to grab my coat and go.

⟫⬦⟪

From the main floor of their house, the Mallory girls pressed their faces against the kitchen window pane as we rolled to a stop in Pastor Charlie's Model T just in time for Thanksgiving dinner. He and I got out.

They dispersed.

"Girls are funny creatures," Pastor Charlie said. "Women, too, for that matter. Still like my little Tin Lizzie?" He shut the engine down and opened his door.

"She's a dream. Two trips in her, and I'm keen on owning one. It'll be a while, though, before that happens." I got out and swept my hand over the fender, savoring the Model T's contour and the sleekness of its black chassis. "I sure appreciate the rides, Mr. Mallory. I mean, Pastor Ch—"

"Okay, okay," he said with a laugh. "How about just good ol' Charlie? That works for me. But it doesn't get you out of coming to church."

"Deal," I said, caught in a weak moment. "How does this baby stay together, anyway?" I cupped the water cap at the tip of the hood in my hands and stepped back to admire the grill at the front end.

"You're the one in the factory. I just drive. Here . . . crank her up, if you want. Wait. Let me pull the choke first. Then I'll show you." He got back into the automobile and in a jiffy returned to the front end. With his left hand on the handle, he tucked his thumb under his fingers. "Like this. Keep your thumb underneath, or you run the risk of getting it broken. That thing swings back." He demonstrated twice around and went back to turn the key and then nodded for me to have a go.

I cranked it, feeling in my grasp the power behind the handle, matched only by the thrill of the engine coming to life—*tatatatata*. I nearly wet my pants.

"You like it. I can tell. You'll own one someday. I'd almost be willing to bet."

I liked it a lot. He had that right. I liked his prediction even better. "They run about two hundred sixty. It'll be a while, Charlie."

"Let me switch her off. We'd better get going," he said—and not a minute too soon.

Virginia appeared at the head of the steps and held the door open. "Are you men coming inside or not?"

Without further delay, we started up the stairs and removed our outer wear at the top. The girls were setting the table in the dining room when we came inside.

Virginia, dressed in high heels and a frilly dress that ruffled under her apron, hurried over to greet us. "You look handsome for this special occasion," she told me. "You and Charlie both do."

I was glad I'd worn a waistcoat and tie—and my best trousers. "Thank you. And you look quite nice yourself, Virginia. How can I help?" I followed her to the sink.

"Here, finish peeling the potatoes." She dropped a couple in my hands and pointed me to the knife on the cutting board. "Girls? Simon is here. Have you spoken?"

Celeste bounced from the dining room into the kitchen like a rubber ball, her brown ponytail swaying from one side to the other. She slowed down just short of the counter, where I was already peeling potatoes, and scrunched her eyebrows at the sight of me. "You need an apron."

"Celeste? No 'hello' for Mr. Hagan? No 'so glad you're here'?" Virginia laughed and turned to me. "We're all glad you're here!"

"I'll get it." Rachel waltzed into the kitchen and pulled a folded apron from a drawer. "Here, Mr. Hagan." Her dark curls were piled high on her head and tied with a green ribbon that matched her dress. "I can help with the potatoes," she said with a delightful lilt. "And I'm sorry you have only us on Thanksgiving, not family."

"Y'all are a very nice substitute. I'm thankful."

"There you go again. *Y'all*." Celeste took a swipe at the whipped cream that sat nearby and plucked a finger's worth. "Well? What about me?"

"It's you, too, Celeste," I answered. "Y'all is everyone, including you."

Satisfied with that answer, she gingerly removed the knife from my hand and began chopping the Idahos.

"Baby," Virginia said, "Mr. Hagan can do that. You check on the broccoli."

Celeste made a face. "He was just standing there." She handed the knife back and took the lid off a kettle. Steam poured out and brought with it the odor of cooking broccoli. "Ugh!"

Rachel opened her mouth to speak. "Mom—"

"Honey, hold on." Virginia craned her neck over her shoulder. "Charlie, we're about twenty minutes away, so don't stray too far. I need you to carve this turkey."

"Just tuning in the radio, Virgie," he said from the living room. "Be there right away."

"Todd County, Mr. Hagan." Celeste, eyeballing me, took a bite of broccoli directly from the steaming pan. "H-hot!" she yelped and dropped the fork. "It sure tastes better than it smells!"

"What'd you expect?" Rachel said. "Move, please. Let me turn up the water for the potatoes. It needs to be boiling."

"How long, Mom?" Celeste turned to her mother. "Fifteen minutes with the burner up?"

"Yes, honey. Then if you'd mash them, we'll be ready to sit down. Charlie, the turkey in ten minutes."

He stood by helplessly as she doled out orders.

"And an apron, please."

"You bet. Let me put a log on the fire, and I'll be right back."

The kitchen was a flurry of activity. After Virginia kindly excused me from my duties, I stepped back to offer some trivia for Celeste to consider. "Todd County's near the Tennessee state line, down in the southwestern part of Kentucky."

She listened attentively, as if she might need to contradict me.

"Elkton's the county seat. The government for the county takes place there." I gestured, as if to say, "*imagine that.*"

She mimicked my crinkled brow and pursed lips.

"And my father's farm is outside Elkton."

Celeste dumped the broccoli into a colander and tilted her head to avoid the rising steam. "Not your mother's farm?"

Virginia rushed past with a full bowl. Whatever was inside smelled delicious.

"Can't I do something to help, Virginia?" I asked.

"No, really, you keep on talking." She brushed past me again, giving cues to Rachel and Charlie as she went.

"Well, it's the *family* farm," I said, wanting to sidestep Celeste's question. "You might be interested to learn that Elkton is named for a nearby pre-pioneer watering hole. A large elk herd used it."

"Speaking of pioneers," Virginia said triumphantly, "let's eat, you Pilgrims." She slung her apron over a doorknob and led the way to a sizable dining room.

Five ladder-back chairs had been arranged in a circle around the table. A white cloth had been draped over it, and serving bowls filled the center. I overlooked neither the savory aroma of roasted turkey, nor what awaited on the sideboard next to it. Pumpkin pie and blackberry cobbler triggered irrepressible memories of home. My mouth watered at the sight.

While Charlie seated Virginia, Celeste waited her turn. Nice manners seemed plentiful in the Mallory household. As self-conscious as I felt doing it, I went over to Rachel just in time to assist her in scooting up to the table. She was light as a bundle of kindling. Our close contact caused a warm sensation in the back of my neck. It promptly spread across my shoulders and slowly down my spine.

"Oh, Lord . . ." Charlie launched into a long, plainspoken prayer. Effortless as it sounded, when he finished, I was relaxed. I couldn't explain its unlikely appeal.

Virginia handed me the mashed potatoes and I piled them on my plate, clanging the spoon against the plate in the process. A sauce boat of gravy followed. Conversation started, forks and knives clinked. I loaded on the gravy and passed it across to Rachel.

Her dark eyes never seemed to change. They went from the gravy boat, to her mother, to me, fixating on each subject. The effect was like soft, thick, rich chocolate—drizzling slowly over hand-churned ice cream. And dish after dish came my way.

"So, Pasto—Charlie." I grinned. "Your church keeps you busy? Big congregation?"

"You can believe it. We're a melting pot of sorts. Different nationalities, languages, denominational beliefs. Eastern Europeans have been flocking here since before the turn of the century. Some by way of Canada. All trying to bond together as Americans." He took a huge bite of turkey and took his time chewing it. "A lot of them are Catholics—but one God."

Virginia wiped her mouth and cleared her throat with an attention-getting volume. "He's got a lot of ground to cover, for sure. Charlie cares about everyone, don't you, darling?"

I felt it. Ol' Charlie had speared a Protestant nerve somewhere between Catholic and God. Everyone was silent.

I had ventured, by choice, as far out on a limb as any backslider could. "Where's the church from here?" I was interested only from the standpoint of curiosity with no plans to attend.

"Not close. Hence the automobile, which my flock purchased rather than buying a house closer to the church. Wasn't one available, anyhow. Between you and me, I like the automobile." He gave me an informed glance. "It's been worth its weight in gold."

"I'd agree." I buttered a roll, mindful of Celeste, who was studying my every move. "I'd gladly take a Model T over a house any day." I winked at her affectionately, same as if she'd been my little sister.

She was having none of it. She rolled her eyes up at the brass chandelier. "Did you, or did you not, hunt elk in Elkton?" She was serious, her fork stuck in midair like a question mark over her plateful of food.

Rachel hid her reaction behind her napkin.

To deliver a hasty answer would have been a sin. I was sure of it. Leaning forward, I stationed my elbows squarely on the table, laced my fingers together, and clasped my hands. Deep in thought, I was more worried about what *not* to say. "Never did. How about you, Celeste? Ever hunt any elk?"

She didn't miss a beat. A good-natured smile crossed her face. "Not yet, Mr. Hagan. Maybe I will, though."

"Forgive me," I said. "With so many brothers and sisters, teasing each other was a means of survival. Toughens you up, but seriously, what grade are you in?"

"Eighth," Celeste said. "I skipped a grade. I plan to go to college."

Virginia nodded her approval. "They both have high aspirations. That's why I'm at the factory."

Rachel looked at me. "I know what you're about to ask. I'm in high school. A sophomore, in fact."

By meal's end, I'd dropped my guard. Virginia was reminding me more and more of my mother, and Celeste of my sister Mary. Rachel was almost too beautiful to look at.

I didn't deserve such a family.

"That was a tremendous feast, Virginia. Best blackberry cobbler this far north." I laughed. "Truth be known, maybe the best ever." I gave her a hug and then the girls. "Thank you, each one, again."

"Each?" Celeste asked. "Not y'all?"

"I'm going to be a slug at work, y'all."

We laughed in unison.

I turned to Charlie. "You've gone way out of your way for me. Let me take the streetcar."

"Nonsense. Go crank her up, and let's get on our way."

Chapter 26

With three full weeks of uninspired work behind me and Christmas just around the corner, I received the first letter from home. It was waiting for me when I returned from the factory Monday afternoon.

Mrs. Butcher had it on the pie safe next to her family pictures. "Afternoon, Mr. Hagan. Looks like a letter from Kentucky."

"Why, hello there, Mrs. B."

With my hat in hand, she'd nailed me. She stood waiting, head cocked, while I took off my coat.

I cocked my head to mimic her. "Something smells good. Need any help?"

"Nah. I appreciate it. Just rustling up some shepherd's pie. Go on about your business, and I'll get back in the kitchen."

The door swung shut with a distinctive minty back breeze.

I took the letter and turned to go, but Mrs. Butcher's head reappeared around the door's edge. "Mr. Begbie said it's cottage pie. On account of it having beef instead of lamb."

"Thank you for clarifying things, Mrs. B. I'll look forward to cottage pie."

I examined the letter all the way to my room. The curtains were closed. I lit the lamp by my chair and slid my pocket knife blade under the envelope's flap. Dad's handwriting was unmistakable—scratchy-looking with most of what he'd written filling the center of the page in a narrow column. Alan's name caught my attention about midway down. I took a deep breath and began reading from the top.

There was the good news of the profits from the crops to sustain the farm, and the sharecroppers' good outcomes, and God's goodness all around, and good hopes for the future, and God's providential hand on my life. I reread it, trying to find a reason to believe the way Dad did and pay it no heed at same time.

"His kind of hope," I said aloud. "So impractical."

His constant reminder of God's goodness and a providential hand on my life had a way of frustrating me. My mind was racing.

Sandwiched between the positive and the perfect of how Hannah was for the children were the concerns. At the mention of Alan, I pictured my brother's rebellion, felt his anger. They spelled trouble.

The margins were huge. When I got to the second and third pages, I saw their usefulness. Afterthoughts had been added as needed. Scribbled in the vertical space was a reminder of Mother's Bible and how she would have wanted me to read it.

No need for it, Dad. I spoke aloud, wishing he could be close enough to hear. The Mallory family, my job, even Mrs. B—I found them. I found this house. I'll find my own way. No thanks to your God.

I flung the pages of the letter into the air and watched them flutter aimlessly to the floor, and Dad's make-believe hopes with them. I went to the washstand, poured every drop of cold water into the bowl, and glared at the man in the mirror, wanting to growl at the resemblance to my father. I let my hands soak, drowning what was possible to drown, then dried them and changed clothes, put on a tie, and brushed my hair till my head hurt. When I walked out the door to go down for dinner, I looked like a new man. Cottage pie sounded terrific.

Chapter 27

"Simon!"

I'd reached the crowded streetcar terminal when I heard Virginia's familiar voice behind me. I waited outside for her to join me. Snow was coming down in sheets of white flakes and sticking to my overcoat. She struggled to stay upright on the slippery sidewalk as she rushed toward me.

The incoming car looked full. Every inch of the black iron on the front and rear steps had been claimed by passengers who were clinging to the handrails. It appeared we were out of luck.

"We'll have to wait," I said, "unless you want to ride on the fender."

"No, but we can try to beat this snow," she said with a laugh. "Come on. Let's get out of it." She took hold of my arm, and we hurried to the far entrance of the terminal. Sputtering and quivering, she brushed flakes from her face and scarf. "How was work?"

I gave her my best agonized look. "I'm being held hostage at Ford Motor Company."

"You're funny."

"I'm not trying to be." I took out a pack of Camels, lit one, and looked as serious as I could. "Yes, ma'am. Factory held me all day and made me beat mountains of rods without stopping until finally, I was let go on my own good merit." I exhaled a mighty puff of smoke and laughed out loud. "I'm no quitter. Not after—what? Three weeks? Three plus? But for sure, I can't see spending my life here."

"You're not leaving, are you?"

"No, of course not. Maybe I'll look into becoming a Baptist preacher. Get myself a Model T."

"Oh, stop being silly. You won't even come to church, and you've dodged Wednesday night prayer meetings, too."

"Maybe if I'm creative, I can do it again." Someone hurriedly brushed past me. "Hey, the car's here."

"That's not fair." She took off in front of me. "Charlie said you made him a deal to come."

"I did. And I will. I didn't tell him when, did I?"

We rushed toward the streetcar.

"How about tomorrow night?" she said. "Prayer meeting."

"Fine, sure. Maybe," I said, buying myself time to find an excuse. "Watch your footing, but hurry. You remember what happened the last time we missed our ride."

She looked back at me and kept moving. We caught the car and, breathless, plopped down on the same bench and settled in side by side. People came on board in droves. "What happened?"

"You met *me*. Remember?"

Virginia loosened her scarf. "Well, yes. I do remember. *Now*," she said emphatically, "prayer meeting, or I'll say I never knew you."

"That's bribery."

"And no more home-cooked meals."

"You drive a hard bargain. The truth is I'm not comfortable with it. I'd be a hypocrite. Church isn't for me."

"I'm not trying to convert you, Simon. Come. You'll like the people. They're sure to like you."

"That's kind. This once. What time?"

"I'll ask Charlie if we can leave a little early. Pick you up at five-thirty." Her eyes danced. "The girls will be beside themselves." The streetcar stopped, and she was up and running. "I'll still see you tomorrow after work, Lord willing."

Maybe it was just as well—her not fully understanding I'd landed a job about as close to making automobiles as dropping rocks in a bucket. Five dollars a day, and a dead end. If factory work was "chasing a dream,"

I thought, I'd better dream again. In the meantime, tagging along with the Mallorys tomorrow night couldn't hurt much.

—❖—

Celeste and Virginia were wedged in on either side of Rachel in the back seat.

Rachel balanced a bowl on her lap. "Hop in, Mr. Hagan," she said over the Model T's purring engine. "I've made meatballs."

"For *you*," Celeste said with a snicker. "Just for you. But I made the spaghetti and the sauce."

Rachel huffed. "Stop it, Celeste. Good thing we don't have far to go."

"She's right." Charlie had a great smile that lit up his face. "Church is two miles at the most. Glad you could join us. It's a cold one." He craned his head to the back. "You girls ready?"

All three chimed in to assure him they were, and we rolled away from the curb on Pasadena Street. The brisk night air chilled the open automobile, and snow flurries floated. No one complained.

Celeste leaned forward. "Did you eat a lot of spaghetti in Elkton?"

Hard as it was to outfox her, I gave it a try. "Mostly the spaghetti we ate we called dumplings. Sauce on it was a little different, too. All the same— southern spaghetti."

"Not true, is it?"

My discussion with Celeste ended at the side entrance of the New Life Baptist Church. We got out, and Rachel made sure I found the way to the basement. Virginia and Celeste weren't far behind. Charlie peeled off in another direction.

"Help me line up the tables," Celeste said. "Food goes on four of them. Here, over here. Hat goes over there. Light's right behind you."

"You're making me dizzy," I said, swinging a table into place.

"I'll go get the cloths." She wasn't missing a beat, was back in no time, and had silverware and napkins piled high on one of the tables.

The crowd had begun to pour in, and the noise level turned boisterous in a matter of minutes. I took a good look at the spread of food that stretched the length of the place: bowls, platters, and pans of it.

"Don't you dare stick your finger into the sweet potatoes, Mr. Hagan." Celeste gave me the well-timed warning with a wicked little gleam in her eyes. She moved in circles around me, energetic as a puppy.

I tried my best to look put out. "Where did you come from? Just show up whenever, don't you?"

"I guess." She moved a few dishes to make room for the large incoming bowl of beans and the friendly face behind it. "This is Mrs. MacCaffrey. We won't be here next week. It's too close to Christmas."

"How do you do, Mrs. MacCaffrey? I'm Simon Hagan."

"It's nice to meet you. My, you're a tall young man," she said, with the plop of a spoon into the beans, then moved on to greet those around her.

I felt possessive. "Your family's going to be gone for Christmas?"

"Nope, just not here," Celeste said. "No prayer meeting that week. Saturday we'll be home, not at church. We'll just be here for services on Christmas Eve. Home on Christmas Day."

"I see." The thought of Christmas tore into me.

Surprising my folks would be good. I mulled over the idea in my head. *Having a talk with Alan would be good.* But going home was out of the question.

I nodded to Rachel, who was coming my direction. "Need my help?" I wasn't sure what to suggest. "Put me to work," I said with my hands out, as if she should put them in chains.

"It's done. Thanks anyway." Her confidence showed in her smile and the way she spoke. "Mother says maybe you'll be invited to Christmas."

"And now what if I'm not?" I said with a laugh. "You'll feel really bad."

She raised her eyelids like weights were holding them down.

I was making a joke, but Rachel remained as poised as a stunned deer. For a second, I wanted to tell her she was as beautiful as one—unfitting as it would have been. "You certainly know your way around the kitchen. Meatballs, coffee, and you're what? Sixteen?" I was on thin ice, and I knew it.

"I am. And how old are you, Mr. Hagan?"

"A fair question. Eighteen. Somewhere in there."

"Charlie's on the platform, you two," Virginia said, hushing us with a finger to her lips. "We're ready to pray."

Charlie appeared through the doorway and climbed up onto a platform. The crowd fell silent. "Join hands. Let's pray."

A stranger reached out for my left hand. Rachel took hold of my right to close the circle. The prayer ended, the food was blessed, and Rachel was gone. The stranger made conversation with me, and one after another, nearly everyone else did, too.

"You were brave to come, Simon." Virginia crossed over to speak. Her voice was sincere. "I hope you feel at home here. These are good people." She searched my face for a reply.

"Of course. I wouldn't have missed it." I smiled, wanting to reassure her. "Besides, I didn't want to lose my chance for your home cooking—or let Charlie down. Does this count for church?"

She was off in the crowd without an answer, effervescent as bubbles in a brook.

Celeste sidled up. "You're so much taller than anyone here. And *Raaa*-chel thinks you're so *hand*-some." With that, she pranced off with her girl-friends, all of them giggling.

Like my Mary, I realized. *Just like her. The boundless energy of young girls.* And I thought of Christmas and Mary with her striped hen, and Charlotte. The idea and the possibility of surprising the rest of my siblings had my mood soaring.

I hadn't known what to expect, but we filled ourselves up on every type of meat and ended with banana pudding. No one thumped their Bible, though every person had one.

Charlie had a lot to say to those of us listening. It sounded familiar—his talk about "the prodigal son, who was still far off when his father saw him and was moved with compassion." Charlie stopped talking for a second to look out at the people-filled room. "And the father ran toward him and fell on his neck and kissed him."

"Charlie," I said on the way home, "you've got a nice way of bringing an old Bible story to life." I turned to the back seat and started to speak, but the wind nearly whipped my hat off.

Rachel and Celeste burst into giggles.

"So glad you could come along," Charlie said, eyes on the road.

"And Rachel's oh, so very glad, too," Celeste said. She wasn't through. "Did you like those old songs, Mr. Hagan? Really and truly, did you? And if you did, why?"

"My father's a man of faith, always giving me a push. So 'Faith of Our Fathers' struck a chord. That one made me think how good he is."

"We'd enjoy hearing more about him," Virginia said. "Won't you plan on coming for Christmas dinner?"

"No. No, thank you. I do have plans. But I'm mighty obliged for tonight. Wonderful meatballs, too—spaghetti and sauce. Wonderful."

Wonderful summed up the evening, and I was not the only contented soul. We rode the entire distance back to the boarding house in quietness. Snowflakes came down like falling stars and melted on the headlights' beams.

The frigid temperature left me no choice but to hurry inside, much as I wanted to bypass any conversation tonight, and I found myself face-to-face with Mr. Begbie the instant the door opened. He was an odd old coot.

"You're a wee late, laddie." He had it in for me, no telling why. "Com'on in. Sit down."

There was enough mint in the air to gag a maggot. I took off my outer wear and let Mr. Begbie lead me into the parlor.

He pointed to a chair with the end of his cane. "What'd you say, laddie?"

"I didn't say anything, sir. Do you have something on your mind?"

"I don't mind a'tall, laddie." He lit up his pipe and settled in.

That alone had me worried.

After taking a long puff, he gave me a notable stare over the top of his glasses. "Mrs. Butcher and me been talking 'bout ye. Aye. Are ye leaving here Christmas, laddie?"

"I'm making my plans," I said, speaking loudly. "They're not firmed up just yet."

"She'd like it if ye be here." He drew in another puff and set the pipe down. "It would make us happy. Tree-dition and all."

I could detect the longing. "Can I get back with you on that, Mr. Begbie? That's mighty nice of you."

"Not any mice here, laddie. Just be the three of us if ye agree to it."

"I'd better be getting on, Mr. Begbie. Hard day of work tomorrow."

Chapter 28

———⟫•◇•⟪———

Tossing and turning through the night left me feeling like a limp dish-rag by morning. Downstairs, Mr. Begbie was at his spot at the table, propped up like a startled squirrel on a limb.

Mrs. B was chipper. "Pancakes and hot syrup, Mr. Hagan," she sang out. "Delighted to see you. And Mr. Begbie tells me you'll be joining us for Christmas. Couldn't sleep a wink—" She stopped herself. "Up in my room, that is, just thinking about what all I'll be cooking."

I shot a formidable eye at Mr. Begbie. "Well, I'm not exactly sure of my plans just yet." I said, as Mr. Palmer came rushing down the stairs. Instinct told me to change the topic.

"Busy day, Mr. Palmer?"

Disapproval formed on Begbie's face.

"You first, Mr. Palmer," Mrs. B said in a deflated voice as steam rose from the large stack of pancakes she'd uncovered.

Palmer straightened his bow tie. "These are delicious." He sat down with outstretched hands to take the platter. "Quite busy."

"Ye don't know till ye eat 'em, do ye? And don't ye be taking all the cakes. Pass 'em over here."

The day was off to its normal start, except for the subject of my where-abouts for Christmas. Arrangements still had to be made, although having dinner with the Mallory family sounded terrific.

"Your mother is doing well, I hope." I had an audience of one now as I talked to Mr. Palmer. The others seemed to have tuned me out.

"She's needing a lot of care," Mr. Palmer replied. "Guess I'll just go ahead and tell you: I'm moving closer to her. Moving out next week."

"Well, I'll be a squattin' toad." Mr. Begbie put his fork down and wiped syrup from his mustache. "Fine 'n dandy! Like I told ye—" he slapped his hand on the table—"just be the three of us for Christmas."

"Please, Mr. Begbie . . . it's not so."

<hr />

Following work, I hustled straight over to the Ford administrative offices to ask for time off for Christmas. My plans to get to Kentucky and back were all mapped out.

Two older men and a young woman stood in line in front of me at the clerk's window, each taking a turn at the cubbyhole-sized opening in the booth. The grill between the clerk and the rest of us was off-putting.

I waited and was glancing around when a woman, huffing and puffing, came up behind me in line. It occurred to me to let her go ahead, but I reconsidered. The clock showed twenty minutes to five. A sign on a small placard to the side of the grill indicated the window would close at five o'clock. I wasn't about to lose my one and only chance to get a four-day pass.

My turn came. The clerk looked at me without expression through the narrow bars that separated us, then down at the paperwork I laid in front of him. After a moment he peered at me with stone-cold eyes. "Simon Hagan." He coughed unnecessarily. "Unskilled laborer."

"Yes, sir." I handed him my ID.

He shoved it back at me as if it smelled like a rotting carcass. "You came here when, Mr. Hagan?"

"November sixteenth, sir."

"And today is December sixteenth. Am I right, Mr. Hagan?"

"Yes, sir. It is." I offered a cheerful nod for the happy coincidence he seemed to be acknowledging.

It took a mere split second to figure out that it was not. His thin lips stretched across yellowed teeth, and the air he drew through them sounded like a hissing snake.

"One month on the job, and you need a four-day pass, correct?"

Heat from the overhead lights seemed to intensify.

"Yes, sir. For Christmas." I shifted from one foot to the other, missing neither his smirk nor the passage of papers coming at me underneath the grill.

"Mr. Hagan, you do not begin to qualify. Not for four days off, not for three days. Not two days." He took a deep breath and let it out so fast the various papers on the counter scattered. "Mr. Hagan, you do not qualify for one day off. If Jesus himself were born right here on this floor, you would not get the day off." He waved me away with a backhanded motion. "Next."

Duly convinced my Christmas plans had just been changed, I turned to leave, feeling like a fool.

The woman who'd preceded me in line, having finished her transaction, had moved a few paces away. She stepped up. "That was unnecessary. I mean, really." Her face was drawn up in disgust. She tucked some papers into her purse and looked up at me. A smile had replaced the scowl. "Pardon me. I couldn't help overhearing. Why are you unskilled when you could be skilled?"

It sounded like a riddle.

I hesitated, making sure she was talking to me. "Afternoon, ma'am." I tipped my hat. "I don't know what you mean."

"You just might be cut out for bigger things. Like applying to trade school. Ford pays you a stipend to learn."

She had to have seen my surprise. She had my attention.

"Of all things. Is that right? A stipend?"

"That's right! It's like a cash scholarship. The school offers technical training." She was wound up like a top. "They prepare you for work in the industry. Things like tool-and-die making and so on." She glanced at her watch. "Not only that, classes in chemistry and history. It's a well-rounded education while you're on the job. My brother's one of their first students." She hurriedly pushed up her coat collar and tightened the sash. "Listen, I've got to run. Go over to the registration office. Ford Trade School. Second floor, next building over. Get a form." And like a flash, she rushed off.

Most everyone, it seemed, had also gone. The lights were being shut down, the building was closing. It was after five.

A person or two brushed by me. For a minute, I didn't budge, sensing my future might have just taken a turn for the better.

⟫◆⟪

Keeping my mind on work the next day was absurd. The more I thought of an opportunity for technical training, the more it resonated. Anything besides factory work.

Four o'clock couldn't roll around fast enough. It was Friday, and the afternoon, like the morning, was uneventful. Eight hours of the monotonous grind, two small breaks, a quick sandwich, and my shift was done. My pocket was empty. I was ready for payday.

A long line had already formed at the payroll window when I got there. I waited, picturing myself at the registration office asking for an application to the Ford Trade School.

Finally, with the week's pay in hand and one arm in my coat, I practically ran to the building. I took the stairs two at a time, then made a passing inspection of the second-floor hallway in search of the registration office. I didn't see one but did notice a door nearby that stood ajar. The sign on its hazy glass window read *PRIVATE*.

"Excuse me," I said, shamelessly tapping at the door.

It opened with a gentle push of my hand, and the stout woman sitting behind the desk looked up from her typewriter.

"I'm lost. Would you kindly give me directions?" I smiled, hoping she wouldn't fling the pencil she had in her mouth at me. "Where might I find the trade school registration office?"

"Are you in need of an application?"

"Yes, ma'am."

"Well, here." She handed me a form. "Go ahead and take this one and fill it out. Bring it back anytime. It won't be looked at now, not till after the first of the year." The telephone on her desk rang, and she turned to answer it.

I pressed the application against my chest, shielded it with my coat, and left the building. Outside it was spitting snow. The sky was darkening. A frozen mist whirled around me as I walked the short distance to the terminal.

I'd missed the streetcar by a long shot. The wait for the next one was sure to keep me hunkered next to a tree trunk for a while until another would be due to stop. I'd be lucky to make it to Pasadena Street in time for dinner, but I was happy as a lark.

Chapter 29

"Laddie, where are ye going all dressed up on a Sat-ur-day mornin'? Got ye finery on."

"That's not your concern, Mr. Begbie," Mrs. B said. "Move on away from the table now. Let me clear it. The man's got a right to go where he goes."

Mr. Begbie gave her a once over, which I was determined to ignore.

"Good breakfast, Mrs. B. I'll be leaving for the city soon. Anyone need anything?"

"Christmas Day," Mrs. B mused. "Lots of fixings yet to do. Only seven days. And dinner's at three sharp, Mr. Hagan, in case I didn't tell you before." Just saying the words seemed to put a spring in her step. She made a dash for the kitchen, leaving me with Mr. Begbie.

I tried to dodge him, but he stretched out his hand toward me. "Help an old man, would ye?"

"Yes, sir," I said, holding his elbow while he found his footing. "Steady there."

"Into town, are ye?"

"Yes, sir. And just between you and me, I'm wondering if there are tools I might find." I bent down closer to his ear. "Maybe there are some here at the house."

"Schools? What for, laddie?" He arched his bushy brows and looked suspiciously up at me.

"No, sir. *Tools*," I said, trying to keep my voice from reaching Mrs. B. "A saw. A hammer." I went through the motions to represent each across the

137

top of the newel post. "And nails, too."

"No tools." He gave me a look over the top of his glasses. "Not sticking me nose in, laddie, but why?"

I got as close as I could, sidestepping his cane. "A Christmas tree."

The paralyzed side of his frame stayed put, like it belonged to a wooden soldier. The rest of him shook in amusement. Slowly he let it relax. "Well, I'll be." A look of conspiracy passed between us, and Mr. Begbie's mustache curled in a smile. "I can 'elp."

Chapter 30

It was late morning before I could finish a letter to the folks back home telling them about my chance to go to the Ford Trade School and how I'd be applying soon. Dad would be proud.

I wrapped up a few chores at the boarding house, got a streetcar bound for the city, and stared out the window at the brightness of day glimmering on ice-encrusted branches. Evergreen trees interrupted the otherwise colorless landscape. The sound of speeding automobiles and honking horns intensified the closer I got to the city. Telephone poles were gaily wrapped in red streamers, Santa Claus's face decorated the shop windows, and people carried packages as they scurried along the sidewalks.

I stepped off the trolley on Grand River Avenue. Frozen dirt crunched under my feet as I crossed the street to the drug and tobacco store on the other side. The door creaked as I entered, and the floor did, as well. An intoxicating aroma of pipe tobacco filled the store.

A gentleman at the back spotted me and came at once.

"Yes, sir." I removed my hat. "Good day to you. I'm in the market for a particular tobacco. Mint. What do you have?"

He gave me a courteous nod and spun around on his heel. With his back to me, he made a selection from the options that lined the wall and then pivoted back as if he were a tightly strung puppet. "Donut. Mint julep. Muscatel. These are offerings from the Snead Carrington Tobacco Company." The man's nose was a bit in the air. "Excellent source. Excellent tobacco."

An expert, no doubt.

I pointed to the mint julep flavor. "This is what I'm looking for. Would you wrap up an amount? One appropriate for a nice gift, please, sir."

"Of course. Excellent choice."

He made several mechanical moves to prepare the package, and the tobacco was ready. "Anything else for you today?"

"As a matter of fact, there is. I need a suggestion for candy—one you could send off for me on Monday. Is that asking too much?"

"Not at all. Come this way." He trotted from behind the tobacco counter and moved quickly to the rear of the store. I followed, listening to his suggestion of a box of horehound sticks. "This would make an excellent choice."

"Odd," I said. "My family does like it. And you're right, it would be *excellent*. But I have my eye on the peppermint sticks. Don't believe we've had that."

He pulled a can from inside the glass case. "Leo Peppermint Sticks. Excellent choice. And in an extraordinary tin." He held high the blue tin so I wouldn't miss the roaring lion pictured on the side.

"That should do it. I'll take two tins. I have the address right here for you to mail the one. If you would post these sticks on Monday," I said, tapping the lid, "I'd be mighty obliged. And now, allowing for the postage, of course, what do I owe you?"

"One moment, if you please. I'll be right back with your total."

With the tobacco nicely packaged and a tin of Leo Peppermint Sticks for the Mallorys under my arm, I was on my way. I stopped by the fender of a parked Model T to shield me from the wind and lit up a cigarette. Admiring someone else's automobile while I smoked was the next best thing to owning one. I told myself that if I got into the trade school, I might own one sooner than planned.

I stood in the freezing cold, taking long draws on my Camel, visualizing my hands on the automobile's steering wheel, and then dropped the butt into the dirt and smashed it with my shoe.

Twenty or so minutes later, with my wages depleted, I left Fletcher Hardware toting a hand-painted biscuit jar with a silver-plated handle for Mrs. B under one arm and a tin of stick candy under the other. The mint julep tobacco was nestled in my coat pocket.

It was dark by the time I got to Pasadena Street, even darker once I'd hidden the packages in the bushes beside the house. With no one in sight, I came around the front corner of the porch and went inside like a cat that had swallowed a bird. The air was steeped with the enticement of popped corn.

Mr. Begbie and Mrs. B were as near to the front door as they could be. Both were keen on getting at me, both in my face.

Mrs. B was first to quiz me. "How was your day?"

Unbeknownst to her, Mr. Begbie had stepped behind her and was acting out a queer little skit all by himself, dipping at the knees, pushing his cane back and forth in a sawing motion.

"Would you excuse me, Mrs. B. I need to have a word with him." I followed Mr. Begbie to the parlor. "What is it, Mr. Begbie?"

"The saw. Did ye get it?" The old man was as impatient as a child awaiting a pony ride.

"No, sir. But I will. And the tree, too. I've spotted one."

He gave me a disheartened look, twisted his mustache, and shuffled over to his easy chair. "Aye."

"I may need advice, Mr. Begbie. Advice on a trade school. Henry Ford's." I watched him, wanting to see his reaction. "If you have any. I may just try to get in."

Mr. Begbie perked up. He took his pipe from his jacket and lit it.

"I have an application to fill out and a test after that in January," I said. "If all goes through, that is. Don't have any idea what I'm doing, but I'd be mighty obliged if you had thoughts on the subject."

"Technical training?" He got a far-off look, and then a halfhearted smile slipped through his mustache. "Don't know a thing about machines. I'm a doctor." He stared down at the floor. "Aye."

"A doctor, sir?"

"In Scotland—Oban. Sits on the dark blue waters of the Firth of Lorn, overlookin' the Isle of Mull. Not needin' to talk on it." He tamped his pipe. "When ye be gettin' the tree, laddie?"

"The hardware store closed at five," I said. "I can still get it and the nails after work the first of the week. And two-by-fours, too. For the base."

"Tooly fours?"

"Two-by-fours." I made an X with my arms. "For the base of the tree."

"Aye."

"I think I'll head on up. Good night, sir."

I left him there to smoke his pipe.

It seemed everyone was asleep when I came back down an hour or so later. The ticking clock on the wall provided the only sound in the otherwise quiet house. Undetected, I went out the front door to the bushes where I'd hidden the gifts and took them from beneath the branches. After hiding them under my coat, I smuggled them back inside.

Chapter 31

"Charlie, Simon here." I leaned in closer to the mouthpiece and pressed the receiver closer to my ear. The telephone connection was weak.

"You all right?"

"Yes." I cleared my throat. "And I hope your sermon went well this morning."

"We missed you."

I laughed. "Oh, maybe one of these days I'll show up. Who knows? Listen, Charlie, I don't want to barge in on you, but I need a favor. Could I bring over an application and let you take a look at it?"

"Why not? How about around three o'clock?"

"Fine. I'll see you then. Thanks a million."

When the time came, I walked the three-quarters of a mile to their house, application in hand, and knocked on the Mallorys' door.

Virginia opened it before I could knock twice. "Come inside. You must be freezing. Charlie could have come for you." She fussed over me while I took off my hat and coat. "Go sit by the fire. I'll make some hot chocolate."

"Don't go to that trouble, please, Virginia. I'm only going to be here a short while."

"Don't be silly! It's no trouble." She left for the kitchen.

Charlie came in, hand outstretched. "Simon, great to see you. What is this about an application?"

"It's quite a story—how this came about—but there's this trade school at Ford. You may know it."

"Sit, please, Simon."

"Would you be willing to help me fill this out?" I held out the papers, still catching my breath. "They would pay me while I'm training. I'd be working and going to classes at the same time." I sat on the edge of my chair. "Technical training."

Charlie stood up. "Let's move to the dining table. Spread it out there."

"Where are Rachel and Celeste this afternoon?" I asked as we headed over to the table.

"I'm here, and Celeste is studying," Rachel said from somewhere in the kitchen. "I'm making you some hot chocolate."

"Mighty nice of you."

Charlie and I hadn't had much of a chance to go over the application before Rachel came in carrying hot chocolate. "Mind if I listen?" She passed out cups to the three of us and took a chair at the end of the table. "I'll be quiet as a mouse."

I let Charlie read to himself for as long as I could. His square jaw was set as he studied the application.

"What do you think, Charlie? Can I do it? The test will be sometime in January."

"You've got a heck of a lot of ambition, Simon. There's no reason on this earth why you can't." Enthusiasm registered in his eyes. "All right. Let's get started." Charlie looked at his daughter. "Rachel, finish your chocolate and give us a chance to bear down here. Boring stuff, honey."

She and I exchanged smiles. I thanked her for the delicious refreshment, and she was gone.

By the end of an hour, we'd filled in all the blanks. I swelled with pride. "This means a lot, Charlie—your taking the time and all. I'll drop it off at Ford's tomorrow after work. We'll see what happens. By the way," I said, putting on my coat, "I missed seeing Virginia on the commute. It was late when I got my hands on this." I gathered up the application. "Be sure to let her know about it."

"And Christmas?" Virginia waltzed in from somewhere. "You're going home for Christmas? No change in plans?"

"It's a long story, too." I laughed at the reminder. "Things have really changed, and now this. But not to worry. Mrs. Butcher's expecting me."

Virginia frowned. "At least you could stick your head in for apple pie. We'd all like it if you did."

A familiar voice echoed down the hall. "*Raa-chel* would love it."

"Hello, Celeste. And how are your studies?"

"Enough, Celeste," Virginia said. "Mr. Hagan was just leaving. Father's going to run him over to Pasadena." She smiled. "Run on back, baby. Finish up whatever you were doing."

I placed the folded application in my breast pocket. "No, but thanks all the same. I'll not hear of it. Going back the same way I came, so I'll be on my way. Have a good evening."

Chapter 32

Two days before Christmas, I had it all planned.

After work, I was on the lookout for a streetcar going the opposite direction of Pasadena—due east to a lumber and hardware store—for a hammer, a small saw, a bag of nails, and a two-by-four. With any luck, I'd make it there before closing. I needed the merchant to cut a six-foot two-by-four into three pieces. If he couldn't, I'd have to get back on a streetcar with a mighty awkward piece of lumber.

Underneath the building's painted letters, *LUMBER & HARDWARE*, a smaller sign read *Grain, Hay, Feed, Poultry Supplies*. I went inside and twenty minutes later came out with my armload of necessities, including the two-by-four, which a salesman had generously cut into three pieces for me. The saw had come with a thick cover. I got to Pasadena, hid my goods in the bushes, and went inside.

Mr. Begbie was out of his chair before I could shut the front door. "Well, laddie? Were you too late?"

"No, sir. I got it," I said, feeling like a crook. "Do I smell popped corn?"

"Where'd ye get the tree?"

Mrs. B entered, almost catching us off guard. She seemed in a twit. "Dinner's early tonight if nobody minds. And Mr. Begbie's filled up on popped corn, I guess. I've got Christmas cooking to get done, so go on. Have a seat, and I'll bring out what I've got."

It wasn't her usual fare, but we ate, not saying a lot. She left the room.

"After work tomorrow," I whispered. "I'll go to the field and get the one I spotted."

Mrs. B was back with no warning. "What about the succotash? Something wrong with my succotash?" She reached across to remove the half-emptied bowl.

"Hands off there, ye. I'm just ready to take me a spoon to it."

"Terrific dinner." I scooted my chair from the table and stood up. "Good night all. Letters to write."

Upstairs, I pulled my valise from the armoire and removed the paper-bound biscuit jar and one soft container of mint julep pipe tobacco folded in lots of newspaper to mask the fragrance. There, also, was Mother's Bible. Behind the valise was the tin of Leo Peppermint Sticks.

I took the Bible and held it, not really wanting to open its cover or delve into the regrets tied to her belongings. After laying it aside, I spent half the night wrapping and then stashing my purchases where they wouldn't be seen. I also wrote a long letter to the folks back home.

When the house fell quiet, I crept out to the bushes for my hammer, nails, and lumber, brought them inside out of the snow, and stuffed them under the bed.

I must have fallen asleep sometime after midnight.

Christmas Eve arrived, and the shift at the factory was a short one, a blur of pulling rods and pounding the hammer. Workers were dismissed at noon, and good wishes passed between us as we exited.

Outside, the sky had released a barrage of white flakes as if a feather pillow had exploded above me. After catching the streetcar, I went slipping and sliding across the sidewalk and up the porch steps to the boarding house. Mr. Begbie was waiting with the handsaw at the front door. I took it without a word and started out across neighboring lawns toward a field in the distance. Snow was coming down faster now, sticking to my shoulders.

The property where I'd seen the cedar was closer to a house than I'd realized, so I trudged to the back door in the blinding snow and knocked. Dogs began barking. I could hear the sound of someone coming.

A man pulled the curtain back just enough to see me, standing with my saw. I tried to appear harmless.

"Let me tie up these dogs!" he shouted. After several minutes, he returned and opened the door about a foot. "They won't attack unless I say so. Stand inside here."

"Thank you, sir." I stomped my feet, propped up the saw by the stoop, and edged inside.

The dogs were mean-looking. They leapt and barked and carried on until the man shoved the palm of his hand in their faces. "Stop! Go sit!"

One look and I was convinced the animals could take me down. "Handsome dogs. What are they, anyway?"

"Boxers. This one's Millie. She's got her babies over in the box. The big one—he's Pete. You don't wanna mess with Pete."

I didn't, for sure, want to mess with ninety-pound Pete. And I could hear the puppies yelping in the box. "No, sir. I wondered if I might cut one of your trees back by the fence. I'd like to bring it over to where I'm living."

The missus, I assumed, came walking in before he could answer. She cuddled a puppy like a newborn baby. "So cute," she said, stroking its muzzle. "Isn't she?"

I admired from a safe distance its beautiful cinnamon coloring and the white markings on its legs. "My, my. She certainly is a fine dog."

"Socks," the woman said. "Nice long socks on her, and the start of a perfect mask. Solid black." She stepped closer. "Ready ta go home with ya."

"Oh, no, ma'am. I came for a tree. I'll be on my way if I can get your permission for that one." I turned and pointed out the window to a medium-height cedar tree standing alone about twenty feet from the house. I turned back, only to start rubbing the puppy's soft, warm ears.

"A dollar," the man said in a raspy voice. "A dollar for the puppy, and I'll throw in the tree for a Merry Christmas. She's worth a whole lot more. What do ya say? I'll even hold her while you hack the tree."

I stood there looking at the puppy, then at the man and his wife, and again at the puppy. A five-dollar bill was all I carried. The rest was back at the boarding house, along with one silver dollar. I could feel the other against my chest.

"One dollar," the woman said, pressing the puppy within inches of my face. "That's all, and she's yours."

"And the tree to boot," the man said.

Irrational as it was, I felt for the silver dollar and handed it over, allowing myself to believe the spirit of Christmas was closer. "Give me a few minutes to get the tree, and I'll be back for her."

Chapter 33

I dragged the six-foot tree to the house on Pasadena Street with the saw under my arm and the pup in my hand, aware I'd definitely stuck my neck out this time. I dropped the tree by the bushes and quickly hid the saw under it.

The animal peed on me before I could set her in the dirt.

Mrs. B had to have heard the yipping the second I opened the door. She was on me like flies on honey. "What on God's green earth is that?" She set her hands defiantly on her hips. "You cannot, *will* not, bring that thing into my house, Mr. Hagan."

"What's the commotion?" Mr. Begbie came hobbling to the front door. "What the—"

"Okay, okay. It's just for tonight. In the morning, the dog goes to the Mallorys as a Christmas gift. Rachel and Celeste will love her." I felt like I'd made my case. "Now, please, Mrs. B, could you spare a box?" I wasn't in any frame of mind to debate. Puppy pee trickled over the toe of my shoe. "Please?"

"Oh, all right! But I warn you, this thing had better not keep me up all night, Mr. Hagan!" She took off for the kitchen.

"Don't worry," I said loudly. "I'll be back after church and take her to my room."

I sidestepped Mr. Begbie, went straight for the telephone, and rang Charlie, who answered on the first ring. Our conversation was brief but fruitful.

Then around the corner came Mrs. B with an empty orange crate. She stopped two steps from my nose just as I hung up. "Church now, is it?"

"Yes, and I do apologize for these little surprises," I said, placing the wriggling puppy in the crate, "but I can't be here for dinner tonight. Got to make arrangements with Charlie." I grasped the doorknob, ready to leave. "He'll be here soon. Good sign that I caught him, don't you think?" I winked at Mrs. B. "Don't anybody worry. I'll be back and take full responsibility."

The dog ran from one end of the crate to the other, yelping.

"Maybe a little towel," I suggested, "or a rag of some sort? Newspapers? A bowl of water? Some cheese, perhaps?"

"Get, Mr. Hagan!"

I nodded to Mr. Begbie, hoping he would smooth things over. He leaned on his cane, shaking his head. I closed the door behind me and waited outside for my ride.

<hr />

"This is a real Christmas Eve treat, Simon," Virginia said as I settled in on the front seat of the Mallorys' Model T. "Wonderful of you to join us."

"Merry Christmas, everyone." I couldn't wait to surprise them with the puppy and was in the best of spirits. "What's Santa bringing in the morning?"

"A lump of coal for Rachel," Celeste said.

"That's not nice, baby, and not true. Let's sing a carol. How about this one?" Virginia burst into song. "'Jingle bells, jingle bells.'"

Charlie and the girls joined in. "'Jingle all the way . . .'"

I took up the melody a second later. "'Oh, what fun it is to ride in a one horse open . . . *Model T!*'"

The bunch of us laughed, giddy as could be, and Charlie pulled in at the back of the church. We piled out and went inside, shaking hands with folks and wishing Merry Christmas to everyone we met.

"Charlie," I said before he could get out of sight, "not now of course, but when you get a minute—"

"Did you get your application in?"

"Oh, yes. On Monday. This is different. Maybe after the service, before we start back."

"Something wrong, Simon?" He pulled me aside, obviously concerned.

"Not at all. And nothing's going to happen with the school till the first of January anyway. The truth is I have a young pup for the girls. Can I do that? Can I give it to them?"

"What? You don't mean it."

"Yes, I'm afraid I do. For Christmas."

"Hmm. Never given that one a thought. Better check with Virgie." He disappeared into the crowd.

⟫◆⟪

The service was short and painless.

Charlie's broad smile after his preaching was more than howdy-dos for the parishioners, more than pride in a well-delivered Christmas Eve sermon. His toothy grin told me what I needed to know: the pup would have a new home tomorrow.

We rode back to Pasadena Street in happy anticipation of what next morning would bring, and the Mallorys dropped me off.

The clock struck eight when I stepped inside the boarding house. I left my coat on and went to the dining room, over to the pie safe. The pup was asleep in the crate with newspaper a quarter of the way up. An upended saucer lay in the corner. I took her upstairs and quickly got her settled. Then I fetched the lumber, hammer, and nails from under the bed and tiptoed back down.

Mr. Begbie waited quietly in the parlor. With the coast clear, he was out of his chair in a flash and swinging the door open before I could pull on my hat. I rushed into the night with him on my heels, and we dragged the tree to the far end of the porch, taking advantage of a bit of light from the nearby window. Mr. Begbie moved unsteadily beside me and watched while I positioned the tree. On cue he began handing me nails, passing them one by one, and I hammered the two-by-fours to the tree trunk.

"What are you doing out there?" Mrs. B shouted from behind the window pane, rubbing away the frost.

Mr. Begbie heaved a heavy sigh. "We'll be there in a minute. The pup needs a house. Ye know it."

That was all we heard from her.

He tugged on my coat sleeve. "Just ye wait till she lays her eyes on this! Aye."

Chapter 34

The hound woke me Christmas morning. A sleepless animal in a crate beside me didn't make anything easy.

"Come on, you," I said. "Let's get to work."

I dressed and started down with the biscuit jar, tobacco, and the wiggling bundle of fur in my arms. It wasn't yet five o'clock but getting up before Mrs. B was imperative. I hid the gifts behind my chair in the parlor and grabbed my outerwear and went out the front door.

The early morning hour was still starlit, and the snow-covered ground shone brilliantly. The Christmas tree, too, was robed in white. I set the puppy down just in time and then put on my hat and coat. With the pup back in the crook of one arm, I shook the snow off the tree's branches, dragged the tree into the parlor, and stood it in front of the window.

Before I could turn around, Mr. Begbie was under my nose. "Here," he said. Four or five strands of cranberries and popped corn hung from his outstretched hand. "Can ye put them 'round?" His eyes glistened. "Gimme the mongrel."

"Mr. Begbie, how on earth—"

He raised his bushy eyebrows. "Strung 'em with me good hand. Aye."

I swapped the pup for the strands. "Let me get started. And a Merry Christmas to you, Mr. Begbie."

"And to ye, laddie."

I wound the cranberries and corn one strand at a time, keeping a lookout for Mrs. B. "These'll make a fine Christmas tree," I said, wrapping the last one. "I'll go find something to cover the base."

"Got it here." Mr. Begbie scooted to the front of his chair, bent over, and hoisted himself up—puppy and all.

I scrambled to help, but he was up, digging at the chair seat.

"A scarf for the missus," he said and pulled the green plaid garment from beneath the cushion, carefully unfolding it. Fringe dangled from its ends. He looked at me over the top of his spectacles, smiling. "Oban, Scotland. Been in me family. It's for her."

I took it and layered it around the two-by-fours. "It's a treasure, a real treasure, Mr. Begbie. Are you sure? On the floor?"

"Don't want your pup a'peeing on it, though."

"No, sir. Let me take her upstairs. I'll make coffee before Mrs. B gets here."

"Take the beast." He shoved her at me. "Bring the crate. She can eat cheese. I'll make coffee. Aye."

Perfect, I thought as he planted his weight on his cane and ambled out of the room. I darted up the stairs and in a couple of minutes was on my way back down with the dog in the crate, which I promptly took to the kitchen. I then hurried to retrieve the gifts from behind my chair and put them under the tree.

I stood back, pleased, and lit a cigarette. No sooner had I taken the first drag than in walked Mrs. B.

"A very Merry Christmas, Mrs. B!" I said, exhaling high into the air. Smugly, I waited for her to notice the tree. "Hope the pup didn't disturb your slee—"

"Heaven's sake! I never—" She gasped and clamped both hands over her mouth. She burst into tears and began inching through the parlor toward the tree.

Mr. Begbie rounded the corner from the kitchen, his cane taking him as fast as I'd seen him move. "Now what?"

He paused when he saw her, and a big smile appeared under his mustache. "Have ye a Merry Christmas."

"Think we could get some coffee?" I started for the kitchen.

"Wait up, ye." Mr. Begbie took a wobbly step and stopped squarely in front of Mrs. B, appearing to have something serious to say. He propped his cane on the side of my chair. "Mrs. B, if I could get me on me knees, I would ask ye to be me wife."

I couldn't hide my astonishment. "I'll leave you two alone, so you can—"

The puppy was howling.

So was Mrs. B. "You'll do nothing of the kind," she said, blotting tears on the sleeve of her fancy red dress. She turned to me. "Can you marry us?"

"No, ma'am. Of course not." I laughed aloud and went over to Mr. Begbie to congratulate him. "But I think this means she's agreeing to it, sir. And if there's not going to be a wedding today, y'all sit. Here." I took a package from under the tree and handed it to Mrs. B. "This one's for you." I turned next to Mr. Begbie and handed him his gift. "For you."

He took the package and pointed a crooked finger at the plaid scarf. "That be for ye. Been lying 'bout it. Aye. It's for a dapper laddie like yourself."

"I don't have anything for anybody!" Mrs. B said. "Not breakfast, not coffee."

"Nonsense!" I said. "You have the best cooking this side of—" I couldn't hear myself over the puppy, who was still howling in the kitchen. "I'll get her. Well, it's the best, Mrs. B." I paused long enough to address Mr. Begbie. "And thank you, sir, for this magnificent scarf. Couldn't be more pleased to own it." I wrapped it around my neck, admiring the luxurious wool as I went off to the kitchen. "See what you have. Both of you. Open up now."

I was back in a jiffy with the crate and the whimpering pup. The newspapers were soaked.

Mrs. B took a seat next to Mr. Begbie on the sofa. She promptly kissed him on the cheek. "There," she said with authority, "that's for you."

"Got more where 'at came from, do ye?"

"Maybe," she said, tearing open her gift. At the first sight of the biscuit jar, she squealed. "Mr. Hagan, this is too much. This entire Christmas morning's too much!" Tears streamed down her cheeks. "Thank you both. It's the best day of my life."

"Glad you like it, Mrs. B. Hope you'll enjoy it for a long time. Now, Mr. Begbie, open up."

It took him a while to unfold the layers of paper holding the pouch of tobacco. He fumbled with it, turning it this way and that. Finally, he got it open and slowly raised his head. His eyes were fixed on mine. "Laddie," he said with humility, "tree-dition."

"Let's eat!" Mrs. B said. "Oatmeal, I guess. Haven't got time to cook another thing."

"Skip it, Mrs. B. It's early, but I'd like to get this pup over to the Mallorys' before we're out of newspapers."

⟨⟩◆⟨⟩

Running, walking, running on an empty stomach to the Mallorys—all too late I'd decided my living gift was madness. Four blocks with the pup wrapped in newspapers and a blanket, its small body bouncing irreverently against the tin of Leo Peppermint Sticks, I realized if I fell on the icy sidewalk, both the animal and I would surely be injured. I was determined to stay upright.

I arrived at the Mallorys' front door and tapped lightly in hopes Charlie might be in his chair by the fireplace, even at this ungodly hour on Christmas morn. My lungs felt like they'd cracked, and steam billowed from my nostrils and mouth.

Before I could tap a second time, he was there with a smile on his face. "Merry Christmas to you. And this is the mutt, huh? You owe me one, Simon." He peeked in at the blanket-shrouded puppy with its two frightened eyes staring back at him. "Please, get inside here. Handsome scarf. I like that."

"Merry Christmas, Charlie." I was breathless.

"The women are in the kitchen. It's your surprise. Want to just go on and take her back there?"

The pup was whimpering. I couldn't keep her quiet.

"I think we'd better." I took off my coat and other outerwear and held tightly to the pup. "Let's go."

I walked quietly down the hallway with the bundle in the crook of my arm and waited until I was in the kitchen doorway to surprise them. "Merry Christmas, one and all!"

Rachel and Celeste screamed in delight. Virginia covered her mouth with her hands.

"A puppy!" Rachel said. "Yippee! A puppy! Can we keep it?" She took it from me as if it were her firstborn and, without warning, kissed me on the cheek.

I felt my face burn with embarrassment. "Well, yes, it's yours and Celeste's. For all of you. And wait, there's more." I went back to the front room for the candy tin and returned. "I hope you'll enjoy this. You have been family to me. This isn't much, just a little something." I handed the Leo Peppermint Sticks to Virginia.

Charlie squeezed my shoulder. "I just have to know one thing, Simon. Did you come to last night's service for this," he said, pointing at the pup, "or because you wanted to hear my sermon?" His solemnness had me going for a second before he burst into laughter.

"I think we should name her Sissy," Rachel said, scratching the dog's ears.

"That's a ridiculous name," Celeste said. "She's no Sissy. Let me think. Give her to me." She pried the puppy from her sister's grasp.

Virginia's breakfast preparations made my stomach growl. "And that dog's had more to eat than I have in the last twelve hours. Hate to break this up, but I need to get on back and let y'all have your Christmas."

"Just happens I'm going over to the church to check on the nativity outside," Charlie said and looked at me. "I'll get the automobile out and run you over to Pasadena. Meet me outside in two minutes?"

"If you insist." His trip to the church sounded a little suspicious, but I hadn't thawed out from the walk over. "Thanks." I turned to the girls. "Let me know what you name her."

"Mr. Hagan, I love her." Celeste kissed the dog's head. "Thank you."

Rachel looked bewildered. "Can't you stay?"

"You can't leave without . . . apple pie." Virginia was insistent. "Let me at least wrap up a piece."

"Charlie's waiting," I said. "Besides, I haven't even had breakfast. I'll be in touch. Again, a very Merry Christmas."

Chapter 35

The New Year, 1921, blew in with little fanfare at the boarding house. Mrs. B's level of cheerfulness had, however, increased considerably. She was whistling when I came down for breakfast—and was still whistling when I left for work. Mr. Begbie was the same crusty Scotsman.

The third day of January was a typical workday, and that afternoon was a typical blustery one. But nothing else about the day was typical. After my shift, I rushed to the building where I'd dropped off my application, tore through the double doors, and hiked up the stairs. My heart thumped so loudly I could hear it under my coat lapels.

The door marked *PRIVATE* was shut. I didn't hesitate to thump vigorously with my knuckles. I could hear voices and someone typing, but nobody responded. I stepped back, considering just how bold I wanted to be, turned the knob ever so tactfully, and opened the door a few inches. The typing was loud. The voices had stopped.

I craned my neck around the door jam. "Excuse me. I'm trying to find out if the application I dropped off two weeks ago has been processed. Would you be able to help?"

The same lady—same pencil in her mouth, same desk and typewriter—ignored me. Another lady, tall, with mousy brown hair and bright red lips, stood behind the typist. She removed her glasses, clearly displeased.

I hesitated, then slipped off my hat and cleared my throat.

The typist acknowledged me with a half-smile. "No."

"No, you won't help me, or no, my application hasn't been processed?"

"You must not be able to read." The pencil bobbed as she spoke. "The

159

sign on the door says *private*."

I smiled at them and opened the door enough to step farther into the small office. It smelled of stale smoke and flowery perfume. I had their attention. "Ma'am," I said, directing my attention to the typist while continuing to smile as sincerely as I knew how, "I was raised on a farm in Kentucky. And I was taught to respect women, so forgive me if I seem rude." I stood straight, feeling my stature empower me. After closing the door gently, I leaned over her desk. "Growing up with a large family made me see life as precious. It's something that got down inside me and went deep."

I'd overstepped my bounds. But whatever had pushed me wouldn't let me turn back. The typist's pencil dropped from her mouth and fell through the typewriter keys.

"It still reaches out in the night," I said, "and wakes me at dawn. It's put a fire in my belly that's telling me I might have to go through doors marked *private* if I'm going to make my own life count for something."

The typist stood up without taking her eyes off me. "What's your name?"

"Simon Hagan, ma'am."

She turned to walk away. "Wait here."

The tall lady stepped aside to let her pass. "She'll be right back," she stammered. "I'm sure of it." She went across the room and absorbed herself in the view from the window.

I fidgeted with my hat brim and waited.

Hardly a minute passed before the receptionist returned and told me to expect a letter. "They're jammed with applications. There will be the letter first, then an exam." She was expressionless. "Perhaps you would have gotten a better reception had you walked down the hall to the door marked *Admissions*. Good luck, Mr. Hagan."

I thanked her and left. If I'd had a tail, I would have tucked it between my legs.

<hr />

Anticipating an acceptance letter from the Henry Ford Trade School made working at the factory purely a means to an end. I went through the motions of pulling the rods and pounding the hammer day after day. No letter came.

Detroit's February was dragging by the same way its January had: bleak and cold, laden with snow. Michiganders took it in stride, bundled from head to toe, tramping the sidewalks in Highland Park, going from the streetcar to the factory and back again. With all the clothes I could put on, I was managing the brutal winter and, as far as I could tell, the only Kentuckian making the commute.

My showing up at the Mallorys' only proved I could make the necessary effort to get through the cold.

Virginia opened her front door and pulled me inside. "Get in here. You've got to be freezing. Just a flimsy overcoat. And you being so thin! Here." She took my scarf and hat. "They'll be over by the fire, drying."

Charlie came walking down the hall with his usual broad smile. "And what brings you out on a night like tonight, Simon?"

The radio was on in the living room, but the puppy's yapping was competing with the pleasant waltz being played. Virginia grinned.

Charlie crossed the room and gave me a sturdy handshake before I could remove my gloves. "Lay those on the hearth. Come. Warm up by the fire." He motioned for me to have a seat. "That Ginger has taken over. We love her. You know that."

"Get comfortable, Simon, please," Virginia said.

"That name suits her. I'm glad she's been fun for you." I squirmed a little and then sat forward on the edge of the sofa. "A dog's a good thing to have around."

Charlie nodded. "All right, Simon. Spit it out. You've got something on your mind. I can tell. You're not asking for Rachel's hand, are you?"

All three of us knew he wasn't serious. Maybe planting a seed, but not serious.

"Better not let Celeste hear you say that," I said. "I'd never hear the end of it."

Charlie sat down. "I apologize. That wasn't right—joking like that. You have to know, though, she has a crush on you. But again, I apologize for—"

"Charlie!" Virginia said, straight-faced. "You shouldn't suggest such a thing, *not anytime*. Rachel would be so embarrassed!"

"You're right, Charlie. There is something." I looked over at Virginia with a lukewarm smile.

"Should I leave?" She started to get up.

"No. Not at all. I need some advice from you both. I've written my father, and we've talked once about it on the telephone. The application you helped with—it's been almost two months. Nothing. Nothing at all." I ran my fingers through my hair and sighed. "The office lady said I should watch for a letter, but how long does it take to get a letter?"

"I wish I knew how to advise you on that, Simon. Have you considered going back over to speak to someone at Ford?"

"Yes, after a week or two, but then I remembered being told applications were . . . *plentiful*, I think she said. I just thought they'd get to mine before much longer."

I heard the girls giggling and the puppy yipping in the hallway, and an instant later Rachel, Celeste, and Ginger were chasing each other through the living room.

"Give us some time, please, girls," Virginia said with a playful tousle of the boxer's ears. "Her strong jaw and black mask make her look so vicious, don't they? Go on now, you two. Greet Mr. Hagan. Then take this lively animal to your room."

"Good night, Mr. Hagan," the girls said in unison.

"Good night. Looks to me like Ginger's in charge!"

Charlie paid little attention to the puppy. "Simon, I feel like something powerful has brought you to Michigan. Don't know exactly what. Drive, vision—"

Rage, defeat, guilt. In my mind, I filled in the blanks for him.

"The trade school could be your calling," Charlie continued. "I know you love automobiles. If that's it, you may need to go pound on some doors. But believe me, there are other opportunities. Have you thought along those lines?" He paused, and the room was quiet except for the soft music.

I hadn't ventured an idea past the end of my nose. "Can't say I have. I'm a country boy, Charlie. Farming's all I've known up to now. Hadn't ever heard of a trade school till this came along."

Charlie glanced at Virginia. "This might be something—hadn't come to me before—but maybe you should talk to Virgie's brother."

She looked at him, then at me. "I can't speak for my brother, but you're right, Charlie. Sam would be someone Simon could talk with."

"Wait. Talk about what?"

"About the police force," Charlie said, "if that interests you. Virgie's brother, Sam Sturges, is a deputy chief at the Detroit Police Department."

"Sounds a bit out of my league."

Virginia moved to the edge of her chair. "Coming up here from Kentucky at eighteen—to me, that says a lot about courage and ambition. Bears repeating: trade school is only one opportunity. And it can happen yet. We don't know, do we? Just give it some consideration. You might want to pray about it."

I didn't have any more questions. I certainly didn't have any answers. And I couldn't begin to think I might want to pray.

Chapter 36

A letter arrived the next day. Mrs. B had the envelope in hand when I came in from work. I hadn't stopped mulling over the conversation about the Detroit Police Department. I was still weighing the odds of someone like me landing a job like that. It was a heck of an idea.

"Now then, I think this is what you've been looking for," she said, waving the letter at me as I hung my hat. "Mind you, I don't *know* that." She handed it over, her head tilted sprightly to one side. "Well, don't you want to see what's inside?"

"Don't ye want to see . . . aye!" Mr. Begbie laughed from the parlor.

"Give me a few minutes," I said. "Think I'll slip up on it, if you know what I mean."

"No! Guess I don't." Her hands went straight to her hips. "Got something in it maybe's going to bite you?"

"Lassie, he means leave him be."

I chuckled. "If I'm not down here, say, by breakfast, come check on me." I started up the stairs with no idea what to make of the letter. So much time had passed.

"No dinner?" Mrs. B sounded puzzled.

"Leave him be. The lad doesn't need your mothering."

It occurred to me as I climbed the last stair—that was exactly what I *did* need. Not another hurdle, not another wall to climb, but a mothering hand.

I went in and shut the door to my room. I stalled for a second, then got on my knees by the bed. *This could be it*, I told myself. The vision of hands-on training and making something of myself shot a surge of energy through me.

"Lord," I said for the first time in a good while, "there's no telling what news is in here. I'm asking for some wisdom about it. Amen."

Still kneeling, I held the envelope under the lamp to read the postmark:

January 6, 1921
6 p.m.
Highland Park, Michigan

What? Disgusted, I read it again. How could it have taken so long to go a few blocks across town? I tore the end off the envelope and tapped it. Leaning into the light, I stood up and carefully unfolded the single page.

January 6, 1921
Mr. Simon Hagan:
This is to inform you that your application letter to the Henry Ford Trade School was received. Bring this Letter of Acceptance to the Radley Building on January 14, 1921, Room 204 at 10:00 a.m. A test to gain admission to the school will be administered at that time.
Best regards,
Byron J. Henson, Admissions
Henry Ford Trade School

"For the love of—"

I tossed it on the bed, sat down on the edge of the mattress, and flicked the letter as if it were a pesky fly. It was clear enough: the mail service had lost it.

I pulled out my Camels and rolled the lighter between my fingers before mechanically pushing the lid open with my thumb. A prompt flame, a deep and long inhale, and I was numbed. Smoke poured from my mouth and nostrils with a vengeance. As I reread the letter, this time in front of the washstand, I reminded myself that I hadn't come to Detroit to go to the trade school anyway. Missing the test date didn't amount to a rejection. I would fill out a new application and be sent another date to take the test.

I inhaled again and watched in the mirror as smoke streamed from what seemed like every part of my being. Miss Hannah's words burned through me like a torch. "A deep search for meaning," she'd said.

Why had I come to Detroit? Questions rolled in my head like tumbling rocks. If I wasn't going to stick it out at the factory or go to trade school—what?

I raised the letter, held the end of my cigarette to it, and watched while a dream went up in flames. Nothing hurt, it simply ended. I wiped the blackened ashes out of the washbasin and walked to the nightstand, put the butt in the ashtray and let it die on its own.

⟫◈⟪

I didn't go down for dinner. It was the last thing on my mind. If I'd been hungry, I wasn't aware of it. At five the next morning, I felt my stomach grumble. By six, I was ravenous.

"Good morning." I smiled a token smile and sat down in my usual chair at the table with the odd couple. "I apologize, Mrs. B, for missing dinner."

Their eyes went from plate to plate, from the chandelier over the table to the floor at our feet. Not once did they meet mine.

Mrs. B passed the toast. Strawberry jam was right behind. Surely, I could eat the entire family-sized dish of hash and fried eggs that was coming my way.

I kept myself from devouring everything in sight and washed down a mouthful with a sip of coffee. "That was delicious, Mrs. B. If you and Mr. Begbie will excuse me, I'm going to head on to work. And by the way, I won't be here for dinner."

They gave each other a worried look.

"Have some business to attend to."

She pushed herself up from the table. "Mr. Hagan—"

Mr. Begbie raised a crooked finger. "Leave him be."

Chapter 37

I was a common fixture at the Mallory household, and following another day at work, I was on the lookout for Virginia at the terminal. For a mid-February day, the afternoon was reasonably mild—at least by Detroit standards.

I spotted her not too far off. "Wait up." I reached her with breath to spare. "The letter arrived. From Ford."

"That's wonderful, Simon!"

"No, not wonderful. It got stuck in the post. Must have gone to . . . who knows where before it got to me. I actually missed my exam."

She gasped. "Oh, Simon. I'm very sorry."

We caught up to the streetcar and found standing room only.

"Could I go over to your house? Maybe go to prayer meeting?"

"Of course," she said, swaying side to side as the streetcar rounded the curves. We got off together and began walking. "I know Charlie's going to want the details. I sure do!"

"You have a visitor again!" I yelled like a child home from school and followed her inside.

"You must be going to church!" came a jovial reply from the back of the house. "Super!"

"Ginger, no jumping, girl." I brushed past her to hang my coat. "And where are your friends?"

I found Charlie waving a wrench over the kitchen sink. His look said he was a mite disgusted with his efforts. "The girls are studying before church."

"Can I give you a hand with that? Not that I'm going to be an expert at mechanics, looks like."

167

"Uh-oh. Rejection?" He bit his lip. "There! Got 'er tight, I think!"

Virginia came in close and propped her elbows on the counter.

"It wasn't rejection. That's the thing. The letter came six weeks late, Charlie. *Six weeks!* It got lost in the mail or something. Missed the test date altogether."

"Hmm. Now that's really interesting." He straightened up and laid the wrench aside. I had his full attention.

"I could fill out another application. But what do you make of the timing on this? I've thought and thought all night and all day today, and I can't tell you how surprised I've been. Disappointed as I was, I'm much more excited about the police opportunity, more than I ever was about the school, if you can believe it." I watched their reactions. "If that letter had come on time, I wouldn't have even heard about a police job."

Virginia smiled ear to ear. "One door closed, and another opened. Our conversation would never have happened. I'm certain of it, too."

"Well, the delay's sure pointed you in a whole different direction," Charlie said. "It's almost enough to make a man believe in a providential hand!"

"Tell that one to my dad," I said.

We all seemed to want to express, "*Well, I'll be!*" But it went without saying.

Chapter 38

⟫·◇·⟪

The last of the snow, piled high, hindered a clear view from the window. We had dealt with the stuff most of March. We'd hoped this was the end of it.

"What do you make of this weather, Mr. Begbie?" I stood up to get a better angle, looking down toward the street. "A sheet of ice. The street and the walk—nothing but ice!" I returned to the chair where I'd sat for the last half hour, lit up a cigarette, and tried to settle myself. The day was turning out as miserable as any I'd seen. I watched the sky through the upper panes in the window, but I couldn't keep still. My interview with a deputy police chief at the Detroit Third Precinct wasn't looking good. "Threatening a blizzard of sorts, looks like."

"Been telling ye, it could hit us some more. Aye. Won't be getting a newspaper, will ye?"

"No, sir," I said, back on my feet. "I don't think so."

"Been waiting awhile, haven't ye, laddie?"

"Weeks," I said, patrolling the window. "It feels longer. Cost me a whole day off work."

Mr. Begbie gave me a significant headshake, as if I'd touched a nerve. "One day's all it takes sometimes, and life goes off track."

I turned to him, deducing. "Your stroke happened quite a while ago, didn't it? Seems like Mrs. B said it was about when you came over."

"Aye, 1908."

I sat down and tried to get comfortable.

His pipe sat idle. His limp hand lay in his lap. "Came here along with me wife from Oban, 'bout a hundred miles from Glasgow." He twisted his mustache and looked away. "Fighting clans needed land for the sheep, forced us out, burned our home." He blinked hard. "Worst night of me life. Had me a stroke as we were a landing. Woke up in a hospital. She was gone."

"Gone?"

His hand went up. "Lost all hope of using me training. Couldn't even doctor m'self—let alone another. Thirteen years. Thirteen."

I was at a loss for words. "Mrs. B's been a good . . . She's been good for you."

"Aye."

I felt my personal frustration over losing a workday sinking like the *Titanic*. Four measly weeks anticipating a police job was squat compared to losing everything.

"You're a good man, Mr. Begbie. A little cantankerous at times. But aren't we all?" I scooted out of my chair and walked over to light the pipe he'd put in his mouth. "I wish things could have been different for you, coming to America, and all."

He was quiet.

"Mind if I call you Doc?"

He nodded.

"You and Mrs. B—quite a pair." I made sure she wasn't in the wings and continued. "When's that wedding going to happen, anyway? I do know a preacher. Bet I can get him here." I paused, certain Charlie would have to know: "You aren't Catholic, are you, Doc?"

"Nary, mind ye." His eyebrows wriggled like caterpillars. "Did ye say preacher?"

"I think you heard me, Doc Begbie, sir."

"Aye." A twinkle shone in his eyes. "And ye finally got yourself a girl-ly." He took a puff and looked at me over the top of his glasses.

"No, sir. Where would you have gotten such an idea? Never mind. This conversation is about you and Mrs. B—"

"Hold on, lad!" He laid his pipe aside.

I braced myself for the colorful advice I knew was coming.

"If ye like her," he said, "don't let her get away."

I was relieved. "Yes, sir. I'll remember that." The topic had me pacing the floor. "I don't have time for girls, but that Rachel's a looker, all right. Hair as black as a raven's, and eyes to match."

He was on my comment like flies on stink. "Eh?" He pressed his ear forward with his hand.

"Doc, stop, please. Don't make anything of what I just said. Maybe I should be horsewhipped for not paying more attention to her, but I've got a long row to hoe first, if you know what I mean." I gave him a no-nonsense look. "The Mallorys have two very nice girls. But I'm really not interested in Rachel—and certainly not her little sister, who's as bad as you. That one never stops poking fun or asking questions. If I were to get on the police force, a lot of things would change." I stopped long enough to consider it. "My dream's to get there—today—by some miracle. After that, if I get a job, I'd sure like to get back to Kentucky for a short visit. Turn in my badge at the factory first, of course."

"Needing to see family, are ye?"

"Yes, sir, especially my brother Alan. Rougher than a cob, that one. May just be on a bad path, but I've gotta get to him." I went to the window, deep in thought. "He's got a wild hair, all right—Wait a cotton pickin' minute!" I yelped in disbelief, surprised as I was by the view. "Doc, I do believe it's clearing up out there!"

"Fooling, are ye?"

"No, really! I'm calling Charlie. And while I have him, it's worth the mention of needing a preacher. That's *preach-er*," I added rather loudly.

"Good thing Palmer found another place to live. Aye. With the two of ye, I wouldn't stand a chance around here."

I went straight for the telephone. "Virginia, good morning. Hate to be short, but may I speak with that rascal husband of yours?"

"You're in luck. He's snowbound. I know you have to be disappointed with the weather. Let me put him on."

Seconds passed. I could hear him clearing his throat as he came to the phone. "Not the best day for appointments in the city, is it?"

"Charlie, have you seen outside? The sun's out. And I just saw an automobile go by, so I'm gonna try to make it in. Hitch a ride. I've got till four.

Just need some good luck—or something—for this interview."

"You've got prayers coming from over here. And maybe someone will teach you to drive in this mess."

"You are amusing. No, thanks. No lessons in this weather. But I'm gonna need them soon. I'll count on you for that." I was so excited by the prospect of getting to my interview I could hardly stand still. "By the way," I said, raising my voice, "I need you to marry this pair I live with. They'd like that." I kept Doc Begbie in my sight, checking his reaction.

"Catholic?"

"No, Charlie, he's not Catholic. I'll let you know how it goes at head-quarters."

"Wait till Mrs. Butcher hears 'bout this!" Begbie was on his feet, yelling from the parlor.

I bundled up and turned to him on my way out. "I've been lucky as the dickens, Doc. Here, in the right place, friends, a nice plaid scarf from Scot-land. And I'm gonna go get a job on the Detroit police force today. Same way you got all those cranberries and popped corn strung with one hand—because you're a hard-driving son of a gun."

"Aye, laddie."

<hr>

If I'd wagered the job on the police force would be mine, the odds would have been in my favor. Recourses—had I not gotten it—would have had me making trips back there as many times as it took, reapplying until I did get one, or till I got my butt kicked out. As it turned out, neither were necessary.

With my factory job obligations behind me a week after I turned in my resignation, I garnered enough time to get on a train to Kentucky with the plan to spend a productive two days at the home place.

Chapter 39

Through water droplets that clung tenaciously to the window pane, I saw Dad standing at the far end of the platform as the train rolled into the station. His hat was in hand. He looked expectant. I almost ran to meet him.

An early April shower had left the air fresh. It wrapped me with everything I loved about Kentucky. Inside, I melted.

"Son, my son." It's all he could say. He buried his head in my neck, his arms enfolding me.

"Was a good trip," I said. "A heck of a long one. It's awfully good to be back home for a spell."

"I do believe you've passed six foot three, haven't you?" He was squinting at me against the glare. His deep laugh sounded like music. "Can I give you a hand?"

"No, sir. I've got everything. You lead the way to the carriage. Don't think I've grown taller." I followed him past the only carriage I saw. "Muscles, perhaps."

He grinned and kept on going.

"Where's ol' Soot?"

"In the barn," Dad said with a ready smile that covered his face like Sunday dinner on a picnic cloth. "Got all the horsepower right here."

I took one look at the Model T and slowly set my valise down in the wet dirt. "Well, I'll be." I stroked the water from the hood and bent down to feel one of its small, hard tires. "When did you get her?"

"We can talk as we go." Full of vim and vigor, he hastened to the front

173

of the automobile and cranked her up. A couple of turns, and out came the beautiful sound of the engine. "Get your bag. Jump in."

And we were off, around the bend toward Elkton, with every bump feeling like I'd landed in a hay wagon. The showers had stopped, and the late afternoon sun was breaking through clouds. Already it was beginning its descent toward the horizon. I tried to recall the last time I'd enjoyed the fragrance of spring as it moved over the meadow after a rain.

I ran my hand over the dashboard and let my fingers skim the smooth glass on the window of the gas gauge while Dad steered the automobile.

He was as proud as I'd seen him since the day he married Hannah. Steadily he held the wheel, confident, working the pedals like an expert—his eyes fixed on the narrow, winding road. A wrinkled brow held the rim of his hat in place.

Against the backdrop of a deep orange sky, I could see leathery signs of aging on his face. He was starting to look older than his forty-four years.

"Detroit all you expected, son?" He seemed to have been putting together the right words.

"Yes, sir. All and then some." I repositioned my bag to give my long legs a little more space. "I left the factory on a good note, and in a few days it all begins." I could feel my chest swell with a picture of what lay ahead. "I never expected I'd be a policeman. Looks like I'll start as a watchman, walking the beat."

Dad shifted his weight and sat up straighter, examining me. His ruggedness melted into a smile. "There'll be plenty to battle as time goes on. But I sure liked the notion of that Henry Ford Trade School, too, back when that was talked about." He got silent. "I'm proud of you, son."

It wasn't the first time I'd heard those words. We both knew I'd done plenty to disappoint him.

"It was a year and three days ago, Dad. Only just a year ago that Mother . . ." I tried to think how to backpedal, and we rode out the awkward moment while I looked out my window. Afterwards, I turned look back over at him. "When'd you get this, anyway?" I slid my hand between the roof and my hat. "They make 'em just right at Ford, don't they? One of these days—"

"Son, you can't change the past. And I can't change the past." He kept his face to the wind, no doubt expecting me to do the same.

I could smell the rich, fertile soil of the farms as we passed, see the freshly plowed earth behind the fences. The beauty of the land I loved was everywhere, and I tried to absorb every speck of it.

Dad honked as a duck waddled across the road in front of us. "Your sisters and Hannah have been fixin' since the minute they heard you were coming." He gave me a sideways glance. "And there's that new young'un on the way, 'round May." He grinned. "It's all Mary can talk about. Of course, Hannah's right happy about it, too."

"How's Alan?" I wanted Dad to tell me Alan had turned a corner—no longer tormented by the moodiness and fits of anger I'd heard about in letters and telephone calls—that my brother had found something to steady him. "He took Mother's passing awfully hard. I wish he hadn't seen her after it happened." I lit a cigarette. "Myself . . . I wish I could have been blinded by a hot poker before I saw."

Dad didn't acknowledge what I'd said. "I'm counting on you to talk some sense into Alan. He positively cannot leave home at sixteen, but that's what he's gotten into his head."

If the weight of the world hadn't just dropped on me, something else sure as heck had. The responsibility for Alan fell heavily on my shoulders. I switched from the picture in my mind of Mother's horrific death to a six-teen-year-old's bad attitude. It was more than I could stomach. I pinched the end of my Camel and tossed it out the window. "What can I do, Dad? Should I tell him there's no world out there, that he should stay here and be a farmer?" I swallowed hard. "And one day, when a black bear comes out of the woods . . . and claws his sister . . . or this new baby . . ." The explosion of emotion overwhelmed me. I pounded my chest with my fist. "Should I tell him barns will burn, crops will fail no matter how hard he tries to save them, tenants will suffer, and there's nothing he can do or say to keep it from happening?" I slammed my hand on my knee. "And God will turn away!"

Dad swerved to the side of the road and killed the engine. His chest rose like it might burst and fell like it might not move again. "Let's get something straight." The look in his eyes could have bored through the stone wall that stood next to the automobile. "The God you're challenging is not going to give up on you, and he's not going to let you *be* God either. The sooner you accept that, the better off you'll be."

He scrutinized me without moving, and we sat in silence while the sky changed from resplendent shades of orange to murky peach and yellow.

When it was clear my insides would not stop churning, he opened the door on the automobile and got out. "Wanna drive her?"

I looked at him, astonished. "You don't mean it."

"I'll take that as a yes." He smiled, got out, and cranked the engine.

With her idling, I jumped in the driver's seat and waited while Dad got his door shut, then pulled the throttle lever down to advance the ignition. The engine acknowledged my command, and we rolled along with dusk catching up.

"Well, Simon," Dad said, holding his hat on his lap, "I see you've had a lesson or two."

I grinned. "Yessir."

As we approached the last turn before home came into view, we gave each other shameful looks. I let her rip, and we took off like a horse with both ears laid back.

The release felt good.

Chapter 40

Alan must have been on the lookout. He was out of the house by the time Dad and I came bumping down the lane, the Model T's head-lights leading the way.

The house was lit from top to bottom, and every lamp on the entire first floor appeared to be burning. Raymond and Marly were next out the door, with Niney barking at their heels. Mary and Charlotte came running down the front stairs as the automobile swung into position next to a low area at the rock wall. The rest of the clan, whooping and hollering, weren't far behind. Miss Hannah brought up the rear.

Alan was beside my door before I could get it open, shouting and waving both arms in the air wildly as if he'd never expected me to return. And when we embraced, he was in no hurry to let go.

Reddish hair fell in unruly curls onto his forehead. He looked like he'd grown a foot in the four months I'd been gone. An immense smile covered his face. Seeing him so happy was like covering an open wound with a sooth-ing ointment. I'd come home for this.

Hugs were plentiful, and everyone took a turn.

My stepmother's came with a high-pitched greeting. "We've missed you," Hannah sang out as I gathered my belongings and we started inside. She looked like she'd swallowed a watermelon seed. Her gait was measured. "So nice to have you home for a while, Simon."

That evening was filled with tales of my adventures in Detroit. When it came right down to it, there weren't many. I was tempted to improve on the truth, to make them worthy, but it seemed my jabbering was enough to keep us up till way past bedtime—reminiscing and eating around the cherrywood table in the dining room.

⬥

I awoke early. Alan lay snoring, curled up on the far side of the four-poster bed. I yanked my skivvies on, carried the rest of my clothes, and slipped quietly from the room we shared with our brothers.

No one stirred, it seemed, as I traipsed down the stairs—shoes, shirt, and trousers in hand—and passed through the narrow back hallway to the kitchen. The house was pitch-black, as if a shroud had been draped over it, and I left it that way, feeling my way along, not wanting to wake anyone. Soon enough, the chores would begin.

I finished dressing by the stove and went out the back door. Niney followed me across the back stoop, her tail wagging.

Outside in the leftover coolness of night, I stood briefly by the well, watching the old oak bucket swing in the morning breeze. Absorbed by the richness of everything in sight, I lifted my face to the sky and inhaled the fragrance of spring.

Then I began to walk, slowly at first, down the steps and out to the back. For no particular reason, I walked along where the dense tree line had stood. I began moving briskly and startled the nesting birds in the only tree that remained along the way. The noise sent them flapping away, the sound of their chirps trailing faintly behind them.

The peaceful pastureland called out to me from one fence to the next, and the barn beckoned me to talk to the animals, put down feed for the hogs, and stroke my equestrian friend from childhood. The countryside wanted to keep me tied to life on the farm, but it was foreign to me now. I dismissed the innocent lowing of a cow and the hoot of a lone mourning dove. I had traded them for an existence far away. And now I thought like a northerner. I lived like a northerner.

Even so, I couldn't deny the spell the outdoors cast on me. Newly thawed earth—plowed, blackened, and still—swallowed the landscape like dark ocean waves, and the essence of the wild rolled toward me from the ends of the earth. Guilt moved in the memory of the trees that had populated the landscape. Now it surrounded me with emptiness, drawing me to the place like a dog to its vomit. I knew the exact spot. I could still hear her screams.

The original chicken coops, torn down, had been replaced by new ones. Mary's striped hen strutted ahead of me as if to show me around. I hadn't been back here since . . . not since last March.

Dad strode along the old tree line and stopped right beside me. "I guessed I might find you here, son." He stared down at the ground, then straight into my eyes. "You had to grow up fast. Not a good thing for you at seventeen. Not for anybody at any age."

I could feel my emotions rising inside me. "If only I'd run faster. She—"

"Son, quit. You're no match for a bear. No man is. Not single-handed." Dad was straining to hold his gaze. Either the beam of the rising sun or his unconvincing proclamation turned his eyes toward the pastureland. "We'll never be the same, but we have to go on."

"If I'd had a rifle instead of a shotgun in the barn . . ." I couldn't say it. I picked up a rock embedded in the new grass and threw it as hard as I could downhill toward the barn.

A hundred yards or less looked so close now. That distance had been so far away at the time.

"Let's go, son. Hannah's probably rustling up some breakfast." Dad was smiling. "She's a good woman. She's been here when I needed her. Guess I've been the same for her."

The discussion of Mother was over. For him, I supposed, Hannah had filled the gaping hole in his heart.

"You'll find a wife, Simon," he said, ambling toward the house, a distinct tenderness in his voice. "I hope she'll be everything your mother was to me."

"Rachel Mallory seems to have set her cap for me, but I'm not really looking for a wife. Not even a girlfriend."

"Eh?" He laughed. "Could've fooled me. Your letters have had a lot to say about this Rachel." He stopped and looked at me apologetically. "Guess I was reading between the lines, as they say. You've got plenty of time for women. Get your feet on the ground first." He started walking again. "I want to hear more about this police job."

"It's got me excited—that's for sure. It took me by surprise when the Mallorys first mentioned it. After I had the chance to really think during the next day or two, it started to grow on me."

He listened attentively, but I knew he wanted to hear why I hadn't reapplied to the trade school, no doubt thinking my piqued interest in being a policeman was nothing more than a flimsy alibi for not persevering. He couldn't have understood how the weeks had dragged on while I waited, anticipating good news about my application, or how hope had died and a new dream had replaced it.

"I don't think I was cut out for mechanics. I sure like automobiles, though." I held the back door open for him. "Your Tin Lizzie has me chomping at the bit. Just like Senator Maxwell's did. And Charlie Mallory's. The streets in Detroit are full of 'em. Guess I was of the opinion I'd like the work, being a small part of the process. Maybe that was it. I was a small part."

The hinges creaked, and the screen door slammed shut behind us. We came through the kitchen and met up with Alan.

"Police work is it, Dad. I'm sure of it."

"Just want the best for you, son. A good, solid foundation."

Alan looked barely alive.

"You awake, Alan?" I said with a slap on his shoulder.

He squinted at Dad and me. "Mornin'."

Hannah greeted us with a smile and a large ladle in her hand. "Food's on the table. Morning, Simon." Her olive complexion glowed. It seemed being pregnant agreed with her. Still, she was big as a heifer.

I stepped to one side to let her get at the sausage sizzling in the pan. "Good morning, Hannah." Calling her by name hadn't been easy. Dropping the "Miss" on the front of it hadn't either. Calling her Mom was unreasonable. "Breakfast sure smells good. I'll just go wash up and take Alan with me."

She seemed relieved to be getting two lanky guys out of her kitchen.

"Si, eat with me." Alan nodded to our stepmother, but his attention was on me. "You're gonna carry a gun all the time, aren't you?" he declared, antsy and jumping around like his feet were on fire. "Holy cow!"

I suspected he'd been lying in wait, eager to restart a conversation we'd begun last night about Detroit and the police.

And Dad wasn't finished with me, either. "The trade school sounded like a fine place for you, Simon. Would it have mattered if I had—"

"No, Dad. It wouldn't have. Don't think so. My mind was made up. And I'm lucky to get the police job."

"Luck? God's providence is probably in there somewhere, don't you think?"

Alan was caught in the crossfire. He wanted to know everything.

"We can talk about it later. Who's down at the barn?"

Alan was quick to answer. "Seth's there, and the hands. Mason should be about done milking." He grinned, and a single dimple appeared like a hole in his right cheek. "I want to hear about your gun."

"I'll take Soot out after breakfast," I said. "But isn't there something to be done down there beforehand?"

"Nah," he said. He looked thin in his overalls—even more so than I remembered. We were skinny kids, all of us, but Alan's long face accentuated his leanness, and his head-full of hair added inches to his height. He looked up at me, waiting for an answer.

"There's no gun, Alan. Not yet, anyhow." I sat down at the dining table. "We both should have shaved before breakfast." I rubbed my whiskers. "And I suspect I'll have a Model T one of these days, too."

"Simon!" Mary screeched as she rounded the corner and ran into my arms. "Let me sit next to you!"

The rest of the herd wasn't far behind.

"I'm coming up there, Si," Alan said, unable to sit at all. "Dad says not now, but soon as I'm seventeen, I'm coming to Detroit."

Chapter 41

I peered out into the night, squirming like a child in my seat as the train pulled out of the Hopkinsville station. The trip back to Elkton, as good as it had been to spend two days with the family, had worn me out. I tried to get myself settled in for the long haul back to Detroit.

My eyelids were heavy, and the steady clickety-clack of the train's wheels on the tracks, measured and fast, should have put me to sleep. But Dad's questions lingered in my mind, nagging at me. In the hours of solitude, I grappled with his concern about Alan's stability and my influence on him. After changing trains in Cincinnati, I pondered Alan's restive spirit. I had no answers.

And I had no answer for myself, let alone for Dad, as to whether I had found peace with God. The question bothered me, but once the train rolled into Michigan Central and I later boarded the streetcar to Highland Park, it needed no answer. What mattered was getting to the Third Precinct by seven-thirty the next morning, and therein lay the answer to Dad's other probing question about where my new job was going to take me.

I slept like a baby in my boarding-house bed, and before the sun came up, I was dressed and out the door, on my way to the Detroit Police Department. Had anyone asked about my destination during the ride to the city, I would have been pleased to answer that today was my first day as a policeman. But without such, I remained quiet, periodically glancing at my newspaper, which I tucked under my arm as we approached my stop.

I stepped off the streetcar, let it pass, and then set out on foot in the direction of 2200 Hunt Street, the weather contrasting rudely with the mild

April days I'd just enjoyed. After crossing Gratiot Avenue, I braced myself against Michigan's blustery wind, which had picked up speed. My overcoat and gloves were a welcome insulation, but I walked fast.

The three-story, block-like structure came into full view. I took the steps two at a time and entered the building where I'd be starting as a rookie. So far, joining the police force held plenty of appeal for me, and the thought of getting involved in daring escapades, even if such opportunities didn't come until later, whetted my appetite. There would be the potential for advancement if, as time passed, I could prove myself capable.

The lobby was as large as a barn and almost as musty. I'd noticed the smell of old wood on the day of my interview. Today, I breathed deeply its richness. I walked with my head held high, like a self-assured Kentucky gentleman—a Senator Maxwell. The ceiling loomed like so many tin squares above busy people with lowered heads, all entering, leaving, or deeply engaged in activity. Some were uniformed. Others were dressed in street clothes. All wore somber faces. No one looked up. It looked to be Monday morning as usual.

After giving myself a minute to survey the sprawling arrangement of file cabinets, extra-long tables, and in-use telephones, I went straight for the desk with an American flag standing next to it. A Michigan flag stood on the opposite side. An officer was seated directly behind it, between the flags. He was occupied, huge, and black. It struck me that he was in charge.

"Good morning, y'all," I said to a couple of passersby as I waited for the officer to notice me. I might as well have been invisible.

He shuffled a few papers, set them aside, and slowly raised his head, sizing me up. "Mr. Preacher-boy," he said, matter-of-factly. "What's up?"

Dumbfounded, I handed him the official document for my employment. It took me only a second to place him. "The barstool. That diner on Woodward!" I laughed. "You gave me directions out to Highland Park."

"You got it, my Dixie-man." He leaned back in his chair until its front legs came off the floor. And when he clasped his hands behind his head of thick black hair, the muscles on his arms could have split his shirtsleeves. "That y'all stuff needs to stay back in *Can*-tuck, if you know what I mean." He let the chair legs drop to the floor and then began studying my papers. His hands were half again as large as mine.

"Yes, sir," I said, cracking my knuckles while I waited.

"That, too, if you're going to be coming to work here. And from the looks of it . . . yup, you are. Deputy Chief Sturges has okayed all this. Almost nineteen, huh?"

"Yes, sir, In June," I said, lighting a cigarette. "I don't forget a face."

His bulging eyes narrowed underneath heavy dark eyebrows. His head didn't move. "Mr. Hagan," he said at last with a chuckle, "the police force just might suit you. Sergeant Roman Davis is the name." He stood with an outstretched hand. "Get your preacher-boy butt through there to check-in, then down the hall for training." He pointed to a map-covered wall with a pair of swinging doors. "And don't look back."

It was a head-scratcher of a remark, but I followed through on what he'd said. The red tape associated with checking in took the better part of the morning, and training ate up the rest of the day. The afternoon was practically over, and I hadn't left the premises. It had been a slow one. Most of the recruits had already left.

I completed the required reading from the handbook, folded the uniform I'd been issued, and was about to get up and go when in walked an officer with two stars on the collar of his uniform. I stood at attention. The remaining recruits did, as well.

He was a handsome man in his late forties, with a slicked-down head of jet-black hair. His shoulders were massive. His legs looked like tree trunks. The gun at his side was impressive. "Hagan," he said with a vise grip on my hand. He looked me straight in the eye. "Sam Sturges here."

The four or five other men left the room, the last one out cutting his eyes at me.

"Chief, good to meet you, sir. You've been a big help. I appreciate it."

"Let's just say Virginia put in a good word. She thinks a lot of you. She and Charlie both do." He checked his watch. "Shall we?" He led me toward the exit of the long, narrow room.

"The Mallory family is mighty special," I said, somewhat distracted by Roman Davis looking our way, as the deputy chief and I passed through the swinging doors. "That sister of yours has been a godsend, Chief. Much as I like automobiles, the Ford Motor Company just wasn't for me."

"Well, we'll find the potential if you have it. Working the street with all this Prohibition crap—it's experience you need for now." He positioned his cap with a dignified tilt and nodded. "Good to meet up with you. And good luck."

"I'll be sure to tell Virginia I met you, Chief."

With our goodbyes said, I doubled back to speak with Sergeant Davis, who was standing near the switchboard, talking with a hefty woman with a telephone to her ear. I walked up and waited, not wanting to interrupt the three-way conversation.

"Saw you coming," he said. "Tall as you are, you're a hard son of a gun to miss." He was four or five inches shorter than I, but a whole lot bigger. His enormous brown eyes protruded like the headlights on an automobile. "Speaking of guns, did you get past firearms training?"

Another head-scratcher.

He laughed and shook his head before I could muster an answer. "Nice range in the basement. You'll get a look at her in a few days."

We traded small talk for a minute or two. Then his tone grew more serious.

"White southerners." He hesitated and then looked me straight in the eye, as if he had singled me out for a lecture. "They're coming in here to the department by the dozens. It's a good thing, I suppose." He seemed to loosen up some and lit a cigarette.

I did the same.

"Crime's outta hand," he said, his jaw in motion, jutting forward with the likeness of an oversized bulldog.

"Then Detroit's in the thick of it?"

"You betcha. Close as we are to Canada, you kidding? Smugglers are bringing in illegal booze. Getting ugly as crap, preacher-boy."

We walked out together.

I caught his eye and kept a straight face. "That preacher-boy stuff needs to go if I'm going to work here."

"Gotcha." He didn't blink once. We seemed to be hitting it off. "One of those goldurn Prohibition agents had his picture in this morning's paper. There he was, standing in a flatbed of confiscated alcohol at the Trumbull Station." He tightened his lips against gritted teeth. "And you'll be finding out about the underworld real fast, my Dixie-man."

Chapter 42

—◆—

The night was as black as an owl's behind, and in the alleyways on my beat, it smelled about like one. Chief Sturges had done me no huge favor in terms of assignment. From the get-go, I walked the four blocks east of Jefferson between Randolph and Grand Boulevard near the Belle Isle Bridge. Practically every step was in clear view of Electric Park with its wild attractions. Even after the first two weeks, nothing about my job on the foot patrol was dull.

The arrests I made—most of them drunks and almost nightly—had me going into court during the day on my own time to back them up. Getting to and from Highland Park, relying on a streetcar for the numerous trips, which had become my jagged routine, was an ordeal and completely impractical. Owning an automobile was the solution. It was that or move into town.

This day in particular, my shoes had a spit shine, my attitude did as well, and my eye was drawn to a parked automobile at the edge of the display lot, obviously a new one, a doozy.

The salesman spotted me the minute I walked over to it.

"That's a fine-looking thing," he said, grinning stupidly.

"It is at that." I returned the cardboard tag with $369.00 written on it to its position on the windshield. The shiny brass radiator and kerosene lights seemed to stand at attention. "Guess it's gonna take a bit more elbow grease before I can pay that kinda price."

He snapped his head intolerantly and pursed his lips. "You've come hoping to relieve me of an automobile at a price less than I'm willing to take."

"I've done nothing of the kind. My funds simply don't allow me to drive your automobile at a price that escapes my ability to pay."

"Does that mean you want the automobile or not?"

"It means I cannot afford to want it. Not at this time. Good day to you, sir. 'Preciate your help." I tipped my hat, skedaddled down the sidewalk, and got on the first streetcar going out to Highland Park.

The next afternoon, Sunday, I was at the Mallorys' house, laughing with Charlie over a cup of coffee at my sprightly conversation the day before, which had yielded no automobile.

"It gave me an idea, though, of just how long before I can own one, Charlie. Did that much for me. Sure did!"

He gave me a quizzical look. "There are loans, but I believe, along with *your* friend Henry Ford, that buying an automobile on credit is morally reprehensible."

"Wouldn't dream of it."

"Mine's a 1917 model. Over four years old now. I think I can justify turning her in on a newer one. Doesn't have to be a '21. Technically, it belongs to my congregation." One of his ear-to-ear grins crossed his face. "Let me see about buying her outright . . . well, just let me work through—"

"No! Charlie I won't hear of it."

"Won't hear of what?" From behind me, Rachel clasped her hands over my eyes. "Guess who?"

I reacted more favorably to her flirtation than I felt. Possibly it was the jubilant thought of actually becoming the owner of a Model T.

Chapter 43

⟫◆⟪

Gangland violence in Detroit began to accompany everyday activities, and illegal liquor was being smuggled onto the city's streets. The biggest port from Canada was giving even the experienced cops a real headache. Compared to them, I was seeing little of the action, watching women coming home from work at one or two in the morning, but my Model T was the prize. I was sure Charlie had cut me a deal: a car for the common man.

Detroit was, however, anything but common. The ill effects of Prohibition were showing themselves, and the law was so unpopular it was nearly impossible to enforce. A tip-off came the night that two detectives were shot and killed by a gang operating out of the Hewitt Warehouse on Clairmount. As a rookie cop, it put me on alert.

Nights shifts, two at a time, alternated with day shifts. My T was more than a ticket to personal freedom, hardly frivolous. Automobile ownership, though, could catch me behaving like a kid with a new toy, but after an average long all-nighter on the beat, I was eager get back to Pasadena Street and roll into the sack.

I arrived back at the boarding house, charged up the front steps, and opened the door. Alan stood there, staring me in the face.

Mrs. B was next to him, close enough to have been brushing his hair—it needed it. "And all this time I've been thinking it's your sister that's gonna show up." Her eyes wrinkled at the corners as if she were in possession of something that didn't belong to her. She had both hands firmly planted on her hips. "You two certainly look like brothers, except for his red hair."

I was astounded, even as Alan and I embraced.

He was already running off at the mouth and looking past me at the Model T parked by the curb. "Daddy-o, is that your automobile out there? I'm getting me one." He looked down at my holster. "Great hugga-mugga! Let's see the gun."

Mrs. B was having none of it. "Shut this door. Do you want me to have to turn the heat on here in August?"

"Alan, does Dad know you're here?" I caught my disbelief a couple of seconds late. "I mean, it's good to see you. Don't know how the heck you got here."

"Same as you: train, foot, streetcar. But now you've got that ride." Alan's dimple came with his smile as naturally as his keen eyes did with every new thought. "Can I try 'er out? Dad's let me since I turned seventeen."

Mrs. B was in the middle of the barrage. "Your brother's going to stay in Mr. Palmer's old room for as long as he needs to."

"Thanks for that, Mrs. B."

"Bumped anybody off yet?" Alan couldn't stand still. He was so excited he didn't notice Doc Begbie slowly making his way toward us on his cane. "Bet you have. I wanna hear."

"Laddie killed two rascals the other mornin'. Aye."

I turned to him, trying to stay calm. "Doc, sir, this is no joking matter. Maybe you'd better stay out of this." I nodded to my brother. "Alan, come on. I'll show you the automobile."

"Sorry," Doc Begbie said, looking repentant. He hobbled toward the parlor and turned to speak to Mrs. B. "Love, can ye give an old man a hand?"

Alan and I went outside without saying another word until the door closed behind us.

"What's this all about?" I asked. "You know you can't stay."

"Killjoy. They're nice folks."

"Yes. I know they're nice," I said, running my fingers through my hair. "Alan, what in the Sam Hill are you doing here?" I lit a cigarette and plopped down in the driver's seat.

"What do ya mean? I told you I was coming." He sat down across from me and lit a cigarette. "Thought you were gonna let me drive."

"Gosh, Alan, this is so uncalled for. So sudden." I glared at him through smoke that swirled in angry circles between us.

Expectancy was written all over his face.

"Okay, okay," I said. "Listen, it's good to see you. Real good. You just surprised me, that's all. I'll show you the city. I'll show you the police department, and you can meet my buddy Sergeant Davis and the Mallorys—the works. But then you've got to go back home. I'll give you money to take the train."

The dimple dug in, and his eyes brightened. The color returned to his cheeks, and if I'd been a swearing man, I would have sworn they'd turned as red as his hair. "I'm thinking I want to be a policeman. Like you."

I took a deep drag and then flicked my cigarette out the window. "You never answered . . . does Dad know where you are?"

"No. I hitched a ride once I got past the fields. Hitched another when I got into Elkton. And then—"

"Enough, Alan. We need to go inside and call home. After that, I'll show you Detroit. But the day after tomorrow, you'll be back on that train. Two at the most!"

Chapter 44

Alan's little surprise visit after my long night on the beat had packed a wallop. I rang up Dad as soon as we were back inside at Mrs. B's. Hannah answered, and after what seemed like several minutes, she succeeded in getting one of the children to round him up.

"We've been worried sick. Started to call but decided to wait and see. There wasn't anything you could do anyway," he said. "Not till he showed up."

"He's fine. None the worse for wear. I'll show him the city tonight and tomorrow afternoon, let him meet the Mallorys. He can get on the train Sunday morning."

"What about your job?"

"I do have the midnight shift tonight. Then I'm off till Monday. He can poke around here in the morning. Landlady will jerk a knot in him. Put him to work doing something." I chuckled, but not much was amusing.

Dad paused. I could hear Charlotte and Mary chattering in the background. "How does he seem to you?"

"Like a thirteen-year-old in a seventeen-year-old's body. I'll watch after him, Dad."

"All right. I trust you will, son. Good to hear from you."

We said our good-byes. I excused myself to go upstairs and get as much rest as I could. Alan had already started making so much noise carrying on with Doc Begbie that sleep might be out of the question.

192 | Annette Valentine

Alan needed grace, I told myself. Perhaps it was the smell of the apple pie baking that had awakened my senses. I came down to find him dishing up a piece. Doc was egging him on.

I got to the dining room table practically unnoticed. "Couldn't wait for me, could you? Eat up. You and I have places to go. Starting with the Mallorys."

"I was hoping you'd let me take your T for a spin," Alan said with a mouthful of pie.

"Not a chance. Well, maybe. Do I get some of that?"

"Here, Laddie. Letting him meet yer girlie?"

"Doc, she's not . . . You bet. Then we're gonna take a drive by the factory so he can see where I got my illustrious start. Oh, and Mrs. B, don't count on us for dinner. Alan needs to see Belle Isle, don't you think?" I was wound up. "And show him Electric Park."

"It's probably the greatest electrical display you'll ever see," said Mrs. B, getting her two cents in.

"We'll eat out there. He can take a streetcar back. I'll be in after my shift."

We finished the pie in overdue peace and quiet, and Alan and I were off.

"You can drive to the Mallorys. Here, catch." I pitched him the key and watched his face light up.

"It's almost as nice as Dad's," he said.

———— ⟫◆⟪ ————

Lights from the Big Dipper roller coaster had Alan's attention before we ever reached the park's main entrance, and when he saw the enormous windmill that dominated it, he was undone.

"Golly-gee! And look, Si, at the sign, *Trip Thru the Clouds—Detroit's Greatest Ride*."

He looked at me with the wonder of a child. "Can we?"

"Well, why not? Needs to be before we eat, though." I parked the automobile, and we wove our way past the curiosities of the amusement park, our eyes peeled to see the ostrich racing and firefighting demonstrations. There was no chance of the novelty wearing off with attractions like *The Inferno* and *Menz Devil*.

By eleven o'clock I had driven him back east across the Belle Isle Bridge and put him on a streetcar to Highland Park. We were both exhausted. Wonder was written all over Alan's face.

A night's work was ahead of me. And it ended not a minute too soon. I drove to Pasadena Street with my head out the window to keep awake, then tiptoed upstairs to bed. Not a soul was in sight. Mrs. B had to have stashed Alan in Palmers' old room.

By Saturday afternoon, revived, I was ready to go again, cruising with Alan past vaudeville houses and nickelodeons that dotted downtown Detroit, past B. Siegel at Livernois and Seven Mile on the "Avenue of Fashion"— showcasing the latest styles in clothing. Alan's mouth never closed; his eyes never relaxed their wide-open inquisitiveness.

The tour of the police department had him reeling, and afterwards I drove us up Grand River Avenue and slowly turned on Washington Boulevard, the most opulent, most successful retail destination in Detroit. I parked as near as I could to the Statler Hotel, and we went inside. It was just past ten o'clock. The place was energized.

"Just wanted you to get a feel for the uptown folks. Let's just sit a spell and watch. Then we need to be heading on back."

We sat on a tufted lounge surrounded by gigantic columns and gawked at the people, the glamor, the glitz. Airy palms arched above our heads.

"You running, Si?"

"Where'd you get that?"

"Dad. Maybe I am, too. To California. Or stay here."

"You can't do either. Tomorrow morning, you'll be going back where you belong."

⟾◈⟽

And so he was. Less than twelve hours later, I doled out the money for his ticket home, and after we embraced, put him on the train at Michigan Central.

I didn't at all like the faraway look in his eyes.

Chapter 45

⋖⟫◆⟪⋗

"He's kissing Rachel, Mom. I'm timing it, too."

The sultry August night added to the heat. Celeste's unexpected presence at the top of the back stairs at the Mallorys made a long kiss short.

I could hear it all: Celeste mocking us from the house to my Model T, and Virginia taking her to task for eavesdropping. Rachel and I didn't find the humor in it. We sat quietly in complete darkness with both doors on the automobile wide open. Rachel tried to ignore her sister, but I wasn't sure Celeste could be ignored. She'd managed to goad a romantic interest between Rachel and me since day one—for nine months and counting.

But it was Rachel at the helm. It made little difference now, anyway. I was here, and this, as far as I knew, was going absolutely nowhere. I removed my arm from Rachel's shoulder and lit a cigarette.

Her smile, which shone in the flame from my lighter, could have chased rain from a thundercloud. Some days that was exactly what I needed, but for now, imagining where our involvement might lead was impractical. I was a policeman in a city so big I could get lost without trying. There were plenty of places to hide the redneck who'd come to Detroit. I took a drag on my cigarette.

I was a farm boy still, but at nineteen, I needed to get the farmer out of me, which meant never going back to Kentucky. Not for any length of time, not for any reason. I wouldn't have traded places with any farmer.

She grinned. "Want to talk? You look so serious."

The Mallorys were a perfect package of good people, and it happened to include a girl who had eyes for me. At the moment, those eyes seemed to want to penetrate my mind.

"Just thinking how lucky I am to have stumbled on your family." I smiled, took another drag on my Camel, and exhaled slowly, buying some time while birdsong in the background played havoc with my concentration. I had no reason to pretend I wasn't attracted to her. I was. But everywhere I turned she was there. She made the hunt a done deal. "You know, you're way too beautiful to be only seventeen."

"*Almost* seventeen." She whisked her black curls behind one ear, bouncing on the seat of my automobile like a two-year-old. "Not till next Tuesday, when you take me to one of those haunts in Detroit. Then I'll officially be seventeen."

"Don't talk like that. You wouldn't want to be there. Some of the places I've seen on my beat are pretty rough. Sure as shootin' not for you."

I couldn't see her response, but I heard her sigh.

More lights came on in the house, giving me the excuse I was looking for to close out the evening. "We'll find something here in Highland Park. I should get going, though, Rach. The evening's been a fun one. Good picture show."

I got out of the automobile and then immediately ducked back in with an afterthought. "Wait. Who said I was taking you anywhere on your birthday?" I dropped the cigarette and snuffed it out with my foot.

She laughed. And so did I. But her aggravating assumption was the same sort that had pushed us this far since April.

I circled her side of the automobile, not finding it necessary to discuss my finances with her, but truth be known, there wasn't a lot of money for extras. Buying my Model T from Charlie had been a stroke of luck, essential to make the after-hours commute when the streetcars weren't running. I was trying to find my way, maybe to emulate a man whose style and polish I admired. But I was no Senator Maxwell. I think I knew that. "Big day tomorrow, Rach. How about I call you after work? Unless something unexpected happens at the department." I continued holding the door while she slowly got out.

"Something's always happening, Simon." Her dark eyes were piercing, and in the shining light, which her father had wisely provided, I could feel them boring straight through me. "It seems like it. Ever since you've been a policeman. I liked it when you were at the factory."

"Now that's not fair, Rachel. There's been very little action come my way in the entire time I've been on the force. But I have a lot going on right now. Your uncle's pulling for me. That's a big deal." I shut the automobile's door and followed her up the walkway to the short flight of stairs. "I'm not going to be on the beat forever. If anybody can get me moved up a notch, it's Sam Sturges."

We stood at the back door. "Why," I asked myself, searching her face for an answer, "do I have to justify my existence for you?"

"Last weekend was just a piece of luck," I said aloud. "Just happened to put me in the vicinity when some detectives pulled a raid."

"Horsefeathers." She looked every bit as beautiful trying to be defensive as she had while watching Mary Pickford in *Pollyanna* at the theater. "You liked being there," she said with a pout. "Don't act like you didn't."

"You're right. Probably always will like action. I've been at the department four months, Rach. What's wrong with wanting more of it?"

"Nothing," she said, implying plenty, and turned to go inside. "Good night, and thanks."

Ginger barked at the opening door.

That's it? I thought. *Good night, and thanks?*

I drove back to the boarding house, wondering about a lot of things.

When I got inside, Doc Begbie was up and waiting.

"Good evening! What's this?" He was ready to talk. Without a word outta my mouth, he went on jabbering as if my long face had baited him. "I'd like ta give ye a tip 'bout women. Aye."

"Doc, I appreciate it. I feel sick to my stomach. *Women.* No, thanks. I'm turning in."

"On the morn, then. Aye."

Fortunately, Mrs. B was nowhere to be seen. I got to my room and flopped on the bed. Even with the affection I felt for Doc and Mrs. B and the Mallorys, I had to find an apartment in town. Purchasing the automobile had been a good step. Now it felt like moving was—and the sooner the better.

Dog-tired, I fell asleep in my trousers, my shoes still laced, my shirt still buttoned, certain no job could compare with being a policeman. My starting position, although it was just a starting point, meant that new horizons were waiting.

⊰◆⊱

The following morning, I hightailed it into the station—not late but not a minute to spare—raced downstairs to the locker room and turned inside. Several of the fellas were already in gym clothes, ready for a workout.

"Well look who's here. If it isn't the big guy from Kentucky."

"Haven't had the pleasure," I said, taking him for a jovial sort. "Simon Hagan here." I extended my hand.

"Pleasure's mine. *All mine*, I'm sure. I'm Lieutenant Dugan. Word has it you're an ambitious character. Or shall we just say you're expecting to climb the ladder?"

There was a definite air about him. Struck me that he thought I'd snookered my way into a job, an elementary one at that.

His face was steely. "Didn't have the benefit of a shoo-in when I came on the force. Guess that's the way the cookie crumbles."

The place was silent. I reevaluated him to be a mealy-mouthed man with a chip on his shoulder. A locker door closing was the single sound. It echoed.

"Watch your step, Hagan."

"Don't believe I get your drift."

"No drift, Hagan. No drift."

Chapter 46

—————⟫•◆•⟪—————

The decision to move into town had been brewing, and by the next day, I'd made up my mind. Even though Tuesday on her birthday was probably not the perfect time to tell her, I planned to break the news to Rachel then.

But before telling Rachel I was leaving, I needed to let Mrs. B know.

She was puttering in the kitchen when I stuck my head around the door. She jumped like she'd been shot.

"Sorry," I said. "Didn't mean to startle you. Good morning. Should have told you before now, but listen, Mrs. B, I've got to slip out before Doc comes in." I stepped into the kitchen. "I hate to break it to you like this. Guess it's best to just say what I have to."

She cocked her head and planted her hands on her hips.

"I'll be looking for a place in the city, moving in where I'm closer to the department."

"I knew it was coming. Soon as you got that dang automobile I knew you'd take off." She walked to the stove, flipped the eggs in the pan, and laid down her spatula. "Suit yourself."

"I really don't have the time right now to go into it with Doc. Later I will. I've got an early appointment with Chief Sturges."

"What on earth am I going to tell him?" She looked glum. "You're like a son. He'll be miserable around here."

"This isn't the last of me. Dinner at six, then. See y'all—if I'm alive." I gave a wink over my shoulder, hopped into my Model T, and drove out of Highland Park and through the crowded streets toward the city.

Alive—I might not be, I thought. With the crime rate mushrooming at the same rate as Detroit's growing population, I lived and breathed the police department. But I was still a rookie and a pawn, another warm body to add to the force: a uniform with a bull's-eye. Any moment could be my last. Maybe I was a fool, after all. But I wanted to be here, and the closer I could get to the fray the better.

The traffic was horrific. I wasn't late, but I was pushing to beat the clock. At 7:52, I was inside the door of the police station. My upcoming appointment left me optimistic—and blind to everybody in my path. There was nothing average about a Monday morning meeting with Chief Sturges.

I arrived at the precinct and stood near his office, idly reading the map on the wall.

Right on time, he called me in. The same two wooden chairs from my initial meeting sat in front of his desk.

He pointed to one. "Have a seat," he said brusquely and sat on the edge of his desk. "Hagan, you interested in more than this?" He offered me a cigarette and lit it and then lit one for himself. The flame was like the fire in me that I wasn't using. Doing more than what I was doing sounded extremely promising.

"You bet!" I said. "Yes, sir. What'd you have in mind?"

His holster with his six-shooter hung rigid at his side. One hand rested coolly on the handle. He and Virginia had the same green eyes. His were fixed, unblinking, on mine. "I'll get straight to the point. I'm waiving some rules. Making you sergeant, starting this week."

I was floored. Compared to being on a farm in Kentucky, this ranked up there with being a senator. "Sir, this is what I was hoping for." I managed to restrain an expletive. "Thank you, sir. You won't be sorry. No slack here."

"Look, Hagan, you know as well as I do, Prohibition's closed every saloon, bar, and tavern in the country since January." He took a drag on his cigarette, stood up, and began pacing. "Illegal ferry services are moving booze from Ontario—Windsor, to be exact—and back across the Detroit River. We're fast becoming a major port for running and distributing alcohol products from Canada. You understand that, don't you?"

"Yes, sir. I've seen it." I stood up and joined him by the window.

"Every drop of it's controlled by bootleggers and racketeers." He pointed out the window, cigarette between his fingers, smoke curling upward. "See that ice cream parlor over there? It's a front, like most every other dance-and-dine place around. You can count on it. Behind the scenes, booze will be flowing. Keep that in mind."

My naive November night in a speakeasy, nine months earlier, flashed in my memory. "Of course," I said, clasping his extended hand.

"I'm bypassing the chain of command," Sturges said. "You know that. Don't flaunt it, or you'll be back on the street."

"No, sir, Chief. I don't know what to say."

He smiled. "You're practically family, according to Virginia. But that has zilch to do with my decision. Get with Sergeant Davis out there. You know him. He'll introduce you to Lieutenant Dugan, if you two haven't already met."

I tried not to let it dampen my mood that, in my opinion, Lieutenant Dugan was the equivalent of the south end of a horse going north. "Yes, Chief. We've met." *And Dugan's going to love that I've been advanced so quickly*, I thought.

With a second handshake, I left his office and went directly to Roman Davis's desk to tell him the news and mention my need for an apartment in the area.

"You don't say? So happens, Lieutenant Dugan's already told me you'll be needing some stitching done on your shirtsleeves—three chevrons a side." He turned his right arm forward to make a display. "Congratulations, Dix-ie-man. I'll keep my ear to the ground for an apartment befitting a sergeant."

———◆———

I finished my briefing with Lieutenant Dugan by early afternoon. My initial impression of him had left me cold. The second one did nothing to alter it.

There wasn't enough time during my break to look for an apartment, but I felt more motivated now than I had before the meeting. I presumed Sergeant Davis knew of lots of apartments. With luck, maybe I would be able to move into one during the weekend.

Sergeant Hagan. I twirled the sound of the rank in my head. It had a nice ring to it.

PART TWO
Chapter 47

⬖◆⬗

ugust 1925—Four years later
A I returned to my apartment building with barely more than a glimpse of Celeste inside the police station all day. As tempted as I was to rap on her door I didn't, not wanting to dominate her every free minute.

But it was the want behind the want. That one had me.

Even for half a day, I missed her. Missed her personality that lit up my world and took away the void that had so long been a vacuum inside me.

I shut off the automobile's engine and sat—watching birds fill the oak tree.

Celeste was all grown up at eighteen, and her decision to come work at the police station had put her near me, working under my nose practically, taken her from the girl who was Rachel's kid sister to the love of my life. I pondered how that had caught me unaware during these last eight months. As if I needed to kill a bear first before I earned the right to her. No one had told me it took so much courage to love. No one had said it would enchant me, like the sweet smell of apple pie baking.

I couldn't fathom how she'd changed me. It was ridiculous.

And if Alan hadn't been doing so poorly, wherever he might be on any given day, groping for some kind of existence that offered short-lived thrills at the expense of his family's constant concern, I'd say all was right with my world. But he was doing poorly. I kicked the gas pedal gingerly—a reminder, somehow, of my need to wring his neck. I got out and headed up.

The telephone was ringing when I opened my door at the Somerset. Dad was on the line.

"Son." His voice was lifeless.

"Yes, sir, Dad. Good to hear your voice. How's—"

"It's Alan."

I felt an immense weight, as if he were leaning on me, struggling for support. I opened my mouth to speak, but my tongue wouldn't move.

"He's in San Francisco. Called collect. That's not all, Simon. I can't judge. So little contact with him. He's a hard one to understand. But I'm scared." Dad sobbed. "Can you go, Simon? He'll listen to you. Bring him home."

"I'll try. I'll go, for sure. Bring him home? That I can't promise. Give me his whereabouts."

After I got the information I needed, I hung up the receiver, stricken, and looked at the ceiling to see if God had crashed through. After a minute, I washed my face, took the elevator down to the third floor, and waited for Celeste to answer my knock.

Ecstatic, she came rushing at me. "I got another raise. Simon, we—" It took her less than a second to notice something was amiss.

I was in too much of a state to give her a kiss. I closed the door with the back of my hand.

She looked strikingly beautiful, but her infectious smile melted. "What is it, Simon? Let me turn the radio down."

"Alan. It's Alan. He's alive. Dad called. He's shaken. From what I can gather, Alan's worse off than ever. At least he's turned up." I dropped onto the nearest chair. "Came directly down here. Hope that's okay. Feels like I've been hit with a board." Reflexively, I stood up and went to the kitchen.

Celeste hurried in front of me. "Sweetheart, let me get you a seltzer. Where is he?"

"San Francisco. Don't know much more than that. Could I call your folks? They need to know, also. They were so supportive of me when he disappeared . . . and resurfaced . . . and disappeared again. It's been tough." I peeled off my sweater, burning up, and let Celeste take it. "There may be more. He could be in some kind of real trouble," I said. I could feel my head drop. "I'll know more details later, after Dad and I can talk sensibly."

"I just met him that once when he came to visit. I know how you've anguished over him." She poured the seltzer until the glass overflowed. "What can we do?" She handed me the seltzer. "How did your father find out?"

"He called collect. Desperate." I pulled a chair up to the kitchen table. "I've got to go to him." I took a sip, ran my fingers through my hair, and stood. "San Francisco. How far away is that? Doesn't matter. I need to go."

"Now? This minute?" She gave me an incredulous look. "It's out of the question to leave now, isn't it? Your work?"

"Work's beside the point." I gulped the soda water and lit a cigarette.

She put her arm around my waist. "This is awful, sweetheart. I'm really sorry."

"Let me call Roman," I said. "See if he'd be willing to go out with me."

"Good idea. I'll rustle us up something to eat."

"Not much, Celeste. I'm not that hungry."

———⟫◆⟪———

Alan, in his few words with Dad, had given our father the address of his whereabouts.

"He told me Brighton-Sussex Apartments on the north side of San Francisco. Number 532 Boling Street. Said there was no reason to come. Just needed some cash to tide him over." Dad had relayed the message to me with some trepidation, and I'd answered with: "Tide him over *what*?"

"Don't know, Son. When can you go?"

"Roman's going. Our plans include leaving in the morning. Early. He and I will switch off driving till we get there."

Dad broke. I tried not to listen.

He had given Alan no reason to know I was driving out. I wondered if I'd find him having the time of his life. Such thoughts had crossed my mind. I didn't know what to expect.

———⟫◆⟪———

The weather was perfect, not a cloud in the sky. The sun was coming up.

We'd been on the road three hours. I figured there were sixty-six more to go. Roman slept; I drove.

I slept; Roman drove.

Three days later, barely having stopped, the trip ended in front of a sorry excuse for housing of human life. I got past the putrid smell of excrement and alcohol. Roman was hanging in there as we climbed the five flights of stairs.

"Alan?" The door was ajar. "Alan," I said, pushing it.

Nothing could have prepared me: Alan lay in the fetal position on bare bed-springs, his face to the wall. A ragged blanket was wadded under his head. His bones looked like they could poke through his skin if I touched them.

"What?" He rolled over, and for a moment a blank stare froze in his eyes. "Si?"

I fought the emotion, fought to stay vertical, fought to get air in my lungs. "Alan! Alan. We've come to take you home."

Roman nodded and swallowed hard.

Alan was still Alan. Mule-headed. "I am home. This is."

"Can you sit up?"

"Sure. Just taking a little nap."

"Where are your things? My friend's going to help me get you out of here." I looked to Roman for back-up.

"You bet. Glad to. I'm Roman Davis, by the way."

"Well, thank you, Mister Roman. But I'm fine where I am. Sorry there's no place to sit." Sweat dripped from his brow, down the sides of his head, trickling off the tips of matted red hair. "Listen, Si, you got any cash?"

"You can go back home, Alan, and—"

A scantily dressed female burst into the room, reeling. The sight was worse than any gritty picture I might have drawn to portray vulgarity.

Alan glanced her way. "You're not welcome here."

"Oh? Since when?"

"Get out. Before Mister Roman here pitches you through the window." Alan turned back to me. "Don't know what that means. No cash?"

"It means, simply, you can go home. You have everything a father could offer you."

"Didn't *you*?" He shrugged. "What else can I want? I have syphilis."

A knife in my gut couldn't have cut any deeper. I sat down on the springs next to him and wrapped shaking arms around him. Roman ducked out of the room and closed the door. Somehow my mouth opened to speak. "You're my brother, Alan. You can leave here." I could feel his shame and understood the remorse that quaked in his bones under my embrace.

"Don't tell Dad. Tell him I'm having the time of my life."

"I can't leave you here. I would never forgive myself. And neither would Dad."

"Not going. I'm sorry you came all this way."

"Roman and I will stay the night. Tomorrow we'll find a doc—"

"No. But cash would help. Whatever you can spare."

"All right, Alan, but I'm coming back in the morning. You can change your mind. It's not too late."

Chapter 48

Alan was gone when Roman and I returned. Like a bird that flew south for the winter, he was gone.

"I don't know what to say. There are no words," Roman offered. "He's a rare one."

We settled ourselves on my automobile's seat. I slumped over the steering wheel for a moment and didn't move.

"Guess it's time we started back," I said after a minute and didn't speak till we were speeding along on the open road. "Who tells you you're on the wrong path? Where do you go when you can't judge things on your own? When home is far away, and the baggage is just too heavy to carry?"

"That's pretty deep." Roman's head wagged sympathetically. "I think you have to let go, one day at a time."

Quiet again, I knew I couldn't dare tell our father the news of Alan's escapades. It would rip him to pieces. Even though he'd never say it, he would think I could have brought my brother home.

"Don't be so hard on yourself. We have to make our own choices, my friend."

"You are certainly that, Roman. And quite a friend to boot," I said, nodding my sincerity. "This has caught me off guard. Way off. Far more than Rachel running off and marrying that construction guy."

Roman sat still while I recoiled.

"Can't imagine why I put her deal in the same breath with Alan. Just stupid sometimes. I don't know, Roman. What a turn our relationship took back then! Just wasn't ready for . . . any of it, I guess. She's married with two young'uns—deserved more than I could give at the time."

He shot me a look from beneath beetling eyebrows. "Well, you and Celeste seem to be made for each other. It's out in the open in case you hadn't noticed. She's head-over-heels in love with you, my man. Don't think you can deny the beautiful thing going on there."

"Yeah, the timing was way outta whack with Rach. The whole thing has lost its sting. I'll just have to see what develops with Celeste. Sure wouldn't want to lose her, though."

I lit up a cigarette. Roman did the same.

"You know what I get a kick out of?" I asked.

"Not a clue," he said.

"That annoyed sigh she does when I want her do anything she's not in the mood for—which on some days is basically everything."

Roman didn't laugh until I did. The levity felt good. I kept my face to the windshield and wiped a tear from my eye before it rolled down my cheek.

After a few hours, he took over driving, and my eyes closed on the day that had brought me more pain than I thought I could bear.

Chapter 49

⟫•◇•⟪

The Grand Riviera Theatre opened on August 24, 1925, with the silent film *Desert Flower*. I wasn't there to see it happen. I hadn't been near the inside of the towering building on Grand River Avenue yet but going there was in my plans. A night on the town, my woman on my arm, and we'd see a show. I could only imagine what the inside was like. A movie house like no other. The outside was a palace, lit up so brightly it was visible from several blocks away.

And that was where I was, several blocks away at Griswold and Fort Street near the Detroit River, riding shotgun next to Inspector Rhodes.

The Riviera Theatre was not my concern tonight. The Detroit River was. As a hot spot for Canada's legal alcohol coming across, rum-running was rampant. Hoodlums brought a load of hooch across and had shown up armed to the teeth. No doubt, they were wise to the fact that they were up against Detroit's underworld led by immigrants from the lower east side. None other than the Bornstein family.

This side of the river it was deadly. Mobsters were controlling the city's illegal drug and alcohol trade, and a large percentage of it was being smuggled in along Lake Avenue and the Saint Clair River. The Roaring Twenties were in full swing. Detroit occupied its core, and we had our own public enemies. The Purple Gang was the worst of them—dubbed rotten by *Lord-only-knows* who, tainted, the color of bad meat.

And the Purple Gang ruled.

As policemen, we were tangling with the scum of the earth, butting heads with people who would have just as soon killed us as not. The underworld

Mafia scoundrels were a ruthless bunch of thugs and killers as bloodthirsty as any known Chicago racketeers akin to Al Capone, a sophisticated gang of bootleggers determined to weed out their competing rum-runners.

Tonight, they'd shown up in the vicinity of Atwater Street.

Rhodes was at the wheel, driving the police car like a bat out of Hades, answering directly to Commissioner William C. Baxter. But for this moment, Rhodes was altogether in charge, foulmouthed and loud. A too-small hat was perched as far back on his oversized head as it could go. He chewed a wad of gum with so much jaw action it made mine hurt to watch.

"The Feds haf'ta get down to the river!" he shouted between chews as we careened off Atwater Street. "And I do mean now!"

He had us in high gear as we roared across Fort Street toward Woodward Avenue.

I was in high gear myself. "We're taking a risk leaving the scene—"

A staccato scream, and another police car streaked past. Adrenaline pumped through my veins. Either the danger or the excitement—one of the two or both—had my temples pulsating. My heart beat at an alarming rate.

"What'd ya say, Cap'n?" He was yelling.

Rhodes drove at breakneck speed across Grand River Avenue, heading over toward Broadway. It was useless trying to holler over the sound of screening tires. Both the car and his jaw were going a mile a minute. "Son of almighty—" He careened around the corner on two wheels, straightened the car, and kept on motoring. "Hagan, you're going to the station. I'm slowing this vehicle down, not stopping. Get inside and on the horn. Get the undercover Feds over to Atwater. Now!"

He began slowing at Macomb, then hung a left on Beaubien Street. As predicted, he was still moving when I opened my door. I took off running like my life depended on it, toward the precinct, got inside, and went straight for the telephone on the nearest desk. I waited impatiently while the switchboard made the connection.

"FBI, Agent Zimmerman," came the voice on the other end.

"This is Captain Hagan, sir. Detroit Police."

"What's up?"

"Get this. Two recognizable Bornsteins jumped the boats in the direction of Windsor. The river's swarming with runners. Goons are all over Atwater Street."

"Not surprising, given the climate. We're on it. Gonna need backup. How many men you got over there?"

"Atwater's covered. A dozen, I'd say."

"Gotcha. Anything else?"

"That's it."

"Thanks, Cap'n."

"You bet. Ten-four."

Chapter 50

⟵⟫◆⟪⟶

D etroit's balmy September nights were anything but mild. The sought-after excitement was at hand, and my stint on the police force had, as of April, moved into its fifth year. The early days so innocently begun in Michigan in 1920 were gone. 1925 was coming to an end.

I hung up and sat down at my desk, staring at the small photograph of my mother and then at another, and a recent one of family. Alan's absence among my other brothers and sisters struck a dissonant chord. He'd not been heard from since the afternoon I'd left him at the San Francisco apartment. I could still envision him lying on the filthy box spring, still see his dimpled face, his red hair vivid despite his disease. I couldn't even begin to count my futile attempts to locate him since then.

The thought of our last embrace overwhelmed me, and I cursed the day he was supposed to have taken a train back to Kentucky. I cursed the day it became clear he had not. I cursed his disappearance. I cursed the reality of his present condition. I wasn't a cursing man, but it felt exceptionally suitable becoming one. Four years and more had proven it was all I could do. When it came to Alan, I was as powerless as it got, and my failure to save him frustrated the hound out of me.

The clock struck midnight. A hubbub of voices, ringing phones, and the persistent yak-yak-yak-ping-yak-yak of countless typewriters was finally enough to distract me. I looked across to the vacant spot where Celeste typically sat on weekdays, ever since she'd started last December, working the switchboard from nine to five. Her image in the nearby snapshot on my desk made me smile. I picked it up, admiring her heart-shaped lips and impish grin that had won me over during her energetic youth. And now, so grown-up, she had an elegant way of lifting my spirits.

I lit a cigarette, impulsively wanting to dash off to Celeste's apartment, knock on her door, wake her, and reach out to her, or at least telephone her for no other reason than to hear her laugh—anything to revive myself with the essence of all that I loved about her. I stared at her chair in the steno pool, the spot that held my reason for living, and took a deep breath. I fingered the weapon at my side, fully aware of my loyalty to the police force. It dominated my existence.

Sweat beaded on my forehead, and a drop fell on the gray metal desktop beside the picture of Celeste. I looked at her, making excuses. Maybe I required work that forced relationships to the sidelines. Maybe I needed to exist this way—to bury and forget, to run until I became exhausted, to lose myself indefinitely in search of my dreams.

Cigarette smoke swirled about me. I dropped my head into my hands, thinking about how things don't always happen the way we expect. Rachel might have been lucky to have avoided settling down with me, I told myself. She'd have been lost in the hum before I could find something to offer her. By the time I'd found it, she was gone. Worked out for the best.

I fought the noise around me. The precinct was steamy, crowded with overworked personnel and overheated bodies. If it was a balmy September night, I hadn't noticed.

Chief Sturges had given me the break of a lifetime, taking me from a wandering farm boy to Detroit police captain. I had him to thank for it. I had him to thank for bringing his niece on board as a stenographer and sparking our romance. God's providence, Dad called it.

At least his beliefs are consistent, I mused.

My career, meanwhile, was claiming my soul. Crime was a messy affair in a town of nearly two million people, and police work was a risky business, about to put me six feet under. Hundreds of miles from home, I was an unmitigated old man at twenty-three.

No more, I vowed, internally kicking the fact that Celeste had put her dreams of going to college on hold so she could be involved with me and my dreams. *I'm not accepting watered-down relationships in order to lay*

myself on the line to stop the likes of the Bornsteins.

That's going to change.

With the nub of my cigarette threatening to burn the hairs in my nose, I crushed it in a butt-filled ashtray and stood. The humidity was intolerable, the heat like a noonday in mid-July. I smelled like a hard-ridden horse.

I set off in the direction of the station's coffee shop in the basement, needing to unwind after an eight-hour shift that had lasted ten, hoping to find Roman Davis doing the same.

⬤◆⬤

"Sergeant Davis," I said with authority, expecting to startle him.

Roman didn't flinch. Unfazed as he was by my presence, he began a sardonic turn on the stool at the counter, and his familiar, bulky frame shifted. A coffee cup was pressed against his lips, and his bulging eyes gaped at me over its rim.

I couldn't help but laugh. "We meet on a barstool once again. So happens you're just the person I need to see after all the crap that's gone down today."

"Oh. You mean you didn't get to the Riviera to see *Desert Flower*? You and Celeste didn't miss much. Colleen Moore wasn't quite up to snuff."

I took a seat on the red, leather-capped stool next to him, nodded to the waitress with an empty cup in midair, and swiveled mindlessly. "Yeah, right," I said with a half-smile. "You didn't go to any movie, Roman. Gimme a break." I tried to change the subject. "You know, I'm thinking a lot about asking her to marry me. Saving a proposal for Christmas, but—"

"Colleen Moore or Celeste?" He slapped me on the back and pulled out a pack of cigarettes. "Smoke?"

"Yeah, thanks. Kidding aside, we've been steady almost a year."

"Why ask me? Not trying to rehash the past, but you did let her sister get away, didn't you?" His lighter clicked shut. He took a deep draw on his cigarette and looked thoughtfully at me. "I know you love her. Told me so yourself."

"Don't bring Rachel into this. I told you in so many words, that gal was keen on marriage from the time she was sixteen. And for crying out loud!

The guy she married swooped in on me just about the time I might'a actually been getting serious. Far as I know, she's happy in Flagstaff."

"So," he said, "did I hear an answer?"

"What? Do I love her? You mean Celeste?" I took a big swig of coffee and nearly choked on the hot refill.

"That's who I mean."

"Like nobody's business. I want to take care of her. Protect her. Know what I mean?"

He slid off the stool, laid a couple of dollars on the counter, and left the seat spinning. "Then don't let her get away, Dixie-man. Hate to run. Gotta meet an informant."

"Yeah. And I have a mountain of paperwork." I turned my back to the waitress and noticed Roman was still chuckling. "Wait. You're meeting an informant at this hour? You're such a hard-boiled son of a gun. Full of good advice, though. Appreciate it. I can never thank you enough for going out to California." I lowered my voice. "But there's something else. Listen, Roman, some things don't add up."

I could trust Roman with my life. "I've got this ugly feeling about—"

He nudged me away from our waitress's earshot and didn't take his eyes off her as she wiped the counter a few feet away.

I spoke barely above a whisper. "Lieutenant Dugan . . . he knows more than he tells. You think he's on the take?" I paused, not liking the sound of my allegation.

"It's late. Get that paperwork done and then get some shuteye, Simon. We'll talk later."

He was right. There were better places to talk. I clambered back upstairs without a word to anyone and sat down at my desk. City streetlights shone through multi-paned windows that towered above me, and bizarre shadows stretched across the vast array of papers and telephones that covered the desks around me.

I ran my hand over my wavy hair, unable to concentrate on the report I had to write. It wasn't the murmur of voices coming from the cluster of nightshift personnel or the squeaks from their shoes on the wood floor that distracted me. And it wasn't the musty smell of stale smoke and old wood or the switchboard that looked like a tangle of poorly strung banjos. Rather, it was my mounting resolve to speak the truth. With no concrete evidence to back me up, I could nevertheless feel my misgivings about Lieutenant Dugan's character eating a hole in me. It sure looked to me like he'd managed to avoid testifying against anyone who might be associated with the Purple Gang. Payoffs were out there. No doubt about it. And if Dugan was indeed on the take, he was providing immunity from the law we'd sworn to uphold.

I picked up the memo pad, scribbled a request to see Chief Sturges tomorrow, and then took the note to his office and taped it on his door.

It was already past midnight. I sat back down at my desk, turned my small clock facedown, and began writing—page after page—an account of the events the day had dished out. With the report complete, I smashed my umpteenth cigarette in the ashtray, folded my notebook and set it in the drawer, and turned the lock.

Chapter 51

⟫◆⟪

It was nearly one in the morning. Outside, the air was refreshing. The streets were as close to benign as they were going to get.

I walked in the direction of my Model T, parked half a block away from the precinct. Restless and too wide awake to go back to my apartment on East Jefferson, I cranked her up and began driving aimlessly through the city streets, my eyes glazing over but my mind at full throttle. Roman was right, there was no reason to wait any longer. I'd made up my mind. If little else in this world was clear, I knew this much: I loved Celeste.

I circled the block, not ready to go home to an empty apartment. It was too late, way too late, to knock on her door. I kept going, unwinding. It felt nice to be cruising the city without the traffic and the honking horns and the eager pedestrians.

I rolled up Grand River Avenue and slowly turned on Washington Boulevard, oddly enthralled by the crimson awnings of the Statler Hotel. A hostile, loud honk from the automobile behind me warned me to move faster or get out of the way. *Aaoogha! Aaoogha!* I veered toward an unoccupied spot by the curb on the other side of the street. After sitting a spell, I shut off the engine, got out, and crossed over to the hotel entrance.

Inside the two-story lobby, a half-dozen people milled about. Whatever I might have been expecting at this wee morning hour didn't come close to the merrymaking that had gone on the night I'd brought Alan.

One among many stops in the city that night, I recalled.

He had been so stupefied by the sights and sounds of places, in such extreme contrast to rural Kentucky, that his mouth had hung open most of the two days he'd spent with me.

What a character, I thought.

He'd vanished after that, in search of a bigger thrill, a car, a this, a that, having looked up to me the way I'd looked up to Senator Maxwell.

Swallowed by the vast and practically empty lobby, I wandered over to the window and looked out at the Grand Circus Park through the lens of a September morning's first hour. Across the way, the newly completed Metropolitan Building pierced the Detroit skyline, and lights twinkled in the many competing tall buildings.

The heavy arches and glittering glass chandeliers canopied like a crown in the center of enchantment, but tonight the gaiety was missing. Dainty hues that had backdropped the scene for Detroiters enjoying boom times now seemed like sleepy tints of faded colors.

I strolled over to the seating area amid enormous columns and airy palms and sat on a tufted lounge. It was impossible to wind down. The thought of Alan and me sitting right here years ago gnawed at my insides.

"*Dad says you're running,*" Alan had said. "*Maybe I am, too. To California.*"

What a kidder. I'd doled out the money for his ticket home, and the next morning I'd taken him to the train station.

I looked toward the mirrored wall to see a stranger looking back at me.

I'm the joke, I thought. *And I can laugh, and I can light a cigarette.*

I inhaled deeply and felt the smoke pass slowly from my nostrils. Lies, like thick, warm, invisible syrup, must've secretly coated Alan's situation with a soothing, sweet, and delicate aroma. It had hardened, making him a victim—immobile, trapped—looking out through a thick, unbendable lens to a distorted world beyond.

When he didn't return home and Dad telephoned me from Elkton, I had heard in his quietness the verdict: *Alan's chasing a dream, son. Like you, he's chasing a dream.*

The city, after four years, had unceremoniously dropped me back at the Statler Hotel and left me feeling completely alone. It was too early to be here and too late to be awake, standing in this place, berating myself for something I couldn't change. I didn't want to count the cost of false pursuits—not for running, not for never scraping off the lies that guilt had used to hold me captive.

Alan had made his own decisions. We all had gone on without him.

⟫◆⟪

After finally arriving home at Somerset Apartments, I parked my automobile at the side of the limestone-and-red-brick building, walked around to the front, and went in through the main entrance's double doors off East Jefferson. The elevator stopped at the third floor long enough for me to hustle across the corridor and stick a note under Celeste's door.

The button lit up for the fourth floor, and I rode the remaining distance to the top, leaning sleepily against the paneled interior. Room 404 couldn't have been a more welcome sight.

Without turning on a light, I went straight to the refrigerator, pulled out a slab of bologna, sliced it in fourths, and devoured it with a glass of milk. Then I took a shower and dropped half-naked onto the bed.

The telephone woke me at four-thirty in the morning. It was Celeste. My explanation of where I'd been for most of the night—while she had been desperately trying to reach me—was irrelevant.

Celeste was hysterical. "Simon," she said through sobs, "it's Roman."

I could hear her taking deep breaths. "What? Celeste, what are you saying?" Nothing. "Celeste?"

"He's been shot. I'm coming up. Be right there."

I set the telephone back in its cradle. The words replayed in my ears. Numb, I walked to the wardrobe.

The sound of the rising elevator broke the eeriness. Then came the faint knock.

"Just a second, Celeste." I buttoned my trousers and opened the door, and we fell into each other's arms.

"Uncle Sammy called me shortly after it happened," she began. "They told him at the precinct you'd gone for the night." She stared at the floor. "Roman died on the way to the hospital, about one this morning."

"And I was riding around," I said, "kicking myself in the butt over Alan.

He's got syphilis. Latent, maybe, but he's got it." I collapsed onto the sofa. "What else? Did Chief Sturges give the details?"

"No!" She practically screamed. "Please! Tell me all this isn't happening! I'm so sorry, sweetheart."

She sat down next to me and wrapped her warm arm around my shoulders. "All that's been said is that Roman was attempting to arrest two men fleeing a robbery on Woodward."

"Sounds like him, trying to do something like that, single-handedly. I have plenty to tell your uncle tomorrow, Celeste. I left a note on his door. It's obviously too late now to save Roman."

"Simon," she said, "what on earth?"

"Not now, baby. I can't go into it. But your uncle has a lot of bases to cover."

<hr />

On Wednesday morning, the *Detroit Free Press* gave tribute to Roman Edwin Davis: *Officer down. Killed in the line of duty. End of Watch: September 22, 1925.*

Some sketchy details followed, along with the names of his surviving relatives. I wasn't among them. Nonetheless, we were brothers, and a part of me had died.

I put the newspaper aside and telephoned Celeste. "Can we see what your folks are planning this afternoon?"

I finished a sandwich as I spoke, and later that day, we drove out to Highland Park. Autumn air and dry leaves had me coughing the entire way. I refused to accept that I might be coming down with a bug of some sort. I had no time to be dragging around like a dying lizard.

PART THREE
Chapter 52

⟫⟩◆⟨⟪

ecember 1928—Three years later

December 1928—Three years later
    Another Michigan day dawned with a threat of snow, and as the morning hours passed, the sky grew increasingly overcast. I turned off the newscast on the radio, disgusted by the truth. One more police officer—shot dead.

Unless I was mistaken, this cop, like Roman Davis, had been set up, bringing the total to absurdity in my opinion. Any number was. I wasn't looking for a confrontation, but the whole thing had me danged eager for some morsel, if it existed, to connect that scoundrel Lieutenant Dugan to the Purple Gang. Maybe Roman Davis had known too much back then. Maybe we'd never be able to substantiate the facts surrounding the informant he'd gone to see after leaving me in the coffee shop that fateful night. His entrapment amid crossfire in an attempted robbery remained unexplained. It had struck me as skimpy information from the outset—and hard to swallow.

A hunch had continued gnawing me for three years.

My new Model T idled peacefully at the corner of Woodward and Michigan, held back by the traffic light whose novelty had captivated me on the day I'd first arrived in the city. Person after person traversed the intersection. Horns blared while I sat impatiently in my automobile, fondling the steering wheel, waiting for the light to change. The instant it turned green, I sped up Michigan Avenue, hung a left on East Jefferson, then took a right onto Bates and headed toward the Belle Isle Bridge.

Winter months were bearing down with a mighty blast off the iced-over Detroit River. Rum-runners were continuing to smuggle by car across the frozen water from Windsor, Ontario, a pipeline that shipped a million dollars' worth of liquor from Canada to Detroit, and our attempts as police to stop them were all but worthless. Mobsters, fueled by the demand for illegal alcohol, were running their specialized boats across the river. We knew all about them, but among us were the well-greased—those cops who played along. The thought made me grimace.

I parked inconspicuously at the back of the Bay Club on Atwater Street, a known rum-runners' transfer spot, and counted on the comings and goings at the club's entrance to divert any attention away from me. After shutting off the motor, I laid my .38-caliber revolver on my lap with a finger on the trigger. If I encountered real trouble, I was woefully under-armed against any gang-held semiautomatic weapons, and there were plenty of them searing the streets half a block away.

The club wasn't overly busy. I'd hoped for more cover. Three automobiles were lined up along the perimeter. A fourth was nosed into the alley. For a Wednesday after ten o'clock, it was relatively quiet. A sliver of fog-enshrouded moon provided the only light.

This was no prayer meeting. Neither was it an opportunity to leave something for God to work out. Officially, I was off duty. Unofficially, I was expecting to target some mighty interesting associations.

I sat rooted to my car seat, waiting in the dark dampness for more than an hour, alone, as far as I could tell, with a decent view from the side of the club's entrance. My overcoat collar was turned over my ears. No hat. I was colder than kraut, blowing warm breath into my gloveless hands. A frosty mist hung in the air. An occasional muffled sound of music stirred the silence.

It had to be approaching midnight. I'd been hanging out longer than I'd planned when a 1928 Lincoln Model L—swanky by any definition—pulled in near the club's entrance and double-parked alongside the string of other black vehicles. Two heavily garbed figures emerged, one with a cigar implanted between his teeth. Fat lips forced it to the side of his mouth. Someone came out of the club, and the three of them moved into the shadows.

All I could see was the lit end of the cigar making erratic movements in the darkness. Eventually, they disappeared inside the Bay Club.

Another hour passed. I squirmed, repositioning my bony butt on the car seat, and continued to sit for another quarter-hour.

The stakeout was looking like a waste of time when suddenly the lights inside the club went out. I gripped my .38. My eyes peeled as I tried to get a closer look at the several figures moving deliberately toward their vehicles.

One in particular, a familiar silhouette, bristled the hair on the back of my neck. Two men flanked him, but the slouch of his shoulders, the arrogant profile, the way he carried himself—all were a dead giveaway.

Dugan! I knew it!

I felt the muscles on my neck take a stranglehold.

He ducked into the back seat of a waiting black Packard, and another figure jumped into the front. Car doors slammed. Motors started up as if a movie reel had begun without warning. Vehicles began rolling, headlights crisscrossing like daggers in the fog. One by one, all five peeled out of the area.

After that, not a sound. Several minutes passed. The lights in the Bay Club came on. I waited twenty minutes or better, then rolled down the alley with my headlights off.

Chapter 53

———◇———

"How're you holding up, honey?" Celeste's call couldn't have come at a better time.

The sandwich bread was stale. I pulled out two slices anyway. The telephone receiver lay wedged between my shoulder and chin. "I'm doing okay. That Dugan character . . . It's tough when you know justice isn't being served. I feel so powerless sometimes."

"I know. Maybe we could go to church with my folks tonight."

"Don't believe so, doll. Sometime, maybe. Not tonight. It'll be great to see them, but let's just keep it to an afternoon visit." I straightened my tie and brushed bread crumbs from my lap. "I love you. You know that, don't you?"

"I do, of course. It's a good feeling. You're my world, Simon. I couldn't go on if something awful happened to you."

I paused just to hear her breathing. The receiver felt like a rock in my hand. I wanted to throw it. "Don't think like that. I'm going to head on down to your place now."

"Good. See you in a couple."

———◇———

The six-mile drive out to Highland Park was as quiet. I reached across the seat to pull her hand to my lips and kissed it, holding on to it for reassurance. It wasn't the dropping temperature that sent a chill down my spine but the cold finality of two bullets in another fellow officer's head.

"This case is so similar to Roman's. Both were good men. I didn't like losing Roman, and I don't like losing this one . . . or anybody, Celeste."

I kissed her hand again and slowly let it go, focusing on the dense housing as we passed building after building.

Her dress fluttered in the wind whipping through the car's open windows, but Celeste was as oblivious to it as a bird on the wing. Long lashes peeked from below her close-fitting hat, and her heart-shaped lips blossomed like red tulips. She wasn't what I thought of as the preacher's daughter. The girlish kid sister, the fun-loving, perpetual teaser and pest had matured into a lovely twenty-one-year-old jewel, and I was going to marry her. I had every intention of finding out what Charlie and Virginia would say about it. I parked at the curb under a shower of autumn's falling leaves. They were, as always, fuel for my cough.

Virginia was out the front door before either I or Celeste had started up the sidewalk. Chatter was constant all the way and didn't show any signs of stopping once we were inside.

Charlie had Ginger on a leash. "Great to see you," he said as he unhooked the boxer's collar. "Come on in. Good girl, Ginger." With a snap of his finger, he sent the dog to her place. "She's a great dog, this one, Simon. Take a seat, you two."

"Glad to see you both." I gave Virginia a hug. "You're looking well."

"Thank you. I'm so sorry, Simon, about yet another death on the force. I know it brings back thoughts of Roman. He was a good friend."

"The best, even if he did call me Dixie-man," I said, hanging on to a bit of mirth. "And thoughts of him . . . well, they've never gone very far. He was there for me. Yep, the best."

Virginia turned to Celeste. "Baby, you look peachy. You're my fashionable little flapper."

Celeste's eyes danced. "Thanks, Mom. Simon thinks I'm almost as pretty as Rachel." She spit on a finger and swabbed the single brown curl that crept forward on her cheek.

I shook my head in disbelief. "She's harassing me something fierce."

"Better leave that one alone," Charlie warned. "We men have to stick together, Simon. Don't you think so?"

Celeste was beaming and unable to stand still. "Mom, Uncle Sammy's seen to it that I got a raise! Isn't that swell? It's been awhile. I deserve one. He said so, and he's chief."

"Of course! I'm so pleased for you. Tell me *everything* that's been happening." Virginia motioned to Celeste. "I get to see so little of you. Let's leave the men. Follow me."

It was an opportune window, and I seized it as soon as Charlie and I were alone. "Charlie, I love your daughter."

He looked astonished. "I do, too."

"No, I mean I *really* love her."

"So do I." His wink didn't help matters.

"Give me a chance, Charlie, please." I was surprised at how nervous I was. "I want to marry Celeste, with your blessing, of course."

"This is out of the blue, or is it?"

"Not really. I think I've loved her, well, since she was too young for me to think about it." That hadn't come out exactly right. I began again. "What I mean is—"

"I think I know what you mean. I should let Virginia speak for herself, but for me, there's no doubt in my mind." He got up and took a few steps toward the kitchen to make sure the coast was clear. "You'll make a fine husband for Celeste. You're a determined young man, hard-driving. You have my blessing. Don't you ever hurt my baby, you hear?"

"Of course. You know me better than most, Charlie."

He shook my hand and then sat back down.

"Then, come Christmas, I'm proposing. Maybe we can get married in the spring."

"Rachel and Albert will appreciate the notice. Their third one—good Catholics." He narrowed his eyes. His bitterness was hard to miss. "Got another baby on the way. Flagstaff's too far to get back here for Christmas. So a springtime wedding will be perfect."

He and I looked at each other at the same instant, registering the same truth at apparently the same time.

He spoke just before I could. "Guess we'd better clear that with Celeste."

I smiled. "I'm stepping out of line here. Just curious. You're not holding any ill feeling for Albert just because he's a Catholic, are you?"

"I dunno. I'm ashamed of my preconceived ideas. Just want this country of ours to hold to the values that make us strong. The old-fashioned family values. New women with their new freedoms, immigrants, Protestants and Catholics, blacks and whites—we seem to be in something of a cultural civil war." Concern shown in his eyes. "Prohibition was supposed to improve family life and reduce crime. Instead, just look at the dangerous criminal class that's developed because of it. You know it better than I: the world is changing. Every day it's changing. Immigrants have crowded our cities—Detroit, in particular. Supposedly, Prohibition was going to assert some control. It hasn't."

I stepped in. "You're right on every count, Charlie. Eliminating alcohol was supposed to turn back the clock to a more comfortable time in history. Of course, we can still drink it." I knew I needed to start backpedaling. "Not that I do. But Prohibition only made it illegal to manufacture and sell it. You can go to any one of Detroit's thousands of speakeasies and get a stockpile of booze." I scratched my head. "But Catholics, Charlie?"

"A whole community's pulling us in too many directions. There's a Catholic church in every neighborhood. Maybe I'm threatened by the thought of America becoming a Catholic country. It's flagrant prejudice, I know. I need to get over it—as a Christian and for the sake of my grandchildren. They'll be raised Catholic."

"How's Rachel doing?"

He gave me a sidelong glance. "She's doing fine, from all I can tell." He drew a breath as if it were his last. "I miss her, Simon. No way will I ever understand why she did what she did. Lord! Flagstaff's two thousand miles away. She could have married someone a lot closer to home."

I didn't dare look him in the eye. *It probably never was going to be me,* I thought.

He stood up as Virginia returned. "I believe God's equipping you for his purposes, Simon."

Virginia looked at me and then at Charlie as if we held a secret, and as Celeste came bounding in, we all looked at each other.

"Did I miss anything?" Celeste asked.

"Celeste, baby, your father's good at summarizing. He's a preacher."

Virginia laughed. "In a nutshell, God's got his hand on this young man of yours. Is that right, Charlie?"

"No doubt about it. What say we have some apple cider?"

Nothing wrong with Charlie's suggestion, but something had come to mind. "I didn't think of this before, honey, but while we're so close, it might be nice to look in on Mrs. B and Doc. You know?"

"Of course, I do," Charlie answered for her. "I married those two characters, and he's Catholic."

"Yes, but he told me he wasn't," I said in self-defense.

Virginia snapped her head in Charlie's direction. It looked like a warning.

"I'm working on it, Virgie."

With our goodbyes said, Celeste and I motored over to my old boarding house, unannounced.

Chapter 54

⟫•◆•⟪

"What the hel—?"

Doc Begbie swung the door open so fast I was almost carried in on the doorknob.

"What in the name o' blazes are ye doing here? Come in this house."

"Who is it, love?" Mrs. B stopped in her tracks. "Well, I'll be skittered." With one of her rare smiles, she rushed at me with a bear hug, scarcely able to reach as high as my chest. "And just look at ye, with your fine-looking hat and your double-breasted suit. Turn around. Let me have a look-see."

"You're starting to sound like your husband, Mrs. B," I said, slowly spinning for her as if I were a horse on a carousel.

Mint permeated the house, and not a thing had changed. Every chair sat in its place. Every rug had its characteristic rumple.

"I should," she said, peevishly. "He's been around forever. Old coot."

Doc Begbie's smile hinted at amusement under his mustache, and without taking his eyes off me, he wielded a smack to her fanny with his cane. "I've missed ye, laddie. Aye."

"And you as well, sir. Both of you. I think of you often. You're not going to recognize this one." I motioned for Celeste to come closer.

She took a baby step forward, striking me as unusually shy for my high-spirited filly, and Mrs. B gave her a once-over. "My, my. You are a lady, all right. Goodness, Celeste. All grown-up. Come, sit."

"Mrs. B, we're not going to stay. I just wanted to stop by and show her off. I'll be back. You know I will. Can't keep from checking in on the two of you from time to time."

"That's good. Ye are like kin. Aye." Doc ogled Celeste from head to toe. "How old are ye?"

"I'm twenty-one, Doc Begbie. And how old are you?"

Her gumption brought the house down. Doc roared. I'd never heard Mrs. B laugh out loud—ever.

"Just a wee too old for ye," the crusty Scot countered with a wink, "but I love ye, no matter."

We left shortly thereafter with laughter trailing us to the car. Doc shouted, "Good cheerio now!" as we got inside.

I shut Celeste's door and went around the car to take my place next to her in the driver's seat. "He's a one-of-a-kind, isn't he? Does darned well for a man in his seventies."

"He's a flirt." Delight expressed, as it always did, like a brook after a spring rain.

I loved that about her.

"I've said it before, Celeste, but I don't ever want to lose you." I turned for a second to look into her eyes and kept on driving.

"You're not going to lose me, silly," she said, jabbing me in the ribs. Her feistiness made me laugh. "Looking forward to the big day tomorrow?" She beamed. "*My* Captain Hagan's going to lead the motorcade. I can't wait. Any chance I could hide on the floorboard?"

I took her hand and kissed it again and again. "What could please me more than having you right beside me?" I sighed and looked across at her, sensing I wasn't sounding as romantic as I'd like. I smiled. "Sorry to be such a stick-in-the-mud. There's just a lot on my mind. There's a big chunk of it that makes me happy. But it's you that makes me the most happy."

<hr>

Ambition hadn't required me to think. It had required me to act. That came with the territory, and some days it was one step forward and two steps back. Tomorrow morning the mindless noise in my head was going to resume, which meant facing the glaring reality that law enforcement wasn't suicide but came mighty close.

Celeste peeled off her close-fitting hat and reclined her head, letting the cool September air blow through her hair.

"My job's demanding, and too much so. And most of the time. And dangerous. Roman's death is a perfect example." I stared straight ahead. "Your job lets you see about as much corruption from your perspective as I do. You type the reports. You dispatch the facts. You're bound to get a feel when something's not right."

She jerked her head toward me. "You don't still think Roman was murdered, do you?"

Of course he was murdered, I thought. "I don't know what to think. It's hard to pin down the facts when there's so much corruption. All I know is this: life's precious. I love you, Celeste. I love you. If you hadn't come to work when you did, we might never have gotten together."

Chapter 55

⟫•◆•⟪

"Coming in? It's not that late, Simon."

I held Celeste's hand in mine as we followed the dim hall to her door. The scent of a disinfectant—as if the carpet had been cleaned while we were out to Highland Park for the afternoon—permeated the place. It got me to coughing.

Our apartment building was located near enough to the precinct that it offered us a convenient commute. I smiled at the thought of her moving in with me in the spring. Marrying her was never far from my mind.

"I'd better get on up to my place," I replied. "For some reason, I'm wiped out. And there's the motorcade tomorrow afternoon. How about if I come down in the morning? Seven-fifteen? We can have coffee before going over to headquarters."

"Sounds good." Her blue eyes twinkled as she inspected me with child-like curiosity. "You okay?"

"Something only a long kiss from my favorite person in the world can cure. It may take more than one."

"I love you, Captain Hagan. Here's one for the road . . . or the elevator." She was still smiling when her lips met mine.

"You're under way too much stress, sweetheart. You've lost weight. You've got to eat."

"Honest," I said. "I'm going to pass on the food. Maybe I should go on up to my place."

"Don't be silly. You're staying right here so I can keep an eye on you." She turned the doorknob and pushed me inside. "Go on. Lie down."

She didn't have to tell me twice. I went to the sofa and curled up like a baby in its mother's womb, and promptly fell asleep.

When I woke up, it was dark outside. Celeste was sitting next to me, stroking my face with the back of her hand. She bent over me—her face so close to mine that I could see her mouth trembling, and then it touched mine— hotly, tenderly, completely. Every move of her lips kindled every fiber of my being. Every second they lingered, the sensation burned more intensely. And when our eyes opened, the depth of passion between them lingered.

I held her, savoring the warmth of her body. "Celeste . . . Celeste, marry me."

She sprang like a jack-in-the-box. "Are you serious?"

I sat up and wrapped my arms around her, pulled her close again, and embraced her, never more certain of how much I longed to have her near me. "I haven't been more sure of anything in my life. I love you, Celeste. I'd planned to wait to ask. It was going to be Christmas. I'm just a few days early." I whispered to her, "Marry me."

I could feel her heart pounding. She melted in my arms and her kiss felt like a yes. The ones to follow did, as well. And the night ended differently. Far beyond any other.

Heading up the glorious motorcade the next day through the streets of Detroit was nothing in comparison.

Chapter 56

⟞◆⟝

Christmas hadn't put Lieutenant Dugan in a Santa Claus frame of mind. When January 2 rolled around, he refused to finger the kingpin responsible for the profiteering that was going down. The nervous son-of-a-mother-load police officer reluctantly took the stand the first day back to work against a gang member and yet again developed a sudden case of the I-can't-recalls in Detroit's federal court. And Aaron Bornstein, the notorious head of the Purple Gang, once again eluded the arm of the law.

Just when it seemed like things couldn't get any uglier, they did.

I got out of bed at the crack of dawn on Friday, January 4, coughing and hacking my way to the bathroom. But before I could make it to the john, I crumpled to the floor and rolled to one side, unable to keep from gagging. I pulled the top of my skivvies to my mouth, gurgling like a newborn. When I looked at the fabric, it was soaked through with wet, rust-colored blood. From where I'd taken hold of the middle of the white cotton knit to where it met my navel, blood spotted every stitch. I sat straight up, hoping somehow I was misreading the evidence.

Staggering to the washbasin, I told myself it was an unreasonable joke, as sinister as staring into the end of a loaded Smith & Wesson. Being lion-hearted for the Detroit police had summoned my valor, I'd planted my feet solidly on the ground—stared boldly into evil's eyes. It was my stance toward the world outside, but the sticky smear I was holding in my hands forced me to take a look at the inside.

No amount of target practice could have prepared me for what I saw.

I called in sick. "Just a bad cough. Probably will see a doctor and be back in on Monday. Pass that on for me. Thanks."

I hung up the telephone, pulled the directory from the niche in the hallway, and looked up the doctor I had seen a time or two for minor ailments. It only took me a moment to find the name: *Johnson, Dr. Burt R.* I jotted down the number on a scrap of paper and called it. No answer. I waited until precisely eight o'clock and then called again. I was unhappy with the response I got.

"Monday? Not before? Is there another doctor who could see me today? It's an emergency. I don't think it can keep through the weekend."

"No, sir, Mr. Hagan. You'll have to come in Monday unless you want to check into a hospital before that."

"Fine, I'll be there at eight a.m."

I went back to bed, tossing for the next hour or so. It was farfetched to think I'd be able to rest, let alone sleep.

The telephone rang at 9:10. It was Celeste. "Simon, what on earth? You have me scared to death. Rhonda told me you called in sick. This isn't like you. Why didn't you call?"

"It's just a cough. I should have let you know. Now don't make a fuss. I'll be back on Monday, good as new."

"Monday! Monday?"

"Well, now that I think about it, I'll have to let the boss know it will be after my doctor's appointment. Gosh. What a mess." I spoke with as much credibility as I could conjure. "Listen, Celeste, I'll be fine. I'll pick you up after you get off. We'll go to Mackie's."

"Something's not right, Simon."

"I'll be fine." I hung up, believing I could make it to our favorite cafe.

But when the time came, I couldn't. Weak, still coughing up blood, and scared stiff, I called Celeste mid-afternoon to postpone.

"Maybe I'd be well-advised to rest this weekend. I may have something contagious." Unable to mask the cough, I begged off. "I'll call you Monday morning after I run in to see Dr. Johnson. I'll see you sometime during the day."

"You don't sound good, sweetheart. I want to come see for myself. You're hedging."

She was right. *Hedging, downright lying*, I thought. The deception was painful. It cheapened the intimacy we'd shared. I wasn't sure where I hurt the most.

⎯⎯⎯◆⎯⎯⎯

The knock on my door around nine was unexpected. Not fully clothed, I cracked it open and peered out.

"Chicken soup from Mackie's." Celeste was down the hall before I could see her face. Gone.

"Thanks," I said over a cough as the elevator doors closed.

Regardless of how I felt Monday morning, I was up and dressed by six-thirty. Weak as a kitten and too bummed to drive myself, I caught a streetcar to Trumbull Avenue and got off. The wind almost knocked me down. I walked against it, then climbed the steps to Dr. Johnson's office—one, not two at a time like I might have if things had been normal. They were anything but.

When I left the doctor's office an hour or so later, the wind had turned into a snowstorm. But as I tramped down the steps, I was not feeling a thing.

Chapter 57

I arrived back at the Somerset apartment, snow-drenched and frozen, needing to be alone. I paced the floor, rubbing my shoulders and patting my forearms until my circulation began flowing. Dr. Johnson's words pounded in my head. I went to the bureau with my hands still in gloves, took Mother's Bible from the drawer, and laid it on the bed in the rumpled covers, hoping to sense her strength.

Eyeing it as if her ghost might creep from between the pages, I considered the several calls to be made. Dad's was number one. I removed my wet clothes, wrapped a blanket loosely about me, and then picked up the telephone.

He must have known something was up. I was calling on a Monday morning. He sounded breathless. "Morning, Simon. Glad you called."

My hand shook. "Yes, sir. Just need to let you know. There's no point in beating around the bush." I pressed the receiver harder to my ear. "I've come from the doctor's. Not so good, I'm sorry to say."

"What is it, son? You don't sound well. Something I can do?"

I was glad he was doing the talking. More than anything else, I needed to hear his voice. I struggled to muster the courage to tell him the rest. "I've had some tests this morning. Looks like tuberculosis."

He was slow to answer. "But not certain?"

"Yes, sir. Pretty certain. Beyond that, I'll be going to a sanatorium. Nothing specific yet, so I haven't told Celeste."

"Sure 'nough got a lotta trusting to do. Maybe the tests are wrong. Either way, we'll get through. Life's hard. Alan, now this. Glad we can turn to God in times like these. The good and the not so good."

I swallowed hard, unable to dismiss the cruelty of the fact. "Have you talked to Alan?"

"No, son, I'm afraid not. Let's get back when you know more. How's that sound?"

"I think that's best, too. I'll call."

"Read your Bible, Simon. Stay strong."

—◈—

Without intending to, I'd fallen asleep to the sound of frozen rain hitting the window pane, bleating like a lost sheep caught in a thicket.

Jolted by the coughing, I woke up feeling the trickle of blood at a corner of my mouth. My eyelids were crusted, and my pillow matted. My hair felt greasy from running my fingers through it. The waves felt limp and heavy. The beard I'd shaven a few hours earlier seemed to have grown with every hand stroke I'd given it. The bones in my jaws seemed squarer.

I thought of the Mallorys, the Begbies. There was no time to visit. A call and a pledge would have to suffice. The urgency to get the help I needed was bearing down. So was scheduling an appointment with Chief Sturges.

Charting my next moves mattered. He would be stunned at my resignation. It was better left until I could be on two feet, not walking into the precinct covered in self-pity. Tuesday at four, I'd be in his office.

I curled up in bed, propped myself on an elbow, and agonized over how to tell Celeste, only just tolerating the wait until I could see her in person this afternoon. Absentmindedly, I pulled the Bible from the folds of the blanket and inspected its worn cover. Mom had treated it like a treasure. I was afraid of it. Even so, I opened it, flipping pages as if I were a predator sneaking up on my prey, and then shut it. I glanced at the clock. With more than enough time to shower and be ready when Celeste arrived, I sat up in bed. Hungry but too limp to get up, I reached for my Camels on the nearby table. The urge was there. Common sense wasn't. I lit up.

Taking hold of the Bible in one hand, puffing with the other, I rested my head on the bed-frame behind me. Smoke curled in the air above me. I looked down at the words on the page where it had randomly fallen open and read the underlined verse from chapter six of Micah:

He has told you, O man, what is good; and what does the
Lord require of you but to do justice, and to love kindness,
and to walk humbly with your God?

I dropped the book to one side, remembering a day in springtime when I'd walked with Mother in the woodland in search of mushrooms, choosing yellow and purple irises for her while she spoke of Jesus's love. I asked myself if anything I'd had thus far was giving me life.

A small piece of paper lay on the bedsheet where I'd dumped her Bible. I turned it over. In her handwriting were these words:

Any man's death diminishes me,
Because I am involved in mankind,
And therefore never send to know for whom the bell tolls;
It tolls for thee.
—Donne

I broke out in a cold sweat.

Mother had liked poetry. I didn't. But I couldn't shed its power—neither the words from the Bible nor the ones from the poet. Not in the shower, and not out.

I chose not to look again at Dad's note, which also lurked inside, and as the time neared for Celeste to arrive at my apartment, I was no stronger. More composed, perhaps, but not stronger.

Chapter 58

I t was late in the day when Celeste entered my apartment, more chicken soup from Mackie's in hand. She promptly set it on the counter.

I was dressed as if we were going out. We weren't. She looked as though she thought we might be. She wore her hat slung low over her eyes and had cinched her sash loosely at the waist of her coat. When she removed them, I was taken by how stunning she looked.

"You're enchanting, Celeste. Purple becomes you." I wanted to pull her toward me. I resisted, knowing it was stupid to get near her.

"It's lavender, sweetheart. Now, golly Moses, what did the doctor say that had to wait till now?" She leaned in to kiss me.

I raised my hand to stop her. "Wait, Celeste." I smiled, hoping to veil my eccentric behavior.

"You look positively ashen. Sit this minute and talk to me." She picked up my Camels, took one, and carried an ashtray to the kitchen table.

I fumbled for matches and purposely sat across from her. "How was work today?"

"Nonsense. We're not talking about me. What's going on?"

"There's not a lot I can do to prepare you, Celeste—"

"Uh-oh. What?" She took a puff and exhaled with a sexy head tilt.

I sighed, unsure if I could find the words to say. "I have to tell you the truth, Celeste."

"Now what can possibly be so grim?" she said, pursing her lips like a fretting child. "You're not running out on me now, are you, sweetheart?"

"Be serious, Celeste. This is not a game. I am sick, and what I have is not going away." I interlaced my fingers so she couldn't see them trembling and leaned forward on the table so she could hear me plainly. "I have to leave this place, this town."

Her look embedded itself in my brain.

"I have tuberculosis."

She gasped.

"The doctor says my only hope is a sanatorium. There's one in New Mexico."

Her bottom lip trembled. "No! You can't!" Her eyes were wild.

"Marry me. Come with me. I love you. I need you."

Through the deadly quiet in my apartment, I could hear the rise of the elevator and the doors opening and closing and voices on the other side of the wall—in someone else's world. And the air in mine went stale.

Again, I pleaded. "Marry me. I can't leave here without you." My head felt like a boulder about to topple from my neck. I lowered it for a second, getting a breath, stifling a cough. "We love each other."

The look in her eyes wasn't reassuring. I could understand how stunned she felt. "I need to think, Simon." She was pale. Her smile, gone. "I just don't know what . . . I'm scared." She slowly rose from the table.

"I'm scared, too. You have to know that I am. The arrangements for the place in New Mexico aren't even made, but it has to happen soon. Dr. Johnson is confirming a hundred percent with tests, but he was all but certain the results will show TB." I walked toward her. "Will you come?"

She backed away. "I can't breathe, Simon. Can we talk when I've had a chance to sort this out?"

"Celeste? What on earth was that but a glowing refusal?" I immediately wished I could take it back. "I'm sorry. My emotions are blown. I can't survive without you."

She stood tall in her stylish boots, gazing at me. A distant look filled her eyes. "I'm struggling with what we did, you know, even if I am a grown woman. And now I'm paralyzed with this news." She eased her hat over her brown bob and snugged it down over her forehead. "Life takes weird turns, Simon. I'm not Rachel's kid sister anymore. I know you loved her. I know she loved you."

"What? Please tell me why you're thinking such a thing." I could feel myself boiling. "You're the one I love more than life itself. I think I have from the beginning."

Celeste was panting. "I'm confused. Just let me go."

I was heating up and started to cough. I groped for a handkerchief. "Go, then. I'm not stopping you, Celeste. Go, if you think I've even given a thought to Rachel. Please, for the love of God, can't you get over what might have been but wasn't? And years ago?"

"I wanted to be beautiful . . . the way you saw her. But I'm just here! I'm just the one who's left." Sobbing, she wrapped her coat sash and gave it a hard pull, and in the brokenness of the evening, she disappeared with the slam of the door.

I stayed unmoving until I couldn't hear the descending elevator. Then I folded on the floor in a heap.

Chapter 59

It was time to go. Unfit to bear the January temperature or the streetcar connections I'd have to make to get to Michigan Central, I hailed a taxi from East Jefferson, my baggage in tow. Bound in every piece of clothing I could put on, including the green plaid scarf Doc Begbie had given me, I was able to flag one down in a matter of minutes. Charlie's offer to drive me had seemed unnecessary at the time. Having declined it seemed perfectly stupid now, but best since I might have unnecessarily exposed him. I climbed in the back of the cab, shivering and weak in the knees.

Detroit led the nation in managing its chaotic traffic issues, but it wasn't apparent today. The driver swerved in and out of cars jamming the streets. *Aaoogha! Aaoogha!* He swung around slow or inexperienced drivers, his horn honking, his vehicle dodging pedestrians in the way.

My early months on the squad, dedicated to traffic control, were a mere fragment in my memory. Almost nine years had passed since I'd joined the force.

The extraordinary evening spent with Celeste, however, was seared into my mind. Possibly forever, never to be repeated. Our derailed future was every bit as severe as my diagnosis of tuberculosis. I'd not seen her since our argument, not even to say goodbye. She'd bailed, refusing to be a part of my tentative future. Maybe she was to blame for it being so precarious. *Someone* was. Too much about it was unfair. Tuberculosis was a killer. This time I was up against fate, maybe even God, facing my own mortality.

I intended to fight. And I intended to survive. I was built that way, no apologies. That meant I'd be settled in a sanatorium in Albuquerque by this time next week. And the mob, the Purple Gang—every last one of them, as far as I was concerned—could go up in flames.

I hadn't seen the last of Lieutenant Dugan, and if his number ever came up, corrupt as he was, testifying against him for his involvement in Roman Davis's death, no matter how many years would have passed, would bring me back to Detroit in a heartbeat. Tuberculosis or no tuberculosis. I had turned in my badge, simply walked out the door the same way I'd walked in. Tied up other loose ends. *A piece of cake.*

Beat from my own mental gymnastics, I laid my head on the back of the taxi seat and watched as we turned toward the terminal. *Who was I kidding?* I couldn't get my hide out to Highland Park to see the Mallorys or the Begbies, let alone testify against anyone right now, not if my life depended on it.

As defiant as my thoughts were, my body was no match. The taxi trip was closer to a roller-coaster dip at the circus than a trip to the terminal. Perhaps my last joyride for who knew how long—or my last. Period. But there was no time to dwell on it or my Model T, which might as well have been my firstborn. It sold to the first looker. The money would help with expenses. I had no use for wheels in a cotton-picking sanatorium anyway. Driving to San Francisco, even if the distance to see Alan was soon going to be cut in half, wasn't going to happen, not with syphilis ending his life and tuberculosis putting mine on hold. Michigan Central appeared in front of the taxi, once again looming large, and I felt smaller than small.

I got out of the taxi, paid the driver in bills I'd wiped on my overcoat, and made my way into the terminal, coughing against the wind in my face, wondering if the bell was tolling for Simon Hagan. I was resigned. It felt like my new norm. The sanatorium in Albuquerque, New Mexico, held the cure, if there was one.

PART FOUR
Chapter 60

⟫⋄⟪

Compared to the dance halls in Detroit, where jazz bands played and nightlife peaked and the happy part of me came alive, I'd earned a one-way ticket to a drop-off point. A train to Albuquerque was confirming it.

If I'd run faster, reacted better, loved more, and grumbled less, there would have been no need to leave my Kentucky roots, I told myself, or pursue wholeness on unstained land. And Alan wouldn't have followed me.

I got up, steadying myself between seat backs as the train raced away from Detroit, onward to Albuquerque. Exhaustion set in from lamenting the past, feeling the weight of Alan's saga. And after the train, a tumbledown bus took me across the plains where the bodacious mountain range lifted itself against the clear blue sky like divine etchings in pen and ink. On past one adobe after another, to the sanatorium at Saint Andrew's where earthy brown layers and scrub trees sauntered up to meet them at the apex of distant dreams and unnoticed requests. I'd come to the place where I said to God, "Move this mountain," and he'd said nothing. All of it made me mad.

Hard sarcasm, and I knew it. I was mad on arrival. Irritability went with the disease. Tuberculosis. It brought me across a smear of burnt sandy colors to breathe dry air, to wander the place that sat high in the desert, to peer into the traces of the area's tribal history and into the faces of the Pueblo Indian.

I felt like I'd come to the end of the earth.

⟫⋄⟪

As cheerful as everyone tried to make it, the sanatorium was a dreary place. Day after day, when even the New Mexico sunshine couldn't brighten my mood, letters trickled in with news from home to rescue me from drowning in self-pity. My father's words, brief as they were, zigzagged down the page of the most recent one that lay face up on the bureau. Letters from family were all I had. Dad's in particular were heartening in their attempts to give me peace, urging me to depend on God.

I'd read and reread all of them a dozen times and didn't need to be sidetracked by this one again. But I was and trying at the same time to keep upright while I put on my trousers. Fatigued and coughing like a croupy child, with my foot caught halfway down the left leg, I could have been a circus act. Moreover, I might have been happier being one, possibly a pirouetting clown or a tightrope walker. But I wasn't, and in the final push to get my foot through the other end of the trouser leg, I made a graceless dive at the bureau. With no one nearby to applaud, I ended my stunt, and the commotion sent Dad's letter floating to the freshly mopped floor.

I let it lay, too spent to retrieve it, tucked in my shirt, and zipped the fly. It took the last speck of strength I could muster to insert my belt through the loops.

Seven weeks of living in this place, in this room, on these premises, had been, at their core, an encounter with mortality. My room could have passed for a surgical ward with its austerity so perfectly laid out, so clean, so minimal. Everything stood in readiness to move one patient out and another one in. No muss, no fuss. Not a particle of dust, not a brightly painted wall, not a rug or a fluffy pillow. Just a bleached white sheet and a short white curtain. Hard. Simple. A single bulb hung from the ceiling. Like a factory for people to come, live if they could, and die if they couldn't. Just die and be moved on.

My reflection stared back at me from the mirror above the bureau. As much as I wanted to be God, I was not, and that alone made me annoyed as heck. I detested the skinny, debilitated imposter of the person I had once been. It hadn't been that long ago, and every ounce of weight I'd lost magnified the effects of tuberculosis. My cheekbones protruded like hardboiled eggs under a dish towel. Circles under my eyes were hollowed like holes in a skull. I glanced away, irked by the sight.

It took a yank, lame as it was, to open the bottom drawer of the bureau. I gave it the necessary extra one to get it completely open and took out a pair of socks. Perspiration saturated my shirt at the armpits, and my hands shook. All the signs confirmed it: if I was ever going to live life as I once had, it wouldn't be soon. I produced a smile to prove to myself some part of me was still in control. Most of me was convinced I was not.

A thump-thump on the door startled me. With my sense of orientation lost, I jumped like I'd been shot. A moment passed.

"Mr. Hagan, it's Nurse Fairweather with your morning milk."

That was what I'd been reduced to—a disoriented, sickly, overwrought man requiring morning milk.

I opened the door as wide as I could without bumping the trash can behind it. "Come on in. Please. Good morning, Mrs. Fairweather."

She required a little extra space to get past me. She had her arms full, and she carried a load as broad as she was.

"I was just getting myself together," I said. "It's still morning. Right? Or have I slept it away?"

"Of course, it's still morning. Sunday morning, in case you've a need to be reminded, Mr. Hagan. It's only a little past eight." She waltzed solidly past me, hawking a tray with a glass of milk and whatever else I'd been pre-scribed to kick off the day's routine. She could be snippy at the drop of a hat, but today she was chuckling. Her cheeks were rosy, and her eyes sparkled. "Beautiful weather. Much warmer than usual for a February morning. Brisk, mind you, but nice. Did you sleep well, Mr. Hagan?" She had a spring in her step. It was all she could do to set the weekly newsletter, along with a glass of milk without spilling it, on the table beside my chair. "Let me open the window a speck. Can't hurt to have a little freshness in here."

"I did sleep well, thanks. Typical night sweats and a few chills tried their darnedest to keep me awake." I moseyed over to the corner where I kept my shoes. "Ten hours of sleep a night must be setting some kinda record for an adult male." I followed her to the chair with my wingtips and a shoehorn in hand. "Newborns require less than that, don't they?" I sat down, trying to put on my socks before my bony feet became a subject for discussion. "If I'd been able to get six or seven hours on any given night when I was working on the po—"

"Do I detect a little mullygrubbing? Negative thinking, as you know, is not allowed here. You have not lost everything, no matter what you think, and your life is ahead of you." She was already knee-deep in one of her textbook lectures. "I guess it must be hard to leave a job that makes you feel valuable to society. Still, it's not good for your morale to rehash those years on the police force." She stuffed her hands authoritatively into her starched white apron pockets and gave me a look.

I nodded and eased the shoehorn behind my heel. "You're right. Most assuredly." With a little force, I slid my long foot into the wingtip. She watched me while I laced it and began the process with the other shoe. "You must get sick of hearing about Detroit." I looked solemnly at her and stood up, towering over her five-foot frame.

"TB is serious. It takes things from you." Her tone was sympathetic. A weak smile pushed at her plump cheeks as she stared up at me. "I'm not making light of your illness. It's sent you into a new direction." She stiffened, striking a soldierly pose. All sympathy had vanished. "But you've got to remember: you must have a forward-thinking, positive outlook at all times."

I had to laugh, first at the suggestion that TB was a new direction, and second at the sight of her. For such a short woman, she was trying to pack a wallop. "Anyone ever call you *Fierce* Fairweather?"

But my laughter changed to coughing, and I couldn't stop. I dispensed with the shoe for the time being and pulled a handkerchief from my pocket. The deep-down churning inside my chest sounded like a lung was loose.

"You're going to get in trouble, Mr. Hagan," she said with a huff. Locks of graying hair jutted randomly from her crisp white cap and shook in perfect unison with the crooked finger she wagged at me. "A lot of trouble. Was there blood with that cough?"

I muffled the next one, deep and rattling as it was, and slid the handkerchief in my trouser pocket. "Trouble for teasing you?" My wink purposely betrayed the seriousness in my voice. "What other fun can I have? Doesn't look like anything else is gonna take me outside these walls. Trouble will be worth the punishment."

"Poppycock, Mr. Hagan. Let me see the hanky." She bent forward, both hands firmly stuck on her hips like anchors to hold her in place.

I was reluctant to produce it. "Looks like a little maybe. See there, Nurse, your harshness caused it."

She rolled her eyes and bit her lip to keep from smiling. Her cheeks turned red. "You're maddening. I'm telling the doctor."

"I thought you required lightheartedness," I said, not wanting to apologize for embarrassing her. "Are you telling him I'm still coughing up blood or that I teased you?"

"You're always so . . . dramatic, Mr. Hagan. You should consider acting, with such an elegant manner about you. And just look at those shoes. Putting on the Ritz right here at Saint Andrew's."

"Got to hide behind something, don't we? It's a big world out there." I paused, knowing I should let the subject slide. "Shoes and a good-looking tie . . . they're just part of my armor."

"Phooey! Lots of rest, good food, and a good attitude are your armor. They're the cure. They're going to pull you through." She turned to go. "Don't overlook your medication, Mr. Hagan. Two pink pills, one yellow, and one white. They're there, under the newsletter." She stalled long enough to pick up my Bible. "Listen to this. 'Wise warriors are mightier than strong ones.' That's powerful advice to remember." She pushed the Bible at me. "It's right there. Proverbs twenty-four."

Resisting the urge to salute, I balanced the Bible on my knees, then resumed the task of putting on my other shoe.

"Now then," she said, "I'm going to continue my rounds. You pay attention to that verse, and the next time I come in here, I want to see that big smile of yours. By the way, it looks to me like you've put on a speck of weight. That alone is something to be pleased about. Maybe I shouldn't be saying it, but since I'm old enough to be your mother . . . well, it's just a thought. You're a handsome man, Mr. Hagan, and so tall. I'm serious. Maybe you should consider going on stage." She paused, and the lines on her face softened. "You'll be out of here in a matter of months. You're going to make it, Mr. Hagan. You are."

The pep talk was most likely protocol coming from a matronly nurse in a tuberculosis sanatorium. But I would have taken it any day. "I do appreciate that. Sincerely, I do, Mrs. Fairweather."

She shook her head and marched past me, snapping up my father's letter from the floor on her way out. Every joint in her body groaned as she bent over to retrieve it. She pushed herself back up with the help of her hands on her knees. Victorious, she laid the letter on the bureau.

"I would have done that," I said, but she'd already reached the door.

Chapter 61

———◇———

I held the Bible the nurse had handed me and stared at its cover and the inscription on the spine. After a second, I turned to the page with my mother's name. Printed on the flimsy paper were the words *Presented to*, and on the next line were the handwritten words *Nellie Virginia Kennan on her wedding day*. Dad's hand had penned that, as well as *Tuesday, May 21, 1899* on the line following the single word *Date*. His signature, *Geoffrey Newton Hagan*, was scrawled next to the word *By*. I lifted it to my nose and inhaled, searching for a scent of my mother that might be lingering between the pages.

The gift of her Bible that he'd slipped inside my valise the day I left home still held the note he'd tucked inside. I'd left it there. The God he had continually pointed me to seek seemed distant now, and uninvolved, and the Bible felt noticeably unused in my hands. It had been almost nine years. Circumstances had a way of changing everything. My diagnosis of TB had been a real kicker, and one slow hour after another slipped by with no guarantee of tomorrows. Imagining them was ridiculous.

Self-pity dug its hooks in. I tried to focus on something else. *Mullygrubber* was not a flattering label. Fierce Fairweather had me pegged. Absently, I laid the Bible and shoehorn aside, thinking my isolation had to mean something more significant than the loneliness I felt.

Part of me wanted to make something of the glimmering rays of sun that were streaming through the window, but the logic in me couldn't attach a great deal of importance to having tied both shoes.

A brilliance reflected off the metal rim of the frame that held a fading image of my mother. I angled her picture so I could see her face from my chair.

Kindness showed in her eyes, and the gaze she held penetrated my soul.

I had toughened after her unspeakable death, and if losing her hadn't matured me, Detroit had. The years I'd spent as a policeman arm-wrestling the Purple Gang in a town of a million people were starting to look like child's play compared to living here, fighting my own demise. Trying to keep optimistic about my life, which hung by a thread, was not for wimps. Heads hit the sidewalk. People died here. Lots of them.

The smiles, the hours in the sunshine, the pep talks, the seaweed under my pillow, and the gun—the gun I no longer carried—all qualified as part of the fight, all certified armor. Every minute was a fight. I looked at the picture of my mother and longed to speak to her, needing her reassurance that my being stuck in Albuquerque was part of something bigger.

Having plopped the Bible on top of this week's newsletter, I pulled out the *Killgloom Gazette* from underneath it to take a look. Irrepressible as it was in its appeal, the sanatorium's publication was not always successful. I leafed through the pages anyway, reading the *Gazette*'s "Cardinal Principles for Health Seekers." Topping the list of recommendations were a hopeful spirit and a peaceful frame of mind. If those principles were going to influence my body to heal, I had some attitude changes to make.

It was the peaceful frame of mind that was hard to come by. Tuberculosis was a killer, and at twenty-six, I wasn't ready to die from it—nor from anything else, for that matter.

Voices, muffled but present, echoed from the corridor. They seemed bent on distracting me. Moreover, the pills Nurse Fairweather had delivered were staring me down. I popped them into my mouth, guzzled the full glass of milk, and then tossed the *Gazette* on the table. Even the rustle of paper irritated me.

Noise was only part of what disturbed me. It went deeper. I got to my feet, agitated and unable to concentrate. The window was partially open and coaxed me to the sweeping view of a spectacular horizon. I gazed as far as my eyes could see, halfway expecting an answer for my future to present itself on the lawn.

A simple mix of motionless trees and growing grass spilled out on the unblemished plains like a wash of green watercolor across a fresh canvas.

The reality of facing tuberculosis alone—facing it at all—bit into my confidence. *Life is a coin toss*, I told myself and inhaled deeply, sucking in the arid potion as if it were an elixir from the gods, letting the curative power of the desert air seep into my lungs till I was certain my chest would cave in.

Strong sunlight went right through my clothes and into my skin, it seemed, and the tightly wound coils in my neck began to unwind. My shoulders fell limp. Breathing in, breathing out, I let my senses fill with everything Albuquerque's out-of-doors had to offer and then leaned my elbows on the sill of the open window.

Unrelenting thoughts of Mother returned.

Not a day in nine years had gone by without some memory of her creeping into my mind. Often a good one. Too often the bad. Details of the appalling incident clung to me. I paced in front of the window, trying to shake them off. Walking to the bureau, I fought them. Looking at the person in the mirror who looked back at me, I fought them.

I tied my necktie—and tightened the knot till my face turned several shades of red—still fighting them. Somewhat pacified, I loosened it and readjusted the knot till I couldn't feel the pain. Pleased with the splash of blue-striped silk, I pulled on my waistcoat and buttoned it high on my sternum.

With that fraction of my appearance intact, and my cough under control, I took Dad's latest letter from its envelope.

Without his encouragement, pumping sunshine between every word he wrote, I would've been totally capable of giving up. He probably knew that, but he had no way of knowing the big chunk of my life I'd kept from him. Getting the icy mitt from the girl I'd intended to marry and leaving Detroit without her were worse than my disease. Blithe as I wanted to be about it now, I still loved Celeste.

I held his letter and unfolded it. What Dad had to say was all about family, and scrutinizing its contents once more wasn't about to change a thing. But it was worth rereading, particularly the part about Alan. It was still obvious, scouring between the lines, that Dad was just as concerned for Alan as he was for me. His sketchy mention of my brother failed miserably to pull the wool over my eyes.

My troubles were difficult enough, but Alan's, from the looks of it, belonged in a category all their own. Alan was as vulnerable as a wounded rabbit, but the optimistic words Dad had written about him dripped with hope.

The letter didn't have to say it—Dad was pushing through. Strong as he was, Geoffrey Hagan had plenty to shoulder by himself with six sons and two daughters. My moving so far away hadn't helped matters. I hadn't intentionally turned my back on any one of them, but I couldn't argue the truth: I had chosen to leave them behind after Dad remarried. I'd gone my own way. Not all of it had made perfect sense, but it was what I'd done. It was a long time ago.

I put Dad's letter back into its envelope and propped it against the other items that were methodically aligned with my souvenir coffee mug. The decal of a Detroit Police badge on the side of it caused me to wonder what kind of influence made two brothers take such different paths.

Poor choices were catching up with Alan, and my efforts to thwart his mistakes had been random at best. There wasn't anything I could do about him at this point. Tracking Alan down was not realistic right now. It taxed me just to get out of bed in the morning—or show up for the next meal.

I walked to the dining room, anticipating a big spread of eggs, sausage, gravy, and toast as I made my way through the corridor. That and milk. Eating had been less of a task lately. My appetite had improved, and I could smell the sausage from sixty yards away.

The staff bustled about, and chaises lined the wide stretch of walkway, where patients were already lounging. My brothers would have laughed aloud if they'd known how much time I spent stretched out on a chaise. Further, I didn't want them to know. Adjusting to the usefulness of lying in the sunshine was not easy. Adjusting to pure uselessness was just as bad.

Such inactivity was not as ridiculous as I'd once believed. It hadn't made me crazy. Some days I thought it might. But this was a healing place, a tuberculosis sanatorium, and I planned to get out—alive—and not on some stretcher. I stopped to admire the view from the enormous windows that flanked the flagstone passage and wondered how much this institution resembled others of its sort. This one, for sure, had a stunning uniqueness: the omnipresent shadow of death. It hovered overhead like a rain cloud, and the many remedies needed to cheer patients who sat in that shadow required an endless effort.

The strong possibility of never leaving was in the air I breathed. It arose from the dozens of others who lay on cots and most certainly were dying with the disease. It floated up from the patients lining the walls like a randomly painted wainscot of human figures lying in iron beds on verandahs. It wasn't a place to expect to form long-lasting relationships.

I entered the dining area, a spacious, elongated room with tall ceilings and hard-surfaced floors. Numerous round tables and dozens of chairs filled most of the space. The rest of it was stainless steel service equipment and rubber-wheeled carts. I wouldn't have been able to name the color of the walls if I'd been forced to. Something between purple and brown. Muddy, maybe.

Only the warm bodies and table napkins absorbed the sound. Clinking silverware and clanging pots brought the noise level to just less than tolerable.

"Mr. Hagan, join us, won't you?" The man who spoke was seated just inside the doors. His table had a place for one more.

I smiled, misjudging the chair's mobility. It rolled, hitting me in the shin.

"Have to watch out for those things," one of the men said. "They can sure take a notch out of a fella. There's milk on the way, and the usual fare should be coming soon."

"Please, call me Simon. Milk, huh? I like milk. Guess it's a good thing." I lowered myself to the chair. "Remind me again of your names."

"I'm Roger," said the man who had greeted me.

"Roger, yes, of course. It's good to see you again. And Raymond," I said, shaking the other man's hand who sat across the table. "I have a brother named Raymond. I'm the eldest of six brothers. Got a whole slew of siblings back in Kentucky. How about you? Where're you from?"

Roger was from Newark and Raymond from a small town in Indiana. We were as different as three feral cats in a barnyard, but we shared the same goal: getting well and getting out. Rest and recovery were all we could talk about. Between us, we'd had thirty hours sleep the prior night and enough milk in the weeks since we'd arrived to have drained half a dozen dairy cows. Before the steam on the bowlful of eggs had disappeared, we'd passed it around twice.

"You chasing any dreams, Simon?" Raymond asked. "Hoping to get back to Kentucky someday?"

"That's a good question. Difficult to predict. Haven't given much thought to going back South." I laughed to myself. Returning home wasn't even close to my dream. "We've got a university right here, practically in our backyard, tempting me. If I get half a chance, I might look into going to school. But who knows?"

"You're an impressive sort of guy," Raymond said, "but you might want to reconsider schooling. If any of us get out of here alive, we'll be lucky to have someone back home to take us. Not any of that pie-in-the-sky ambition for me. Nah, not me. I'm just wanting to get home."

Roger spoke up. "Those little ladies back there in the kitchen make the best durn eggs I ever tasted." He scooped another fork load into his mouth and swallowed hard with a big swig of milk. "I'd bet you guys I've eaten seven or eight hundred of these things in the six months I've been here. They're putting the weight back on, that's for sure. It'll be hard to eat eggs those New Jersey chickens lay. At least I'm going home, though."

Survival and family. We covered it all, and I didn't notice how quickly the time passed. Our conversation finished over the last drops of coffee, and I wandered out to the veranda.

The cure for TB had everything to do with being outdoors. Eight hours a day of it—weather permitting—couldn't be overemphasized. Preferably in one of the chaise lounges which dotted the lawn. Even with the sunshine it was way too chilly to sit out, but the rocking chairs were taken. Patients with bundled heads and blanket-covered knees sat like upright mummies, breathing like their lives depended on it.

I couldn't have sat another minute, anyway. Compared to Detroit's pace, this pace was for snails—or people in straitjackets. I walked toward the banister, buttoning my coat and turning up my collar as I went, and then stopped to admire the picturesque prairie. The tranquil vista called for a cigarette. There had been dozens of those times since January, but I'd forced myself to ignore the urge. Spitting up blood was one heck of a deterrent. That first smear of red on my handkerchief almost two months back had sent a shiver down my spine that didn't stop for days.

I hiked my foot onto the banister, giving my long legs the stretch they needed. The minimal effort gave me something to do while I pulled a stick of gum from my pocket and methodically unwrapped it. I twirled it between my index and middle fingers, rolling it, smelling it, regarding it as a poor substitute for a Camel, and then propped my elbow on my knee to enjoy once again the sensation of a cigarette. I dropped my head backward, relaxing my neck, and blew an imaginary puff of smoke, enjoying freedom in the immense, wide-open sky, inhaling liberty in the breeze that played with my wavy dark hair.

Chasing a dream.

I rolled the accusation around in my head and dismissed it. Merely envisioning myself a studious college man left me fully charged, and I was savoring the thought when, out of the corner of my eye, I caught sight of a lad heading my way. At first, he blended in with other people inside the building. Then it became obvious that he was moving past them at a hasty clip. He hustled across the corridor and whipped through the exit like a gazelle in flight.

Once outside, he ran straight to me. "Good morning, sir. I hope you're having a good day. Quite a nice one, isn't it, sir?"

"I am, and it is. And how might I help you?" I was certain he had more on his mind than my take on the weather.

"I only need to verify your name." He took a step back and waited for my answer.

"Simon Hagan. Newton's the middle name, if a middle name matters."

"No, sir, just Simon Hagan. This is for you, sir." He pulled a telegram from inside his jacket and handed it to me. "Have a good day." And without another word, he turned and was soon out of sight.

I stared at the name *SIMON HAGAN* on the telegram for what seemed like a lifetime. There was no denying the thing was intended for me. I thought of Dad. Family. Home. A blaring alarm began sounding within. Something was amiss. My hands grew weak, and the telegram shook in their grasp. Eyes were on me. Possibly every patient's eyes followed me as I turned to go.

The walk across the veranda was a short one, past the patients in rockers, past the staff with pasted-on smiles. I lacked what it would take to break into a run, or I would have. It seemed like a mile-long walk to my room, down a never-ending corridor.

The doorknob felt like a rock in my hand, one I wanted to throw at the bad news I held in my hand.

I stood with the telegram in the privacy of my room, dithering for as long as I could. Letting it remain unopened another minute wasn't going to change its contents. I took a deep breath and unfolded the yellow parchment. My heart stopped beating. Beneath the Western Union heading and *DETROIT MICH 347P Feb 28 1929* were a scant five words.

I dropped to my knees. The telegram drifted down to the floor beside me.

Chapter 62

———⟫·◆·⟪———

The nurse must have seen me enter my room. Not just any nurse. The almighty Fierce Fairweather.

The knock on my door was hers. Not another nurse could, or would, rap nonstop on it the way she did. It must have echoed down the entire length of the corridor at Saint Andrew's Sanatorium. I was surprised she could get away with making that much noise with so many patients trying to get tens of hours of sleep.

"Mr. Hagan, it's Mrs. Fairweather."

Living here for weeks had taught me to recognize her voice with the first word out of her mouth. I didn't doubt for a second she wanted in. She surely wasn't knocking for the sake of disturbing all the victims of tuberculosis.

I got up from my knees, still clutching in my hand the telegram I'd been handed not ten minutes ago on the veranda. "Come in," I said as I purposefully walked in the opposite direction. Five words on a Western Union parchment page had bowled me over. I'd since regained my composure.

"Time for milk or exercise? Or do I get to go with you for a walk on the lawn? Perhaps a game of croquet?"

"Mr. Hagan," she said, serious-faced, "I'm checking on you. That's all. About half the time I can't tell if you're kidding." She nodded at the telegram. "Not trying to stick my nose in, but you're surely in a happy frame today. We recommend that, you know. Good news there?"

"A precise diagnosis if I've ever heard one," I replied. "Good news, indeed, and happy doesn't quite do it justice." I had no reason to hide my overwhelming joy. "Mrs. Fairweather, my girl's going to marry me! Celeste

Mallory is going to marry me!"

"My goodness! That's wonderful, Mr. Hagan, absolutely wonderful! But you need to simmer down. You're a sick man, I must remind you. But this should go far in helping you along the road to recovery."

"I couldn't agree more," I said, studying Celeste's telegram, burying her initial reaction to the news that I had TB. "Listen, thanks, Mrs. Fairweather. If you'll excuse me, I need to call her. On second thought, there's way too much to say in three minutes."

"Now, Mr. Hagan, don't overdo it. Don't underestimate the consequences." Her set mouth and stern fixation on me served as a warning. "In any case, you're so much better off without stress."

I took Nurse Fairweather's concern in stride and listened as she continued on to the next door in the corridor. Already I was fighting thoughts of the last time Celeste and I had been together. Confusion stung like the dickens. And tracking Alan was a whole other ball game. If his circumstances weren't stressful, I didn't know what was. Avoiding stress seemed unrealistic.

I left the telegram on the bed, walked down the corridor, and took a seat in a rocker on the veranda. In the wide openness of New Mexico's outdoors, I breathed the refreshing cool of the February air and let it clear my head.

On top of everything else, I was still chasing a simple dream: staying alive. And with Celeste's answer, I had another reason to try.

Chapter 63

Friday morning, the first day of March, the sunrise failed to awaken me. Fifteen minutes might have passed before the chirping birds outside my window fussed enough to roust me. The agonizing despondency that had robbed me of a reason to live since the day Celeste had turned her back on me was gone. Although there was no hurry to seize any part of the day ahead, personally, I had an agenda.

I wrapped my robe around my skinny frame, which seemed to want to remain that way, and opened the curtains on a beautiful Albuquerque day. The birds, still insistent on making their presence known, took flight. Not a creature or foe on the sanatorium grounds showed any signs of life. But the spring dew on the grass and the fresh leaves on the trees were a sight to behold. Compared to the frozen tundra that was Detroit's springtime, this was heaven.

Celeste's telegram lay open where I'd left it, the gold parchment reminding me of my neglect. Yesterday's date, along with the Western Union heading, was significantly imprinted on my brain.

WESTERN UNION DETROIT MICH 347P Feb 28 1929
MISERABLE CANNOT LIVE WITHOUT YOU
CELESTE

Five words. Five little words, and my world was turned upside down. I'd needed the hours since their arrival to unpack their message, and now, in a letter to Celeste, I tried to put into words the desires of my heart.

I paced like a caged animal in the confines of my small room, untangling the emotions that had split us apart on our last night together, pondering what to say, and how to say it.

She can't marry me out of pity, I thought. *She has to understand the depths of my love.*

I started the letter and began to let go of the hurt. In forcing my soul through the wringer, I put to the test my ability to trust her again. I expressed my love as clearly as I could, hoping its power could cover the multitude of my shortcomings.

Finished, I licked the back of the envelope and sealed it, grateful for the solitude that had given me single-mindedness. After addressing it, I dropped it off at the front desk to be posted.

⟫◆⟪

Having mailed the most important letter ever, I went through the remainder of the morning, determined to face the reality of tuberculosis. I rested on a lounge in the wide-windowed corridor until I thought I'd go insane and napped in a rocker with a book, my head slumping on my chest with drool running from my mouth. I'd consumed enough milk to gag a nursing gorilla and had basked in the sunshine until my earwax melted. I'd had the course.

Compared to being a policeman, this inactivity made me feel like a pansy. But seeing the repercussions of not taking care of myself—or not letting others take care of me—made me want to cooperate.

I folded the blanket that had wrapped my body and was on my way inside when, from where I stood, I could make out the familiar gait of a lone figure striding across the lawn toward me. The slope of his shoulders, the tilt of his head told me it was my father.

I went out to meet him, walking at first to be certain my eyes weren't deceiving me, running when there was no doubt.

And when we embraced, Dad broke. "Son," he said, overcome with grief, "Alan's gone." He stepped back, holding my shoulders—the only thing he had within a thousand miles to hold on to. "Simon . . ." Longingly, his gaze met mine. "We lost him." He embraced me again, his body quaking.

We stood together in the noonday sun, his tiny suitcase lying in the grassy shoots on the embankment beside it, clinging to each other as if our world had come to an end. Close to a year had gone by since I'd seen Dad. The last time had been in the summer, on the farm, when the corn crops had been harvest-ripe and the burley tobacco had waved low and dark green.

We started toward the sanatorium, and the only sound came from the soles of our shoes on the grass.

Chapter 64

❝Nice weather here for March," Dad finally said. "You're looking as well as can be expected. Wiry. But fairly good color." He nodded to the patients aligned in their wheelchairs and enjoying the view of the Sandia Mountains.

Unlike me, Dad hadn't come here for the plentiful sunshine and arid climate. His hair was tinged gray at the temples, and new creases had formed in his face. But for a man in his early fifties, he appeared sturdy. Even so, it wasn't easy knowing he'd come an extremely long distance to be here with me to soften the blow.

I directed us up the ramp to the sanatorium's side entrance and past a simple colonnade that shielded those patients whose delicate balance between life and death required privacy.

We turned a corner, and I pointed toward the commons. Dad gave it a once-over and commented on the comfort Saint Andrew's afforded. It was old—who knew *how* old.

"This way, Dad."

We were eye to eye, although he seemed inches shorter now. We reached the dining area and seated ourselves in the open-air section, which was noticeably newer-looking, fresher. Pale yellow walls and light-stained hardwoods reflected the sunshine. Food arrived on a cart, and a server set plates in front of us.

Dad immediately helped himself to the offerings.

"When did it happen?" I asked.

He sat across the table eating cauliflower. Weariness showed in his eyes, but at least he was eating. From the looks of it, he was hungry. He wasn't answering and instead, buttered a biscuit.

The food was decent, but for me it had no appeal. Niceties of any type couldn't alter the finality of Alan's senseless death at twenty-four. I felt sick to my stomach. I let Dad be and sat still, not having the wherewithal to make idle conversation.

"A week ago Wednesday," he finally said, wiping his mouth. His eyes moistened. He took a sip of coffee and blinked hard. "Syphilis. It's a dreadful death." He looked away. "Wednesday the twentieth at four in the morning. The hospital waited till six to telephone." He began rolling out the details as though they were on a scroll in his mind. "Alan came home in a pine box. Saturday. We buried him the same day."

I wanted to know more, but I didn't think either of us was up to it. A glass of milk stood in front of my untouched plate. It was all I could do to drink it. My hand shook the glass as I lifted it to swallow. Guilt at the ending to my brother's story wracked me.

"Whoever in San Francisco took his body ruined everything about him. His hair was larded down. Red curls were a slick mess. His . . . No dimple. No—"

"Dad—"

"Don't know how I even recognized him, 'cept for that scar on his neck where the blasted mare kicked him."

I wished I'd skipped the milk. I could feel it souring inside me. "In a way," I said, "I see it like this: Alan would be alive if I'd stayed on the farm. Maybe if I'd stayed another year or two—"

"Wait just a minute, son."

"No, sir." I wanted my say. "If he hadn't followed me to Detroit, he wouldn't have been exposed to nightlife and city women. Whores, so prevalent and so available. There for the taking. We couldn't walk down the street that they didn't come swanking. He saw too much. Not that anything like that happened, but he came to Detroit with an obsession. He seemed bent on a life of constant pleasure. It's my fault, Dad."

"Are you finished?"

Dad's Adam's apple rose and dropped. "Alan frequented the low-life dives. Stuffy, smelly, airless, titillating dives. Loose women enticed him." I could tell what he was saying ripped him to pieces. But he pressed on.

"Apparently they were his addiction. Him—not you. That wasn't your fault. This is why I came, Simon. You're at a fork in the road. Lots of decisions after the dust settles here, with your health and all." He pushed his plate aside and propped his elbows on the table, clasping his hands. "Alan is gone. You've got to go forward, son, for your own sake, not mine. But I have to say this much. Doesn't matter how you see it now. God's divine providence pulled you out of Detroit."

I cracked my knuckles, trying to guard the force of unchecked anger that rose inside me. "God's providence wasn't there when Mother was torn to pieces, Dad. Probably not there when Alan died, either."

He looked sorrowfully at me. "Are you shaking your fist at God? Is that it, Simon? God's to blame?"

Out of the corner of my eye, I picked up on Mrs. Fairweather coming our way.

"You were a God-fearin' youngster, Simon. I don't know where you stand now, but you can't run from God. Something ugly happened with Alan that none of us can change. My reckless, redheaded boy will never return."

I heard every word he was saying, and I knew it was true. Even so, I was distracted. Lack of concentration seemed to accompany my illness.

While I fidgeted, Dad shifted gears. "Alan's life was based on lies," he said earnestly. "It was consumed by them."

I saw my nurse coming to our table, but she pivoted away at the last minute, her white shoes squeaking. The fleeing form in a white dress and cap disappeared behind a service cart, and I breathed easier.

Dad was still talking, unaware of what had transpired in the background. He spoke with deepening frankness. "And the woman I've loved with all my heart, even to this day, is gone." He paused. "Hannah's sure a fine wife for me now, but your mother was my love, my joy." He leaned back on his chair, rubbing his chin. "She'll, of course, never return, either," he said quietly. "I'll see her in Glory . . . be with her in Eternity. I can't say that, for certain, about Alan." His eyes locked with mine. "I want to be certain, son, that I'll see you there."

⇒◆⇐

The racket around us had been steadily increasing as dishes were scraped and cleared from the unoccupied tables. Patients were making their way past us and out of the dining hall. Dad continued to watch my every move, ignoring the disturbance.

I saw Fierce Fairweather across the way speaking with another lady garbed in white, their mouths moving in rapid unison. My favorite nurse appeared to be tracking me.

Grateful to have a chance to avoid Dad's admonition, I motioned to her.

"We have a guest," I told Dad. "Fierce Fairweather is coming over."

She sidled up to our table, apparently not eager to engage in conversation. "Mr. Hagan, you've not eaten a bite," she said in a scolding tone.

My father stood up. "Hello, ma'am. I'm pleased to make your acquaintance. I'm Geoffrey Hagan, Simon's father."

"I think I see a resemblance. I'm trying my best to fatten him, Mr. Hagan. Can't if he doesn't eat. Please, sit."

"Dad, meet Mrs. Fairweather, lovingly known as Fierce Fairweather."

"Pleased, ma'am, but we best be going. I'm wearing him out." He pushed his chair to the table.

"You can't refuse to eat," she said, cutting her eyes at me. "He's a fighter—this one. Mullygrubs every now and again." Her tattling got a wink from my father.

I took my pills, downed my second glass of milk, and was done with it.

Her fierceness continued unabated. "But he's a charmer, and I'll bet that girl he's marrying thinks so, too. Now, if you'll excuse me, I need to get on with my rounds." She turned and strode across the corridor.

"Marrying? And Fierce Fairweather?" My father's curiosity was piqued.

We walked the short distance beyond the main corridor and then turned onto a narrow one. The pungent odor of medicine floated through the air as a reminder of ill health and affliction.

"How long are you here, Dad? Not meaning your question has a long answer. Simply put, Celeste sent a telegram. The rest of it is complicated." I nodded to my room just as we arrived at the door. "So, this is where I sleep my ten hours, write letters, and such. I wrote one back to her after she told me she'd changed her mind. I posted it this morning."

The room suddenly struck me as exceedingly sterile. Dad's all-black clothing contrasted starkly with the room, like a tree trunk set against a snowy backdrop.

"I'm here for the night. Train leaves at ten after nine tomorrow morning." He propped his bag against the wall.

It was an odd arrangement. I wasn't sure of the rules for accommodations. It didn't matter. Dad was staying with me, even if I had to sleep on the floor. Humbled by his immense effort to bolster my spirits, I was determined to be respectful. This time, I hoped I could leave God out of it.

"Take that chair, please," I said. "Have a seat."

"I could be wrong, but I don't believe whatever held him could possibly have satisfied his yearning. Depravity's an addiction." Dad noticed Mother's Bible on the table beside him. "It took him further than he wanted to go and cost him more than he was prepared to pay. Bondage cost him his life, son."

I had nothing to add that hadn't already been said. "How are Mary and Charlotte taking it?"

"Who can say? Your sisters . . . and brothers, too . . . were just pups the last time they saw him. They'll move on. All but the youngest, and of course, Hannah's and my two babies, have families of their own. We have no other course but to go on."

He picked up the Bible. "It's been nine years, son. Nine years since your mother passed. This is the best thing of hers you can own." He took a laborious breath before continuing. "You left home and carried a burden that no young person should. *No one* should." He returned the Bible to the table and tapped its cover. "This book right here is truth. Lies are just another form of bondage if you believe them. Don't, Simon. Don't believe them." He couldn't sit still. He got up and went to the window and for a time stood motionless before the view. His gray hair shimmered in the setting sun. "Alan saw the awful thing that happened to your mother. Even if he didn't see the bear maul her, he saw plenty when you carried her into the house. Not wanting you to misunderstand what I'm saying here, but he was never the same." He stepped away from the window. "What are your plans, son, once you leave here? Sure sounds like Celeste is in the picture."

"Yes, sir. If we can get over a few hurdles. My letter should reach her in a few days. Then we'll have a lot to discuss. Right now, there's just a lot up in the air." I went to the window and draped my arm around his shoulder. "Dad, it means everything to me that you'd come all the way out here."

"Well, there's no greater joy than knowing you walk in truth." He studied me intently. "My deepest desire for you, son, is that you'll live the life God has planned for you."

"Don't give up on me, Dad."

Chapter 65

———◇———

"No, Mr. Hagan, nothing." The oversized lady behind the desk at Saint Andrew's was clearly humoring me. She double-checked the mail cubbies, A-Z, searching for a letter for me. "I'm sorry. There's nothing here today. Perhaps tomorrow."

"Ma'am, it's urgent. Would I be able to make a collect call?"

She raised her eyebrows at me, doubtfully and disgustingly businesslike. "Three minutes. We can't tie up the lines. And it will have to be after seven."

"Seven it is. I'll be back. Much obliged, ma'am."

Having waited several weeks and certain my letter had reached her by now, I couldn't wait any longer to call Celeste. Not hearing its effect was killing me. If she'd changed her mind again, I needed to know.

Promptly at seven I was back at the desk, explaining to a different lady my dilemma. After insisting that my call was urgent, that it would be brief, that it would be collect, and that I needed a tiny bit of privacy, she caved in.

"All right, young man. Give me the number."

She tried Celeste's number while I paced—and waited.

"How many times has it rung?" I asked. "What are they say—"

The lady lifted a hand to shush me. "That number is no longer in service. I'm sorry."

For a minute I felt like puking. Not sure what my next step would be, I returned to my room. Unable to sleep, I prayed. It seemed like the thing to do.

The next morning, I was back at the desk with a plan. Fortunately, a new face awaited me with the same old repellants. Won over, the polite lady picked up the telephone along with the Mallorys' number written on a slip of paper.

I could hear Virginia's voice coming through the receiver, but I couldn't believe what I heard. "Flagstaff. Miss Mallory's in Flagstaff, Arizona."

I leaned on the counter between me and the polite lady. "May I talk to her? Please. I'll pay for the call."

Misgivings showed in her eyes, but she handed over the receiver.

"Virginia, it's Simon."

"Simon, hello." She sounded different, reserved. "Certainly hope you're on the mend."

"Yes, doing well." I jumped in with both feet. "Where's Celeste?"

"Flagstaff. With Rachel."

"But why?"

"Well, Rachel has her hands full. Children and all. Celeste's helping." She hesitated. "You love her, don't you?"

"Of course!" I said emphatically. "You know I love her! And I've got to reach her."

"She decided to go to Rachel's after she didn't hear from you. She's not here."

The polite lady was now waving her arms in protest, and I was struggling to get the whole story inside three minutes.

"I see. Well, there's a letter." I wiped the sweat from my face. "I know she's not there, Virginia. I've tried telephoning. What about my letter?"

"I don't know."

I thought I might've stopped breathing. "Okay, my letter should forward to you. And when you get it, you'll see that she gets it?"

"I will. Sure."

"Okay. Thanks, Virginia. Sorry to cut this short."

Left with the clear understanding that Celeste and I had become like ships passing in the night, I had no recourse but to wait for my letter to go from Celeste's now-vacated apartment to the Mallorys and on to Arizona. Everything else felt sketchy. It was like putting puzzle pieces together in my brain. Rachel, I figured, needed help with her children. Maybe Rachel's husband Albert needed help with his road construction office, and Celeste, not hearing from me, had decided to make a fresh start.

Exasperated, I went to my room, retrieved her telegram, and sat down to stare once more at it. Her five words held me no less spellbound than they had the moment when I'd first read them almost three weeks ago.

I stared at the ceiling. Police work, I decided, had been far more predictable than loving a woman.

Meanwhile, my eyelids closed on a sorry situation.

Chapter 66

Hindsight told me I should have called Celeste the minute I'd gotten her telegram. Bad judgment seemed to be defining my choices. Blaming it on tuberculosis wasn't getting me anywhere. Treatments hadn't stopped me from blaming everything on anything. On the other hand, the regimen of the Albuquerque air, March sunshine, a healthy diet, rest, and more rest had weakened the bacterial infection in my lungs. It was confined, and the threat of more disease spreading through the lymph nodes and bloodstream had been reduced. The risk of death was gradually decreasing, and the more I learned about medicine, the more I considered becoming a doctor. The thought didn't seem as unrealistic as it once had.

I couldn't do diddly-squat, however, about the insipid crawl of events that had failed to restore my relationship with Celeste. After a month of misguided communication and misinterpreted advice, the convoluted mess showed no signs of improvement. As far as I knew, my letter was still on its way to Celeste.

I was making a nuisance of myself at the telephone desk, talking to Virginia, trying to track my letter to Celeste. Eventually, I pushed Virginia to give me the number so I could contact Celeste at Rachel's home.

Most of the desk personnel made it clear they weren't excited to see me coming.

"This, Mr. Hagan, is not a public telephone." The large lady I'd dealt with initially glared at me. "Even though you're willing to pay for calls, the point is, we cannot allow misuse of lines that are intended for other purposes, not personal calls." She turned her back to me, satisfied our conversation was over.

"Mrs. Curtis," I said softly, "I'm sure you, being a married woman and all, understand a whole lot more about love than I do."

She waited perhaps a second before turning to face me.

"I've failed miserably trying to convince the girl that I love to marry me," I explained. "That telephone right there is my only hope."

It was true. My redemption hung by a telephone wire. Talking with Celeste, even only briefly, was all-important. I was desperate to hear her voice.

"Three minutes." She hunkered on the desk and, with the receiver in hand and a whale's eye look for me, asked, "What's the number?" Mrs. Curtis reached the operator and connected with someone at Rachel's home.

A moment later, Celeste came on the line. Her voice was as musical as raindrops on an open windowsill.

I could barely speak over the lump in my throat. "Celeste, I love you more than life itself. I've told you so often before." I cupped the receiver and spoke in a whisper. "We can only talk a couple of minutes. Just know this: I want to marry you. I wrote it all in a letter."

I could hear her crying. "You could've called the minute my telegram arrived," she said through sobs.

"I know that now, of course! I should've sent a telegram, but I wanted to pour it all out to you, so I wrote it in a letter. We can sort it out—together. Not apart, Celeste. Your telegram changed everything." The words tumbled from my heart.

"You should've called."

"Looking back, yes, but there was too much to say in three minutes. I thought a letter would reach you in a matter of days. That's why you didn't hear—"

Mrs. Curtis abandoned her post without making eye contact. I last saw her shuffling resolutely across the corridor.

"I need time, Simon."

"Yes, take all you need." I could feel her mistrust. If it wasn't a stand-off, it could have fooled me. Our conversation hadn't resolved a thing, and opportunity was slipping through our fingers like the days of March that had come and gone.

I couldn't make good on allowing Celeste to take her time. Lively telephone calls going between the Mallory household and myself were enough to keep a switchboard operator in business. Virginia was my ally in Michigan. Mrs. Curtis was my ally at the desk here in Albuquerque.

"A call, Mr. Hagan," someone said, rapping on my door. "Hurry."

That was all it took to get me back to the desk. Mrs. Curtis had her purse under her arm when I got there, ready to leave as soon as she handed me the receiver.

But it was Charlie Mallory, not Virginia, waiting for me to answer, and when he finished informing me that it was high time for me to be reconciled with Celeste, I wasn't taking too kindly to his interference.

"With all due respect, Charlie, you're outside the boundary. I don't want to lose her, either, obviously, but it's a little difficult to reconcile with Celeste when she's pushing me away, don't you think?"

"You need to reach her, Simon. My daughter's in love with you."

"Well, if she hadn't rejected me the minute she found out I had TB—"

"Listen here." Charlie's intensity caught me off guard. "You can't treat her like you did Rachel."

"I agree. She's fragile," I said, trying to remain civil. "But she most certainly can come across otherwise, Charlie. I think we need to give this a rest." I paused a moment and then tried to change the topic. "Any update on Sam's probe into Lieutenant Dugan's criminal amnesia?"

Too late. Poorly timed. There was a sickening hush on the other end of the telephone. Our conversation took a nose dive, and the sour note on which it ended drove a stake in my heart.

———⟫◆⟪———

If Charlie's unsolicited advice wasn't enough to rile me, the next bout of family interference was. This time it was Rachel on the line.

"Celeste is my baby sister, Simon," came the familiar voice over the telephone line. "I love her too much to let the ridiculousness of this whole thing continue. Your letter arrived."

I was listening. I hated the pause. Rachel was hedging.

"When she opened it, Celeste wanted to quit her job at my husband's office and go straight to Albuquerque to be with you. But the two of you are so peculiar! She changed her mind. Now that it's been weeks . . ."

The reception was garbled, but I got the gist of what Rachel was saying. I pulled Mrs. Curtis's empty chair over and sat down, pressing the receiver closer to my ear.

"Simon," she said in a tone that made me feel weak, "Celeste is pregnant."

My heart stopped.

Before I could speak, Rachel continued. "There are complications. She almost lost the baby." Rachel began to cry. "Yesterday. She almost miscarried yesterday, Simon, after your letter came. She's in the hospital. It's not my place to tell you all this, but there it is. Celeste wanted to give up on you. When she didn't hear from you, she thought, well, you know what she thought."

I sat as if I were a stone. "When can I talk to her? I have to talk to her, Rachel. When will she leave the hospital?"

"Tuesday."

I stood up, feeling stir-crazy.

Nurse Fairweather was approaching me at a purposeful pace, a tray in hand.

"I can't leave here, Rachel, not for two months, and not with TB. I shouldn't get near Celeste." I tried to dismiss the nurse with a look, but she motioned me to sit back down. "We'll talk, please, on Tuesday after Celeste gets home." I stood up once more, resisting Fierce Fairweather's instruction. "Rachel . . . thanks." I hung up the phone.

"Sit down, Mr. Hagan," my nurse said. "Now! And drink this milk." She shoved the glass at me. "You look like you're going to faint. And for your information, Mr. Hagan, you'll not be here for two months. It'll be four, at least. You're looking at July. Maybe August."

Chapter 67

Dust gathered above the treetops as the evenings grew late. Week after lonely week crawled by until time was on my side.

Springtime pushed flowers outside my window toward the sunlight. Days were getting longer.

I could feel my strength retuning, and nothing but the slow ticking of the clock could wreak havoc on my spirit.

A smattering of patients and staff were milling about outside the sanatorium in the June sunshine. With dinnertime nearing, I had the long expanse of the open-air sanctuary to myself. The boarded floor passageway creaked as I walked across to the railing on the other side.

"Celeste," I muttered to myself as I walked out to the veranda, "don't give up on me."

I fished a stick of gum from my shirt pocket. Even after all the time I'd spent not smoking, the urge had come back with a vengeance. I chewed on my knuckle, gazing at the Albuquerque sky.

"Dear God in heaven," I said under my breath. The longer I stood, the longer I prayed, and the more I prayed, the more I argued.

Hazy peaks of the glorious mountain range in the east mesmerized me. I sensed a power so near I could almost reach out and touch it. But to the west, where crimson and orange blazed on the early evening horizon, four hundred miles of rugged road separated me from Celeste and the baby she was carrying—so far away that I couldn't begin to reach them.

The sun began dropping behind the trees that bordered the grounds at Saint Andrew's. I went over and sat on a porch rocker. I was seeing every-

275

thing differently this evening, and in my mind, I found very little consolation, being confined to a sanatorium.

"Celeste," I whispered again, after such a long time of brooding that I'd lost track of it, "don't give up on us. Just a few short weeks to go."

With every reason to believe I would regain the momentum to do what I'd set out to do, I waited, as if I might absorb from the powerful view a way of controlling the future. My shot at my share of normalcy was just around the corner.

⟫◆⟪

"Good morning, Mr. Hagan. How about getting dressed?" Nurse Fairweather was rapping on the door. "It's a beautiful day out there. Check in with me later, after you've finished breakfast."

I crawled out of bed and pulled back the curtains. It was early, and the July sun had only just begun to rise. It didn't matter. This day had taken forever to arrive, as I'd expected it would, without much of a send-off, let alone one remotely similar to my father's in Hopkinsville so long ago. Not only was *he* not here, but no one was, save the staff of nurses I'd come to know over the past seven months.

With plenty of time to think while I packed my suitcase, I reflected on my fight for justice in Detroit's lawless arena. Those years had become foreign, belonging to history, except for the lingering suspicion of Roman's death. I couldn't let that remnant go.

Repulsed, I shook off the thought and skimmed the acceptance letter from the University of New Mexico that topped the stack of mail on the bureau. Next to it was my itemized list of anticipated expenses. If I had wanted to ditch my plans to enroll in premed, I might have let the dollar signs discourage me, especially with a baby due in late September. But I was dead set on working my way through college.

As I neatly packed the mail and miscellany on top of my clothing, I told myself an acting role or two at a local theater shouldn't sap every tidbit of my energy. Auditions that had been printed in the newspaper intrigued me. I wasn't expecting to be a celebrity, but there was money to be made.

With Nurse Fairweather's encouragement and coaxing, I was somewhat persuaded I had enough good looks and talent. I could even carry a tune and whistle like a bird. If other attributes were called for, I fully intended to acquire them. I'd applied by mail and gotten a date for an audition.

I pressed the latches on my suitcase in place, took hold of the handle, and made a final study of the cube that had been my healing retreat since January. It was closure on a lengthy chapter in my twenty-seven years and two months on this earth. Hopes were reemerging like the green faces of crocuses that had poked through frozen crusts on that wintery day when I'd left Detroit. Life had whirred past, and my youthful pursuits had changed. Celeste and the baby were my priority.

With my health restored, I made some promises to myself. In a matter of a few hours, I would be back in the running, jobless and financially shaky, weak but healed.

I rounded the corner and ambled through the corridor in search of the fierce one.

"You've sure got a lot of determination, Mr. Hagan," she said. "For a man as sick as you've been, you're going to have to watch yourself. Going to college and getting married . . . I'm just saying."

But mapped out, the plans looked perfect after a long, dormant existence. Now so close to being released from the sanatorium at Saint Andrew's, I couldn't imagine bad judgment would ever be my downfall.

"I'm going to keep close tabs on you," she said. "And of course, Dr. Siebel needs test results and evaluations after a month."

"You've been the best, Mrs. Fairweather. You know, of course, it was all in fun—the fierce part." I reached out for a hug.

She welcomed it.

Chapter 68

⟫⬥⟪

I stepped up to the counter, unable to miss the bright yellow calendar that hung on the wall above the clerk's head. Lettered in black was today's date: Monday, August 19. After buying my ticket for the westbound ride to Flagstaff, I boarded and, along with several other passengers, rolled out of the bus station on a Pickwick-Greyhound at 12:05 in the afternoon.

Albert was there to meet me in his pickup when I arrived in Flagstaff at 6:23 that evening. Had it not been for his heavy, muscular build and immense shoulders, I might not have recognized the guy who'd married Rachel. Not one thing about him screamed Catholic.

I must have looked like a beanpole as I stood next to him while the driver retrieved my suitcase from beneath the bus. He reached to pick it up as the driver dropped it along with other bags on the curb.

I was quicker. "I've got it," I said. "Thanks." My thoughts were less amicable. *I can handle my bag, sonny, whether I look like it or not. Thanks just the same.* It had nothing to do with Rachel. Bygones were bygones. "Nice roadster you've got here. New one." I ran my hand across the tan leather seat. "How's the road-building business?"

"Good. We're on one of them. State Route 89, soon to become 79." He gave me a bigheaded glance. "Model A. Right, it's new. Ford makes 'em good. And the stock market—it's going nuts. The thing's hit a peak, and now prices are declining. I dunno." He kept on rattling off the facts, eyes on the road. "Unemployment's on the rise, weak agriculture, large bank loans that can't be liquidated. Not here, though. We're sort of insulated. You doing well, Simon, all things considered?"

"I recognize how good they are. Agreed. About Ford, anyway." I concentrated on the earth-moving equipment to my right. "I don't keep up with the stock market. But yes, Ford makes a great automobile. And all things considered, yes, I'm glad to be alive. The main thing now is Celeste and the baby. Very excited about that."

"Been a while, huh? I know she's . . . Simon, honestly, I can't even describe it. Happy's too tame for it. She's one thrilled little momma. You're doing the right thing, marrying her."

I shifted on the seat, agitated. "Well, it's not out of a sense of obligation, Albert. I love her. That's it. Celeste is quite simply the spark in my life."

He pulled into a nice-looking neighborhood and drove a block. After he turned into the driveway and switched off the engine, I jumped out. Rachel was holding the front door open. All I saw was the gladness in her eyes.

I ran through the front door of her home, bypassing her with a hurried greeting, and rushed in the direction she pointed. Celeste was sitting up in bed, her girlish grin spread from one side of her face to the other, her arms outstretched. It had been eight long months.

I sat on the side of the bed and sunk like a flat tire against her body. Tears streamed from my eyes, and I held her so close it scared me. "Am I hurting you . . . or him . . . or her?"

"No," she whispered. "I thought I'd never see you again. Hold me till this baby comes, if that's possible."

The faint scent of her skin was as sweet as a flower. The adoration in her eyes thrilled me, and when we kissed, I wanted it to never end.

I curled up next to her, feeling the baby kick as my hand lay across Celeste's tummy. "I love you more than you can possibly know," I said between our sweet kisses. "Can someone close the window, and we'll let the world go by?"

"What could we possibly want but this? Simon, I love you so much."

———◆———

Dawn broke shortly after five a.m. the next day. I couldn't have imagined the elation I felt.

By nine I was knocking on Celeste's door. "Can I see the bride? Heck! Let me in, or I'll break down the door."

"Ah, sweet prince. Where hast thou been? Come in at once, or I shall faint."

Her laughter was contagious. I flung the door open, laughing like I hadn't in a hundred years. "Most beautiful bride, where hast thou been all these many months whilst I languished, deep in TB?"

"You are beyond silly," she said. "Come here and suffocate me with a kiss."

And the morning passed with the giddiness of two lovers waiting to begin our lives as one. Between spilled orange juice on the sheets and toast crumbs on the pillowcase, we couldn't keep our hands off each other.

"Stop it!" she said. "You're upsetting this baby. You'll make me deliver before we're married."

I stopped with the tickling, and we talked. We reminisced, and we planned. We kissed through lunch and beyond. At one o'clock in the afternoon, the justice of the peace showed up with Bible in hand. Rachel followed him into the room, laid a bouquet of white flowers in Celeste's arms, and stood on the far side of the bed. Celeste, propped against a backdrop of pillows, couldn't have looked more beautiful.

I was as nervous as any bridegroom. Lodged deep inside was the desire to salvage the sweetness of the first moment we were one, a desire that had caught us both off guard. I respected what I knew Celeste held in her heart for the man she loved—the beautiful union with the person she would spend the rest of her life beside.

I was thankful to be that person.

The ceremony was short. Neither of us were taking the old-fashioned vows lightly. Our vows were sacred. That much I'd learned from my father, and that much I held on to more than I could, or ever would, say.

I knelt by her bedside, and a skinny little man in street clothes pronounced us man and wife. And I kissed my bride while Rachel cried like a baby.

The tenderness of the four days that followed were all we had before it was time for me to return to Albuquerque. Torn by our passion to be together, we planned for my return to Flagstaff and, along with it, our move with the newborn to my apartment in Albuquerque.

"I'll have it ready for the three of us," I told her. "You, me, and our baby.

As long as my health checks remain as good as the last one, we're set." The sound of it was marvelous. "An apartment with the Sandia Mountains for a backdrop, and a tiny bed for you and me. So tiny, Celeste, that you'll be everywhere I turn."

Her heart-shaped lips melted me. I kissed them over and over.

"You'll make a fine doctor, Si," she said, teasing me. "Such a nice bed-side manner."

"Whoa, Nellie. I think we're missing a few steps, don't you think? Picture a few years of college. Then medical school. Then—"

She stopped me with a kiss, pulling away to ask, "And who is Nellie?"

"Maybe this one." I laid my hand on the immense balloon that was Celeste's tummy.

———⊷◆⊶———

Asinine as it was, my audition was scheduled for four o'clock on Saturday. If the bus wasn't late, I'd make it back to Albuquerque with an hour to spare. Financially, I was depending on the opportunity. Celeste and I both felt it was one I couldn't pass up. On top of that, my classes were set to begin at the University of New Mexico the following Monday.

Chapter 69

⟫•◆•⟪

Backstage hand. Gopher. Two-bit acting role. If it paid, I found a way to do it during the remaining days of a sweltering August in New Mexico. As steamy as the weather was, it was no match for the love-filled letters and telephone calls going on between Celeste and me. We found ways to communicate while Celeste remained on bed rest in Flagstaff and I prepared a place for us in Albuquerque.

As September 20 approached, all I could think about was my desire for her, if only to be near her and hold her in my arms. Barring any relapse on my part, I'd be on the 12:05 p.m. bus to Flagstaff to be with her on her due date.

⟫•◆•⟪

The trip was not unlike the one I'd taken a month prior, and Albert's gunmetal-blue roadster pickup was waiting when I got off the bus.

He looked anxious and didn't take the time to shake hands. "Grab your things! Celeste went into labor at two-something this morning. We need to get you to the hospital. I don't know the latest."

We hardly spoke as the Ford zigzagged through the streets of Flagstaff. Once inside the hospital, I raced down the maternity ward, dodging nurses and carts until a woman half my height stopped me.

"If you're Simon Hagan," the tiny nurse said with a smile, "you have a six-pound, one-ounce baby girl. Your wife's expecting you. Room 211."

The sight of Celeste lying in the hospital bed asleep—the mother of my child, so delicate, so spent, so beautiful—brought me to my knees. The

282

wasted year on the sidelines of my life along with the thrill of being a police-man were irrelevant, and Nellie Virginia's baptism in the hospital room made my entire past irrelevant. A fastidious nurse held her, wrapped in a blanket, while Albert took a photograph.

The aftereffects of a troubled delivery kept Celeste in the hospital with the nursing baby for two weeks. Once the complexities were overcome and the baby gained a few more ounces, the three of us returned to Rachel and Albert's home.

Begrudgingly, a few days later and in the wee hours of the morning, I boarded the Pickwick-Greyhound back to Albuquerque to strengthen the foundation I'd begun. In my wallet was the small photograph Albert had taken of Nellie Virginia. I took it out, adoring the face of my child, and then turned it over and wrote the initials *NVH* and *Sept. 1929.*

I woke up five hours into the trip, stiff-necked and dry-mouthed. I could see up ahead the overhang of the train station in the small Pueblo settlement of Isleta. With no reason to stop, the driver slowed the bus as I and the other fifteen or so passengers bump-bumped across the tracks. The quiet reigning over the sunny fields of the age-old Indian town left me a bit heavyhearted—if for no other reason than my observation of its seemingly slow-paced desolation.

With fourteen miles to go, I sat up in the seat, trying to alter my dishev-eled appearance, anticipating the happiness we'd share when Celeste would arrive on this same bus in a few weeks.

Chapter 70

And the day couldn't have come too soon. With my family reuniting, in addition to my having landed a small part in a play, delivering my first spoken lines, life was good. Except for my somewhat crabby neighbor, Ronald Reagan, and my concern that he would continue to be a nuisance, I was on top of the world. The apartment I'd painstakingly prepared was ready.

Waiting at the station for the eastbound bus from Flagstaff, I paced from one end to the other, on the lookout for the rounded, cream-colored top of the familiar motor coach. My eyes were peeled for the first glimpse of it coming from the west.

I took a look at my watch, holding its face so the sun's glare didn't distort its hands: 11:09. The bus carrying Celeste and month-old Nellie was overdue.

I went to the desk for the third time.

"No, sir," the clerk said, "please be patient. They're just a few minutes behind schedule. It's usually on—"

The ring of the telephone behind him got his attention.

He pressed his ear to the receiver and, without turning his head, shifted his gaze toward me as he listened. His faraway look made my blood run cold. The ring of another telephone cut through the close space like a shrill omen, taking from me the air that I breathed.

I couldn't hold back. "My wife! My baby! They're on that—"

But he raised his hand to silence me. Sweat ran down the sides of his face. It saturated the armpit of his shirt and soaked through to his vest. He

284

beat the desk with his hands like a drummer. Other people, also waiting to board or waiting for loved ones, were gathering with panic on their faces.

Yet another telephone rang, and one of the bystanders, with no one left to answer, leapt to get to the other side of the desk. He picked up the receiver— listening, frowning, and gasping. Dazed, he continued to listen while the rest of us stood by with our senses on fire.

"The bus originating in Los Angeles," the clerk began, turning to us with the face of a tortured man, "collided at ten-twenty-seven with a train at the Isleta crossing."

I knew the spot. It was grafted on my mind's eye. I could see the tracks. The bump-bump jarred every bone in my body. I felt the isolated settlement, the heat of the sun-drenched fields, the pain on rugged Pueblo faces.

Chapter 71

<hr />

Three days later, a train left Albuquerque's station Wednesday, bound for Detroit and carrying the bodies of Celeste and Nellie Virginia. I sat across from Rachel in one of the passenger cars, a copy of yesterday's unread *Albuquerque Weekly* under my arm. It was four o'clock in the afternoon. Exhausted, I rested my head on the back of the seat and wept.

Rachel stared blankly ahead as the train began to pick up speed, her dark eyes bloodshot, the cruel reality of the prior three days left in our wake.

I didn't talk. I didn't think I could. There had been inquisition with the ugly truth of dashed dreams and lost life, of firsthand accounts of the crash, and on and on. I had identified Celeste's body at the morgue by her wedding ring and her heart-shaped lips—lips I'd only recently kissed. It had been all I could do to withstand the sight. And I'd held next to me for as long as I could the lifeless baby we'd conceived in the only time Celeste and I had ever been one body. Nellie Virginia had had her mother's precious lips.

Rachel came over and sat next to me. "I can't bear it, Simon." She inched her hand through the crook in my arm, and her head fell on my chest. "She loved you, Simon. I hope you know that."

"It's God, Rachel. As far as I can tell, he's taking with one hand what he gave with the other." I felt better letting go of the anger.

Her face became contorted. "Who talks about God that way?"

"I do," I said flatly. "My mother, my Celeste, my child—those are sights I'll never forget. I talk about God that way, Rachel. Your sister was my life. We had everything ahead of us."

286

Rachel cried. There wasn't a tear left between us, and the train kept roaring with a sympathetic wail, moving us like waterless clouds on the winds of fate.

⋙⋅◆⋅⋘

Rachel fell asleep on my arm.

I must have dozed off, as well, because sometime after midnight, I woke up, too limp to make my way into a sleeping berth.

Rachel was scrunched up in the seat next to me. I covered her with a thin blanket and sat back down with my face against the vibrating window. It merely added to the dull ache that ran the length of my body. I drifted back to sleep, not caring.

When the morning arrived, bright light streamed unsympathetically across my face. Unable to block it, I sat up.

The *Albuquerque Weekly* lay folded where I'd left it in the seat beside me. I pulled it from underneath Rachel's knee and began reading what I would have given my life to undo:

> *Tuesday, October 22, 1929*
> *A loaded Pickwick-Greyhound bus, which had departed from Los Angeles en route to Denver, was demolished by Santa Fe mail train No. 7 on Sunday morning. According to local authorities, there were ten fatalities. Among the survivors, nine were seriously injured.*
> *The crash occurred at the Isleta grade crossing, where Indians were tilling the soil nearby, and shattered the quiet community with the eerie wail of a locomotive whistle and the sound of the thundering impact. Half a dozen ambulances were rushed from the Wily, Owens, Stierwalt-Harrison, and Martinez and Sons mortuaries.*
> *The train's engineer had slowed to thirty-six miles an hour when his locomotive struck the motor coach, sideswiping it. Parts of the bus were carried half a mile down the track by the speeding train. The accident is reported to be the worst*

in the history of Western-Ox Bus transportation.

Witnesses said the bus driver attempted to turn parallel with the track when he realized he could not beat the train. The locomotive, enveloped in a sheet of flame, ground along the rails before it came to a stop. Ambulances from Albuquerque and nearby communities arrived half an hour later.

Horrified onlookers gave morbid accounts of the aftermath of the scene. Gas was ignited by flames . . .

Chapter 72

⊰·◈·⊱

Thirty-plus hours after leaving the station in New Mexico, we pulled into Michigan Central.

I shielded my swollen eyes from the familiar lights of Roosevelt Park across the way and walked with my bag and newspaper through the corridors of the station with Rachel at my side. We hardly noticed the magnificent architecture or the bronze chandeliers. Within our eyesight of the waiting room, Virginia and Charlie slowly rose from their seats. In my haste to reach their embrace, I came close to tripping. Charlie caught me. Virginia clasped Rachel to her bosom.

It was just past five-thirty a.m. by the time the necessary papers were signed and procedures for the bodies of Celeste and Nellie were completed. We left Michigan Central and set out on the short trip through the city, on our way to Highland Park.

The predawn hour rendered Detroit's skyline unimpressive—an oversized, abandoned Erector Set. Charlie drove us through the still-sleeping streets where once I'd thought myself so strong, so self-sufficient, where I'd hidden my inadequacies behind honking horns, revving engines, and a policeman's badge. The big-city lure and crime-stopping challenges no longer enticed me.

We rode past the memories of my nine years spent camouflaging my guilt with a backlog of worthless pursuits, and out to the neighborhood I knew like the back of my hand.

Ginger barked once and raced across the backyard at the Mallorys as the automobile pulled in next to the fence. All of us spoke to her, giving her the

289

attention she had no reason not to expect. Even in our grief, the old boxer made us smile, and the distinct *tur-tur-reet, tur-tur-reet* coming from the leafy elm tree suggested a whippoorwill awaited the new day.

⟹◆⟸

Later that same day, Charlie, Virginia, Rachel, and I rode up the short, winding road beside the New Life Baptist Church to the cemetery. The Friday afternoon traffic put us there a little behind schedule. No one seemed to notice. A somber crowd gathered with an outpouring of support for the Mallory family.

There was a slight chill in the air, and Virginia and Rachel huddled together under the shade of a tent over the open grave. Beside the fresh earth was the single wooden casket holding Celeste and Nellie Virginia.

The burial was a short service. Charlie lifted his Bible toward heaven and spoke of the interference God sometimes makes in our lives.

I thought of the sour note on which Charlie's and my relationship had been left unresolved, how he'd interfered where I wanted control. "*Outside the boundary*," I recalled having said.

He spoke with a strong voice. "These two people, precious in God's sight—" Charlie walked to the casket and chose a lily from the ones that lay on top. "God's in control, my friends, and whether we like it or not, he interferes in our lives because he loves us. Sometimes it's painful. Unbearably so." Still holding the lily, he laid the Bible in Virginia's lap. "I want to tell you a story." He fixed his gaze on Rachel, then Virginia. "Virginia and I love our girls with all our heart. We love this infant granddaughter." He brought the lily to his nostrils, indiscriminately looked at me, and kept talking. "Go with me back a number of years. Virgie wanted Celeste to have a special gift for her thirteenth birthday. A surprise gift. Behind the scenes, Virgie worked every night on fancy curtains for Celeste's room, sewing after she came home from the factory and later, after the girls had gone to bed. Week after week, she prepared the curtains. The surprise was going to be beautifully put into place on the appointed day—while the girls were at school.

"But one evening, Celeste, barefooted, tripped on a needle that Virgie had been using. It had fallen on the rug and gotten embedded. That needle stuck up from the nap enough to prick Celeste's foot—not seriously, but enough to upset her. Anger sent her railing against her mother."

I could feel Virginia's body quaking next to me as Charlie spoke. Rachel was sniffling on the other side of Virginia.

"Being a preacher, I'm not going to repeat the exact words Celeste said to her mother. Let's just say she was angry. She brandished her almost-thirteen-year-old clenched fist at the very one who knew every piece of fabric to choose and every stitch to make in order to prepare for Celeste the best possible gift." Charlie stood still, composed but drained. "You see, Celeste knew only the pain in her foot. Not until the appointed day would she know what was being prepared for her. Oftentimes pain overshadows what's going on behind the scenes. God's in control of that. Not you, not me." He brought the lily to his nostrils again and inhaled.

The movement sent fragrance into the air.

"God has taken the lilies of the fields, clothed them in beauty." He looked at his family members individually and then out to those gathered. "And that's helping to remind me today of his unfailing provision in this heartbreaking interference. We be awaiting the beautiful gift he's preparing behind the scenes."

He returned the lily to the bouquet and bowed his head as if he were going to pray, but no words were spoken. After a bit, one by one, we stood.

As we filed back to the car, friends extended open arms, and everywhere, kind faces reflected serenity. Somehow, serenity eluded me.

Chapter 73

⟫•◆•⟪

We arrived back at the Mallorys' house. Food was spread from one end of the counter to the other and covered the table—more than ample to feed us for days. But I didn't intend to stay. I planned to leave on the train the next day. Rachel hadn't seen her parents since springtime when she'd brought her two youngsters and infant son for a visit. Seemed like she and Virginia needed time together.

I wasn't sure what I needed. Whatever it was, it wasn't at the Mallorys. After the service I just wanted to get away.

"Have a seat, Simon. Please, your favorite chair." Charlie sat next to the fireplace, and everything looked so darned normal at his house. "It's a hard time," he said.

I shot him a look, my thoughts swirling. *Hard?* I could feel the heat crawl up my spine and across my shoulders. *This is a needle in my foot?* My palms went from cold to clammy. I took out a handkerchief and, not about to sit down, blotted my brow. *Interference?* "I don't know, Charlie. I'm gonna have to do a lot of thinking. But I cant' stay here. This God of yours—and my father's, for that matter—lets horrible things happen. I'm sorry. I just don't happen to believe the way you do."

Voices coming from the kitchen, their numbers increasing, were getting louder by the minute. It was all I could do to keep from bolting.

"Please understand. I've got to go. Probably now." I extended my hand to shake Charlie's. "Being here, in this house with y'all, it's all wrong."

Charlie sat quietly. I could see the hurt I was causing.

"Listen, Charlie. How does one say it? This wouldn't have happened if . . . I'm responsible for—"

"Simon, don't. We all need time. We all could ask *what if?* Don't you think so?"

"I can't stay. I'll get my bag and go over to Mrs. B's before it gets too late."

Charlie stood. "Allow the grief, my friend. Running—" He stopped himself. His hand was heavy on my shoulder, as though he'd dropped an unnecessary weight. "You can't exit the pain, Simon, if you don't enter it. Neither can I."

"Running? Maybe you were right the first time, Charlie. *Hard*'s an understatement. Harder every time God lets this happen. My mother. Celeste, Nellie. Alan. And what about Roman? Where is God, anyway?" I braced myself for an emotional goodbye. "Never mind. I know your answer to that one: God's in control." I shook Charlie's hand and turned to go, then turned back. "I hope you'll cover for me, Charlie. Use your good words to explain my actions to Virginia and Rachel. I have a job to get back to. And that's *all* I have."

I left through the back door, bag in hand, undetected in the fervor.

Ginger, penned and looking indignant, perked up as I neared her.

"Stay, girl. Take care of things."

She raised no objection. The only sound was the chatter coming from inside the house. That, and the pounding of my heart. Not half a block away, as I walked dispirited through the October night toward 73 Pasadena, I heard her bark once, as if to challenge the situation over which she had no control.

I was convinced we had the same God.

<hr />

The moon shone above me like an enormous egg yolk in a star-filled sky. I tried to disregard it and kept on walking as the cold penetrated my lightweight coat. Selfishly, I hoped Mrs. B had no boarders at the house. My old room could easily belong to someone else by now, I told myself. If she was still up, brooding over her flock, it would be absurd for me to covet the familiar space while I waited for the right time to take a taxi to Michigan Central.

I was too numb to know how I felt about surprising Doc Begbie with my presence. Boarders kept Mrs. B busy, and Doc, in his own way, kept her happy. Catching him off guard would give him plenty to say on the subject. I wasn't sure if I cared. Putting this ordeal behind me was my foremost concern.

As I turned the corner and got closer, I could see his form through the transparent folds of the curtains. The front porch lights were off. I knocked twice, hoping to roust the old guy.

I watched as he stood. His shadow moved away from the curtains. I heard his cane hit the floor, and I heard him tapping the hardwoods unevenly as he walked to the front door.

"Doc Begbie!" I called to him through the door. "Simon Hagan here! Doc?"

The porch light came on, and the door opened.

"Aye, 'tis ye, laddie? Come in, come in. Good to see ye."

I followed him to the parlor, inhaling the pleasant wave of minted fragrance as if it were a missed friend. For the next hour, with the house quiet around us, we talked of tragedy. Lost love, lost dreams. Mine first, then his. He had no answer for why things had happened the way they had, but he listened to my heart. We'd traveled a similar road. We had both come to a place where the bridge was out. I knew that part of his story. Knowing it made us kindred spirits.

I don't recall climbing the stairs later on that night, but the room at the top was the same, and when morning came, it was the same Mrs. B at the bottom of them.

"So, you just burst in and didn't call or anything like it. Fine." She started off with her usual kick, but it was short-lived. "I want you to know I haven't the words to tell you. Sit down, Mr. Hagan, would you?"

Not needing to think about it, I seated myself at the end of the table, and Mrs. B dashed off to the kitchen, from which wafted the aroma of perking coffee.

Doc was left to pace the floor with his cane, stopping every few steps to peer at me. "Got something up her sleeve, aye," he said, having worn out the both of us with his fidgeting.

She was back with a tray of scones and a jar of strawberry jam. "Made yesterday. Eat. I've got something to say while the coffee's coming." She sat down next to me and leaned in close to my face. "Mr. Hagan, you're at another crossroads. First TB, and now this. We all come to them. Things happen. We can't explain." She gave Doc Begbie a soulful stare. "The two of us—we've both had our share of sadness. No say-so in the matter."

Doc opened his mouth to speak.

She stifled him with a look and continued. "I'm not a smart woman—not dumb, either—but I know this much: I know you're not a man to be broken." She threw her hands in the air, practically hitting my cheek with one of them. "Why, I've seen you go from that tall, skinny kid in man clothes, begging on my front porch for a room, to a hard-working factory man to a fine, brave policeman that would take a bullet for a friend if he had to." She took a deep breath, her eyes watering. "That young woman you brought here for us to meet—she completed you."

Doc nodded from his chair.

"I'm sure sorry about this," she said, blotting a tear with the edge of the tablecloth. "Breaks our hearts, but you're strong, and you'll look for the right way. You'll cross over, Mr. Hagan." She took my head between her hands and pulled me close to kiss my forehead. Then she was off to the kitchen.

"Always something up her sleeve," Doc said with a wink over the top of his eyeglasses.

<hr />

By noon, I'd readied myself and gotten a taxi. I wasn't quite sure what, if anything, I'd given of myself in this place that once had been home. The visit had given me closure. I wasn't sure when I'd be back—if ever.

With the midday Michigan wind hitting my face, I ducked into the Model T cab that was sitting at the curb at 73 Pasadena Street. "Take me to Michigan Central, please."

I laid my hat on the seat, settled in for the ride to the train station. Then my heart suddenly changed course. "Go up two blocks and turn left, then one more block and take a right. I've got a quick stop to make."

"It's your dime," said the cabbie."

"Yeah. Right here. Next house on the left. I'll be right back."

"Meter's running."

Charlie must have seen me get out of the cab. He was at the door. "Come in out of the cold."

"Can you talk? I'll not stay but a minute."

"Of course. At least sit."

"She went to live with Rachel because of me. None of this would have happened. Not only that, Celeste would've gone on to college if it hadn't been for me."

"Nothing's easy about losing Celeste and little Nellie Virginia. You need to talk. I'm hurting, too. We're all hurting."

"I want to apologize for bolting after the funeral. I had to. Losing Celeste and the baby—I don't think I can go on. There's no point."

I could see his chest rising, his eyes softening. "Who's going to save you, my friend? Who's going to save you from these lies you're believing? Lies that are robbing you of abundant life. Put your burden down, Simon. No one blames you. God doesn't. Who am I to? Who are you to?" He paused with a heavy breath. "God loves you regardless of what you've done, or think you've done, or wished you hadn't done. He loves you regardless of what you might ever do. But you aren't going to be rid of this guilt till you decide to face a forgiving God. You're hanging on to guilt—that and lies— listening to them as if they owned you. Refuse to believe them. Cooperate with the fact that God loves you."

I couldn't think of anything to say.

"You don't know this, I guess, but that crazy boxer of ours saved Virgie back a month or so. Hear me out. The cab can wait. It was late. Virgie should have been at home. She wasn't. She was at church in the parking lot, loading donations of clothes for immigrants. She'd just opened the car door when a man came at her from behind—"

"What? No!"

"Listen. His intentions, most likely, weren't good. Little did he know, our vicious-when-need-be dog had her beady black eyes on him, watching his every move. Ginger lunged over the back seat, nosed her way out the partly opened door, and was on the ground in a flash, backing the man down, baring her teeth, growling, ready to attack. The guy took off with her chomping at his legs. Virgie said she'd never seen anything like it. And I'm convinced Ginger saved her. The very act of love you provided years ago saved my Virgie. Might be an odd comparison, but true. Love's a saving grace. It's waiting and willing. Consider allowing God to unleash the truth of his mercy. Swap its truth for the lies you're believing, Simon. It's waiting for a partly opened door." Charlie was dead serious. "Think it over."

I was sure he wasn't saying God was a boxer in the back seat, ready to lunge. But I'd met my match. Charlie's God—and Dad's God—was after me. My hands were wet with perspiration. "You've been a big help. There's a lot to sort out.

"How about you? And Virginia? How are y'all holding up?"

"There aren't always answers to the question of why God does what he does. We trust his sovereignty. But we hurt. What else can I say? Anger isn't the answer though. Forgiveness is. Yourself first."

"Well, you should despise me for what's happened. I don't deserve forgiveness. But I've kept you. Let's talk again soon."

"Rachel's leaving for Flagstaff tomorrow. Yes, we'll talk. I'm glad you came."

"Charlie . . . thanks. Give my best to Virginia. And Rachel."

"Take care, my friend."

Chapter 74

⬤◆⬤

The return train ride from Detroit to Albuquerque left me bone-tired. I exited the taxi, climbed the stairs, and unlocked the door to my apartment, having noticed Mr. Reagan's trash was nowhere to be seen.

All six hundred square feet of the apartment were dark. I turned on a lamp and set my bag on the couch, not wanting to go near the bedroom I'd prepared for Celeste and me—or near the crib I'd assembled for Nellie Virginia and set in a corner close to our bed.

Nothing about the place was luxurious. A half wall separated the kitchenette from the living room. I wandered over to the sink and stood at the window, peering out at the early morning haze over the Sandia Mountains to the east.

"God," I said aloud, as if he might have some reason to listen to me or tell me a reason—any reason—why I should go on.

But no response came. All I could hear was my own breathing. If I could have stopped it, I would have. My shoulders closed in around me. My legs folded.

This is what it feels like to be a hundred years old, I thought as my fist came down hard on the sink.

God's silence left me empty. The future left me hopeless. And I wept, replaying in my mind Charlie's story of Celeste with the needle stuck in her foot. I savored my recollection of the day she and I first met. The memories, the years, the events that had so drastically altered the course of our lives churned in my head, and alongside them I saw a beautiful vision of us together—and the accompanying death of that vision. Celeste's existence had been but a brief spark.

My strength to continue was gone. It was all I could do to stand and look through the window and out across the rows of automobiles and building tops to the mountains where the sun was rising over them.

Strong? Good ol' Mrs. B's voice echoed in my head. "You're strong, Simon. You'll cross over."

The rays of morning light bathed my face and streamed across the rest of me, tranquilizing me with an amazing view of creation.

Strong? I felt so small, like an ant, easily squashed, easily erased from the face of the earth with little to prove I'd ever been here. What would it matter if I had a cigarette now? And why had I regained my health for this? Battled for my life for this? Been spared while others around me had died? For what? I started to search cabinets for a cigarette, mindful of the fact I wouldn't find one, telling myself I'd hurt everyone I touched, wondering why I was here.

No cigarette and no answers. I turned off the living room light, dropped onto the couch, and slept there until the next morning when, out of sheer habit, my eyelids mechanically snapped open. It was five o'clock, still dark. I reached for the lamp and accidentally knocked Mother's Bible from the table to the floor, having previously placed it there for no other reason than it looked nice. It was the only book I owned. I picked it up, held it for a second, and then put it back where it had been. But the irrepressible small paper insert—the daunting poem I'd read when tuberculosis had struck— lay next to the table leg.

With a flutter of uneasiness, as if Mother had handed me the note herself, I slowly unfolded it and read the lines:

> *Any man's death diminishes me,*
> *Because I am involved in mankind,*
> *And therefore never send to know for whom the bell tolls;*
> *It tolls for thee.*
> *—Donne*

I refolded it. Diminished? Yes.

Chapter 75

I cleaned myself up and started across town on foot, pushing myself to begin again. It wasn't my first day on the job, and it might have been a normal Monday morning for someone else, but I'd been gone for a week. Nothing about it was normal. I made my way on foot down Albuquerque's Central Avenue, turned into the alley behind the Franciscan Hotel, and ducked in through the back door.

My boss hadn't been pacified by my phone call to cover my absence. If authority were a banner, he lifted it high at every opportunity. Thin-lipped and sneering, he was near the door when I entered.

"Thought you might show up today, Hagan," he said and pointed to the soiled wine glasses and silverware stacked near the sink. "Have at 'em."

Grateful for work, I didn't waste any time digging into the mass of dishes to be washed. The overlap of last night's food scraps and this morning's breakfast plates, saucers, cups, and juice glasses kept the work coming. Just as the breakfast rush ebbed, the lunch rush began.

"Looks like the stock market's gone into free fall." The boss was back, rigorously directing waitresses with armloads of plates. "Dining room's got one of those highfalutin' bankers out there talking to the other guests about how the market's rallying. Everyone's in a panic." My boss was a small man, edgy and effeminate. The pressure from somewhere made him extremely unpleasant. He was talking more to the high-pitched ceilings than to me. "Seems like that one," he said, referring to a patron he'd singled out for rebuke, "others like him, and the dad-burned investment companies didn't do a thing to stabilize it. Just bought up blocks of stock to make the exchange look good!"

He was making little sense to me. His hysteria was not about the dishes, and the stock market was the least of my concerns. Still beat from the trip to Detroit and back, I rounded out the afternoon by washing the last of the lunch utensils and pans and scrubbing and putting them away, unsure if my sinking spell was exhaustion or coming from the deep hole in my heart. But the pay made ends meet. I had only to Bon-Ami the counter, get something to eat, and walk back to my apartment. Tomorrow promised to be more of the same and would end with a class at the university in the evening. I had theater rehearsals on alternating nights. Weekends were the icing on the cake: on stage for a brief appearance. Today, the brief lines I recited seemed tasteless.

Having talked to my father only once since the accident, I studied until seven o'clock and then picked up the telephone. "Call, please. Yes, connect me to Geoffrey Hagan at Crestwood 5774."

Hannah answered. "Simon, good to hear from you. I 'spect it's your father you're looking for, though, and he's down at the barn still. I can holler at him."

For an impotent few seconds, I felt like an actor standing speechless on the stage, unable to adjust the urgent part of me that wanted only my father and his strength. Time and distance had not diminished the need. Hope of having him to myself frittered away. "No, that's okay. How are you, Hannah? And John? He's got to be getting on up there. And little Patty?"

"Fine, fine. I'm doing just fine. John looks more like ten than eight," she said of my half-brother. "Gonna be wearing shoes as big as his father's before long. And someday, tall as you. He's already past four and a half foot. We don't call him John anymore. He's Big John." She laughed, and then her tone changed. "You doing as well as can be expected? I'm so sorry, Simon. There aren't words for your loss."

"Don't know . . ." Decency wouldn't let me stall long enough to cover the crack in my voice. "Don't know how much more God's gonna throw at me. I'll get through," I said, struggling to keep composed. "Got plenty of experience, I guess. But school and work'll keep me busy. Still performing with the best of 'em, too."

Performing. That said it all, covered it all. "Everybody else doing well? Bring me up to date," I said, racing on with my own questions to avoid hers. "I want details."

Hannah summed up the latest on each of my siblings. Hardest to picture was Mary with a husband and a newborn. I could still see her cradling the black-and-white-striped hen, and I wanted to smile. Life on the farm seemed like a performance ended too soon. Abruptly, no applause. No curtain call necessary. I'd just walked away and the show had gone on without me.

Hannah and I said our goodbyes before I could talk to Dad, and the unmerciful swell that pushed inside me slammed my heart against a private place where dreams go to die.

Chapter 76

The Franciscan Hotel was in a state of a frenzy at half after eight the next morning, Tuesday, October 29. I went around the back of the building, as usual, attributing the fervor in the streets to the events on the New York Stock Exchange the day before. The sky was cloudless and the air unusually chilly with a twist in it that made me grateful to get inside the warm kitchen. Even the dirty dishes from the breakfast had a cold clamminess that chilled my spine. I tied my apron strings around me and got to work, rustling up soapsuds in hot water. It took the edge off, and by mid-morning the influx of dishes had stopped.

My plan was to wind up here and go straight from work to the university. After class, I'd sign up for an audition or two and search out any other means of getting myself near the stage. I was about to leave when the swinging doors to the kitchen flew open.

The boss stomped in like a madman. "Stock prices have collapsed!" His eyes were wild, his arms gyrating uncontrollably. "Completely! One hundred percent collapsed! Do you hear me, Hagan?" He ranted, as if he expected me to do something. "It's incomprehensible! *In-comp-re-hen-si-ble!*" He careened back through the doors as quickly as he'd come.

The news stunned me, although the ins and outs of Wall Street weren't part of my world. With only minimal amounts of money to keep myself in school and even less to put back for the future, I had no idea what was in store as a result of the market's losses.

But it was not business as usual. Black Friday was a household word. The industrialized world spiraled downward as billions of dollars were lost in its wake, and Albuquerque was no exception. In the coming months, the Great Depression stretched its tentacles over all of America, snatching away whatever hopes lay in its path. By late winter, the devastation was hard to fathom.

I and most young men of my day began living by a new set of rules. Jobs were nonexistent. Many men had no recourse but to sell pencils on the street. I was among the more fortunate, still washing dishes at the Franciscan Hotel. At least it was work. It covered my expenses, nothing more. How on earth, I asked myself, would I have managed to care for Celeste and Nellie Virginia? And once more, my heart fell to pieces.

"Riverside 4426, please, ma'am."

I waited, expecting Charlie to pick up the telephone at the Mallory home.

"Hello," came Virginia's voice on the other end.

"And hello to you. It's Simon."

A few slow-moving seconds passed. We hadn't talked since the funeral. I'd been unable to bring myself to call her. "Virginia . . ." Words wouldn't come.

"We're well, all things considered," she said, filling the void. "There's plenty of opportunity for the church to reach out and meet needs. So many people are without food for the table."

"I've seen it. Don't know what it's going to take to get our country back on its feet. I hope you're keeping Ginger close by. Sounds like she's quite the guard dog."

"She is at that. You looking for Charlie?"

"I was, Virginia, but I'm glad I got you. There's so much I'd like to say. I wish things had been a lot different. Truth is, I don't know if the pain will ever stop—for any of us."

"You'll be interested to know that I'm not at the factory any longer. What about that?"

"No kidding?"

"No kidding. But, hey, I don't want to run your telephone bill sky-high. Charlie's gone for a couple of hours at least. Want me to have him call?"

"I'm better already, having heard your voice. Just ask him if they ever got anything on Lieutenant Dugan. Or maybe I'll give your uncle a call one of these days. Just curious. He'd be shocked to know I'm washing dishes and pumping gas. School and this blatant ambition to act are keeping me going, though. Chief Sturges will get a kick out of hearing that."

"He knows it, Simon. Just don't try to hid yourself behind someone you're not. We're all just glad you made it out of the sanatorium alive. Detroit's not a place to come back to, in case the thought crossed your mind. But I'm sure my brother would welcome you back at the police department."

"That's very nice. Guess I'm not thinking of doing police work again," I said. "Still planning to make a doctor of myself. At least that much has come out of my having beat TB."

Even as I said the words they sounded lifeless. Underneath, I felt my facade crumbling. I was angry still, and pushing to prove there was something more. Angry and pushing. As cordial as our conversation was, Virginia's tone sought to override the obvious sorrow we shared. Talking to Charlie would have helped. He might have told me that, in spite of my condition, there was a reason for me to climb the next mountain. He might have reminded me to lay down my burden—the lies, the guilt, the person I was hiding.

Dugan was flying free as a bird for all I knew, free to continue his low-down conspiracy with the Mafia, free to get other innocent people besides Roman Davis killed. He still drew breath, while so many people I loved no longer did. The injustice ate at me.

Go back? I mused. *You bet your sweet bippy. In a heartbeat, if I could breathe Albuquerque's desert air in the streets of Detroit.*

"No, Virginia, I guess I won't be coming back to Detroit anytime soon. Too much has changed in a year. It's been great talking with you, though. And best of luck with your work at the church. I'll keep in touch."

"Promise you will."

Chapter 77

———◆———

Acting roles surfaced sporadically as winter passed. My hours had been cut back at the Franciscan, and my second part-time job pumping gas was as near to an automobile as I was going to get. That was what the foreseeable future held in store. Financially speaking, I was narrowly keeping my head above water. The Great Depression loomed as a reminder I was not in control. It stuck like a briar in me, in the soul of the nation. For the ones who could afford it, the theater provided entertainment in a nation otherwise profoundly saturated with the sad reality of hardship.

But springtime in Albuquerque energized me, despite a cough here and there and the misery dominating the daily news. Lavender, bell-shaped flowers burst on a profusion of desert willows outside my apartment.

Everyone should be so lucky, I thought.

The second semester at the university was going to end soon. I was never far from a dream, having enrolled during the summer semester and wanting badly to graduate in three years. I planned to explore the high desert country if I got any down time.

Just when I was about to think acting was a waste of time, my big break came. I picked up a part with a speaking role in the production of *This Thing Called Love* on stage next to Vivian Vance. Such good luck put my world in a tailspin. Juggling rehearsals, more auditions, and elaborate parties meant I was playing roulette with a relapse of tuberculosis.

I got Dad on the telephone. He needed to be the first to know I was going to perform at the Albuquerque Little Theatre with an honest-to-gosh star. He answered after several rings.

We were both breathless.

I turned the receiver to keep him from hearing my wheezing. "It's unbelievable, a real game changer. We started rehearsals last week. They'll go through the end of the month. Show's scheduled to open in June. Things are looking up. I couldn't be more pleased."

"Well, I'm proud of you. If that's what you want, I sure hope it works out." Dad sounded reluctant to share my enthusiasm. "These are hard times. Don't much see how people can afford plays and such. Personally, I think it's a bad choice."

Bad choice? Or simply another bad choice in a string of them that stampeded my memory? The guilt was as loud as the hooves of a thousand horses. *The Great Depression. Is that my fault, too, Dad?* My face burned with anger.

"What would you have me do, Dad? Come back to Elkton? Live on the farm? Maybe see what damage I can do to the rest of the family while I'm at it?"

"How's your health, son?" he asked, taking me down. "Seems to me you're spreading yourself pretty thin."

"Opportunities like this one are too promising to ignore," I replied. "Vivian Vance is big. My health is good. Fine." At best, it was still on the rebound. There was—and always would be—the danger of jeopardizing my health. "Dr. Siebel says I'm fine."

"Don't know much 'bout big names and stars. Just want you to make good choices. Continuing your education—that's good for sure."

I stifled an annoying cough. "Yes, sir. And work, too. I've got it all under control. How's everyone back home?"

"It's a right hazardous thing to think you're in control, son. That's God's place. Careful you're not being led astray." Dad had an annoying way of picking and choosing topics. "Your home, the family—we're 'bout the same as always. God's been faithful."

After we said goodbye, it took me three tries to get the telephone receiver back on its cradle.

My confidence—and everything I was holding on to—was a complete fraud. Dad saw it. I guess I did, too.

⟹◆⟸

June 1930, and I was on stage. Performing was second nature to me, and I took the grandeur in stride as if it were a well-deserved break from unfairness. But Albuquerque had never felt less like home. Ensnared by the glamour and glitz, I dropped out of summer classes at the university with no intention of reenrolling in September and gave barely a thought to investing all my energy in acting. The show ran its season, but by the end of it, the Great Depression had dealt the theater industry a solemn blow. July passed with none of the flair of the previous month. Acting roles were unheard of.

September arrived, and funds were too slim to support my livelihood. I was back on the streets of Albuquerque, looking for work like everyone else, going daily to the side door, rear door, any door of any theater in search of a bit here or a role there. Behind me, the KiMo Theatre stood like a monument to extravagant living that had emptied my pockets and shredded my ambitions. The highlife and its raunchy, seductive appeal had looked a whole lot better than it felt. And I didn't see God's hand in any of it.

I sat on a bench by the curb of Central Avenue and watched the cars speeding past while my dreams simply evaporated.

Chapter 78

It was after dark when I opened the door to my place at Anson Flats. I was ready to accept the death of yet another vision, and in the quiet nothing-ness, I wrestled with the thought of waking Dad with a telephone call. The handy receiver hung on its cradle—too often, too easy to rely on. Never-theless, I took and held on to it, not wanting to wave a white flag of surrender in the face of my failure. I wrestled with the reality of shame, of bad choices, of calling home for moral support. With not much more money than I'd had after leaving home at eighteen years old, I felt a tremor of uncertainty run straight through me.

Mother's old Bible lay under a dust-film across the room. I stared at it for the longest, then put the telephone down so that I could pick up what I knew was inside it. Dad's note.

> *"I sustained you in a desert land, in a howling wilderness,*
> *and shielded you, cared for you, guarded you as the apple*
> *of my eye."*
> Those are God's words, son, not mine. Don't ever forget
> them.
> —Dad

I had indeed forgotten them.

From where I was, the telephone operator's voice was coming through loudly and clearly: "Number please?"

Nothing else seemed to be quite so clear, except the shallowness of my existence. In the condition I found myself, there was a lot I didn't like. I blurted out the number that would travel the wires from Albuquerque to Elkton and send its alarming ring through the entire first floor of my Kentucky home. Surely Dad would wake with a start.

The connection was faster than I expected.

"Hagan residence." He didn't sound much like himself. "Geoffrey Hagan here."

"Dad." I addressed him as if his name were a foundation under me. "Hope I'm not calling too late."

"Not a'tall. As a matter of fact, I was just praying over you, son. You all right?"

The lump in my throat grew. The wider I opened my mouth, the more antagonizing the strain became. "Here it is: there's not much for me these days—work-wise. Money's tight. I'm pumping gas two nights a week. I have the dishwashing job at the Franciscan, but it's not enough to pay tuition and make ends meet. I'm not going to be any doctor, Dad. We both know it. I'm thinking about going back to Detroit. Chief Sturges would take me back without a question. Besides, I left unfinished business there, not to mention a wife and baby."

He cleared his throat. "I'm glad you called. These are tough times, mighty tough. You'll get through, though. And if you're needing my advice, I'd have to say you'd better ask the Lord. He's got his hand on your future. You can count on it. If it's him you're listening to . . . and if Detroit is where you need to be . . . you'll know it."

I hung up the receiver, fixating on the cradle that held it. *And if Detroit's where I need to be . . . I'll know it, will I?* The question jabbed a touchy scar somewhere between the sarcasm permeating my existence and the overgrown hedge of resistance to Dad's ongoing providence theme. *Why the note, Dad? How can I expect God to guide me, let alone guard me?*

I stared until the glossy black finish on the telephone had me going cross-eyed, looking for answers. *Would the future ever offer a less precarious cradle of uncertainty?* I pushed the receiver and watched it rock back and forth to a halt. *What if Dad were right this time? What if he'd been right all along?*

Chapter 79

I took off for work, walking to save gasoline—down Central Avenue, passing through alleyways, past beggars with tin cups, past men in suits selling apples on street corners, and mothers with distraught faces and crying babies, frail elderlies and skinny canines with distended bellies—a bleak close-up encounter with those who'd lost their way.

As usual, I entered at the back of the hotel's restaurant. I closed the door behind me, put on my apron, and started washing the stacks of the previous night's dishes.

My boss's high-strung voice came from the hotel pantry. Mr. Gronseth was in a foul mood, again. Nothing new there.

"Don't screw up, buster! That water's got to be hot enough to get the crap off those plates. They've been sitting there all night, just waiting for ya." He surfaced from behind the shelves of canned goods. A scowl spread across his face. "And don't think for a minute you're better than the next. You're the one washing, and it ain't gonna get any better than that."

Silently, I bristled but kept on washing and rinsing. "Yes, sir. You bet."

He left the room with a hostile air without looking me in the eye. I felt the thermometer rising.

By the time the breakfast-hour traffic ground to a halt, I'd mounted piles of scrapings on one huge platter and worked feverishly to finish washing the stacks of dirty plates. Despite all the dishes, business had dwindled. Following the stock market crash and the ensuing onslaught of the Great Depression, hotel guests and restaurant patrons began staying home, traveling less, eating less, smiling less. Everything was less.

I scrubbed the few remaining pots and was almost ready to inform the boss it was time to collect the cash I was due. After that, I'd be on my way. Payday was welcome anytime but in particular today.

"What now, Hagan?" he snarled, name-calling, spouting off a blue streak. "What are you waiting for? Looks to me like you're slacking, *Mis*-ter Hagan."

"It's close to ten," I said. "I'll get rid of the garbage, but I'd like to go ahead and take my meal for today, along with the pay I'm due. Pretty darned hungry about now."

"Oh, I see," he said with a nasty laugh. "Hungry, yes. Well, there you have it, Mr. Hagan. Your meal's right in front of you. All you can eat. Look! It's even on a silver platter." He pointed to the pile of scraps.

His arrogance was nothing new, but today I wasn't putting up with his groundless disrespect—not from an employer, not from anyone.

The clock on the wall struck ten. The reminder was divine. I'd had it up to my eyeballs.

I glared first at the mire and then at my boss. "Why, you dimwit piece of crap! We had an agreement: a decent meal as part of my pay. I have no intention of eating what your patrons left on their plates." I tore off my apron and flung it on the dish rack. "I'll take my pay now. And if you want to discuss it in the alley, I'd be pleased to take you on, *Mis*-ter Gronseth." I stepped so close to him that his nose touched my chest. "Well?"

With his eyes glued to mine, he reached into his pocket, pulled out his wallet, and picked out a two-dollar bill. "This is all you're getting from me." He dropped it and took a step backward. "Don't bother coming back. There're plenty more where you came from, dipstick. A dime a dozen out there on the street."

"Dipstick? You mean, like a rod for measuring the depth of oil in a vehicle's engine? That kind of dipstick, Gronseth, or another kind? Maybe one I don't know about. Or did you mean like the spot that hurts so bad when it's pinched that you have to cry 'uncle'? It's right here."

My clasp on the nerve near his collarbone brought him to his knees, and the only remaining cook left the kitchen.

"You're in no position to call me a dipstick, Gronseth, now are you? Hand me your wallet, or I'll break this wee collarbone."

He slowly handed me the wallet while I maintained my grip on the nerve at the base of his neck.

I fished out a couple of bills with my free hand and dropped the wallet next to him. "May I have these? Seeing as how you're unable to hold up your end of the bargain and all." I intensified the pinch.

"Yes," he said with no respect.

"'Yes, uncle, perhaps?'"

"Yes, uncle," he managed to say.

"How about, 'Mr. Uncle'?"

"Mr. Uncle."

"Much nicer than dipstick, don't you think?" I let go, tucked the bills into my pocket, and walked over to the tray of scraps. "Think about your uncle while you're cleaning this up." I dumped the platter of garbage on the floor and stepped over it.

"I'm calling the cops!"

"Yeah? Tell them to look up Captain Hagan, Detroit Police Department. That's in Michigan, pipsqueak."

<hr/>

My buttoned-up collar was unnecessary, as were my tie and long sleeves. I loosened my tie and walked through the alley behind the Franciscan, shaking off the events of the morning. They had hardly elevated my disposition or affirmed the direction of my future. God didn't seem to be indicating his approval, either.

I nodded to a gentleman on the corner as I turned up Central Avenue. Dry air, milder than normal, whisked past me. It was not over seventy degrees, but I was hot as a firecracker.

"Good morning, sir," the man said, taking an apple from his crate as I approached.

Sir? I mulled over the unearned respect and laughed. *Beats dipstick.*

"A nickel apiece," the man said. "And might I add this from the Bible: ever seen the verse that says God cares for you like you're the apple of his eye?" He polished one with the sleeve of his shirt and held it high for my inspection.

314 | Annette Valentine

I could almost smell the apples stewing on the stove those many years ago when Mother was killed and my life seemed to take a detour away from God.

"I do believe I know that verse. And I'll have a couple of your apples."

He took my dime and gave me the apples, and I continued on my way with one in my coat pocket, the other in the palm of my hand. Halfway down the block, I took a bite of my breakfast and lunch while dinner bounced against my hipbone.

The day was still young when I reached my apartment door. I tossed the apple core into a bush, went straight to my bedroom, and stopped at the bureau. I set the second apple on top and bowed my head. The time had come to cooperate with the fact that God loved me.

Chapter 80

My days in Albuquerque were numbered. They included a few more nights of pumping gas to fulfill my obligation, but my mind was made up. I had one last appointment with Dr. Siebel. After that, I'd be dismissed from his care. I expected Nurse Fairweather might want to get in her two cents.

I trekked the long, dusty road to Saint Andrew's with my thumb in the air, hoping for a lift. Two miles later, I was still walking in the heat of New Mexico's afternoon sun, my chattels slung over my shoulder. Every step reminded me that I'd chosen the hottest day in September thus far to leave my Model T parked.

Nurse Fairweather seemed to be expecting me. She took aim. "You're in no condition to be walking in this heat, Mr. Hagan. Don't you know about taxis?"

"Fierce as ever, I see. And how's life treating you?"

"Are you the doctor now, Mr. Hagan?"

I saw no reason to humiliate myself with my less-than-stellar choices in the four months since I'd seen her. "Guess not. That would be a stretch in any direction. But I do have some pretty exciting news."

She stuck a thermometer in my mouth and took it out as Dr. Siebel entered. "You're going back to policing? Detroit?"

"Uh, no. Afternoon, Dr. Siebel. No. Elkton, Kentucky," I said with all eyes on me. "I'm a new man. Right, Doc? Clean bill of health? Got my whole life ahead of me."

He pulled the stethoscope away from my chest, looked at my chart, and smiled. "I'd say you're good to go. You'll need to watch for signs of weakening stamina. Rest is still going to be important. Other than that, you've been lucky."

I smiled without correcting him. "Thanks."

With a quick scribble on my chart he was gone.

Nurse Fairweather was not. "What will you do back home?"

"That remains to be seen. One day at a time."

"It's true for all of us, especially in times like we're in. I wish you the best, young man."

"You were an inspiration to me, Mrs. Fairweather. One never knows what a word of encouragement can do for a person. I'm grateful for your care while I was here."

"You still look like an actor to me. Handsome—"

"You're still such a flirt. Better be on my way. A hug?"

"Are you still sweating?"

"I guess I am."

"Doesn't matter."

<hr />

A final glimpse of the vista from the corridors of Saint Andrew's and the walk past the rocking chairs on the veranda sprung a tinge of bitter-sweet nostalgia. I sensed it would be the last time in this place where my will to rise was born, my desire to continue—nurtured, and the power to love again—restored.

I hitchhiked back into town with better luck getting there than I'd had getting out to the sanatorium. After I reached my apartment, I began packing my belongings, envisioning the next morning when I'd board the train. Only one loose end remained. It was September 20, 1930. Nellie Virginia would have been a year old. I picked up the phone.

"Hello from sunny New Mexico," I said to Charlie.

"You sound chipper," came his friendly voice on the other end of the line.

My smile was widening by the second. "Got a minute or two?"

"You betcha!"

"Well, I've made a decision." I let that sink in.

"Coming back to Detroit? Virginia's sure her brother would put you right back on the police force."

I pulled a lone silver dollar from my breast pocket and rubbed with my thumb the embossed words *E PLURIBUS UNUM* across its top, as I spoke. "That's great! Thanks, but listen. This is going to sound half-baked. Believe me, it isn't. So here goes. My father gave me two silver dollars the day I left home for good. One went to buy Ginger for y'all. I've got the other in my hand."

I took another look at the silver dollar, not only the face of Lady Liberty and the year embossed on it—1884, when my mother was born—but the word *LIBERTY* that arched like a crown on her head.

"This thing's gone with me to every port in the storm, but here's what's struck me about it recently—*providentially*, I must say. I had this fella—my boss—tell me I had to eat garbage, and not ten minutes later, another guy told me I was the apple of God's eye." I switched the receiver to my other ear. It felt like a perfect time for a cigarette, but I didn't dare. "Lies and truth hit home for me. That's it in a nutshell. Dad tried before to make the point. I guess I was content eating garbage and listening to lies till just a short time ago. My father wasn't giving me a good luck charm when he gave me this, Charlie. In a way, he was passing down his legacy of liberty."

"I can see that. You've accepted forgiveness. It sure takes a load off. Does it also mean you're coming back? Going to nail that Dugan character, are you?"

"I could do that. But I'm not going to." I paused to reflect on the gravity of what I was about to say. "No, Charlie, I'm going home."

He was silent while he absorbed the news. "That's a new wrinkle. Good for you, Simon. Starting over's okay. You go home, and let God show you the next steps. This journey of yours hasn't been a waste at all. You've loved and been loved. I hope you'll accept that, Simon. You've lost some people— we all have—but we're better for knowing them. One day loved ones will lose you. And they'll be better for having known you."

"That's a good send-off," I said. "Much obliged for it. And there's nothing I'd like better than to see Lieutenant Dugan convicted. One of these days I'm going to try to see that happen. Nice of the chief to take me back. But those Kentucky roots are nagging." I hesitated and took a deep breath. "There's a favor I'd like to ask."

"What's that?"

"Nellie Virginia—"

Charlie jumped in. "Her birthday."

"Her birthday. Would you put flowers on her grave?"

"Virgie and I were there this morning. Did just that, my friend."

"Give my best to Virginia. I'll be in touch."

I hung up and considered what had happened to Celeste, my child, my mother, my good friend, and my brother. I had no answers. I'd searched my conscience without understanding why they had perished and why I still lived, aware only that I had been diminished by their loss and increased because our roads had crossed. The eastbound bus from Flagstaff that carried the loves of my life had changed me forever.

Mother's Bible lay on the table, still waiting to be packed. Before putting it in my bag, I opened it and thumbed past some of its pages to the underlined words in chapter six of Micah:

> He has told you, O man, what is good; and what does the
> Lord require of you but to do justice, and to love kindness,
> and to walk humbly with your God?

I'd gone halfway across the country to discover that God's mercy was wider than my wanderings. I'd been gone close to a decade.

Chapter 81

The day I arrived home was an ordinary one, if *ordinary* can adequately describe the visible effects of the Great Depression on the town I'd left behind, or the humidity compared to the arid, healing climate of New Mexico. It was Saturday, and Carver's Grocery and Hardware was the hub of activity. For the sylvan Kentucky town of Elkton, like so many one-crop towns in the South in 1930, this particular morning had sprung to life.

Main Street teemed with the comings and goings of local folk and farmers, perhaps most of whom had wheat or tobacco farms that were pulling through by tight margins, many unable to find work. They were, though, in the courthouse square, a few in mule-drawn wagons, some on foot, more by horse-and-buggy.

None of the nodding passersby showed a sign of having ever known me. They were just unassuming folks with friendly greetings for a stranger. But I was no stranger to the inside of Jim Carver's store, and as odd as it was to breeze through the front door in a déjà vu state of mind, I felt quite comfortable. I traipsed to the rear, past the familiar candy case and the aisles of fresh produce and packaged offerings—no less appealing now than when I had been a boy—hoping to find Jim Carver needing an extra hired hand. I could hear him in the back room politely dickering with a man over some fish in a bucket, so I occupied myself by watching a lanky adolescent in overalls pick out a handful of square nails from a keg.

Suddenly my eyes were drawn toward the front of the store as a young woman swept through the open door and glanced in my direction. In the next instant she was strolling toward the candy counter. It was impossible to take

319

my eyes off her, but common sense reminded me why I'd come. The odds of meeting her were slim. The thought that an impromptu chitchat might lead to something more was preposterous, but before she could finish her purchase, I began to finagle a way to introduce myself. Drawing on my recent stage experience to charm her, I moved toward the front of the store.

She saw me approaching and calmly continued to study the candy display.

"Please excuse me for interrupting," I said, trying to sound as gallant as possible. "May I offer a recommendation for the chocolates before you make your decision? The finest of the fine is right before your eyes—your beautiful eyes, if I may be so bold." I didn't flinch a mite, in spite of the cold shoulder she was giving me. "I'm something of an expert on the subject. But first things first. My name is Simon Hagan."

She gave me a brisk once-over. "How do you do, Mr. Hagan? I am Gracie Maxwell."

I wanted to suggest to her that she was the essence of full-blown color set against a drab backdrop of economic depression, not to mention a breath of fresh air in my personal world of uncertainty. But I offered her a bar of chocolate, knowing full well it would take a chunk out of the few coins in my pocket.

She left with the chocolate bar and some sticks of horehound candy, and I went to look for Jim Carver—with Gracie on my mind.

⊰◈⊱

Mr. Carver lost no time connecting me with the Hagan farm and the relationship that had existed over the years. I'd bought my first Camels from him, and he had extended credit and seed for our sharecroppers. He and Dad had done business for as long as I could remember.

"Well, well! Mighty fine to see you, Simon. Mighty fine. I see you met my sister-in-law. And what brings you back to these parts?"

"You wouldn't believe how I met this beggar selling apples," I said. "God must've positioned him in my path. All in the timing, I guess, but that's what pointed me home."

"I've gotta hear the whole story sometime. Lend me a hand with these crates, would ya?"

"Sure thing," I said, distracted. "Your sister-in law?"

He straightened. "My wife is Miss Maxwell's sister, Senator Maxwell's daughter. Hand me that, please. Your dad send you?"

I hadn't made the connection with the Maxwell name. It took me aback. "No, sir. Funny thing. He doesn't know about my coming. I'd like to get some work, though. Would you have any need for a strong back and a weak mind?"

"Fact is I could use a strong back, but I'd insist on a strong mind, too." He laughed.

I swelled like a puffed-up toad. "Well, put me to work! I'll be going out to the farm for a bit to figure out my next steps, but I intend to stay in Todd County."

"Then help me put these in the back room." He indicated a few bushels of produce. "How ya gettin' out there?"

"Walking, hitching a ride."

"Nah. Take my truck. Don't need her on Sunday anyhow. You can drive, can't ya?"

"Yes, sir. It's been a while."

"Well, she's a rowdy piece of equipment. Be careful and bring her back with something I can sell. Pumpkins, some of Hannah's canned goods—anything. Finish up here and be back here day after tomorrow. We'll settle on a fair wage then. Deal?"

"Yes, sir. That's a deal if ever I heard one. Thank you, and—"

"Enough. Here's the key. Go on now. And it's spark up, key on, gas down."

Chapter 82

━━◆━━

I took a seat behind the wheel of Jim's rowdy piece of equipment out back, started her up, and rolled tentatively past upturned crates and tall, brimming cans of debris in the alleyway. In an unstoppable wave of exhilaration, I had the truck motoring along cobblestone city streets at a cautious little clip and then beyond to the outskirts of town. Loose rocks chortled beneath the tires for a mile or so before the road turned to well-traveled dirt, at which point my thoughts turned to the lovely Miss Maxwell.

Every breath of country air confirmed I was exactly where I wanted to be. I felt my homeward-bound spirit embracing the pleasant planting of my youth, felt it reaching for the touchable Hagan legacy. I stuck my hand out the window to let it bounce at liberty off the ripples of wind and released the sense of unworthiness that had spawned my search for authenticity.

As I came to the lane and the familiar rock wall on the last leg of my trip home, I felt like I was back in the saddle again, soaking up the rich smell of tobacco crops, basking in October's offering of splendid midday color in falling leaves and fading grass. The red barn and silo stood off to the left. The butterscotch stone bungalow beckoned like a lighthouse in the distance.

Out by the gate, with a horse's bridle in hand, Dad strolled toward the barn. Gray hair waved at the temples under the wide brim of his hat. He frowned against the glare of the sun. A boy walked in step.

I drew closer in the borrowed truck with *Carver's Grocery and Hardware* lettered on the side and could see my father standing like a statue in the brilliant daylight. A rough-hewn handsomeness bore well his fifty-three years. No longer evident in his soft brown eyes were the longings of a husband for his wife who would never return, or the father for his lost child. Filling the void left by Alan was the young redheaded lad at his side. Freckles the size of the end of my little finger clustered on the bridge of the boy's nose, and his ears looked like wide-open doors on a Model T coming 'round the corner.

"It's Mr. Carver, Papa!" the boy shouted. "Ain't it?"

I stepped from the vehicle, and Dad's baffled face lit up—deep-wrinkled in smile lines. His gaze locked with mine. "My son. You're home."

His arms enveloped me as his tears fell on my neck. Beyond him stretched my own backyard, my own garden where I was sure answers grew plentifully.

"Hey, y'all!" came an impatient voice from behind.

I turned and extended my hand to my young half-brother, awed by the massive paw that gripped mine. "So, this is Big John. You were about *this* big last time I saw you." I formed a shape about the size of a watermelon. I could tell he wasn't impressed.

"Yes, sir, that's me," he said, full of the likeness of the spirited soul I'd once known as my brother. The boy could have been a replica of Alan at that same age.

Dad towered over him, and pride for his son shone like sunshine off the tailgate of Jim Carver's truck.

"You're Simon, right?" asked the boy.

I blinked away the recollection of Alan and his careless attitude toward lies that had so easily robbed him and allowed me to escape. "Yep. I'm Simon. Shouldn't you be in school? Well, of course not! This is Saturday, isn't it?" I pulled my two bags from the truck and followed Big John to the house. "What grade are you, anyway?"

Niney spied us from the porch as we climbed the stairs. She hobbled back to her spot and flopped down, head on her paws.

"Second." He twisted a bag from my fingers. "I'm in second grade. Where've ya been?"

"It's a long story. Been in a desert land, Big John, a howling wilderness. But God shielded me and cared for me and guarded me as the apple of his eye."

THE END

About the Author

————⬥◆⬥————

Annette Valentine is the author of a trilogy entitled *My Father*, with *Eastbound From Flagstaff* being her debut novel and the first in the series. Her writing began with a knack for believing in spine-tingling ghost stories and Nancy Drew mysteries. At the heart of this creative and intensely energetic writer is her purposeful compassion that launched an advocacy of the anti-human trafficking movement, for which she is heavily involved. She is a retired professional interior designer and lives in the Brentwood suburb of Nashville, Tennessee, with her husband, Walt, and their beloved Boxer who prefers to be on par with mortals. Annette and her husband have two grown children and six grandchildren.